An H&G Mystery
book one

CHRISTINA ROST

Published by Scrivenings Press LLC
15 Lucky Lane
Morrilton, Arkansas 72110
https://ScriveningsPress.com

Printed in the United States of America

Paperback ISBN 978-1-64917-409-3

eBook ISBN 978-1-64917-410-9

Editors: Susan Page Davis and Heidi Glick

Cover design by Christina Rost.

All characters are fictional, and any resemblance to real people, either factual or historical, is purely coincidental.

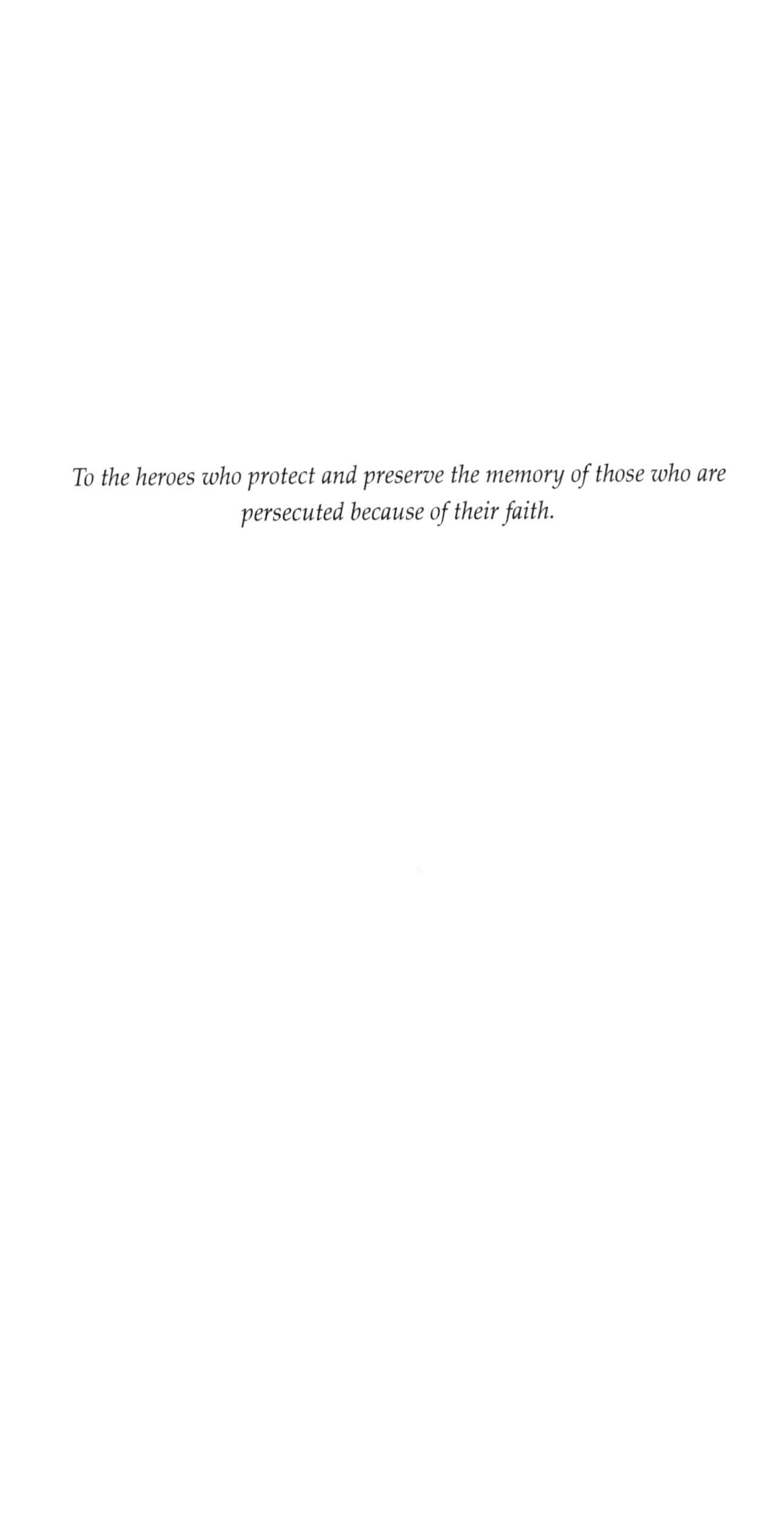

To the heroes who protect and preserve the memory of those who are persecuted because of their faith.

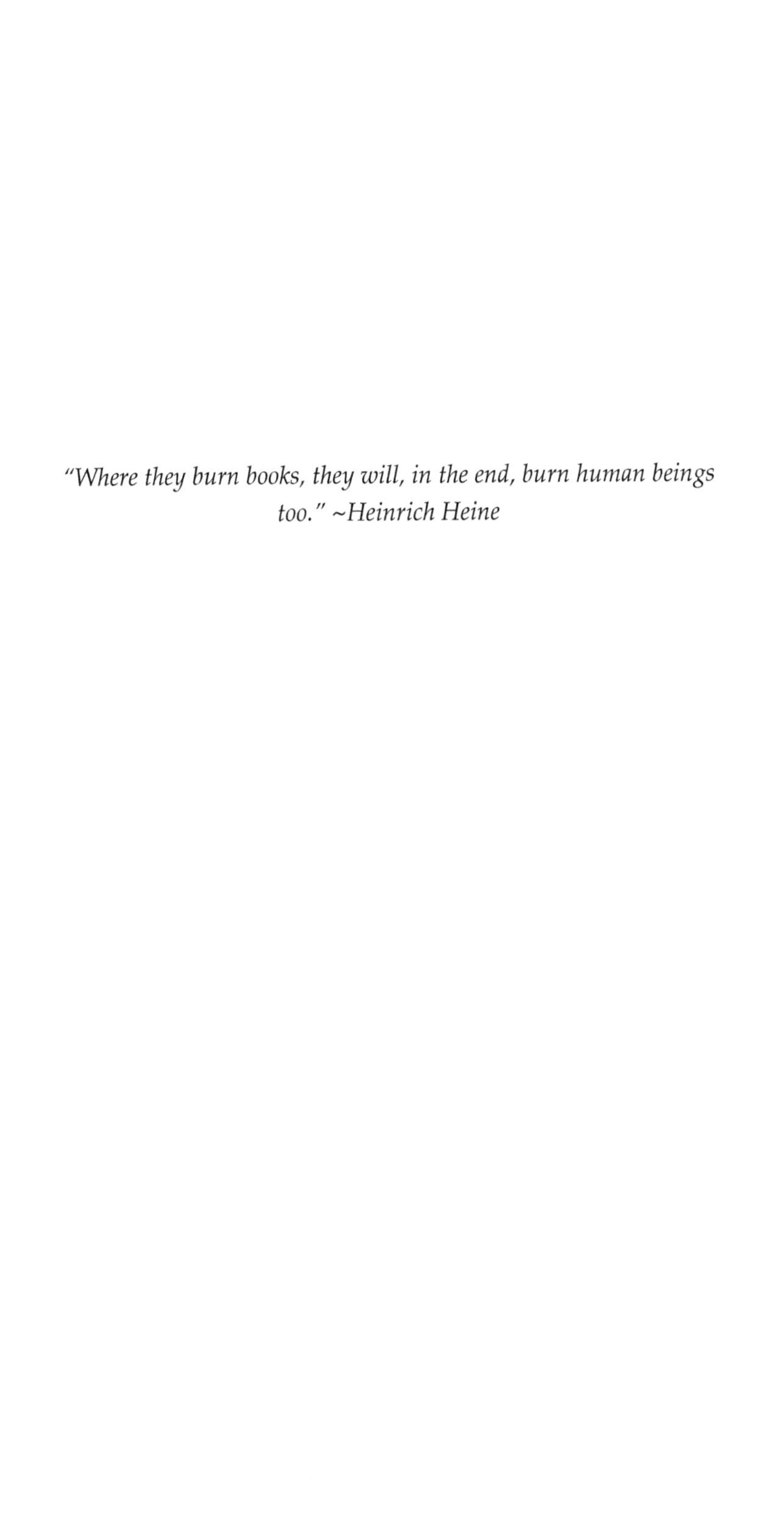

"Where they burn books, they will, in the end, burn human beings too." ~Heinrich Heine

PROLOGUE

Germany 1933

Flames and hazy smoke licked the ethereal sky. Ten-year-old Abram Zucker stepped out from behind his mother and stared at the streams of people herding into the village square.

"What's going on?" Abram looked up, hoping to read his mother's expression. Her brow wrinkled, but she didn't answer. Instead, she draped an arm around him and drew him close. Cozy warmth encircled him as the lingering, homey scents of flour and sugar drifted up to his nose. He leaned closer.

Disturbing the tender moment, a group of university-aged men pushed past them, their arms weighed down with stacks of textbooks.

"Where are they going?" Abram scanned the street while several more curious onlookers strolled out of their shops and homes.

As three cargo trucks rumbled across the cobbled streets, his mother's posture straightened. "I'm going to get your father."

Abram turned to stop her, but she broke away and scurried across the lane to their apartment above the bakery.

Slicing through the hum of activity, the town clock's chime struck nine, and a gentle breeze picked up the pungent scents of burning paper interlaced with charred wood. When Abram stepped into the street, Henrich and Karl, his neighbors, fell in step beside him.

"Do you think we can bring the *buchs* from Mrs. Fischer's class?" They bobbed and weaved past the adults, pulling Abram along. "Then we don't have to read them next year."

Abram snorted and shook his head. The waning sunlight cast a blood orange glow over the town as he struggled to make sense of the scene unfolding in front of him. Neighbors and friends milled about, with expressions of pensive expectation. A man he recognized as the grocer knelt and laid a spark to one of the books. The group cheered and applauded.

Glancing over his shoulder, Abram skimmed the crowd for his mother. Feeling the brush of a small hand sliding into his, Abram glanced down. "Rachel?" His heart dropped when the girl peered up at him through wet lashes. "What are you doing here?"

She sniffled, and a handful of tears trickled down her flushed cheeks.

"You shouldn't be out here." Abram looked around, hoping to see her parents.

Rachel tugged on his hand and pointed to the mound of books. "They took my book."

He followed her gaze and spotted a children's book poking out of the bottom of the pile. "That one?" Abram pointed to the thin hardback then cut his eyes to the crowd pushing in on them. "Is that your book?"

When he glanced back at her, she nodded. Her forlorn expression pressed a lump into his throat. He'd known Rachel since her family had moved into town a few years ago, when they'd opened a dressmaker's shop across the street. She was only a few years younger than him, but the urge to act as her protector clung to his soul.

"It's my grandmother's. She gave it to me before she died."

Rachel nibbled on her bottom lip while she fiddled with the long braid sloping over her shoulder.

Someone shouted across the street, and a sea of heads turned like a wave crashing onto the beach. Abram followed their gaze. A group of soldiers lifted tinted glass bottles and yelled out a hoot of victory. The crowd shouted and raised their right arms in unison as if yanked by a conjoined string.

A shudder shook Abram's spine despite the heat wrapping around him from the rising flames. What was going on tonight? In only fifteen minutes, the crowd had doubled in size. He lifted Rachel's chin with his forefinger. "I want you to go back home."

"Will you get my book?" Rachel leaned forward, and her breath brushed across his cheek. "I'll love you forever if you do, Abram."

He stifled a chuckle. "I'll get your book, little lamb." He tousled her wispy bangs. "Go home before this crowd gets any larger."

She slipped her hand out of his. Abram watched as she weaved in and out of the throng like a medieval sprite bent on escaping a foe.

"Here, throw it."

"What?" Startled out of his thoughts, Abram turned. Karl had sidled up next to him and thrust a book into his hands.

"Just throw it in like this." Karl stepped back and hurled a book into the flames. The pages fanned out then ignited in an array of cool white and orange. Karl nudged him and pointed at the pile. "Do it."

The bonfire reflected in Karl's pupils, and like a brush of unseen fingers, a shiver worked its way across Abram's skin. He glanced down at the book in his hand and shook off the troubling image. *I need a diversion.* He drew his arm back and launched the textbook into the center of the flames.

"Nice throw." Karl whooped and threw up his hands.

Abram pointed to the books not yet touched by the flames.

"Let's grab the ones on the bottom and see who can throw them the farthest."

"I'll win for sure."

"Grab that one." Abram pointed to a hard-bound art book. "It's big."

As Karl yanked the book free then pulled back to launch it, Abram snatched Rachel's book from the fire. A sharp flame licked the inside of his forearm and a cry wedged in his throat. He shoved the book under his shirt and tore through the crowd. Determination propelled him forward as the singed corner of the hardback pressed like a firebrand against the tender skin of his belly.

"Abram, are you okay?"

Abram ran headlong into his mother's open arms. *"Mutter."* The endearment fell off his lips in a whispered gasp.

His mother and father wrapped their arms around him and steered him through the door of their bakery. As soon as the door slammed shut, he ripped the book out from under his clothes and yelped in pain.

"Abram." His mother sucked in a breath when she examined the glossy welts on his arm and across his belly. "What did you do?"

"I had to." He swallowed hard and tried to hold back the waterfall of tears threatening to break free. "It's Rachel's book."

His father took the book from him and stared at the cover. *"The Twelve Story Stones."* Abram's heart thudded as he struggled to read the expression on the aging man's face. His father handed the book back to him. "You can return it tomorrow."

He nodded as his mother went to the cupboard. "Sit down, son. Let me look at those burns."

After she finished applying a sticky balm, Abram climbed to his room on the third floor. Through the window, he watched as golden flames soared higher in the ebony sky. He looked down at his hands. The fingers he'd wrapped around the book were white-knuckled and shaking. *What have I done?* He took a deep breath and tried to organize his competing thoughts.

We must obey authority. Recalling the words of his schoolteacher caused his blood to ice.

As he glanced across the street toward the dressmaker's shop, Abram's heart stalled. Where there was once a window display of fine fabric and dresses stood a board painted with angry words. Gripping the book with a clenched fist, he slumped onto the edge of his bed. Pinching his eyes shut, Abram forced a swallow. *Don't be a baby. They're just burning a few books.*

Abram's eyes shot open as he recalled Rachel's words. *My grandmother gave it to me.*

A sour taste settled on his parched tongue. It was more than just a book; it was a family heirloom.

Collapsing to his knees, he yanked up the floorboard loosened years ago to hide his childhood treasures. Carefully, Abram slid the book into the dusty crevice and clicked the plank back into place. He made a promise to himself—no matter what the cost, no one would ever take Rachel's book again.

1

Kelly Landon sat at her desk in her home office and groaned. The main character in her latest crime fiction novel wasn't cooperating today. And neither was her word count.

Her phone rang twice before she succumbed to her literary agent's ringtone. After mulling over the same scene for the last hour, an interruption from *this* caller was a welcome one.

"Hello, Declan. This better be good." She pressed her black-rimmed glasses back onto the bridge of her nose, while balancing the phone between her cheek and shoulder. "I told you, no calls until I finish this rough draft." She covered her mouth, attempting not to laugh at her forged displeasure.

"I know. I know. I'm glad you're focused, Writer Girl."

Declan McNeary's lyrical voice ignited a flame in her veins. She imagined him leaning back in his chair with his long legs propped up on his polished oak desk while the sun from the bay office window bathed him in a golden light.

Daydreaming about his unassuming Irish charm, she sighed. "That's me. Focused."

"Good to hear it. How's the story going today?"

"Adam's being interrogated."

Declan snickered.

Unlike her story's main character, Declan didn't model brawny masculinity. He was fit without the bulging muscles, and he looked more at ease in expensive suits than changing a tire. Her agent was tall, handsome, and loved reading the classics. She blew out a breath, putting to flight the wispy bangs on her forehead. Didn't hurt to dream. Did it?

"I have a favor to ask."

"Hmm?" She spun a pencil between her fingers, then plopped it into the jar on her desk.

"I've received a request for your writing services."

"What does that mean? I have no interest in ghostwriting."

"Hear me out. I know how you feel about interviews and fans, but this is different." He paused, giving her anxious thoughts ample time to multiply. "Mr. Abram Zucker's looking for someone to collaborate with on a historical memoir about his parents' life."

"But … I write fiction."

"So?"

She slumped back in her chair. "It's a memoir. I have no experience writing something like that."

"It'll be something to stretch that inquisitive mind of yours."

Declan's amusement floated over the phone, and she envisioned his mouth curving into a seductive smile.

"Mr. Zucker's a wealthy man. Very involved in the local arts council. He has what he's described as a group of historical love letters he'd like you to review."

"The idea of writing about a couple's life doesn't sound the least bit intriguing." She blew out a long breath. "It sounds more like a … a love story."

He guffawed at her answer. "Love stories aren't so bad. Are they? Besides, the Zucker's story unfolds in the middle of World War II. There's bound to be some intrigue there."

Adjusting her grip on the phone, she took off her glasses and pinched the bridge of her nose. "I'm just not sure … You said he wants to meet me?" Her messy bun bobbled on her head as she shifted in her chair. "Can't he just send the letters over, and I can see if I want to take the job?"

"This will be like an interview, not really a meet-and-greet with a fan. He wants to see if you're someone he can work with."

"That doesn't sound intimidating at all." Her tone dripped with sarcasm.

"You're a fantastic writer. This should be easy. Besides, you'll beguile him with your witty intelligence, I'm sure."

Butterfly wings blossomed in her chest. "I don't know about that. I've only written two books. Five, if you count the three YA disasters." Her previous young adult books were science fiction, but after feeling alienated in the world of aliens, she'd left that cosmos behind and attempted to write something new.

"Kelly." Declan's mood turned serious. "Abram's a fascinating man. He has some old journals and documents from the war he wants you to look over."

She rubbed her sweaty palms on her sweatpants then switched the phone to her other ear. He knew right where to hook her.

"From what I've gathered, Abram has a world of information locked away in his brain—stories from his childhood. Maybe you can unearth any skeletons hiding in his closet."

His melodic voice dipped into a villainous tone, and her toes curled in her slippers.

"Are you sure he asked for me?" She wandered into her living room, where she sank into the sofa and pulled a soft angora blanket over her lap. "I mean, there are so many other capable writers out there. Carmen Sanchez and Julia Winters have written memoirs for retired senators and athletes—"

"Kelly Rea Holt Landon."

Her lungs constricted.

"You're Treasure House Publishing's leading author. Your two novels are climbing the lists, and there are readers out there clamoring for a third. I've shopped your series at a few production companies. Do you hear what I'm saying? You could have any one of the *New York* publishing houses eating out of the palm of your hand *if* you played your cards right."

The fervor in Declan's voice carried over the line as a tremble of nervous energy shot through her. She imagined he no longer sat at his desk but instead paced in front of his large office window. Most likely, he'd taken off his reading glasses while he ran his fingers through the soft waves of his dark, honey-blond hair.

"Kelly? Are you still there?"

"Yes."

"What do you think?"

I was thinking about your sun-kissed hair. She fidgeted with the drawstring on her sweatpants.

"I don't think you understand how good of a writer you are and what you mean to Treasure House."

But what do I mean to you? "Okay, I'll do it."

"Really?"

"Yes. If you think this is a good opportunity, then I'll do it."

Declan continued to explain more about the interview and the eccentric—and very wealthy—Mr. Abram Zucker. "I want you to know I'll work closely with you on this. You'll probably get sick of having me around."

I doubt it. "That would be nice. Thank you." She frowned and glanced down at her clothes. Her favored sweatpants and university T-shirts didn't hold a candle to the sophisticated clothes of the women Declan kept company with. She'd need to change her wardrobe.

"By the way, what crime is Adam solving this time?" Declan asked.

"Actually, I'm thinking about crafting it into a romantic thriller." She swallowed hard. Flirting didn't come easy for her, and neither did lying. *Could I ever tell him how I feel about him?* Her heart galloped like a herd of mustangs. *Probably not.*

"Ah, I didn't think you were the romance type."

"Well, there's a lot about me you don't know, Mr. McNeary." She smacked her palm on her forehead. The slapping sound echoed, and she hoped it didn't carry through the phone.

"I'll bet there is, Writer Girl. When you get a few chapters done, send them my way. I'll let you know what I think about your *romantic* thriller."

His words washed over her like ribbons of silk as she walked back to her office and stammered out a goodbye.

Laying the phone down, she settled into her desk chair. Instead of placing her fingers back on the keys, Kelly picked up a fashion magazine and sifted through the pictures, trying to ascertain what style fit her.

Punk rocker? "Nah, too bizarre." Make-up model? "Too plastic." The First Lady? "Too matronly." Surveying her outfit once more, she grimaced. "Anything would look better than this."

Declan's words of admiration rushed at her while her fingers landed on the keys, and tapped, tapped, tapped, in a marching cadence across the keyboard. She imagined her tall, Irish literary agent cast as the hero who saved her from her ho-hum life of sweatpants and dusty journals.

The Winter the Flower Bloomed …

Scratch that. Too adolescent.

The Summer I Woke Up …

Nope. Sleeping Beauty.

She typed on the keys late into the night and compelled her mind to find the perfect mix between romance and crime.

2

A week after her conversation with Declan, Kelly drove up to Mr. Zucker's looming estate. Her first instinct—put her SUV back in drive and hightail it for the exit.

I've received a request for your writing services. Declan's words slipped through her mind as she turned off the engine. Had it been anyone else asking her to step out of her comfort zone, she would've passed.

Flipping down the visor, she swiped a trace of cinnamon gloss across her lips. Then, she turned in her seat and surveyed the Zucker estate. To say the sizeable Georgian home impressed her was an understatement. The mansion sat nestled in the center of lush, sprawling acreage, blanketed in trees on the cusp of changing color. As she stepped out of her vehicle, she stared at the ebony shutters flanking the windows. They resembled enormous bookends, holding up a row of glossy-spined books. She checked her watch. Five minutes before ten. At least she wasn't late.

The door opened after a quick knock, and a stout older woman greeted her. "Welcome, Miss Landon. Right this way."

Kelly stepped into the foyer. A smooth, buttery blue covered the walls and wrapped around her like a breezy summer sky. Snow-white molding lined the ceilings and entrances and encased everything in clean lines. Large black-and-white squares, polished to a high shine, spread out like a gigantic checkerboard beneath her feet. She resisted the urge to slide from one square to the next like a chess piece.

"My name is Donna." The woman flashed her a warm smile and led her up a broad staircase. "If you need anything during your visit, please let me know. I'll have you wait in the sage room. Mr. Zucker will join you shortly."

As she climbed the stairs behind Donna, Kelly studied the black-and-white photographs lining the walls. Several showed men in uniform—circa World War II? The other photos exhibited landscapes and old buildings. When she noticed a photo of a lone oak tree, she paused. *My tree.* The oak resembled one she'd danced around with imaginary friends and played make-believe beneath as a child. She blinked. A coincidence?

"Miss Landon?" Donna stopped a few steps ahead of her. "Is something the matter?"

"This picture looks familiar."

"Mr. Zucker dabbled as an amateur photographer for years. I'm sure he'd be glad to give you the history behind the photo."

Kelly stole one more glance at the massive tree, whose bushy branches mirrored a tangle of outstretched arms.

I'm a fairy princess, Father. I'll climb the branches of my magical tree and hide from the ogres roaming the countryside. She shoved the memory away. Even as a child, she'd let her imagination run rampant with tales of faraway lands and unexplored galaxies.

"I'll fight your ogres, and your mother, the queen, will live with you in your magical tree."

A pang of sadness gripped her heart as the provincial farmhouse her family lived in on the outskirts of London flashed across her mind. *Before Mom left. Before my world turned upside down.*

After her mother left, she and her father relocated to the city, where he quit playing make-believe with her. In London, Father only believed in ogres and monsters and not in magical trees.

Stepping onto the second floor, Kelly took a moment to admire the massive crystal chandelier dangling from the ceiling. The chiseled glass reflected the sun and projected cascades of sparkling diamond waterfalls across the walls.

"Mr. Zucker had that chandelier commissioned for his wife."

Kelly dragged her eyes from the glittery reflection and looked back at Donna.

"When the moon hits it just right, it looks like a thousand stars."

"That's wonderful." She followed Donna into a sitting room with towering sage walls.

Donna gestured toward a chair near the floor-to-ceiling windows. "You can sit here."

Kelly slipped into the seat and glanced outside. The room overlooked a meticulously landscaped rose garden. "The gardens are amazing."

"Mr. Zucker loves roses. Every color has a meaning. He tells me you can communicate a whole story just by choosing the right color combinations."

"That's interesting. Almost like a code."

"Exactly." Donna uncovered a bone china plate stacked with miniature cookies. "May I get you some tea or coffee?"

"Coffee would be wonderful."

"Cream or sugar?"

"Both, please."

After Donna poured her coffee, she filled two glasses with water from the crystal pitcher on the table.

"Thank you."

"Of course. Enjoy your visit." Donna turned to leave just as a young man dressed in scrubs wheeled an elderly gentleman into the room.

"Good morning, Miss Landon."

Her pulse raced as she stood and stuck out her hand. "Good morning, Mr. Zucker."

When their palms clasped, a mound of unnaturally

pigmented scars along his wrist caught her attention. He followed her gaze, and she winced. She'd not meant to stare.

"Marks of a well-lived life." Beryl Abram Jakob Zucker's oceanic blue eyes danced with symphonic energy.

Those eyes. Her cheeks warmed as a childhood memory tugged at her thoughts. "I'm sorry, Mr. Zucker. Have we met before?"

After holding her gaze for several seconds, Abram released her hand. "If we had, no doubt you'd remember." He waved to the chair. "Please, have a seat."

No doubt she would have remembered. She lowered herself into the chair and attempted to steady her nerves with another drink of coffee.

"It's nice of you to meet with me. I'm a huge fan of your writing." A symmetrical, white-grey beard outlined his smile, reminding her of a seasoned sea captain.

"Thank you." She set her mug down and smoothed the imaginary creases in her slacks.

"Books have always been one of my simple pleasures. Your crime novels intrigue me." Abram grinned at her. "You have an uncanny ability to draw a reader right into the drama of your story."

"I, well … I'm glad you enjoy them."

"My family has a lot of history, Miss Landon." He lowered his chin, and sunlight filled his eyes, turning the blue iridescent. "There might even be some mystery for you to write about."

Her body relaxed. "Please, call me Kelly."

"Very well, Kelly." Abram sat back in his chair, folded his hands, and steepled his fingers. "Where should I begin?"

She shrugged. "The beginning."

"The beginning. Of course." Abram's baritone laughter bounced around the room. "My parents lived in a small village outside of Berlin during World War II. It was a dark time in history for my family." He frowned. "For many families, as you can imagine. With a new regime in place and war on the horizon, our simple life was about to go up in flames." His eyes darkened as he rubbed at the scars on his arm. "If you decide to take on this project, I'll work closely with you over all the details of the book."

"I understand."

"We're not on a timetable, my dear." Deep crinkles formed at the corners of his eyes. "Outward appearances may suggest otherwise, but my time is in God's hands."

She shifted in her seat.

"Take your time. Gather as much information as you need to," he said. "There will be several documents and newspaper clippings for you to look over as well as records my parents kept."

"I'll be honest with you, Mr. Zucker—"

"Please, call me Abram."

"Abram. I've never collaborated with anyone before, and I've never written nonfiction." She didn't want to cut her chance off as soon as it was offered, but she wanted to be sure he understood what he was signing on for. "I've never written about anyone's family history."

"Ah, but this is not just a bit of history, the story of my family," he stopped and leaned in as if relinquishing a profound secret. "It's an incredible love story."

Her muscles tensed. Love stories were the farthest thing from what she was comfortable writing.

"Not a fan of romance?" His eyes twinkled with mirth.

"Well, I just don't have any ..." *Any experience in love.*

"I know you can write a whodunit."

"Yes, that's what I prefer." She took another long drink of her coffee. Solve the crime and get out. No hearts on the line. No emotions to shatter.

"Ah, but Kelly, love is a mystery. Isn't it?"

Abram's words ribboned around the room and sent a tingle of goosebumps across her skin. "I'm not sure what you mean."

"For instance, Mr. Declan McNeary." Sitting back, Abram shot her a sheepish grin. "Do you have feelings for him?"

"Why in the world would you ask me that?" *How could he know?* She placed her mug back on the table.

"He seems very fond of you," Abram said. "Why would you not?"

She tried to read Abram's expression. But couldn't.

"He's a nice, handsome man—an Irishman, if I judged correctly—and you're a clever and beautiful young woman."

Her heart sank. *No one could know about my feelings for Declan. Could they?*

"Mr. McNeary gave a glowing recommendation for you." He seemed blind to her uneasiness as he continued. "I've talked to him several times, and he can only say good things about you. Very complimentary."

She swallowed. "I would hope so. He is my agent. It would be a little awkward if he disliked me." Prickly heat crept across her neck as a flash of Declan's beautiful face traipsed across her mind.

"Well, it's a mystery why you two aren't together. Isn't it?" His brows rose. "Do you know much about him? He seems to know a lot about you, Kelly dear."

She opened her mouth, then clamped it shut. This was ridiculous. Who does Abram Zucker think he is? A matchmaker? This interview wasn't what she'd expected—or prepared for.

After a moment, the lines around Abram's eyes softened. "I'm an old man. I may have spoken out of turn. Forgive me?"

"Uh, yes." She relaxed her shoulders. Was this some bizarre test to see how she could handle herself under pressure? "I'd love to talk about Edna and Otto. Your mother and father." She forced a weak smile, hoping to redirect the conversation.

"Right. A love story but not quite a mystery." Abram winked at her.

"Or a whodunit."

"Oh, you might be surprised."

"Really?" Her heart skipped as she dug through her bag for her notebook and pen.

Abram stretched out his wrinkled hand and placed it on hers. "No notes today. Let's take a walk."

"A walk?" Her pen and paper mimicked a protective sword and shield, and she hesitated to put them away.

"Yes, it's a little cooler today. Don't you think?"

Her eyes darted to the window. She hadn't noticed the weather.

Without being summoned, the same man who'd brought Abram in entered the room.

"This is Trevor." Abram waved a wrinkled hand in her direction. "Trevor, this is Kelly. The author I told you about."

"Nice to meet you, Kelly." Trevor shot her a smile then secured the blanket around Abram's feet. "Abram's told me a lot about you." Trevor gripped the handles of Abram's chair and moved him toward the door. "Where are we walking today?"

Abram gestured for her to join them. "Let's walk in the rose garden."

Kelly stashed her pen and notepad in her bag and met them by the door. Today's interview hadn't unfolded the way she'd expected. She'd planned to gather information to determine if she and Abram would be a good fit. What she didn't expect was a quirky, older gentleman who would derail those plans.

She followed Trevor and Abram down the hallway leading to the elevator. What would the rest of the day bring? Maybe a shift from the normal wouldn't be so bad.

3

Kelly walked next to Abram as Trevor pushed him along a winding path. Abram had been right. It was cooler today, and the fresh breeze was working to calm the reservations in her mind about the possibility of working with Abram.

After they walked a while, Abram spoke up. "So, tell me, how did you come to be such a fascinating authoress?"

Fascinating? Entertaining, maybe, but not fascinating. "Well … I …"

"I've done some research on you, Miss Landon—I mean Kelly. You graduated at the top of your class at university. You have a degree in …" He hesitated for a moment as if drawing the information from the back of his mind. "Library science with a minor in creative writing."

He *had* done his research.

"Tell me about your writing process. I think I should know what it is if we're to work together."

"I just consider the world around me. There are so many puzzles I want to piece together. I like to pick a setting before I begin—like an off-the-beaten-path town or an old, abandoned home." She glanced over her shoulder. "Or maybe a Georgian mansion." Then, looking up at the sky, she added, "For a while, my head was in the clouds, though."

"Ah, yes, the science fiction novellas." Abram chuckled. "I enjoyed those very much."

"Thank you. You were one of the few."

He laughed. "Tell me more about how you begin a story?"

"I do research. A lot of research. I want to make the story believable."

Abram brushed his beard with his hand. "Good to hear you're not afraid of a little investigation."

"In fact, that's my favorite part."

"Another by-product of your remarkable intelligence."

She quieted for a moment. At times, she regretted the quirks in her brain and the super-charged memory that cataloged snapshots of history in her thoughts. The pink rosettes on the cookie plate. The number of buttons on Donna's sweater. The crisscross pattern on the teaspoon she used to stir her coffee. Most of the useless details she could pull up at will. Except meeting Abram. Why couldn't she pull that memory forward?

"It's okay to be smart. And to remember things." His expression softened. "As we get older, those memories are harder to hold on to."

She fumbled with the delicate gold chain dangling around her neck. She never wanted to forget the smell of her mother. Soft rose water and mint. Or the way her father's eyes danced with excitement when he talked about faraway places.

"I'll admit I questioned Mr. McNeary about your writing style. I wanted to make sure you'd be a good fit for the story I'm about to release into the world."

Abram's statement yanked her back from her distant thoughts. "Well, let's hope I don't disappoint you." *Or Declan.*

"I'm not worried about that in the least." He looked up at her as they continued along the path. "What do you think is an important element in every good story?"

"I think it's important to leave something out until the very end. The readers can come to their own conclusions." She stopped walking. "Like a missing piece to a puzzle."

"That's perfect. Like a treasure hunt for your readers."

"Exactly."

As they came to a square garden lined with rose bushes, Abram glanced up at Trevor. "You can leave us for now. Thank you."

Trevor nodded and tucked Abram's blanket snug around his legs before he turned to go.

"Why don't you take a seat?" Abram motioned toward the bench next to the three-tiered fountain.

She studied his profile as he sat in silence, looking out over the manicured grounds. The lines on Abram's face compressed into neat rows as he glanced up into the sun's rays and squinted.

"What story do you see here?" Abram gestured to the rose garden.

"Let's see." Kelly considered how she should proceed. Since everything about today struck her as unconventional, she decided to let her guard down. "If I were to start here, I might say this garden holds a dark secret." She shifted and moved her gaze back to the mansion. "A secret about the family who lived here for generations."

Standing, she walked over to the vibrant, purple-hued rose at the center of the garden. "Imagine a treasure hidden—yes, buried—just beneath this florid rose bush." She caressed the silky petals with her thumb and forefinger as the spicy scent from the bloom drifted up to her nose.

Abram turned his wheelchair to face her, his eyes alight with pleasure. "Treasure. That's a good place to start."

"Imagine an antiquated family heirloom hidden here. Some bauble holding a deep connection to the past." She looked around the garden. Her imagination twirled to life. This was her favorite game to play, and she'd played it since childhood. "This rose was planted on the exact day the treasure was buried, to throw off the evidence of loose dirt." Dipping her voice into a hushed tone, she added, "The amaranthine purple resembles the color of the dress—the dress of the woman who buried the treasure."

She closed her eyes while a fresh story looped in circles in her mind—a story cloaked in mystery and wrapped in the anticipation of solving a crime. When her eyes fluttered open, she breathed in the intense, floral aromas gliding around her in the breeze.

"Bravo! Bravo!" Abram clapped and cheered. "You almost convinced me we should dig up that rose and find out what treasure lay beneath it."

She took a quick bow before she returned to her seat on the bench next to Abram.

"Now, let's try something else."

She turned to face him. "Like what?" Somehow, she'd slipped down a rabbit hole and landed in a garden of make-believe.

"Tell me what love story you see."

Her chest tightened. *Declan.* His name skipped across her mind, and her stomach clenched. Allowing herself to imagine him as anything more than her agent would lead her down a path of disappointment.

"Take your time." Abram's quiet voice broke through her thoughts.

"I could see two people falling in love here. This garden would be a beautiful place to have a proposal, or maybe a wedding."

"Very good. Now, what about an ending?" He patted her hand as he asked, "Would it be a happy ending?"

I'm afraid to imagine a happy ending. Kelly shook her head. She'd discarded her belief in fairy-tale love long ago and exchanged it for a more realistic expectation. "I've got nothing." Her shoulders fell. "I guess this means the interview is over?"

"Hardly, my dear." Warmth ensconced his words. "We're just beginning."

A weight lifted from her as they continued to talk about writing and travel for almost an hour. As morning neared noon, she sensed a gentle attachment blossoming between her and this grandfather figure who'd shaken her world with his quirky personality.

"I need a quick rest. Would you mind taking me back to the house?" Abram gestured toward the paved path.

"Of course." While she pushed his chair down the path, she studied the beauty of the Zucker home with its perfectly bricked three-story walls and twin rectangular chimneys. "How long have you lived here, Abram?"

"Long enough to know there aren't any secrets hidden beneath the *Ebb Tide* rose."

She brought the wheelchair to a standstill and stared up at the white pediment framing the portico. *What mysteries are behind that stately façade?*

"Is something wrong?"

"No—no, I'm sorry. I'm just admiring the beautiful design of your home." Her mind flashed back to the picture of the tree in Abram's home. Should she inquire about its origins? Or was she only being suspicious?

"I think this is the start of a beautiful friendship. What do you say?" Abram tilted his head to look at her.

"I—uh, yes." With whitewashed knuckles, she pushed Abram through the front door. A beautiful friendship. Or an unsolved mystery. Releasing her death grip on Abram's chair, she moved to retrieve her handbag that was now hanging on the hook by the door.

Abram spun to face her. "Maybe we should bury a time capsule."

"What?" She blinked, trying to keep up. This man was full of riddles and plot twists.

"Beneath the rose."

"Um … okay. What would we put inside?"

His face lit up with a boyish grin. "I'm sure I have some secret treasure around here somewhere. Something for my great-granddaughter to find when I'm gone."

A familiar ache pressed against her chest. When he was gone. They'd only just met. "A time capsule could be fun."

"Ever since I was a boy, I've hidden treasures for safekeeping." His eyes sparked with mischief. "Shall I see you in two days?"

"Two days?" His question startled her. "Sure."

"We'll take lunch on the veranda. I have something exciting for you to read." He winked at her then lowered his voice to a cryptic pitch. "I might even have a mystery or two for you to unravel."

There was no doubt she'd have plenty of mysteries to unravel with this man. "Okay. Two days. I'll see you then."

After she stepped across the threshold, Kelly walked to her vehicle in a daze.

She pulled out her keys and pushed the button to unlock her car. *Why can't I remember if I've met Abram before? When did he take a picture of my tree?*

Her mind circled through a throng of questions, as she slipped into her SUV and stared back at the Zucker mansion. There were hundreds of trees resembling the one she remembered from her childhood garden. Her imagination was just running wild. Right?

Kelly shook off the thought and started the car. If she'd met Abram before, she'd remember. Her mind wouldn't let her forget. Would it? "Maybe the picture was just that—a picture."

She drove around the circular drive then pulled onto the desolate highway as a final question popped into her mind. What made Abram ask about my feelings for Declan?

A warm tingle crept its way across the back of her neck. How had he known the secret desire of her heart? To love and be loved.

Pulling back her shoulders, she fought to ignore the ache pressing on her chest.

The easy and honest way Abram knit himself into her heart today almost made her want to believe in the mystery of love.

Almost.

25

4

"What's all over your desk, Writer Girl?" Declan waved a hand over the leatherbound books stacked in front of her.

"Just a couple of old journals." She glanced up from her computer and casually tried to shift the books closer to her. Following her second meeting with Abram, a box of journals had arrived at her house along with a request—*Please keep these journals safe. They contain treasures my family's kept secret for years and are for your eyes only.*

"Looks like more than just a couple."

"True. There're about twenty."

He moved around her desk, inspecting the stacks. "Are these all from Abram?"

"They are." Her eyes roamed over the words on her monitor. She frowned when she caught herself reading the same sentence more than once.

"Have you unearthed any mysteries yet?" Declan picked up a journal and flipped through the pages. "You've been at it for weeks."

She shot up from her chair and laid a protective hand on the worn leather. After their meetings, a bond had formed between

Abram and her. A bond she couldn't quite explain. *It sometimes feels as if I'm conversing with my dad again.*

She tugged the journal out of Declan's hand and laid it back on the pile. "Don't mess up the stacks. They're in calendar order."

Declan held her gaze for a moment before lifting his hands in surrender. "Understood."

She lowered herself into her desk chair and glanced back at the screen. *Where was I? He's so distracting.*

Moments earlier, Declan had appeared out of the blue, standing on her doorstep and holding out a cup of coffee like a peace offering. She appreciated anything with a shot of flavor and lots of milk. Today, he'd brought a hot, toffee-nut latte with extra whipped cream. When she snatched the drink out of his hand, she took note of how effortlessly handsome he looked in his slim-fitting navy suit and invited him in.

I'm going to get nothing done today. Zilch. Kelly pulled her gaze from her screen to Declan.

"I didn't mean to interrupt your research." Small creases crinkled at his eyes. "I guess I'm a little overzealous to find out what you might dig up."

"I hardly think it will be earth-shattering." She waved him off and tried to sound nonchalant. "It's just a love story."

He unfastened the buttons of his suit jacket, then slid into a chair near the window. As he crossed an ankle over his knee, the body-hugging sleeves tugged at his arms. Kelly's mouth dried, and she looked away. *Where was I?* She glanced back at the cursor, and it blinked at her like a warning sign. *Focus.*

"Love stories have put a lot of authors on the shelves, Writer Girl."

"Ha! Not this author." Keeping her eyes averted from his, she typed a few words. *Once upon a time …* She backspaced. *While German troops marched into the town …* That's better. In her peripheral vision, she caught the corner of Declan's lips as they twitched into a cool smile. She lifted her chin. "You're distracting me."

"Am I?" He tilted his head and shot her a playful look. "I'm curious. You won't write them, but do you *read* romance novels?"

She stilled and silently begged the rush of fire filling her cheeks not to give her away.

"Is that color painting your expression a yes or a no?"

Her cheeks flamed hotter. It was hard to spar with a man who made her stomach feel as though it hatched a kaleidoscope of butterflies.

Dropping his foot to the floor, Declan leaned forward in the chair and rested his elbows on his knees. "What about tragic romance? *Romeo and Juliet*?"

Before she could counter with a witty comeback, he catapulted out of the seat and strolled around the room. After a second, he whistled a soft tune. Kelly rolled her eyes. With his hands clasped behind his back, Declan appeared self-assured and just a tad arrogant. A look that suited him. She returned her attention to her computer and tried to recall where she was in her notes.

"Aha!" Declan's hoot of victory carried across the room. He withdrew a book from her Jane Austen collection. "I knew it." He strolled over and laid a copy of *Pride and Prejudice* on her desk. "Writer Girl *does* read romance."

"How do you know I'm not just a collector?" Kelly forced her clammy palms to rest on the keyboard as she angled her face to meet his. "Everyone likes Jane Austen." Then, with one hand, she waved him off. "This memoir isn't going to write itself."

"The lady doth protest too much, methinks." His jade eyes darkened to the color of a moonlit, stormy ocean.

"If you want me to write this book, I need to get back to work." She'd get nothing done with him quoting Shakespeare.

He arched an eyebrow then continued his perusal of her library.

I wonder if Hamlet would sound better in Shakespearean English or Irish Gaelic? She shook off the question and tracked Declan as he sauntered around the room. He pivoted and caught her staring at him. Her pulse jumped.

He turned back to the bookshelf and in one languid motion, traced his fingers over a specific row of books. She took that moment to admire the smooth lines of his suit and the angles of his well-chiseled jawline. *Beautiful.*

He tugged at a book on the top shelf. For a brief moment, he considered the cover, then strolled back to her desk. As if handling a rare artifact, he laid the book in front of her. "It's true. You *are* a collector of Austen, Miss Landon."

The skin around her collarbone flamed with heat. He'd stumbled upon her treasured, rare edition of *Pride and Prejudice.*

He opened the first book he'd brought over. It had a bright blue cover with a white title, but the corners were worn with use. He turned a few pages and stopped about a third of the way through. Beneath his finger, a folded dog-eared page, then a few pages over, an old ace-of-hearts held a spot. Finally, he fingered through a couple more pages and pointed to a cluster of maple-colored coffee stains. "But, Miss Landon, you are also a partaker of Austen." Declan flashed her a cat-that-ate-the-canary grin. "You cannot deny the proof."

Her veins pulsed with fire. Pulling her eyes from his sultry gaze, she stood, picked up her cherished collectible, and darted around her desk to the bookshelf. Straining, she balanced on her tiptoes and slid the book back onto the top shelf. "I guess you've found me out, Mr. McNeary." When she turned, he'd swooped in and stood only a few inches from her. Her breath hitched.

"Yes, I guess I have." His expression was a mask of brooding self-control. A look even Austen would find unnerving. "I wonder what other mysteries you're hiding."

I'm afraid to believe in happy endings. Her pulse quickened, and she struggled to piece together an intelligent thought.

"Kelly." The sun's rays from the bay window waved across

his eyes, transforming their hue from a shadowy green into a watery jade. He leaned in, and his lips parted as if he was going to say something more, then he closed them again.

"Yes?"

He stepped back, bowed theatrically, then fastened the buttons of his suit jacket and tugged at his cuffs. "I can see I've invaded your space, Miss Landon. I'll leave and let you get back to reading your … *romantic* journals." He shot her a wink, then just as quickly as he arrived, Declan let himself out the front door.

Kelly laid a hand over her erratically beating heart. "What was that all about?"

With jelly legs, she returned to her desk and attempted to read the second line on the screen for the fourth time that afternoon.

5

Donna led Kelly into the sunlit room on the second floor. A chill still clung to her after the short walk from her car to the house, and she tugged her sweater closer. The holidays were approaching, and winter's sunshine, while inviting, had done little to ward off the crisp afternoon breeze.

Abram sat by the window, glancing out over the gardens and looking lost in thought. As she approached him, he pulled his gaze from the sprawling acreage and turned to face her. "Hello, Kelly, dear. How are you today?"

"I'm good." A shadow of concern stole over her. The circles under his eyes appeared deeper, and the blue irises that normally flickered with life had dimmed. "How are *you* feeling today?"

"Well, you know," he gestured to the chair next to him, and she sat down. "Good days and some not-so-good days. But every day is a gift. Is it not?"

She smiled. Abram's positive tone always brought an airy cheeriness to their conversation even if it tore at her soul to see him so weak

"Did you enjoy the journals?"

His question pulled her away from her melancholy thoughts.

"I did." After poring over the Zucker family journals and boxes of newspaper clippings, she couldn't wait to start writing.

"What did you learn from them?"

"Well, they weren't only letters about a simple courtship as I first believed." She tipped her chin and threw him a chiding look.

"True." His brows lifted. "They *were* love letters, but there's much more to my parents' story. Don't you think?"

"Yes." She let her mind drift to everything she'd read about the Zucker family. Otto and Edna Zucker, owners of a small bakery, exemplified a simplistic family unit, but as they stepped out of those roles, their choices made them enemies of a very dangerous régime. "Your mother and father took a great risk to save those children."

"They did. What do you think compelled them to take such a risk?"

She considered his question. "They were daring and courageous, but their unwavering faith directed every decision. Otto and Edna believed helping those children escape was their calling."

"You're right. What about the theme of the letters? What stuck out to you as you read them?"

A lump expanded in her throat. The resounding phrase *God is love* was peppered throughout their correspondence. Those words pried at the door to her heart—a door she'd long ago sealed and whose key she'd discarded. *Where was God's love when I begged Him to bring my mom back?* A shadowy memory of a little girl kneeling on the floor beside her bed petitioning the Almighty with heartfelt requests to bring her mom home floated across her mind. Clearing her throat, she shoved the image away.

"Kelly, dear, is everything okay?"

"Yes, yes, I'm fine." Looking up, she waved off his concern while a long-ignored ache continued to grip her chest. After her mother left them, her father became distant, pouring himself into his job and hobbies. When he was around, she sensed his thoughts were always a million miles away. Now that she was on her own and an orphan, God's love felt that way to her too. *But who walked away? Me or God?* As a little girl's longing for security and love bubbled to the surface, she pinched her eyes shut to suppress the wave of unwanted tears.

Abram reached out his hand and laid it on hers. "Do you remember how Edna and Otto signed their letters?"

She opened her eyes and nodded. She was afraid her voice would betray her if she replied.

"God is love." He squeezed her hand then pulled a handkerchief from his pocket and handed it to her. "That's the theme of God's letter to us as well. God's love is interlaced through every story from Genesis to Revelation."

Shifting in her seat, she dabbed her eyes. The kind of love she'd seen exemplified in the story of Edna and Otto Zucker—a trustworthy, genuine, and unconditional love—made her wonder if God's love *was* something she could put her trust in.

"I'm here. If you ever need a friend to talk to, you have one in me."

She bundled the handkerchief in her fist. "Thank you. I appreciate that."

"What else did you learn about my parents?"

"They loved God more than their own lives, which, in turn, is how they loved those children."

A twinkle of joy flashed in his eyes. "I think you're beginning to see the heart of their story."

"I think I am too." The cumbersome weight of sadness pinning her emotions to a singular place in time, loosened. "Are we ready to write?"

Abram's tone shifted like the wind in a hurricane. "Before we begin, we need to discuss the journals."

"Okay."

"They must stay in your possession."

"You don't want them back?"

"No." Concern crept over his features. "I want you to keep them."

The request sounded odd, but she'd grown accustomed to his idiosyncratic personality. "If that's what you want, I'll hold on to them."

"Remember what I said." The urgency in his voice stepped up. "You can't let anyone else read them." Abram held her gaze for a heartbeat, then he looked out the window. "For now, at least."

She leaned forward and tried to read his expression. "I'm writing the story of Edna and Otto. Their story, if I do my job well, will be published and available to everyone."

"Yes, yes. Of course." Abram looked back at her, his expression a mask of weariness. "I just pray the *right* person reads their story."

An uneasy shudder crawled down her spine. *The right person?* "Abram? Are you having second thoughts about me writing this book?" Although she'd be disappointed to have taken months away from her own writing, she'd respect his wishes if he wanted to put a pause on the project.

He shook his head. "No. I want you to write it. It's just as much your story as it is mine."

Leaning back in her seat, she considered his words. "Don't worry about the contract, Abram." Her chest squeezed. She'd come to care for the eccentric old man, and she'd be willing to intervene if he wanted to walk away. "I can talk to Declan, and he—"

Abram held up a hand, cutting her off. "No, I want to move forward. Just keep the journals safe. They, along with my parents' story, are yours now."

He talked as if he were leaving on a long journey. Kelly's heart sank. "Of course. I won't let anyone else read the journals."

"Those journals hold secrets." Abram waved her closer. "Hidden treasures from the past."

"What secrets?" Mimicking his tone, she kept her voice low. "What treasures am I supposed to be looking for?"

"Sometimes the treasures are hidden within the story." Abram sent her an imploring look. "You should know that."

"I've read everything. Twice." She rubbed her temples. "What did I miss?"

"I don't want the secrets to die with me." He straightened, and with trembling hands, Abram fiddled with the woolen blanket in his lap. "My parents were wonderful people to help those children the way they did. I don't want their sacrifices to be in vain."

She mentally shuffled through the letters she'd read between Edna and Otto. Nothing seemed out of the ordinary. Young and in love, they found themselves immersed in a war they didn't anticipate or want. They became enemies of the German government and risked their lives to save Jewish children who could not fight for themselves. The Zuckers were selfless heroes, and their story deserved to be told. In her mind, they and others like them were the hidden treasures of that war.

"Abram, I don't think there are any more secrets in their story." Her heart broke as a forlorn expression stretched across his wrinkled face. *Is he forgetting the war is over?*

He reached out his hand to pat hers. She observed more signs of aging in his pale, translucent skin. "Someday, it will all make sense to you, Kelly, dear. When you solve the mystery." He turned his gaze toward the window, appearing to focus on something beyond the now barren rose garden. "Someday, after I'm gone, history will collide with the present, and you will understand." He cut a look back in her direction. The intensity in his stare sent an icy shiver through her. "In time, you will know what to do with the information I've given you. Just keep researching."

She sat in silence while her mind spun with questions. *Know what to do?*

Abram seemed in no hurry to reveal the secrets locked

behind the veil of his mind, and she was running out of time to retrieve them.

As the grandfather clock's chimes echoed down the hall, her heart tore in two. *I don't want to lose him.*

Determination welled inside of her.

She'd start writing tonight. Then, she hoped, she'd unearth the secrets he'd alluded to before it was too late.

6

K elly took a long drink of her coffee and placed it back on the coaster. It was her second cup of hot brew that morning. No doubt there'd be another one to follow. *I wish he would say something.* She tapped her foot lightly on the floor. It's a good story. No. It was an intriguing story. Something she could imagine played out on the History Channel in a documentary. A morsel of history to pass on to other generations.

Declan peered at her over the laptop then lowered his gaze back to the screen, his stoic expression giving her no hint of his thoughts.

She slumped back onto the couch. He'd been at it for hours—reading her work and tapping on the keys like an agitated woodpecker. She'd already finished two crossword puzzles and cleaned out her fridge in a weak attempt to occupy her mind.

Inhaling deeply, Kelly shifted forward in her seat and turned her attention to the window. Bluebirds tittered the arrival of spring while the fresh buds of green waved from the trees. A new season. A new story. Where had the time gone?

She flicked a look at Declan. There were eighty thousand words on those pages, indicating exactly where her time had gone. Eighty-three thousand, two-hundred six, to be exact. A perfectly reasonable amount of writing to put into print.

Moreover, with Abram's family linked to wealth both in America and abroad, there was no doubt the memoir would turn out to be a best seller.

She blew out her breath and stared at the clock. Time was a curious thing. Some days it slipped through her fingers, and other days, it idled like an indolent cat. She'd spent most of her time this winter tethered to a laptop, piecing together the story of Edna and Otto. It hadn't been a waste of time. Had it?

"Has he given you any more information he wants you to include?" Declan pushed back from the desk and morphed from an easygoing friend into a resolute Olympic coach.

"No. Why?" Her gut twisted. "The story was simple. Boy meets girl, boy falls in love and—"

"And they are caught up in the middle of a horrific war." He rose and paced the length of the room. "You wrote about them making risky decisions and how they helped several Jewish children escape death."

"Yes." She picked up her mug and took a slow drink. "I also included a lengthy account of how they skirted the authorities by using their bakery as a front."

She understood this dance of push and pull. The way he tried to glean from her all the details of the story. His method of drawing more from her could be exhausting, but it was worth it every time.

"I even included postwar newspaper articles detailing what they'd accomplished directly under the nose of the German authorities."

"Where are the details? The hidden gems of this story." Declan's eyes glinted with energy. "Where are the words that make me want to jump into this book and experience it for myself?"

She set her mug down and rubbed her sweaty palms on her jeans. "This is what Abram wanted published."

"Yes, but there has to be more." Declan walked around the room and raked his fingers through the loose waves on top of his head. "You focused on their spiritual heritage, about how they were led by God to preserve life, even if it cost them theirs."

"Yes?"

"That's all very endearing, but where's the hook?"

"The hook?"

"Yes, Miss Landon, the hook." He did an about-face and glided toward her like a panther on the prowl. "The story makes me want more." He sank into the sofa beside her. "Is there more to tell? Are there any unsolved mysteries in Abram's story? Did he leave anything out that would shoot this book to the top of the best-seller list?"

"I ..." Her voice caught in her throat. "I put everything in that Abram and I discussed." It was true. She'd included everything Abram wanted her to add—every minuscule detail. Some of those details, even as odd as the type of buttons his Uncle Gerhard, who was a bookbinder, wore on his jacket. If the facts were important to Abram, she added them.

"As the writer, it's up to you to unravel the secrets of a story." Declan shifted to face her. "I can see it in your eyes. You've got something you're holding back from me." He reached for her hands. "Memoirs are tricky. It's up to the author to act as an investigator."

Kelly took a quick breath as he caressed the back of her hands with his thumbs. She wasn't sure what flustered her more, his touch or the fact he sensed she kept something from him.

"You knew this wasn't going to be a mystery or a thriller when you asked me to write the Zucker memoir." She tried to lighten her voice. After months of collaboration, she'd only gleaned one mystery from her eccentric friend about the journals —they needed her protection. As for Edna and Otto's story, if there were any mysteries hidden, once the story was published, they'd no longer be a secret.

"Yes, yes, I know." Releasing her hands, he leaned back against the cushions and rubbed his temples. "I wish there would've been more information about the war itself. How did they evade the Gestapo so many times? Were there others involved? Who helped the Zuckers? What about the families they helped? Are there any names?" He turned to face her, his eyes alight with interest. "Where are these kids now? Wouldn't that be a story?"

She pursed her lips. *Someday, it will all make sense to you.* Abram's words echoed in her memory.

"Do you have a list of the children?"

Declan's question jolted her. "No. I wrote what Abram wanted." She rose and walked over to the window. "I spent months on this project, and the man who hired me has already read the final draft."

Declan stood and joined her.

As she turned to face him, her heart hammered against her ribs. "Abram's pleased with what I've written, and so am I."

"Oh, it's a good piece." Folding his arms, he leaned against the molding. "I thought maybe with your genius for solving puzzles, you would've extracted something a little more controversial." His lips pulled into a lazy grin. "A diamond in the rough, so to speak."

She pulled her gaze from his and glanced out over the front yard. She couldn't let him see the deceit cultivating inside her. *Don't list the children. We need to protect them.*

"Kelly, you know I'm only trying to help."

"I know."

"It seems I may have pushed my Writer Girl a little too much this time."

"I'm fine. I ..." When she pivoted to face him, moisture gathered in her lashes.

"I'm sorry. It wasn't my intention to hurt your feelings. Only to draw out more from the story." He studied her for another second before he stepped back and moved to the entryway. "I should go."

A longing to ask him to stay flooded her heart. *Be careful.* She frowned. She hated acting like a clumsy teenager when Declan's presence made her tongue-tied and her knees weak.

"Declan, I …" Unable to finish, she shifted on her feet and wrapped her arms around her middle.

"Let's finish this critique tomorrow." His unhurried tone tugged at her heart like a symphony. "It's good writing, Miss Landon. I hope you understand I'm only doing my job."

"I know you are."

A battle raged inside her. She wanted to tell him everything. To share with him every undisclosed detail Abram ever let slip past his lips. She wanted Declan to join her on this mysterious journey as she tried to untangle the puzzle of the Zucker family history.

But she couldn't.

"It's all in there." Her chest tightened. "The story is complete."

"Okay." The muscles in Declan's jaw twitched. "I'll send it off to the editor tomorrow. We'll aim for a late fall release."

She nodded then waited while he turned and let himself out the door. As she listened for the hum of his car engine, she stood rooted to the floor.

She'd just lied to the one person she'd wanted to grow closer to.

If he found out, would he forgive her?

Or had she just crushed any possibility at a happily ever after with her agent?

7

As Kelly opened the taxi door, sounds of the city pelted her senses, along with the crisp fall air. *It's just a business dinner. It's just a business dinner.* The mantra played in her mind like a record with a skip.

"Why did I get so dressed up?" Stepping out of the taxi, she tugged her coat tighter. They were discussing the memoir's release, but it was Friday night, and Declan had made reservations.

"It's only Declan. Your agent. Relax." She fidgeted with the pins in her hair, then smoothed her hands down the front of her coat.

Her gaze landed on the windows, where she surveyed the tables through the partially drawn curtains of the restaurant. It was busy. Somehow he'd garnered a table.

Taking in a long cleansing breath, she turned and followed the lights of the taxi as it drove away. "I guess I can't run away now." She searched for her rehearsed confidence and pulled it to the surface. *You splurged on a new dress. So what? People buy new clothes all the time.* She squared her shoulders and glided across the pavement to the restaurant's door.

"Good evening." As she entered, the host slid an appraising look over her. "Do you have a reservation?"

Breathe. "I'm meeting someone."

"Wonderful. The name?"

"Mr. Declan McNeary."

The host's face brightened as he stepped out from behind his podium and held out his arm. "He's expecting you. May I take your coat?"

With shaky hands, she undid the buttons and slipped her arms out of her double-breasted, swing cloak.

"Right this way." The host passed off her coat to the woman lingering behind the counter, then guided Kelly to a secluded table by the window. "Enjoy your evening."

Declan stood as they approached. "Miss Landon." His usually smooth voice hitched. "You look—that dress is stunning." While he kept an appreciative gaze on her, he pulled out her chair.

"Thank you."

He looks incredible. She blinked, praying nobody in the restaurant could read her mind.

After she slid into her seat, Kelly looked out the window. Headlights lined the busy street, and the night sky had transitioned from a warm tangerine into a shadowy magenta. *Stop fidgeting.* Still feeling his eyes on her, she turned to face him.

"I'm sorry." Declan adjusted his tie. "I didn't mean to stare. You look amazing. Is that a new dress?"

"Yes."

"You have impeccable taste." He lifted the menu and cleared his throat.

Her insides vibrated. A new outfit had been a good idea.

"I've never seen you this dressed up before. It's kind of rattled me." He peeked impishly over the menu.

Rattled herself, she lowered her gaze to the menu and tried to focus on the descriptions of French cuisine.

"Your necklace."

She looked up.

He nodded toward the pendant while his gaze lingered on her neckline. "It's exquisite. Is it a family heirloom?"

"I guess you could say that." The delicate gold chain led to a pendant twisted into the shape of an outstretched tree. Six emeralds were set as leaves, while hand-cut diamond accents dappled the sparkling vines twisting around the trunk.

"Care to elaborate? I love a good story, you know." Declan's engaging smile unwound the nervous tension coiled inside of her.

"It was a gift from my father."

"Really?" He leaned forward to take another look. "May I?"

Her body tingled as she lifted the necklace and brought it toward his extended hand.

"What a magnificent piece of art. You probably don't know this about me, but I'm a bit of a gemstone enthusiast."

"Are you?"

"I am. I sometimes collect items that catch my eye." He flashed her a roguish grin. "Tell me about your father. You don't talk about your family much."

"There isn't much to tell."

"That can't be true. Family means everything."

Did it? At one time she believed that, until hers fractured into an unrecognizable shell of childhood memories. Straightening in her chair, she attempted to unpack a few safe layers. "My father worked a lot. I saw him only occasionally. Sometimes, I imagined him as an eccentric uncle who swept in on occasion to whisk me off to faraway places."

"Were you and your mother close?"

The memory of her mother pressed an uncomfortable ache in her heart. "She died when I was a teenager."

"I'm sorry, I didn't realize." He shifted his tie again and looked away.

It didn't surprise her he'd started to fidget. Nobody liked to discuss the death of a parent.

"It's okay." When he looked up, she shrugged, hoping to

lighten the mood. "I had a wonderful nanny, and my father provided well." She fiddled with the menu and held back the story of how her father's moods swayed to the irrational during the latter years of his life. Or that she longed for his attention while he worked unusual hours and obsessed over their safety.

Declan's features relaxed. "That's something to be grateful for."

"Yes, I suppose it is."

"Did your father give you the necklace on a special occasion?"

His question pulled her from her thoughts, and she redirected her gaze back to the necklace. The candlelight between them caused the emeralds to dance and sparkle.

"Actually, he gave me just the emeralds." She reached up to the earrings hidden behind the tendrils of her hair. "There are twelve total."

He reached over to study the earring. After he released it, his finger brushed across the soft skin below her earlobe. "They're beautiful."

She swallowed past a shiver. "I designed the settings myself."

"Did you?"

She nodded. "I took a few sketches to a jeweler shortly after my dad passed, and they pieced it together for me."

"Is there meaning behind the design?"

"The tree resembles one I remember from my childhood." A brief flash of the photograph in Abram's house tumbled into her thoughts. When she'd asked him when he'd taken the photo, he'd acted as if his memory had escaped him.

"The deep green suggests their level of purity. Have you had them appraised?"

"I did." She took a sip of her water and waved him off. "I don't wear them often. I'm afraid to lose them."

"No one wants to lose a priceless treasure." He smiled, leaning closer. "I want to know more about you, Writer Girl. You're still such a mystery to me."

"I hardly feel like a mystery."

"To me, you are. I want you to let me into that beautiful, enigmatic mind of yours." Reaching across the table, he took her hand and curled his fingers around hers.

Kelly stilled. From the moment they'd met, she could think of nothing more than letting him in—into her mind, into her life, and into her heart.

"Tell me more about your father's pursuits. They sound fascinating." His thumb twirled lazy circles in her palm while he waited for her to answer.

Releasing a long breath, she felt the weight of loneliness lift like the fluff of dandelion seeds caught in the wind. "My father combed Europe for rare antiquities. He seemed bent on finding the one valuable object that would finally give him peace. It was his passion." *Or obsession.* She studied their hands. The warmth from Declan's touch continued to pry open the doors of her guarded heart. Lifting her gaze back to his, she added, "I never cared for it much—chasing after outdated objects. It was a dusty, dirty hobby."

Declan released a low ripple of laughter, and the melodic sound glided around them. As he pulled his hand back, he lifted his glass and took an unhurried drink of Cabernet Sauvignon. When he lowered his glass, he shot her an inviting look. "So, you don't see the allure of *old* relics?"

"I don't."

His brows lifted. "That's too bad. We have a couple of years between us."

"Oh … I …" Her heart knocked against her ribcage. "I meant, no—to the relics. But as for you, well, you're barely in your thirties. Hardly an antique."

Curving his lips into a grin, he lifted his glass again. "To antiques, just not the dusty ones."

She laughed. "I thought objects needed to be at least a hundred years old to be considered antiques." She picked up her water, and the pitch of glass clinking echoed between them. "I say, here's to priceless treasures."

"I like that. Priceless treasures." His gaze heated as he lowered his glass. "Tell me more about the treasures your father searched for."

Kelly relaxed as she waved her hand across the table and envisioned a scene from long ago. "My father would bring home books, papers, pictures, trinkets—if it was antiquated, it was strewn across our dining room table."

"That doesn't leave much room for family meals."

She frowned. "No, it doesn't."

"Did his search include gemstones?"

"Sometimes. He'd dismantle jewelry, then study and date the various stones. I have pages of his ledgers in storage."

"What an interesting pastime your father dabbled in."

The waiter approached to take their orders.

"Do you recommend something?" Kelly asked. "I haven't been here before."

"I've never had anything here I didn't enjoy." Declan winked at her. His overt confidence and charm intermingled with the opulent setting of the restaurant.

With the menu's descriptions already tucked safely in her mind, she decided quickly on a seafood plate with a side of steamed vegetables. The waiter took Declan's order then scurried away.

"Your story about your father fascinates me. I can't imagine why anyone would take jewelry apart."

She shrugged. "He was an odd man at times."

Declan asked a few more questions, then he talked about his early years as a literary agent. She enjoyed his stories about his past clients, and his ideas about how history influences fiction.

After their dinner arrived, she continued to expound on her life, growing up with a brilliant yet eccentric father. "My father loved history. He searched high and low for old books and old photographs. It was as if the past was somehow calling out to him. As he grew older, the call became stronger."

Declan leaned back in his seat as the subject morphed from antiquities to their love of classic literature and coffee.

"Speaking of." He bent his head and cocked an eyebrow. "I know it's late, but would you care for a cup of coffee?"

"It's never too late for coffee."

When the waiter brought them their cups and a small pitcher of cream, they reached for the porcelain decanter at the same time. As their fingers touched, they exchanged a knowing look.

"What's coffee without cream?" Declan pushed the pitcher toward her.

"Exactly."

"It's almost as bad as jewels without a setting."

Their relaxed conversation draped around her like a toasty fire on a winter's night. "I agree."

While the two of them chatted over a cup of creamy coffee, the waiter cleared their dishes, and Declan ordered a dessert for them to share. When the dish arrived, he moved the ramekin between them. "Try some. They make the best *crème brûlée* in the city."

Leaning forward with her doll-sized dessert spoon, she broke through the crunchy outer crust and scooped out a small portion.

"What do you think?"

She let the dessert linger on her tongue a moment before she swallowed. "It's perfect."

He scooped out a bite. "I'm glad you think so."

When they'd taken the last bite of the dessert, he reached inside his jacket and pulled out a flat envelope with a shiny black ribbon looped around it. "Now, the reason I asked you to dinner, Writer Girl."

"What's this?"

"You'll see."

She unwrapped the ribbon, pulled out the note, and scanned the words. "Already?"

When she glanced up, his lips quirked at the corners. "Yes. Already."

Upon release, the Zucker memoir sat comfortably on the national best-seller list. She set the envelope down, and a small tear escaped down her cheek.

"What's the matter?"

"I hoped my pen would honor their story."

"I guess the proof is in the numbers."

"Yes, I guess it is."

Declan sat back and folded his hands in his lap. "So, Writer Girl, maybe a bit more romance in your future?"

"Maybe." At his heated look, her heart cartwheeled. "If the right story comes along."

He shot her a playful grin as he turned and motioned for the waiter to bring the check.

Was she imagining things, or did Declan's question hold a possibility?

8

K elly stepped out of the elevator and sighed. It was late, and she wanted to slip into her pj's. Spring break had not been a break for her.

It was the final night of the writers' conference in Philadelphia. She'd spent most of the evening chatting with college students who believed they had the wherewithal to make it as mainstream authors. Bright-eyed and full of dreams. Did they know writing meant hours bent over a keyboard in a self-imposed life of solitary confinement with little fame? She sighed. *Unless you're a best seller.*

Her brief jump from crime fiction novelist to memoir collaborator with one of the East Coast's wealthiest men had opened a floodgate of opportunity—and fans, a thought that made her grateful and terrified at the same time.

Fumbling with her laptop bag, she grabbed her key card out of the front pocket. "I can't wait to get out of these heels." She huffed her complaint while she balanced her notebooks in one hand and slid the card into the lock with the other. Not bothering to flip on the lights, she clicked the door shut behind her and kicked off her shoes.

"It's time we had a little chat."

She froze. A deep, melodic male voice floated across her ears as a towering figure glided next to her in the shadows. She reached behind her to grasp the door handle. Before she could turn it, a steady hand clutched her arm and led her across the room.

"What do you want? Who are you?" Kelly jerked her head to the side, straining to catch a glimpse of the intruder.

"Keep moving, Miss Landon." After he maneuvered her farther into the room, he lowered her into a chair and emptied her hands of their contents.

"Just tell me what you want. Please."

Instead of answering, the interloper draped a silky material over her eyes and tied it at the back of her skull. "This is for my safety—and yours."

She angled her head to follow his voice.

"Keep your face forward." The man's gloved fingers curved around her jaw to stop her. "And put your hands in your lap."

"Please. Don't hurt me." The plea came out raspy, as her imagination bombarded her with all the sordid ways this night could end.

"I'm not going to hurt you. I just have a few questions." He drew his hand back, but the imprint of the smooth leather lingered on her jaw. "Tell me what you know about Abram Zucker."

"What?"

"Who else gave you information for the book?"

"I don't ... I don't know what you mean."

"Why would you make the information public?" The man's well-spoken British accent glided around her as the warmth of his breath caressed her cheek. "Your best seller was a bad idea."

Her heart stalled. "Please. I don't understand what you want from me." After a sharp intake of air, she added, "I'm just the author."

"Kelly." His breathy whisper trailed with the sugary scents of caramel and chocolate. "Tell me everything you know about Abram's family. It may just save your life."

White-hot panic surged through her while she strained to see beyond the shadowy fabric. "Everything Abram gave me is in the memoir. I don't know anything else."

"I think you do."

A whoosh of air circled around her as the man moved away.

For a few labored breaths, his footfalls traversing the carpet were the only sounds she heard.

That and the thunder of her beating heart.

Think, Kelly. Think. It's the details in life that will keep you alive. A quick sound bite of advice from her overly cautious father shot like an arrow through her mind.

Before he'd passed away, her father had grown increasingly suspect of a hidden, unnamed danger. Meticulous about locking and relocking doors and windows, he also grew suspicious of neighbors and friends. Her father had taught her how to survive something like this. She just never believed she'd need to use his instruction.

This man knew Abram. But he hadn't asked about the journals. *Keep them talking.* Another snippet of advice from her wary father darted through her scattered thoughts. *You're smart. But they don't need to know that.*

Her captor's presence drew near again.

"What did you say you wanted to know? I don't think I understand." *Breathe in. Breathe out.*

The man slammed his gloved fist down on the desk. "Kelly! Stop the charade." It sounded more like *char-rod* when the word escaped his lips. "This is not a game."

A tremor racked her body as perspiration dotted her forehead. *I should scream for help.* She shook off the thought. What if he gagged her? Or worse.

Focus on the details. London English. Someone from the city. Methodically, she chronicled everything around her. Every smell, sound, and caress against her skin. Forcing the details into an invisible stack of files in the caverns of her mind. As her captor moved in next to her, she breathed in the subtle notes of citrus mingled with an arboreous fragrance—something high-end and expensive.

"Whose side are you on? Can you at least tell me that?"

His questions were steady and unhurried. *He's done this before.* Kidnapping or interrogating—or both.

She shoved away the unsettling thought. "I wrote the book with Abram's permission. It's only a memoir about someone's parents." Kelly sniffled again, but this time she forced her voice to sound more in control. "The book included several love letters I arranged into a story. That's it. That's all I know."

"You really don't know. Do you?" The room grew quiet. "I've seen you on the telly, talking about that blasted best seller of yours. Printing this story has opened a Pandora's box."

He's a fan. Her heart slammed against her chest. *Not just any fan—a demented fan.* She'd been on a couple of talk shows promoting the book, but she hated that sort of thing.

"What I don't understand is," the mattress creaked as he lowered himself onto the bed. "Why did you go public with what you know? It was downright idiotic. For what? A couple of quid?" A low chuckle escaped his lips. "I know you. You've got plenty to live on."

Does he want money? She gripped her hands together as sweat pooled in her palms. "Please. I don't have any more information about the Zucker family."

Her captor placed his hand on hers, and she froze. "Relax. I'm not going to hurt you." For a moment, his silky voice soothed her, but then dread churned to life in her belly.

"God, please help me." It was the first prayer she'd uttered in years.

Releasing his grip, he asked, "Don't you understand what you did by printing that story and connecting yourself with Abram?"

She pulled in her bottom lip and bit down. *God, I know I've been silent for a while ...*

"You've put yourself and those around you in more danger

than you can even imagine." The timbre of his voice quickened, blending the inflection in his speech even more. "Others will want to know what clues Abram might have deposited in that sagacious mind of yours."

Her thoughts swayed on a pendulum of conflicting moods. While her captor complimented her intelligence, he acted concerned for her well-being. And as he talked of more danger from others, he'd blindfolded her and held her captive in her hotel room.

"It's just a memoir."

"It's not *just* the memoir." He released a sigh. "It's what you didn't say in the story that's put you at risk."

Confusion wrapped itself around her like a death shroud. *What didn't I say?*

"There are nefarious people out there looking for information about the Zucker family." He leaned in and whispered, "I'm not the bad guy, Kelly."

Then who are you? Why not go straight to Abram?

"I know what you're thinking." The bed shifted as he sprang to his feet. "You're wondering why I didn't ask Abram for this information."

A tremble tiptoed down her spine. *Now he's reading my mind.*

"Abram's a nice, frail, and, at times, senile old man, but you ... you're brilliant. Your memory is off the charts. You're able to catalog and decipher information in your mind in a truly unique way."

"What did you say?" The therapist she'd met after her mother died had used those exact words.

"I know everything I need to know from Abram's angle, and I have no desire to frighten the man into an early grave. However, there are others I fear may go that route." He paused. "Because they don't know about you."

This man irritated her with the way he talked in riddles. *It's like Abram and he are cut from the same cloth.* She pursed her lips. In her mind's eye, she tried to imagine what her captor looked like. British. Tall. Imposing. She needed something to tell the police when—if—he released her. She inhaled the rich scent of leather. From his clothing? Or his car?

She groaned. None of those clues would lead to anything.

"Okay, have it your way, Miss Landon." Her captor's words sliced through her frustration. "I was hoping we could work together on this. It seems as if you've given me no other options but to continue as before."

"Are you going to let me go?" She blinked and strained to view anything through the cloth.

Like a phantom spirit, the man swooped in beside her and whispered in her ear. "Remember, others *will* come for the information Abram gave you. Don't trust anyone." Hesitating for a heartbeat, he added, "Count to one hundred then take off the blindfold. If you tell anyone about tonight, your boyfriend might end up dead."

9

Kelly gasped. "What boyfriend?" Her question hung in the air like a stagnant London fog. Heavy footfalls strolled across the hotel room floor. The door opened, then clicked shut.

She counted quickly to one hundred in her head. *Seventy-two, seventy-three …* "Hello? Is anyone there?" *Eighty-five, eighty-six, eighty-seven …*

Finally reaching the last set of numbers, Kelly tore off the blindfold and scanned the room. She stood, and her legs wobbled.

"Get it together. He's gone." For the first time all evening, she breathed a sigh of relief.

Her laptop bag, purse, notebooks, and red high heels sat in a neat row on the bed. With shaky hands, she stared at the closed door and strapped on her heels. *He's gone.* She dug through her purse and pulled out her cell to check the time. Eleven thirty. The whole tormenting ordeal took less than thirty minutes.

With balmy, trembling fingers she attempted to dial the police, but as she reached for her laptop bag, she stopped. "No." Her cell slid out of her hand and landed with a soft thud on the floor. "Declan?"

A black-and-white photo stared up at her from the bed. In the snapshot, Declan leaned forward in his chair with his arm outstretched across a table.

"The night we shared dessert." She collapsed onto the edge of the bed. Even now, she could recall the warmth of his hand on hers.

Kelly blinked back a few tears as she bent over and fumbled around the floor, searching for her phone. Checking to make sure the call canceled, she traced the red circle drawn around Declan's face. Her heart sank. "What does this have to do with my agent?"

As if in a trance, she threw her notebooks into her laptop bag and slung the strap over her shoulder. She dropped the photo into her purse then set about to gather her toiletries and clothes in her overnight bag.

She pulled open the door and checked both ways down the hall. It was empty. In several quick strides, she reached the elevator and pressed hard on the button more times than necessary. *Keep it together, Kelly.* The ping of the elevator announced its arrival, and she jumped. Taking a brief glance inside to make sure she was alone, she stepped over the gap and whispered a silent prayer for her protection.

In the parking garage, she weaved through the rows of parked cars until she found hers. "Keys. Where are my keys?"

While she dug through her purse, a horn echoed from the street. Her heart banged hard against her ribs. *Get in the car. Just get in the car.* With wobbly fingers, she hit the unlock button on the fob. She threw her bags into the passenger seat, slid behind the steering wheel, and relocked the doors. *You're safe now.*

A night guard moved out of the shadows, and she bit back a scream. He threw her a courteous nod and rounded the corner.

"No, wait." The words floated off her lips as perspiration gathered in pools under her arms. *Don't say a word, or your boyfriend will end up dead.* Blinking back fresh tears, she started her car and pulled out of the parking garage.

As she drove through the vacant city streets, she fished

through her purse and pulled out the black-and-white photo. Her throat burned. "Who would want to harm Declan?" Kelly tossed the picture back into her purse and drove up the on-ramp to the interstate.

With a trembling breath, she thanked God she was still alive, and with the same ragged breath, she begged God to keep Declan safe. "What am I going to do?" The adrenaline racing through her veins kept her alert on the six-hour journey south to her home.

When she pulled into her neighborhood, she kept her eyes glued to the rearview mirror and revisited the question that had haunted her for miles—Why Declan?

Nobody knew the feelings she had for him. Nobody. It was a crush. A silly fantasy she kept locked safely away in the confines of her heart. He was way beyond her reach.

She pulled into her circular drive and turned off the car. After she grabbed her purse and her laptop, she sprinted for the front door. *How could anyone know?* Kelly fumbled with the key as she struggled to unlock the door. As she stepped into the entryway, an eerie quiet wrapped around her.

"Hello?" She peered at the darkened hallway. *You're overreacting. Philadelphia is miles away.*

She closed the door, secured the lock, and switched on the lights. Declan had insisted she install a better alarm—something she balked at. She didn't want to live like her father, with three deadbolts fastened on each door. But now, after her captor had broken through and shattered her peaceful world, she wished she'd listened.

"How am I going to get any sleep?" As she ambled toward the kitchen, yellow and orange rays peeked through the clouds and filled the window above the sink. She jerked open the junk drawer and searched for her pepper spray. When she found it, she gave it a shake. "It's full." Nerves sparking, she catatonically walked toward the living room couch.

Please, God, keep me safe. Crumbling into a heap, she reached over the back of the sofa and pulled her grandmother's well-worn quilt across her lap. *Please, God, keep Declan safe.*

After she set her phone next to the pepper spray, she ran her fingers along her temples, retracing the place where the smooth fabric had covered her eyes. "Why? Why me?"

Taking deep, deliberate breaths, she forced herself to quiet her anxious thoughts.

Did Abram know what he'd pulled her into? Did Declan?

Tonight, the dangerous world her father had warned her about had finally shown itself to be real.

Now she needed to figure out who to trust to keep her safe.

10

After only one knock, the door to Declan's office swung open.

"Kelly, please come in." Attractive as usual, he greeted her wearing a pale gray suit and mossy-green tie. "How are you?"

"I'm okay."

"That didn't sound convincing." He flashed her a concerned look. "Would you like some coffee?"

"Sure." As she sank into the chair in front of his desk, he poured her a cup of coffee.

"You seem a little off, Writer Girl. What's up?"

She tried to mask her discomfort with a shrug. It had been a few weeks since the writers' conference in Pennsylvania, and she'd barely had a peaceful night's sleep. Most nights she spent curled up on her sofa with the TV on for comfort.

"How's the Zucker memoir doing?" She blurted out the question, ignoring his. All she could think about was that book.

"Numbers are still doing well." He slipped into his desk chair and studied the computer screen. He pushed out a few clicks on the keyboard. "Thinking about sales today?"

She took a long drink of her coffee and nodded. *More like creeps who linger in hotel rooms.*

Turning the screen, he pointed to a row of columns and numbers. "We're releasing it into the foreign market next month. That should ramp up sales, but more importantly, give it more exposure."

She tensed, feeling the color drain from her face.

"That's not the response I expected," Declan said. "Something on your mind?"

"Uh, yes. I mean no." She set the coffee mug down and fidgeted with the letter opener sitting on the corner of his desk. "Have there been any odd … or bad reviews?"

"I didn't think you concerned yourself with reviews."

"I don't." The muscles in her neck twisted. "I was just wondering what the readers are saying."

"I get it. The temptation to know what people think is a strong pull." He angled the screen back in his direction. "Are you sure you want to know?"

"No."

He stopped clicking the mouse and looked at her. "Probably best. Besides, it doesn't matter. The sales speak for themselves."

She took another sip of her coffee. "You're right."

"Let me worry about the numbers. You focus on writing. Deal?"

"Deal."

Declan's expression turned serious. "Speaking of writing. I asked you in today because I wanted to discuss your contract with Treasure House—and me."

"What about my contract?" Her mouth dried.

"I know I had you veer off course a bit with the memoir, but Treasure House has been asking about your final installment in your crime series. Since the memoir is doing so well, they want you to ride the wave of new readers." He blew out a sigh. "Those were their words, not mine."

Chilly moisture sprouted across her forehead. *Maybe I should ask for an extension.*

"I need an update on your progress, but I'm not trying to push you." He leaned back and clasped his hands behind his head. "Business never meshes with art."

Her stomach sank. *My progress? I've barely punched out a couple of chapters. I haven't done anything since ...* Looking down at her feet, she wrestled with how she should answer.

"Kelly?"

"Yes?" Startled, she lifted her gaze. "I mean, I'm sorry. Is there any way I could get an extension?"

"Got some old-fashioned writer's block?"

Her neck warmed, less out of embarrassment and more out of guilt. "I guess you could say that."

"The romantic thriller not going the way you planned?" He cast her a playful look then waved his hand in the direction of the window. "Maybe you should get out there and date a little. It might jump-start your creativity."

She opened her mouth to say something, then closed it.

"On second thought—" Declan shook his head, appearing flustered. "You probably don't need that kind of distraction in your life."

"Well ..."

"Unless, of course, you're already dating someone, then I—"

"No."

"No?"

"No. I'm not dating anyone."

"Oh—good." He raked a hand through his hair. "I don't mean good. I just mean ..."

Did he just ask me if I was dating someone?

"Well, I botched that. Didn't I?" He smiled wryly.

"I'm not sure. Did you?" A match ignited in her chest. *What's going on?*

"I need to go out of town for a few weeks."

"Okay." *Did he just change the subject?* "What about the extension?"

He held her gaze for a few seconds then looked down at his phone. "I'll check on that." As he scrolled his finger across the screen, he said, "Let's say we meet again in a few weeks and check on your progress."

"That works." *Liar. You've lost focus. What makes you think you'll get it back in a few weeks?*

"Good." When he looked up, his dark peridot eyes glinted in the sunlight. "I'll try not to sound like a bumbling idiot next time."

"A what? What do you mean?"

Declan laid his phone down and sighed. "Would you consider going to dinner with me? After your contract is satisfied, of course. A proper dinner this time. Not a business dinner."

"Dinner? I'd love to."

"Wonderful." Declan stood and walked her to the door.

Did he just ask me out? Her knees turned to jelly.

Before he opened the door, he reached for her hand. "Do you think you can push past your writer's block and give me something to read when I get back?"

"Definitely."

"Good." He lifted her fingers to his lips and brushed the back of her knuckles with a kiss. "I'll see you in a few weeks, Writer Girl."

She nodded, lost in his gaze. After a breath he released her hand and opened his office door. She almost pirouetted into the hallway. *Dinner. Not a business dinner.*

In a daze, she walked down the hall and pushed the button for the elevator. She stole a look back at Declan's closed office door. *A date. With Declan. Is this a dream?*

As she stepped into the elevator, her lips curved into a slow smile. "Not a dream."

While the doors closed, Kelly envisioned all the ways the final installment of her crime series should end. *With the hero falling madly in love.* She brushed a finger over the knuckles Declan had kissed.

Nothing—not even a lingering, faceless shadow—would stop her from writing this book and fulfilling her contract.

Or falling helplessly in love with Declan.

11

As Kelly stepped through her front door, a cold shiver walked its way down her spine. *Something's not right.*

She'd woken up early that morning, hoping to get in a quick trip to her favorite bookstore and pick up her dry cleaning. Declan was due back in town tomorrow, and she'd finally outlined the end of her story—Adam, her rugged hero, had fallen in love.

Kelly hung her dress bag on the coat tree and walked into her living room.

"No!" A vice wrapped around her throat as her eyes scanned the ransacked space. "Please, no."

She darted to the kitchen. Morning sunlight broke through the half-opened back door. Fumbling for her phone, she scrolled through the numbers and pushed Send.

"Hey, Kelly, what's—"

"Declan—" Her voice caught when he answered.

"What's wrong?"

"Someone's been in my house."

"What?"

With shaky hands, she gripped her phone tighter. "I came home from the bookstore, and when I arrived …" She inhaled, trying to catch her breath. "My house. It's a mess."

"You need to get out of there. Did you call the police?"

"Not yet. You were the first person I called."

"I want you to get in your car and lock the door. Do you understand me?"

Immobilized, she examined every corner of the kitchen. *Someone's been in my house. Was it him? Does he know where I live?*

"Kelly?" Declan's voice yanked her out of her tormented thoughts.

"Yes, I'm here."

"I need you to get in your car."

"Yes, yes. Okay." The memory of that night in Philadelphia shot through her mind like a bolt of lightning. She darted out of the house, crawled into her driver's seat, and locked the doors.

"Call the police and stay in your car until they get there."

"Okay."

"It'll be okay. At least you weren't home when they broke in."

Thank God, I hadn't been.

"I need you to hang up and call nine-one-one."

She nodded, barely comprehending his words.

"I'll catch the next flight out," Declan said. "I'll be there soon."

She ended the call and robotically dialed the police. "Hello, I'd like to report a break-in."

While she answered the dispatcher's questions, she scanned the backseat through her rearview mirror. She didn't feel any safer in her own car than in her tousled living room. Hadn't the man said he didn't wish to harm her? Her stomach curdled. He'd also said writing the memoir had put a target on her back.

"Please stay on the line, Miss Landon, until an officer arrives."

"Okay."

A cool shudder traveled through her as she looked up at the still-open front door. *How did they get in? Did they have a key?* The yowling sirens grew closer, and with heavy legs, she stepped out of her car and waited for the officers to park.

The first officer exited his vehicle and approached her. "I'm Officer Pierce." He gestured to his partner. "This is Officer Glendale. Did you see anyone fleeing the scene?"

"No."

"How long ago did this happen?"

Kelly retraced her timeline.

Officer Pierce looked toward the front steps. "Was the door open when you got home?"

"No." She wrapped her arms protectively around her torso.

"Is there someone we can call for you?"

"No, I've already called my ... I called my friend."

The officer nodded, then he and his partner told her to wait outside while they went in and looked around.

After several minutes, Pierce poked his head out the door. "Miss Landon, please come in so we can see if anything is missing. Please don't touch anything while you look around."

She pulled her arms in tighter, feeling like a stranger in her own living room. Her home, her sanctuary, looked as though it had been turned upside down and shaken. Books lay on the floor, cushions were off of the couch, and drawers were pulled out and turned over. She moved to the kitchen, where cabinet doors stood open, and the cans in the pantry were tipped over. Some cans were scattered on the floor.

"Do you see anything of value missing, Miss Landon?" Officer Pierce took out his notepad and scribbled something down.

She shook her head. Her laptop sat, as usual, on her desk, and the flat screen television was still on the wall. The few antique baubles she'd kept from her childhood remained untouched on the mantel. "There's a safe in my closet."

Officer Glendale followed her upstairs to her room.

The master suite was a mess. More drawers were emptied, and her intimate belongings strewn all over the floor. Her eyes burned. *This can't be happening.* She walked into her closet and ran her hands across the safe. The door was still closed and secured. "The safe is still locked."

"Maybe you should open it and make sure nothing was taken."

She complied and opened the safe.

"Is it all there, Miss Landon?"

She fished through a few important pieces of paper, her passport, and a small bag of jewelry. "Yes, it's all here."

Officer Pierce joined them outside the master bedroom. "If you could look around the upstairs and see if you notice anything missing."

"Sir, I don't have anything worth stealing up here."

"Miss Landon, I know this is tough, but I need you to give the rooms a once-over. If you notice something odd, other than the mess, I need you to tell me."

"Okay."

Both officers followed close behind as she surveyed the rooms.

One spare room, the one next to the master, had gym equipment and an old desk she'd planned on refinishing. Nothing had been touched. The next room, near the hallway bathroom, was a guest room. The final was a library. Books lay scattered all over the floor and chairs.

"Miss Landon, do you see anything peculiar that would help us find out who did this?" Officer Glendale took a glance around the library.

Kelly shook her head. It would take her more than just a hasty perusal to notice if any specific books were missing.

The three of them descended the stairs. She fidgeted with a loose string hanging from her T-shirt as Officer Pierce repeated her story.

"Have you had any other incidents that we should know about?"

Her pulse echoed in her ears. "No."

"Can you think of any reason someone would want to break into your home?"

"No, nothing." *The journals.* Her throat constricted as she swallowed back the lie.

"Have you lost your keys, or maybe your purse? Anything that might have given someone access to your home?" Officer Glendale looked toward the back door. "The door isn't damaged. It seems as if someone walked right in with a key. Maybe one of your windows was left unlocked?"

She shook her head. She'd never be that careless.

Officer Pierce continued to take notes. "An old boyfriend? Disgruntled family member."

"No, neither."

Officer Pierce called in the information over their radio while another vehicle pulled up, and the additional officers did their best to find fingerprints around the home.

Only hers and Declan's would be found. If the same man who'd held her captive in her hotel room had done this, he would've worn smooth leather gloves. A menacing shiver migrated from her neck to her vertebrae as she recalled the silky texture of his gloves on her skin.

Trying to steady her breathing, she inhaled and exhaled slowly. A trace of rustic cologne wafted across her nose. She glanced at Officer Pierce. Was that his cologne? Or had it lingered from the intruder?

After a few seconds, Officer Pierce looked up and caught her staring. She blinked and looked away. Chaotic thoughts bounced around her mind as tears threatened to emerge once again.

"Are you sure we can't call anyone for you?" Officer Glendale's voice snapped her out of her internal tug-of-war.

"I'm fine. I'll be too busy cleaning up this mess to worry about being alone."

The officers nodded and walked toward the door.

"I do have a favor to ask," Kelly said.

Officer Glendale's expression turned sympathetic. "What's that?"

"If you could be sure this doesn't get to the press, I'd be grateful."

"We'll do our best, Miss Landon."

Both officers promised to get in touch if they had any more information. Then, before they ducked into their patrol car, they tried to reassure her it was most likely a random event, and she didn't have to worry about it happening again.

Officer Pierce glanced around at her front gate. "In this neighborhood, probably just some kids looking for fast cash. Be sure and call us if you find out they took something."

Kelly nodded. She wouldn't find anything missing, and these weren't just a group of kids. As the patrol car pulled away, she closed the door, grateful for the reprieve.

Again, she surveyed the mess, then made a beeline to her beloved collection of rare edition books. She was thankful to find they weren't damaged. In fact, they appeared almost carefully placed in small piles around the floor.

She picked them up—Austen, Dickens, and Brontë—and like close friends, she cradled the books to her chest as a round of tears began to fall. She couldn't imagine all this turmoil was because of one best seller.

As she glanced around her office, her thoughts cycled into overdrive. Her instincts told her that whoever broke in was searching for the journals. But, even if they'd taken apart the whole house, they'd never find them. She moved toward the bookshelf and systematically placed the books in their proper order.

As she shuffled the last remaining books in her arms, a small piece of paper floated out of one of the novels—*Hard Times,* by Charles Dickens—and landed on the floor. She bent over, picked up the scrap of paper, and scanned the words.

IS HIDING THE JOURNALS A GAME TO YOU?

I GUESS IT'S TIME TO PLAY.

Cool perspiration fell over Kelly's skin. The ghost-man from her hotel hadn't mentioned the journals, which meant today's intruder might have been someone else.

There will be other people coming for this information.

Her tormentor's words floated through her thoughts like a heavy October mist. *But who?* She folded the piece of paper and shoved it into her back pocket.

"So, this is my life now? A real-life whodunnit."

Writing about cat-and-mouse games thrilled her, but she dreaded playing the part of the mouse.

After she'd spent several hours replacing drawers and organizing shelves in the upstairs library, the buzzer from her front gate echoed in the intercom. She trotted down the stairs and pushed the button on the security screen.

"Kelly. It's me, Declan."

A wave of relief washed over her. She didn't need to open the gate. He knew the code and came on through.

Yanking open the front door, she fell into his arms and let her tears fall.

"Oh, Kelly, it will be okay. I promise." Declan murmured, drawing her closer.

As she stepped back, she motioned for him to enter then closed the door.

After they settled on the couch, Declan asked, "What happened?"

She hung her head. *Should I tell him everything?* "I came home and …"

He patted her knee, then stood and walked into the kitchen and brewed two cups of coffee. "Here." Declan returned and held out the steaming mug like a sacred offering.

"Thanks."

"I'm sorry about all of this, but I'm glad you're all right." When he sank back into the seat next to her, he reached out for her hand. "I've been thinking. I want you to stay at my place tonight."

Her cheeks warmed to the same temperature as her coffee mug. "I'm not sure that's a good idea."

"Why not? I have two guest rooms and space big enough for the both of us."

She shook her head. "I just don't feel comfortable with that. The two of us. You know, it's not, well …"

"Well, I don't feel comfortable leaving you here by yourself." He glanced around the disheveled room. "Look at this place. It looks like a crime scene."

She winced. It was still hard for her to believe that hours ago a stranger had been in her home, rummaging through her belongings.

"If you won't use my guest room, I insist you stay at a hotel for a couple of nights." He gave her hand a gentle squeeze "You can get a room downtown next to my office. Then, I can check in on you when I head into work in the morning."

She knew she wouldn't sleep a wink if she stayed at her own house tonight, but the thought of staying in a hotel conjured up apprehensions she didn't want to think about either.

"Kelly?" Declan tilted his head, his eyes searching. "Is there something wrong with staying at a hotel?"

Releasing a held breath, she shook her head. "No. That's fine. I won't get much sleep here."

"Would you like me to make a reservation for you?" He pulled out his phone and flipped through the screen. "I know just the place."

"Sure."

After punching in a couple of things on his phone, he glanced up. "You can finish cleaning up tomorrow. I'll wait here while you go pack a few things."

She nodded then moved numbly up the stairs. The crumbled note shifted in her back pocket. Should she show him? No. She only wanted to deal with one crisis at a time. If she showed him the note, she'd need to explain what happened in Pennsylvania. Then she'd need to tell him what her captor thought about their relationship. She didn't have the energy to discuss either one of those subjects right now.

Shoulders back, she shoved the note deeper in her pocket. Her father had shown her snippets of the world of enigmatology, and if Abram had given her a puzzle to solve in those journals, then she'd learn how to crack it. If a game was what the intruder wanted, then a game was what they'd get.

Some mysteries are better left buried in the grave.

Her father's foreboding warning called to her from the past. But, ignoring caution, she thought about the journals. After she finished writing her current crime thriller, she'd spend all her free time unraveling the secrets of Abram's family. Then, maybe, she'd be able to get back to living her normal, humdrum life.

The life she had before the best seller.

12

Kelly walked into Declan's office after a quick knock on the door. It had been a week since the break-in, and she still hadn't been able to find her bearings.

He looked up and flashed her a concerned look. "How's my Writer Girl?"

Her stomach clenched under her ribbed crew-neck T-shirt. How was she? She couldn't shake the persistent worry when she thought about the faceless stranger ransacking her home. She didn't feel any safer in a hotel than she did in her own house. If she was honest, she wasn't doing well.

"I'm fine." Her mouth dried while she fell back into one of the velvety, emerald chesterfield chairs next to the window. As a yawn escaped her lips, she extended her legs and stretched her toes as far as they could go in her sneakers. Feeling at peace with Declan so near, she fought the urge to curl up in the sun like a cat and take a nap.

"How are the rooms at the hotel?" He sat in the chair next to her. The color of the tufted fabric intensified the jewel tones of his eyes. "You look like you haven't slept much."

"They're nice, but I can't wait to get back to my own bed." She brought her hand to her mouth to stifle another yawn.

"My offer still stands. There's plenty of room at my place."

"Declan, I …"

He held up his hands. "I know, I know. It wouldn't be proper."

Her cheeks burned as she changed the subject. "I think I might be ready to go back to my place tonight." She'd already tried to go back a few days after the break-in and reluctantly called the hotel for an extension on her reservation.

"That's what I wanted to talk to you about this morning. You've had a lot on your mind lately, even before the break-in." Declan leaned in and pushed a stray strand of hair away from her cheek. "I know you've been reluctant to add more security to your home, but after what's happened, I hope you'll reconsider."

"I think it's a good idea." She didn't want to travel down the dark road her father had been on—a road where suspicion lurked around every corner. But after recent events, she needed to be more vigilant.

"Okay, good." He didn't hide the relief in his voice. "There's something else. I've hired someone to keep an eye on you until we find out who broke into your house."

A bodyguard? Before she could object, there was a knock at the door.

"Come in." Declan stood and walked to the door.

A suit-clad, broad-shouldered man opened the door and stepped across the threshold.

"Right on time. Thanks for coming in this morning." Declan shook the man's hand.

"Of course." The man clicked the door shut and stepped farther into the room.

Kelly stood and assessed the newcomer. His hair, a deep walnut brown, was cut military style, with a few waves on top. When he caught her measuring glance, he pulled himself to his full height and towered several inches above her.

Declan turned toward her. "Kelly, I'd like you to meet Nathaniel James."

Nathaniel threw her a curt nod.

"Nathaniel, this is Miss Kelly Landon, the author I told you about."

Nathaniel stuck out his hand, and reflexively, she shook it.

"Nice to meet you, Miss Landon." A cutting New England accent permeated his words.

She nodded and withdrew her hand.

"Nathaniel tells me he's from up north." Declan cocked his head. "Where did you say you were from again?"

"Maine. Just outside of Bangor." Nathaniel addressed her directly. "My job ended early in DC. When I heard an author at Treasure House Publishing needed more security, I applied." His deep voice was buttery smooth, a perfect complement to his cool demeanor.

"Nice area, Maine. I've not been that way yet." Declan leaned against his desk and asked about Nathaniel's previous jobs.

Kelly appraised Nathaniel while Declan made small talk.

He wore a charcoal tailored-to-fit suit with a crisp, white button-down shirt. The satiny fabric of his sapphire tie looked as if it had been handpicked to accentuate his eyes. Eyes that danced with a hint of mischief. And ego. When he caught her staring, the edge of his mouth tipped into a roguish grin.

She blinked and looked at Declan. "Is this really necessary? A bodyguard?" Taking a few steps toward the window, she studied the street below. Everyone's lives seemed to be moving at a natural pace. Everyone's but hers.

"I think it is." Declan drew next to her. "Someone was in your home. How do you know it won't happen again?" He waved a hand toward Nathaniel. "Nathaniel will head over to your house this afternoon to set up cameras and install new equipment on your gate. If you want to go back tonight, at least I'll know you're secure."

"Cameras? Really?" She lowered herself back into the chair and laid her forehead in her hands. "I can't believe this is happening."

"The cameras will only be on the outside of your property, Miss Landon."

She lifted her chin and caught Nathaniel's intense gaze. If she judged his look correctly, he understood her reluctance to give up her privacy.

"We're updating your alarm and adding motion sensors to your windows."

Her vision blurred. *Just like my dad's house.*

Declan crouched in front of her. "I only want what's best for you."

"I know."

In her peripheral vision, she watched as Nathaniel placed his hands behind his back and fell into parade rest. Of course. Ex-military. He'd watch her like a hawk. And all this because of one best seller.

She waved a hand toward Nathaniel. "What's this going to look like exactly? Having a bodyguard? Will he go with me —everywhere?"

"He's here to accompany you to events on your schedule. On occasion, he'll stop by your place and make sure your security is working properly." Declan stood and flashed her an easygoing look. "When I'm out of town, at least I'll know there's someone local for you to call if you have any more trouble."

"This is only until we have answers. Right?"

"Of course." Declan gave her shoulder a quick squeeze. "As soon as we find the person responsible for harassing you, Nathaniel will be relieved of his duties. I promise."

She looked at her handsome new companion. "Did you say the security at my house will be done today?"

He brought his arms in front of him and tugged at his cuffs. "Yes, ma'am. I'm heading to your place directly to install all the equipment Mr. McNeary's supplied me with."

She slouched back in the seat and turned her attention back to Declan. "I just want to go home and put this behind me."

"I know you do." He faced Nathaniel, and they shook hands.

"Thanks for stopping by. Give me a call as soon as everything is up and running."

"Of course." Nathaniel shot her a quick look.

Declan turned back to her, and his expression lightened. "When this is over, you can get back to doing what you love most—writing."

She faked a smile then let out a long exhale as both men walked out into the hallway. *So, this is my new normal?* The thought made her cringe.

Would she ever get her quiet life back?

Or would looking over her shoulder be something she'd need to live with for the rest of her life?

13

Nathaniel pulled onto the interstate while Kelly sat rigid and quiet in the passenger seat. "I really should insist that you sit in the back for your own safety."

"Have I encroached on some unwritten bodyguard rule, Mr. James?"

He'd been Miss Landon's bodyguard for over a month. It had been an easy job so far. She'd insisted on him not hovering and only shadowing her when she went to book-related events. He'd accompanied her to a signing and a three-day conference. Nobody seemed off at either of those events. Other than that, she'd spent the majority of her time at home writing, where he'd only need to check in on her. However, he could sense the loss of some of her independence out in public had chipped away at her usual pleasant demeanor.

Not wanting to spar with her, he ignored her question. "Mr. James makes me sound ancient. I'm guessing we're about the same age. Please call me Nathan."

"Okay, Nathan." She turned to face him. "Is there a reason you'd prefer me to sit in the back?"

He glanced at her sidelong. *Because you're distracting.* The short time he'd been with her, he'd come to know Miss Landon as more than just a quiet writer. She had an easy way about her. One he was drawn to.

After he'd read her crime novels, he found she had a dose of humor hidden inside her too. She'd once told him she'd considered penning him into one of her stories and killing him off if he didn't give her some space to breathe. He smiled. He hadn't been hovering at all. He had a job to do, and he performed it. Thoroughly.

"Tell me about yourself, Miss Landon." Nathan dismissed her inquiry. Again.

"Not much to tell." She fiddled with her purse strap. "And please, call me Kelly."

"Of course. So, you're a crime fiction writer. How did that start?"

"Boredom, basically."

He laughed, then halted when he realized she was serious. "Did you grow up in Virginia?"

"No, I was born in Pennsylvania."

"Go, Steelers!"

She shook her head. "My family moved when I was eight months old. Hardly enough time for me to start wearing yellow and black." By the inflection of her voice, it sounded as if she'd rolled her eyes at him.

He already knew the basic things about her, but it was vital for her to feel at ease in his presence. He needed Kelly to trust him so he could connect the dots and find out who was harassing her.

"What about *your* family, Mr. James? I mean Nathan." He caught her smiling. "Do *you* have a family?"

"I do. A brother." He let a grin slide across his lips. He liked how she turned the tables and started asking him the questions. "He's younger than me and yet somehow wiser. He works in IT."

He pulled up to her gated entrance on Lincoln Lane and

pushed the backlit numbers on the gate. "How long have you lived in Virginia?"

He'd done a simple background check, but he hoped she'd fill in the details.

"A few years. Why?"

"Where did you live before? Any angry boyfriends or crazy ex-fiancés I should know about?" He drove through the gate and waited for it to swing closed behind them.

She chuckled. "No. No angry boyfriends or crazy ex-fiancés."

"Good." After he threw the car in park, he turned off the engine. "Angry boyfriends are not my cup of tea."

"Not mine either."

Nathan chuckled as he got out of the car. After doing a quick scan of the front yard, he opened her door and held out his hand. "I'm going to do a quick look around since I'm here."

She placed her hand in his and stepped out of the car.

A tingle traveled up his arm, and he frowned. He released his grip and followed her to the door. As soon as she unlocked it, he stepped through the door first, flipped on a light, and glanced around. Kelly followed him in and pulled the door shut behind them. After he checked all the windows and doors on the first level, he ran upstairs to inspect the rooms.

When he came back downstairs, he noticed she hadn't moved from the entryway. A weight pressed on his chest. He'd seen that look before. It happened when his clients realized their lives would never be the same again.

"Everything looks good. Is there anything else you need?" He moved toward the entryway, ready to leave and give her some space.

She sniffled and wiped a tear off her cheek with the back of her hand. "This isn't what I signed up for."

Nathan's heart sank. He could relate. This wasn't what he'd signed up for either. But he was here now, and he'd protect her with his life if necessary. "I'm sure it won't be like this forever."

"Really? How do you know?" Frustration rolled off her question. She shuffled into the living room, where she dropped her purse and phone on the coffee table. "It's been months since the memoir released, and my life has been a mess ever since. I like to write thrillers, but I don't want to live one."

He shoved his hands in his pockets and followed her into the room. "Can I ask you something?"

"Ask away." She flopped onto the couch and sighed.

"Has anything else happened other than your house being broken into?"

Her chin darted up, and a flash of something in her eyes made him uneasy.

"I feel like it's overkill to have a bodyguard when it could have been a random break-in. People burglarize affluent neighborhoods all the time." He glanced around her home, studying the cozy décor. The brick intermingled with crown molding made him want to sit back with a warm drink and a novel. "Did they take anything?"

"No."

He freed his hands before sitting in the club chair opposite her. "Is there something else going on here? I need to know everything if I'm to do my job well."

She inhaled, then exhaled slowly. "There was a note. Left at my house after the break-in."

"A note? What kind of note? Was it threatening?" Internally, he counted to ten while the muscles in his neck twisted like a pretzel.

"Not really."

"Have you told Mr. McNeary about this?"

"No." She clasped her fingers together and stared at her shoes. "I don't want Declan to get hurt."

"What did the note say?" When her gaze lifted, he fought the urge to reach out and cover her wringing hands with his. "Did someone say they wanted to hurt you or Mr. McNeary?"

"I can't tell you. Not until I know for sure what it means."

She's scared and *headstrong—not an ideal mix.*

"The person who sent the note is looking for something I have."

"Okay …"

"I don't have it here."

"Maybe the person who ransacked your house has come to that conclusion." He flashed her what he hoped was a reassuring look. "That could be in our favor."

"So." Her voice caught. "What do I do now?"

Let me in, Kelly. Tell me everything. "Is said item in a safe location?"

"Yes."

"Does Mr. McNeary know this location?"

She shook her head. "No one does, except me."

"You can't tell me what the item is, can you?" He wanted to share her burden, but he also wanted to get the target off her back.

"No. I made a promise to someone *I* would keep it safe."

He stood to stretch his legs, attempting to piece together everything in her story. Her strength and tenacity in the middle of her fear surprised him, but he wished she didn't feel as if she had to face her battles alone.

"I'm going to talk to Mr. McNeary about your schedule this week." His gut twisted. *How can I protect her if she won't tell me everything?* "For now, we'll just remain vigilant. I don't want you to go anywhere without security."

She stood, and a flash of irritation traced across her features. "I hardly think that's—"

He held up his hand. "Kelly, we don't know who's sending these notes or their threat level. If they've been in your house, they know where you live. They may be watching for you to go out alone."

Her bottom lip quivered. "This is a nightmare."

"It's only until we eliminate the threat." He shoved his hands back in his pockets. "You've got my number. No bookstore or coffee runs without me."

Her eyes widened as if she'd been caught.

He bit back a smile. "I've been to The Bookend a few times myself. Great place. But there's an alley behind it. Too secluded."

"It's the one place I can be alone."

"Exactly." He pulled his car keys out of his pocket. "Thank you for telling me about the note." If she'd not told her agent—whom he guessed to be more than just a colleague—he'd obviously gained her confidence.

"I just want my privacy back." Her brows furrowed as she followed him to the door.

"I'll do everything I can to keep you safe." He pivoted to face her before he reached for the handle. "Call me. Anytime."

She nodded.

His heart pounded in his ears. This was a job. That was it. He needed to finish what he was here to do and nothing more. Defend and protect. Not fall into some emotional chasm with a beautiful writer.

He cleared his throat then added, "You need to tell me if you receive any more notes."

"I will."

"I need to know if someone directly threatens you or Mr. McNeary." He held her gaze. The anguish kindling in her hazel eyes wrenched his heart into a knot. *This is just a job.* He couldn't look away. The golden sunbursts brushed across the earthy green, reminding him of autumn. *She has beautiful eyes.*

Kelly blinked, breaking the spell.

"I need you to trust me." His fingers twitched as he fought the urge to reach out to her. "That's the only way I can keep you safe."

"I trust you."

Rankled by the unexpected tug at his emotions, Nathan turned, yanked open the door, and stepped onto the porch. Without a glance back, he waited to hear the door shut. After the lock engaged and the familiar beep of the alarm echoed behind him, he ambled down the steps to his SUV.

He had one job.

Keep the author safe.

After that—if God allowed—he'd try to sort through the game his heart was trying to play.

14

Kelly slid into the passenger seat while Declan held open her door. After the door clicked closed, she released a long, frustrated breath. It had been a month since she'd let down her walls with Nathan and shared her concern about the notes she'd been receiving. Nathan had insisted he accompany her whenever she went out, which made her feel like a caged rabbit. She understood both Nathan and Declan just wanted to protect her, but she needed space.

Her thoughts drifted to this evening. Abram's book was gaining popularity, and readers posted positive reviews on all the social media sites. Treasure House aimed to place its authors in the public eye to keep the sales flowing, and tonight was no different. For the past few hours, she'd put forth a brave face through chapter readings, book signings, and the unveiling of the book trailer to the soon-to-be-released third installment of her crime series. The publicity was great but exhausting.

Declan joined her in the car and leaned back against his headrest. "That was more hectic than I expected. But what a night."

"Yes, it was quite an evening." As she craned her neck back and forth, she attempted to let the stress of the evening roll off her. "I'm glad we went together."

"Me too." Declan said. "Your idea to have Nathan meet us there and just blend in with the crowd made sense."

"I didn't want to detract from the book." She swallowed the half-truth, and it traveled down her throat like sour bile. She also didn't want to draw the attention of her fans and turn every question into an inquiry about her safety.

"That was smart. You had a line leading to your table. Lots of new readers." He flashed her a grin. "I know tonight was a lot to take in, but the fans want to hear from the authors they follow."

"I know, I just …" Kelly fumbled with her words. Large crowds bothered her. What if the perpetrator who'd haunted her nightmares stared back at her from the sea of faces? "There's been so much going on lately. Now that I've honored my contract, maybe I need to step away for a while and get my bearings back."

"Are you sure this is a good time? Your next release date is quickly approaching." Declan shot her a worried look. "I'm doing everything possible to try to make you feel at ease."

"I know you are."

A weight landed in her gut. Two letters had been sent directly to Treasure House Publishing, challenging the Zucker family history's validity. Declan had tried to reassure her it was normal for non-fiction books to garner that kind of attention. Especially if somebody disagreed with the author's viewpoint.

However, a cloud of deceit still hung like a weighted blanket over her. She hadn't told Declan about the alarming notes she'd received personally. The latest one accused her of printing misinformation and made a direct attack on her research. The message wasn't threatening to her personally, but it mocked her lack of knowledge about World War II history. It nauseated her to think there were still people in the world who sided with the atrocities of that war. When she'd shown the note to Nathan, the fury in his expression proved he felt the same way.

"It bothers me how much this publicity is upsetting you."

Declan raked his fingers through his hair, leaving a few of his waves mussed. "I feel helpless. I don't know what else to do."

"You're doing plenty. It's just me. I want to go back to the way it was when I could write in peace and live my life under the radar."

"I'm beginning to hate that book." He wrapped his hands around the steering wheel until his knuckles turned white. "And I resent that man for pursuing you to write it."

"Don't say that." She studied Declan's chiseled profile in the moonlight. "Abram is a dear friend to me. I'm glad I met him."

He dropped his hands and turned to face her. "Have you told him about how your life has been turned upside down since the book was published?"

"No, of course not." She shifted in her seat and gazed out the passenger window. Bright moonlit rings encircled the streetlights like misty halos. "I told him it was a best seller. That's all he needs to know."

"Maybe if you told him what's happened, he could help us figure out what's going on."

"No." She jerked her gaze back to Declan. "He's a kind, old man who doesn't need to be involved in this."

Abram grew weaker every day. The time she'd have him as a mentor and friend was growing short. The thought of losing such a kindred relationship cinched a tight band around her heart.

"Did he ever give you anything of value?" Declan shot her a pleading look. "Maybe the break-in *is* connected to the memoir. Is there anything you have of Abram's? What about the journals? Where are they?"

She pressed her back into her seat. Memories of the night in the hotel room came flooding back to her. *Why does everyone assume I have something of value?* "I gave them back to Abram." Swallowing the lie, she added, "I don't have anything else of his."

"Okay. We'll leave Abram out of it." His tone softened as he wrapped his fingers around hers. "For now, we'll just keep our wits about us and make sure the writer doesn't get hurt." Declan released his grip then started the car and pulled out of the parking lot.

A pang of guilt sliced through her. *Maybe I should tell Declan everything. Doesn't he deserve to know?* Her pulse raced as the question looped on repeat in her mind.

His outburst over the book had startled her, but he was just being protective. *How would he act if he knew about the man in my hotel room? Or that I still have the journals?*

The last thing she wanted to do was drag Abram into her chaos. He would never have put her in harm's way intentionally. Would he?

What if Declan confronts Abram? The errant thought tumbled through her brain, making her shiver.

"I hope, with time, whoever has an issue with the book might just go away."

Declan shot her a sideways glance. "That would be ideal. Wouldn't it?"

Kelly swallowed hard. She didn't believe the problem would ever just go away. She had to do something. Finish the puzzle. Figure out what was so important in those journals that someone wanted them. Up to this point, she'd not uncovered any other skeletons in the Zucker family closet. She didn't even know what she was looking for. *I need to ask Abram.* A dull ache pushed against her ribcage. *Before I run out of time.*

When they arrived at her home, Declan punched in the gate code and drove up the pebbled drive. Before he turned off the engine, he asked, "How's the bodyguard working out?"

"He's fine. Why?" Her heart jumped. Nathan had been there tonight but acted as their shadow. Recalling the protective way he tracked her this evening sent a tingle across the exposed skin of her forearms.

"I wanted to get your opinion of him and how you two are getting along."

"I wouldn't say we're getting along." *I've told Nathan about every note—that's more than getting along. I trust him.* "Having a bodyguard is not something I've grown accustomed to. I'll be happy when I don't need one." The words rushed out to conceal the pounding of her blood through her veins. *Are you sure about that?*

He turned off the engine and faced her. "I just want to make sure you feel safe."

"I know you do. I appreciate that."

"I have a couple of out-of-town meetings coming up. I'd like you to let Nathaniel accompany you to any events you have on your calendar while I'm gone." He paused as concern blanketed his features. "Maybe you shouldn't head out alone to that bookstore you love to frequent."

Her shoulders pulled taut. She craved freedom, not more constraints.

"Have your bodyguard take you," Declan said.

"I'll think about it." Nathan had suggested—no, almost demanded—the same thing. But The Bookend was her retreat, and even that bit of solitude was being ripped away from her.

Declan didn't push. After he hopped out of the car, he strolled over to the passenger side and opened her door.

They walked up the stairs in silence.

After she unlocked her door, she turned to face him.

Declan's lips parted then closed as if he was going to say something but changed his mind.

"What?"

"Nothing."

She waited.

He leaned on the stone pillar next to her front door and crossed his arms. The relaxed posture made his fit body resemble the outline of a Grecian statue. "I was just thinking about how stubborn you can be sometimes."

"Oh, really?"

"Yes." His eyes darkened. "You, Miss Landon, are a puzzle I haven't quite figured out."

A warm, late summer breeze wrapped around them, heating her skin.

"One minute, you're insecure. A damsel in distress. The next, I sense your hesitancy to let anyone beyond those walls you've erected around your guarded heart."

While she considered what he said, she frowned. Had she not let him in?

"Don't look discouraged. It's okay I haven't figured you out." His mouth tugged at one corner. "Everyone likes a bit of mystery in their life. Don't they?"

She stifled a laugh. *I don't need any more mystery in my life, thank you very much.*

As he continued to rest against the column and study her, an awareness danced in her middle like a pile of wind-tossed leaves. She would survive losing her privacy, and she would even survive this real-life mystery, but she wasn't sure she'd survive the feelings Declan stirred to life inside her.

Stepping forward, he placed a whisper soft kiss on her cheek. "Have a good night. Stay safe."

She nodded then retreated into her house. After she heard his car drive away, Kelly leaned against the closed door to catch her breath.

Was she a puzzle he hadn't figured out? More like a puzzle she was hiding the pieces to.

Closing her eyes, she considered the two men in her life—Declan and Nathan. Both were trying to protect her, but which one could she trust to help her solve the mystery of the Zucker memoir?

The mystery *she'd* been entrusted to protect.

# 15

Kelly scrutinized her reflection in the full-length mirror. The single-shoulder, midnight blue bodice hugged her silhouette while the airy chiffon skirt rippled to the floor.

"I think this will do." She slipped in a pair of diamond earrings and swiped her lips with a shimmering gloss. She was a grown-up fairy princess awaiting her prince. Even though they didn't need more color, she gave her cheeks a quick pinch. Was this real? Or was she floating on a dream?

The doorbell chimed, and with it, her heart grew wings and beat against her ribcage. *He's here.* She moved one more stray hair into a pin then glided down the stairs to answer the door.

"Good evening, Miss Landon." Declan stood before her dressed in a glossy lapelled tuxedo, holding a bouquet of red and yellow roses. "I've heard yellow stands for friendship and red for love. Which would you prefer this evening?"

Heat prickled the back of her neck. "They're beautiful." She took the flowers and inhaled their intoxicating scent. "Please come in."

"You look amazing." After he stepped over the threshold, Declan placed a tender kiss on her cheek.

Feeling like Cinderella, she did a quick turn. "Thank you for the dresses. They were an incredible surprise."

Last week, she'd received three luxurious gowns, with a handwritten invitation to the art gala black-tie event. Just as always, Declan had thought of everything.

His gaze lingered on the A-line gown. "You definitely chose the right one."

"You think so?"

"Absolutely."

She blinked away from his dreamy look. "I better get these flowers in some water."

Escaping to the kitchen, she grabbed a vase from the cupboard and filled it with water. "Tonight feels like a fairy tale." *Be careful. Fairy tales aren't real.*

She dropped the stems into the vase then smoothed her trembling hands down the front of her dress. *Just breathe.* They'd only been dating for a few weeks, but every hour she spent with him had her tap dancing on a cloud. If she wasn't careful, she'd forget how to tread on land.

"Is everything okay?" The nautical scents of Declan's aftershave circled through the air as he slid behind her.

"Yes."

"I know crowds aren't your thing." He skimmed a finger down the bare skin of her arm, sparking a ripple of gooseflesh. "I'll be by your side the whole evening."

She spun to face him. "You promise?"

The threats had quieted from her stalker, but the fear and anxiety still lingered like a shadow.

"I promise." Slipping his arms around her, he drew her close and pressed a gentle, yet lingering kiss on her lips.

Fireworks shot off in her brain as she melted under his touch. *A fairy tale.*

When he pulled back, his mouth quirked into a grin. "If you prefer, we could skip the gala and stay in."

"Well, I …"

"Of course, I'd hate for you not to show off that dress." He stepped back and raked an approving look over her. "Did I mention you look stunning tonight?"

Sizzling heat circled from her head to her toes. She'd never been in love before, but she was sure this was exactly how it was supposed to be—holding hands, impromptu lunches, and sweet, lingering kisses.

With a reluctant look, he inclined his head toward the door. "We should go. Our audience awaits."

Our audience. Tonight, the publishing world, at least the small niche that mattered to Declan and her, would see them for the first time as a couple. The thought made a cool tremor twist down her spine.

He grabbed her wrap and held it out for her. As she draped it over her arms, he leaned in and whispered something unfamiliar in her ear. The dialect sounded antiquated—almost medieval.

"What did you say?"

"That's a mystery for you to unravel."

When she turned to look at him, she noticed a smattering of gold in his eyes she'd not seen before. "I guess I should study up on some of the more archaic languages, Mr. McNeary."

"Aye, maybe."

Every nerve beneath her skin hummed to life.

She was falling. No, cascading. Make that careening into the orbit Declan's lyrical Irish brogue sucked her into. *Don't fall too deep. You may not recover.* She grabbed her purse and turned off the lights. Would that be so bad?

He opened the door and followed her onto the porch. "Your carriage awaits."

She gasped. Turned at a showroom angle, a glossy, white limousine took up most of her driveway. She glanced back at him and tried to smooth her shocked expression.

"Too much?"

"No. It's perfect." As they approached, the driver popped out and opened the door. What else could make her fairy-tale night complete than a pearlescent carriage ride to the ball?

When she slid into the limo, a shadowy figure shifted near the window, causing her heart to jump into her throat. "Hello … Mr. James."

"Miss Landon." Nathan gave her a curt nod.

"I asked Nathaniel to join us tonight." Declan scooted in next to her and smoothed out the ripples in his slacks. "It's a big event. I thought it would be wise to have security."

As the driver turned up the soft interior lights, they painted an amber glow over the length of her bodyguard.

Nathan redirected his steely gaze from her to Declan's left hand. "That's a nasty bruise you have there."

Declan glanced down at his knuckles. "This? Oh, it's nothing."

Kelly gaped when she saw the bluish purple splayed out across his fingers.

"I lost a fight with the lid of an old wooden trunk." Declan shrugged. "The hinge springs must have rusted out years ago."

How did I not notice his injury? A slow burn traveled from her neck to the tips of her ears. *You were too busy thinking about his kiss.*

When Declan caught her staring at the bruises, he reached for her hand and lifted her fingers to his lips. After caressing her skin with a soft kiss, he smiled. "Nothing to worry about. It doesn't hurt."

Embarrassed by his attention with Nathan sitting next to them, she stilled. "That's good."

"Sorry about the wait earlier." Declan shifted to face Nathan. "Kelly was a little distracted."

Her face burned as Declan continued to hold her hand against his thigh and make tiny circles in her palm with his forefinger.

"No need to explain. I'm on the clock for the whole evening." Nathan looked away from Declan and stared past her out the tinted window. "It makes no difference if I sit in here the entire night. It comes with the job."

She drew her hand from Declan's grip. Why did it feel as if Nathan's tone was a reprimand? *What is going on with him? Is he irritated with me? Is he upset with Declan? Wait. Why do I care?*

As they continued their drive, Nathan and Declan conversed back and forth about unimportant things like the weather and politics.

Nathan cut a look her way, his expression a mask of stoic professionalism and—What was that? Confusion? Hurt? *Maybe he's going through something. Should I ask?*

Nathan's jawline turned stony, and he looked away.

When they arrived at the gala, a handful of bloggers and influencers stood poised with their phones, hoping to snap photos of artists and authors to splash across their online magazines.

Nathan stepped out first, then extended his hand to help her out of the car. She looked up at him, but his gaze was focused on the small crowd gathering on the steps. When he turned to face her, his expression softened. "Be careful tonight, Miss Landon."

Before her mind could linger long on his words, Declan reached out and placed her arm in the crook of his. "Are you ready?"

She pulled her shoulders back and forced a confident smile as he led her up the steps and through the tall glass doors.

"By the end of the evening, everyone will know it was I who stole the heart of the talented author Kelly Landon."

She nodded, but his silky words did little to quell her nerves.

The entryway was packed with people, and before they entered the main hall, Declan had already introduced her as his girlfriend and favorite writer to more than a dozen people. As he navigated her through the crowded hall, Nathan stood dutifully to the side, scanning the throngs of formal dresses and black ties. The night unfolded precisely the way she'd imagined—a stream of small talk and bubbly drinks. It was exhausting.

After they'd taken their seats and the meal was served, Declan leaned toward her. "Are you having a good evening?"

"I am." She blew out a quick breath. She'd never imagined herself like this, being treated like a princess, and on the arm of such a confident and handsome man.

"You are the most beautiful woman in the room tonight." Declan's whispered words glided over her like honey. "And I'm the luckiest man at the gala."

She let his declaration hang in the air for a moment as questions raced through her brain. Could she really become a socialite authoress, dating one of Hampton Roads's most eligible bachelors?

Declan was wealthy, charismatic, and ambitious—not to mention the owner of a nationally recognized literary agency. Could she push aside her insecurities and learn to be the confident woman at his side?

Taking a deep breath, she tried to rein in her nerves as she scanned the crowded room. Everyone around them looked at ease. *I feel so out of place.*

As she glanced toward the exits, her gaze locked onto Nathan's. Instantly, her anxiety fled. He held her stare for a few seconds, then he nodded. The gesture made her feel as if she was doing everything right, and it was okay to breathe again.

Watching him, poised to intervene, reminded her of all the ways her life had changed since she'd written the best seller. Ways that required her to have a bodyguard at public functions.

Nathan took a step forward, and she shook her head. "I'm fine." She mouthed the words in a breathy whisper and feigned a look of tranquility.

Like a sentry, Nathan stepped back and reclaimed his post along the wall. He'd caught her staring and thought she needed him. A rush of heat washed over her, and she looked away. Did she need him? For protection? Or just as a friend?

The string quartet played a melodious piece by Tchaikovsky that drew her gaze to the ballroom floor. The enchanting rhythm of the song ebbed and flowed as couples glided together in tempo to the music. "Declan, I love this piece. Would you like to dance?"

"What was that?" Declan glanced down at his phone and frowned. After reading the text, he looked up. "I'm afraid I have a fire I need to put out." Jumping to his feet, he plucked his jacket from the back of his seat.

"You're leaving?" She rose and tried to quell the tremble in her voice.

"Oh, Kelly, don't look so dispirited." He changed his tone from hurried to tender as he lifted his hand to her cheek. "I wouldn't leave if it wasn't pressing." Declan flagged Nathan, who was there by her side within seconds. "Nathaniel, I have a bit of a crisis to attend to. I need you to escort Kelly home." He glanced back at her. "Don't worry, I'll catch a cab."

She opened her mouth to protest, then clamped it shut.

"Oh, and can you dance?"

"What?" Both she and Nathan asked in unison.

Declan pulled her close and gave her a hasty kiss on the cheek. Several people at their table turned to gawk at them. An older lady with hand-painted eyebrows flashed her a haughty look as he picked up his things and readied to leave.

"She loves this song, Nathaniel. Would you do the honors?" He winked at her then departed quickly through the side entrance.

Tears gathered in her lashes. To be passed from her boyfriend to her bodyguard for a romantic twirl around the dance floor made her want to crawl under one of the fancy tablecloths and hide.

Nathan didn't take his eyes off her. Instead, he offered his arm and led her out onto the open floor.

"You don't have to do this." As he turned to face her, she

lifted a hand to his shoulder and slid her other hand into his palm.

"I know." Nathan's penetrating stare sparkled with kindness. "This is a lovely piece. I can see why you wanted to dance to it."

Pulling her toward him, Nathan pressed his hand to the small of her back. She was thankful he didn't mention Declan's hasty departure but instead took the lead and started to dance.

"I love this era of music." Her lips trembled as she fought to focus on the melody and mask her embarrassment.

"I do too." His mouth tugged at one corner as he continued to lead her in graceful circles around the floor. "Tchaikovsky was a master. The notes of this piece carry a range of emotions."

"You're right. They do."

He flashed her a knowing look, then lifted his gaze above her head as their steps continued to move in rhythm with the song.

"It sounds almost sad. Melancholy. It reminds me of a tragic fairy tale." Heat wrapped around her as she studied the carved silhouette of Nathan's smooth jawline. From this angle, she noticed a small, white scar traveling below the slight clef in his chin.

As if sensing her perusal of him, he tilted his head down to look at her. "I didn't realize you were such an admirer of the Russian romantic composers."

Her heart fluttered as if it had grown wings. "I am."

"I'll need to keep that in mind."

They glided across the floor, and her heart pumped in tempo with her bodyguard's agile steps. She'd almost forgotten Declan's impromptu exit.

Nathan drew her nearer for the song's final beats. When the music stopped, he stepped back, and bent forward in a quick bow. As he did, she realized she'd been too preoccupied that evening to notice how debonair he looked in his jet-black tuxedo.

He winked at her. "At least it won't be obvious you're dancing with *just* your bodyguard this evening."

"You look …" She steadied her voice. "Very nice tonight."

"Thank you. And you look breathtaking in that dress." He held out his arm and guided her back to the table.

Before they reached her seat, another guest at her table, an older woman with garish makeup let her eyes trace over Nathan in a long, raking glance. "It seems, Miss Landon, you've misplaced your agent this evening."

She bristled at the comment. Had the people at their table been gossiping about them?

"It looks like you've found someone just as handsome to take his place." The woman waved an insipid, wrinkled hand in Nathan's direction. "Care to introduce us?"

Kelly cringed. Judgment dripped from the woman's every word.

She glanced down at the place card. Foster. Mrs. GG Foster. Co-owner of Foster Publishing House. One of the largest regional publishing houses on the East Coast. The same publishing group whose name had been splattered all over the evening news only two weeks ago over a scandalous book they'd published about the former president of the United States. Obviously, the legal debacle hadn't kept her or her husband from attending social functions. Or looking down their noses at others in the business.

Before she had a chance to muddle through a response, Nathan swooped in and caught GG's hand in his. He lifted her pale-skinned fingers to his lips and brushed them with a kiss.

As GG's eyes widened, Kelly fought to withhold a ripple of laughter.

"My name is Nathaniel James. Miss Landon is a friend of mine." As he released GG's hand, his lips lifted into a well-practiced, arrogant smirk. "Our families are connected through many generations."

"I wasn't aware Miss Landon had any family nearby." GG raised a badly stenciled eyebrow at Kelly.

"There is an extensive, well-known history of the Landons in

New England," Nathan said. "And I'm sure you've heard of the James family from northern Pennsylvania. We can trace our lineage to the landing of the Mayflower."

Kelly tried not to let her mouth drop open into a surprised oval at his well-spun words. Where had he come up with this story? It didn't matter. The look on Mrs. Genevieve Grayson Foster's wrinkled face was priceless.

GG paused for a moment and lifted her nose a few millimeters higher. "Do you mean the James family who own the expanse of orchards in the northern part of the Keystone State?"

GG was struggling to compensate for the lack of knowledge of the supposed James family. Kelly smiled. He'd clearly made up the whole story, and the hilarity of it made her want to double over with merriment at the ruse.

"I'm afraid you have the wrong family." Nathan leaned in and held his voice down to a dull whisper. "We deal in cargo ships and antiquities. I'm ashamed to say that I've been told our family may have a few—" he winked at her mid-sentence. "How shall I say it? We have a few *pirates* in our closet we don't like to talk about in polite company. If you understand my meaning, Mrs. Foster?"

Mrs. Foster pressed her thin lips together as if she'd sucked on a lemon then turned to face Kelly. "I hope you enjoy the rest of your evening, Miss Landon. Treasure House is lucky to have you. And so is the infamous Mr. McNeary."

The woman's dismissive words slinked through the air. When Kelly glanced up at Nathan, he threw her a wink, hooked her arm into the bend of his, and pulled her away from the table.

"What was that all about?" She leaned into him as they walked to the outskirts of the ballroom.

"Let's just say I know exactly how her family made its fortune." Nathan chuckled as they both glanced over their shoulders at Mrs. Foster.

"Do they really have pirates in their family?"

"They do. From generations ago." When they took up their

post at the edge of the room, he leaned in and deepened his tone. "And they don't like anyone to know about them."

"Then, how did you—"

He stopped her with a wicked grin. "It's my job, Miss Landon."

"Of course, it is."

His smile broadened as they both turned. "I know all the details about everyone at your table."

"You take your job quite seriously, Mr. James." Lightening the mood, she leaned toward him and whispered, "Do *you* have pirates in your family?"

For a brief second, Kelly imagined Nathan as a swashbuckling captain of his own Jolly Roger vessel.

"Hmm … I think that's a secret for another day." When he glanced at her, his eyes darkened to a deep blue.

Like a stormy ocean. In a pirate novel. Swashbuckling indeed.

She chuckled, enjoying how much he reminded her of Abram. As they stood in silence, a wave of fatigue washed over her. "I think I'd like to go home."

"Are you sure?"

"Yes. I'm not comfortable in large crowds right now."

Nathan moved closer, and the piney scent of his aftershave tickled her nose. "Is there someone here making you uncomfortable?" Throwing her a sidelong glance, he added, "Other than Mrs. Foster."

She shuddered. The images of her pirate bodyguard were making her uncomfortable. "No." She did a sweep of the room. "This is a lot to take in. These events are Declan's idea of a good time. Not mine. I'm more comfortable at home with my laptop and a cup of coffee."

"Understood." A flash of something she couldn't name fell over his expression as he sent a text to the driver.

Was he thinking about Declan running out on their date? A fresh wave of embarrassment fell over her.

They walked to the entrance, and she accepted her wrap and her purse from the attendant. As she slipped it over her shoulders, another thought raced across her mind. How long had Nathan been waiting in the limousine outside her home? She tried to count back from when Declan arrived on her doorstep until he met her in the kitchen and—

"The driver's out front."

Kelly jerked her head up.

"Are you ready?"

"Yes." She smoothed a hand down her dress in an effort to level her thoughts.

Nathan guided her to the front door then wrapped a protective hand around her waist as they descended the stairs to the street.

"Nathan, I ..."

Did she feel the need to explain about her and Declan? Why? She nibbled on her bottom lip. When they reached the limo, he opened the door and waited for her to step inside.

She stopped and looked up at him. "Thank you for stepping in tonight." *Stepping in? Stop rambling. He did his job. That's it.*

Nathan threw her a quick nod but didn't reply.

She ducked into the car and waited for him to join her. He hesitated. Then, after a heartbeat of a second, he shut the door.

Kelly's heart sank. Was he not riding back with her?

She watched out the window as he shoved his hands into his pockets and paced the length of the limo. After a few seconds, he walked to the front and slipped into the passenger's seat.

As her snowy white carriage pulled away from the curb, the weight of loneliness pressed in on her like a north wind. She glanced down at the shimmering sparkles on her dress and blinked back the moisture gathering in her eyes.

Tonight was supposed to be magical. A fairytale.

Instead, it ended with an absent prince, a moody bodyguard, and the longest ride home she'd ever endured.

16

"Good evening, Miss Landon."

Kelly smiled at Donna as she stepped into the now familiar entryway. "Good evening. I hope it wasn't an imposition, me calling last minute." Needing a friend, she'd reached out to Abram and slipped away for a visit on her own. No bodyguards. No agents. No deadlines. Just a quiet visit with a friend.

"No imposition." Donna glanced out the window at the partly cloudy sky. "There's a late summer storm brewing, but they say it won't be here until well after dark." When she turned, her eyes were misty. "Mr. Zucker's nurse set up a convalescent bed in the blue room, giving him an additional place to relax other than just the master wing." Donna continued to chat about how the room overlooked the pond and the apple trees. "Blue is Mr. Zucker's favorite color. Did you know that? Well, Mrs. Zucker's favorite color was blue and …"

Donna's voice faded to the background as Kelly prepared herself to see Abram confined to a bed. No more walks in the garden. No more lunches on the veranda.

The familiar scent of fresh-brewed coffee greeted her as Donna pushed open the large French doors. Kelly's gaze roamed around the room. The deep indigo paint shone with the natural light streaming in from the opposite wall of windows. Sweeping a glance at the far wall, she took note of the oversized, milky white fireplace. It stood in stark contrast to the subterranean hues anchoring the room.

"Miss Landon's here, Mr. Zucker." Donna looked back at Kelly and grinned. "He's been chatting about your visit all afternoon."

Kelly picked up her pace and walked over to Abram's bed, where he sat upright against a wall of pillows.

"Hello, Kelly, dear." He sounded winded, but happy to see her. "What should we talk about today?"

She smiled at him. "Love or mystery?" She cherished their riddled conversations every time she visited.

"Or the mystery of love?" Abram laughed at his own play on words.

Kelly waited for Donna to leave the room before blurting out the question she'd wrestled with for weeks. "How did you know you were in love, Abram?" Sinking into the oversized chair next to his bed, she reached for her already prepared cup of coffee. A caramel blond roast with two dashes of Madagascar vanilla and enough steamed milk to make it the same color as almond biscotti. And with it, her favorite, a plate of shortbread cookies.

"My love story? You already know *my* love story." He paused a moment, and she imagined he was thinking about his wife, Rachel. His eyes glistened. "What about you? Has your Mr. Declan put a happy blush on your face today? Or is there another?"

She was taken aback by his perception. His eyesight was failing, yet he saw things others around her missed. It had been over a week since the black-tie gala, and she could not get her mind off Nathan and the dance they shared. It made her smile when she thought about Mrs. Foster and her pirates.

"From your pause, I suspect another."

She took a quick sip of her coffee before placing the ivory mug back on the side table. "It was just a moment. A jolt to my emotions. I can't explain it. We had a connection." Her words sprang off her lips in short bursts, and she shook her head. The elegant image of her bodyguard in a tailored black tuxedo dangled at the forefront of her thoughts.

"Something mysterious, perhaps?"

"Perhaps." Now Abram had *her* speaking in riddles.

"How did you meet this other man?"

"He works for Treasure House."

"Ah, that could be dangerous if it doesn't work out."

So could dating my agent. "Yes, I guess it could. Thankfully, his job is only temporary."

"Tell me about this jolt. I'm losing my eyesight, dearest. I need all the vivid descriptions you can give me."

Kelly's heart sank. She didn't want to lose Abram. Not yet. However, seasons continued to change, and the clock ticked quicker each time they met. "Of course." She patted Abram's wrinkled hand while she unpacked her story. "I was at a dinner … no, maybe I should call it a dance."

"A dance? That sounds very adolescent for a woman your age."

"It was an art gala. A black-tie event. Declan also thought it would be good for my career."

"Work and pleasure? Was it a date with Mr. McNeary?"

She hesitated. "Yes. In fact, our first public appearance as a couple."

"Interesting. Let's call it a ball." Abram loved to embellish her descriptions. Maybe he should've written his parents' story.

"Okay then, a ball."

"Yes, that's better." Abram shifted against the pillows and closed his eyes. "Describe everything. What did you wear to this ball, Miss Landon?"

Playing along, she described all the details from that night. She even included how Declan had surprised her with a group of dresses to choose from along with the invitation.

"I bet you looked marvelous." He cleared his throat. "And Mr. McNeary?"

"What about him?"

"How was he dressed?"

"He wore a tuxedo."

"It *was* a ball. Very debonair of him for a first public date."

"If you call trying to mingle with the city arts council an elegant evening, then yes."

Abram's laughter caused his body to shake beneath his blanket. "You're in a gown, and your date is wearing a tuxedo. How much more romantic can that be?"

She continued to describe the limousine, the food, and the music. "Declan looked so handsome, and the evening was going so well ..." *And there was that kiss.*

"This sounds like a great beginning to a respectable love story." Abram's eyes slid open as he folded his hands together in his lap. "Who interrupted our leading man?"

She took a breath before she rushed ahead with her description. "Declan received a text. After he read it, he looked harried and distracted. He passed me off to Nathan at the beginning of the dance. It was awkward." She picked up her coffee and took a hasty sip. "I think Nathan believed it was his duty to dance with me."

"Who is Nathan again?"

"Remember, he works for Treasure House Publishing?"

"Yes, that's right." Abram rubbed his chin. "Declan gave up your dance. Sounds like Nathan won the duel."

"Hardly a duel." Angel's wings flapped in her belly. If they had drawn pistols at dawn, Nathan most likely would've won. She imagined the two men dressed in waistcoats and cravats while standing opposite each other in a misty field.

"Tell me about this dance."

Her cheeks heated as she blinked away her Regency era daydream. "Nathan stepped in. It was all very uncomfortable. But he stayed with me and completed the dance."

"And that gave you the jolt? How odd."

She heard the humor in Abram's voice as she let her thoughts wander back to her bodyguard. Recalling the way his strong arms led her through the dance like a classically trained professional sent a wave of warmth across her skin. "No, it was during the dance. He seemed so—earnest."

"Earnest?" Abram lifted his brows as if waiting for her to elaborate.

"As he held me close, my uneasiness vanished along with my disappointment." Kelly walked back through the memory to where their bodies moved in tandem with the strings of the quartet. "Nathan didn't move mechanically like I anticipated, but ..."

"But?"

"But poetically. Like he'd danced that way a hundred times."

"A good dancer always wins the girl. At least in my day." Abram's lips curved into a boyish grin.

She tried to imagine Abram as a young man dancing with his sweetheart. "Nathan was a wonderful dancer. He remained serious and professional, but he was also kind and attentive." She glanced out the window while the image of Nathan's muscular form draped in black fabric filled her thoughts. "He smiled at me in a way I'd not seen before."

"Was it a mysterious smile?"

"Yes." She turned back to face Abram. "It was like he knew what I was thinking. Although, I don't even know what I was thinking."

"You were thinking *he* was a great dancer."

Her pulse sprinted through her veins. "Yes. I was. All this time, I'd only thought of him as just my bodyguard."

"He's your bodyguard?"

She winced. "Yes."

"Since when did you need a bodyguard? Are you in danger?"

She looked away. "That's a long story, my dear friend." When he cleared his throat, she turned back to face him. "Maybe that's a tale for another day?"

Abram's brows crinkled. "So, your bodyguard, Nathan, surprised you?" He allowed her to switch the subject but still eyed her with concern. "By being good at something unexpected?"

"Maybe. It didn't fit his personality." She paused, thinking back to how he'd spun a yarn about pirates.

"Even you should know not to judge a book by its cover, Kelly, dear."

She chuckled. "That's true. Nathan carries himself in a reserved and professional manner, but for a few minutes, he seemed at ease, passionate, and creative."

"Creative?"

"Yes. He made up a story out of thin air about pirates."

"Who doesn't like a good tale about pirates?" The enthusiasm in Abram's voice made her wish he'd been there to witness Nathan tell his anecdote in person.

"I'm usually a good judge of character, but he surprised me."

"What do you think of his character now?"

"I'm not sure. He's always been kind to me." She picked up her mug and took another sip. "On the night we danced, there was something different about him." As she remembered his decision to sit up front with the driver, she replaced her mug on the table. Why had he not stayed with her? Had he also felt the spark of energy humming between them? She sighed as she waved her hand in the air, trying to clear away her tangled thoughts. "Anyway, I'm not sure what to think."

"Nathan sounds like a puzzle."

"Yes, I guess he is."

"A puzzle you want to figure out?"

She bit down on her bottom lip.

Abram nodded, accepting her unvocalized response. "Mr. McNeary. What of his character?"

"Declan can light up a room. Everyone loves him." *And he can kiss like a poet.*

"But can he dance?"

She considered Abram's question. They'd only danced once that evening. "He can. But he wasn't as confident or as attentive. He seemed … well, he seemed distracted."

"Now, there lies the mystery."

A mystery indeed. She shook her head. The real mystery was this man, Abram. Most of the time he spoke in riddles, yet he was so easy to converse with. She glanced down at the small table next to her. After a couple of shortbread cookies and a hot cup of coffee, she was spilling her heart to this man. He'd become one of her truest friends.

"Sir, you have another visitor." Donna's voice sliced through the room. "It's Mr. McNeary, sir."

They both turned to look at the door.

"Yes, please bring him in."

Sweat beaded on Kelly's forehead as she looked from the door to Abram then back again. *What is Declan doing here?* Before she could take another breath, Declan ambled around the corner and walked into the room.

Abram sat up straighter. "Mr. McNeary. What brings you for a visit today?"

Declan shot her a surprised look. "I had no idea you'd be here today, Kelly. Is there another story you've been keeping from me?"

Her cheeks stung. Had he heard any of their conversation? "No. No story. Just a coffee date with a friend."

An unreadable expression shadowed Declan's face before he pulled his gaze from hers and spoke to Abram. "I wanted to stop by and offer my thanks again for the privilege of allowing Miss Landon to write your family's story."

She exhaled a long breath then reached for a cookie. *Was that all he wanted to say?*

"Of course. I appreciate you lending me one of your best authors."

"It took some prodding, but I'm glad Kelly agreed to it." Declan shoved his hands in his pockets as he continued to rattle off mundane information about the publishing market.

Abram listened and nodded. Every so often, he'd glance at her and smile. "I do appreciate you keeping me in the loop, Mr. McNeary."

Abram's eyes shut in an extended blink. She placed her uneaten cookie back on the platter.

"It looks like we should finish our conversation a little later."

Abram turned and urged her closer. "Maybe I should meet your bodyguard and give you my opinion."

"I, well …"

Abram chuckled then threw her a playful look as he glanced past her to Declan. "Mr. McNeary?"

"Yes?"

"Kelly's shared with me that she now has a bodyguard."

Declan tipped his head and shot her a curious look. "Uh, yes, that's true."

"I think next time, he should be the one to escort her for her visit." Abram glanced at her and winked. "She should be as safe as possible. Don't you think?"

Declan's phone buzzed, and he dipped his head down to check it. "Yes, yes, of course." When he lifted his gaze, he smoothed his expression. "If you come back to visit, you really should bring Nathaniel. You can't be too safe on these winding roads."

She looked back at Abram and narrowed her look. Abram's muffled chortle floated through the air.

"We'll leave you to rest, Mr. Zucker. Kelly, can I walk you to your car?"

"Sure." Grabbing her purse, she rose and joined Declan by the door. "Thank you again, Abram, for letting me stop by."

"It's my pleasure, Kelly, dear. And don't forget to bring your bodyguard next time."

Her palms slicked with sweat as she gripped her purse. "I will."

Declan waited for her to step out into the hall before he slipped his hand into hers. "I had no idea you two were still meeting."

"Yeah. It's not really about the book now. Abram has become a dear friend to me."

When they reached the entryway, he released her hand and opened the door. "Is that so?"

His tone made her stop just past the threshold and pivot to face him. "Do you have a problem with that?"

An amused look traced across his expression. "No. Of course not." He pulled the door shut then reached for her hand. "I'm just not accustomed to you being so social."

They walked down the steps and out on to the gravel drive.

"Abram's been good for me. Creatively. I guess after we spent hours together researching and writing, a friendship formed." When they reached her car, she released his hand and turned to face him.

"I understand." His brow pinched as he lifted her chin with his forefinger. "I didn't mean to sound like a jealous lover."

Declan's gaze flickered to the Zucker home then back to her. "I had to be sure I wasn't losing my favorite writer to a rich old man living in a million-dollar mansion." Wrapping his arms around her waist, he tugged her closer. "I don't know if you understand how much I've grown to care for you, Kelly."

Lately, she wasn't sure what to think. Declan's moods ebbed and flowed with the tide. But then again, so did hers. He drew at her heart strings with that mesmerizing look in his eyes. Had she finally fallen completely under his spell? *What about Nathan?* The unexpected thought made her still. *What about him?*

Declan ran a gentle finger down the line of her jaw. "A penny for your thoughts?"

She blinked. Sharing her thoughts would be a bad idea.

He leaned in and pressed his lips against hers.

Her thoughts zig-zagged like a roadrunner. *It would take more than a penny. You'd need to pry them out of me.*

When Declan stepped back, his mouth tugged into a wicked grin. "Or you can keep them to yourself."

"I … wasn't …" She worried her bottom lip between her teeth. What was she doing, thinking about Nathan while she kissed Declan? It was foolish. Impractical. He was just her bodyguard. Although he'd been kind to her, it didn't mean he felt affection for her.

"I'll call you tomorrow." Declan pulled out his phone and glanced at the screen. After he sent a quick text, he brought his gaze back to hers. "Will you be okay to drive home?"

"Yes. I'll be fine."

"I could have Nathaniel meet you at your place." He looked out at the setting sun flanked by a backdrop of threatening clouds. "I heard we might be getting some bad weather from the tail end of that hurricane. It might be dark and stormy by the time you get back."

Her heart skipped. The last thing she needed was to see Nathan right now. She waved off the suggestion. "No—no. There's no need to call him." Her throat dried as she croaked out the rest of her words. "I'll be fine." *Liar. What if we lose power?*

Her chest squeezed. She wanted nothing more than to have Nathan and the security he offered waiting for her when the storm started. But wouldn't she feel the same if Declan had offered to follow her home?

"I don't need a bodyguard. Remember?"

"Right. And as soon as we have some answers, he's fired."

As he strolled toward his car, Declan's words seared a hot brand across her heart. *He's fired.* Wasn't that what she wanted? Her privacy back? Yes, of course she did. She was a fool for not being content with her relationship with Declan. A relationship she thought she wanted more than anything else in her life. *What is wrong with you?*

Kelly waved a quick goodbye as she watched him slide into his two-seater sports car and drive off into the sunset.

A fresh idea took root and sprouted as she slipped into her SUV. "Maybe it's time to flip the script." A rumble of distant thunder answered back. "When the story hits a snag, have your protagonist do something out of the ordinary."

As she started the car, she glanced back at the Zucker family's sprawling mansion and rehearsed her last conversation with Abram. So much about her meetings with Abram created more questions in her life than answers. Had Nathan won the duel? Did he intend to? Was Declan jealous of her friendship with Abram? And why had he shown up today?

Shaking off the unsettling inquiries, she shifted her SUV into drive and glanced in her rearview mirror at the approaching late summer storm.

Whatever the answers were, one question still lingered at the forefront of her mind.

If love truly was a mystery, then how did one solve it?

17

Kelly opened the door to greet Nathan. "Good morning."

"Good morning." He shot her a sheepish look and held out a paper cup.

"Is that for me?" She took the cup from him and breathed in the tangy scents of pumpkin and nutmeg.

He nodded. "I guess they brought the flavor out early this year."

"Thank you." She took a drink and sighed. The weather hadn't cooled much, but this reminded her fall was just around the corner. "It's delicious." She held the cup up and read the stamp. "Oh, this is the new place next to The Bookend."

"I remembered you stopped in the last time we were out."

Warmth circled through her as she waved him in. "My purse is upstairs. I'll be right back."

He stepped in and held out a hand to take her coffee.

She laughed and handed it back to him. "You can have a sip but save some for me."

"Don't worry. Your coffee's safe with me."

Kelly took the stairs with a skip in her step. After muddling through her jumbled feelings, she'd finally come up with a way to implement her plan. A plan she hoped would finally shed some clarity on the two men tugging at her heartstrings like well-trained puppeteers.

When she returned to the entryway, Nathan handed her back her coffee. "Are you sure you want to do this?"

There'd been no more scribbled notes about the journals, no more break-ins, and no more menacing men lurking in the shadows, yet the paranoid feelings remained. She wanted to get back to writing in peace. To do that, she needed to know how to protect herself. Once that happened, Nathan could leave.

A dull ache pressed on her chest.

Or if he wanted to, he could stay.

"Yes." *Yes, Mr. James, it's all part of the plan.* "I'm sure." His brow furrowed, and she waved him off. "I need to do this. I need to get control over my own life." Staring into the liquid blue of his eyes caused her to blink and take a few steps back. "I can't have you with me forever, and I don't want to be afraid anymore."

A shadow passed over his expression, then just as quickly it vanished. "I understand."

"I've been alone most of my life. I'm not going to allow some faceless person to invade my peace with a few threatening words and gestures." She switched off the lights. "The memoir's not a novelty anymore. Whoever had their feelings rankled over the story has most likely moved on."

"I'm sure you're right. As long as you remain cautious." Nathan paused before he stepped across the threshold and onto the porch. "Even after I'm gone."

"Of course." Her guts twisted into a pretzel. "I'll remember everything you taught me. Safety first." Kelly locked the door and followed him to his car.

After several minutes of driving, Nathan's voice sliced through the silence. "I don't mind, you know."

She turned to look at him. "Mind what?"

"I was hired to protect you, but I also *like* being with you."

The crinkle of skin at the corner of his eye twitched. When he pulled up to a red light, he turned to face her. "What I'm saying is, it's not just a job for me. Not anymore. I enjoy spending time with you."

"You do?"

The light turned green, and he turned back to the road. When his skin darkened to a deep red around his collar, she looked away.

Had Nathan been thinking about her too? A quiver twirled in her belly and settled. *What about Declan?*

Declan was her dream man. Most days, he looked as if he'd walked out of an upscale menswear magazine. He was attractive and self-assured. He made her feel special. Like a treasure. She loved how he pushed her to be a better version of herself.

Kelly pinched her eyes shut. She'd asked Nathan over today for two reasons. One, so she could take charge of her own security. And two, to find out if their connection was all in her imagination. *Which is where I tend to live a lot of my days.*

Her eyes fluttered open, and she stared out the windshield. He was her bodyguard. She was unexpectedly dropped into his life—or he was into hers. He was cool and mechanical, but she'd uncovered a different side of him. A side that had her questioning, well—everything.

She took a long drink of her latte then returned it to the cup holder. When she was around Nathan, she felt secure. Seen. Free. Like she wanted to let her guard down. Didn't that mean he was just good at his job?

Kelly studied Nathan's profile. A five-o'clock shadow trailed along his jawline, giving him a relaxed, weekend vibe. She contemplated what he might look like with a full beard.

"I'm sorry." The muscle snaking down Nathan's neckline yanked taut. "I think I may have crossed a line."

"What do you mean?" Her mouth dried as she blinked away the moisture gathering in her eyes. *Please don't take it back.*

"What I said. It wasn't very professional." When he stopped at another red light, he turned to face her. "But I did mean it."

Her soul screamed at her to confess. "I like being with you too."

One corner of his mouth tipped up before he turned his attention back to the road. When the light turned green, he accelerated and followed the on-ramp onto the freeway.

What am I doing? With clammy hands, she smoothed down the imaginary wrinkles in her jeans.

After several miles of silence, they found their exit, and Nathan pulled into a parking lot in the warehouse district. He turned off the car, and for a few moments, didn't say anything but sat there fidgeting as if he might.

"Thanks for asking me over today."

"Thanks for agreeing to come." She didn't hold back her grin. "Off the clock."

A deep chuckle escaped his lips. "I'd still take a bullet for you if the need arose."

Kelly's toes curled in her sneakers as she turned her attention to the warehouse. "Let's hope that's not necessary."

He laughed as he got out of the car, walked to her side, and opened the passenger door. "It's a little breezy. You can head inside if you want."

"Okay." She didn't rush ahead. Instead, she waited while he retrieved his gun case out of the trunk and walked with him to the front entrance. Once inside, she took a deep breath, and released it. *You can do this.*

Nathan sent her a reassuring look. "You got this. I'll be with you every step today."

Her uncertainty sprouted wings and flew away. She *could* do this.

And having Nathan here would be all the assurance she'd need.

A tall, lanky man stood behind the counter. Nathan shook his hand and watched Kelly out of his peripheral vision. She walked around the U-shaped entrance and examined the firearms in glass cases as if she was inspecting artifacts in a museum.

"I need a lane and a couple of targets." Nathan paid and turned to face her. "Are you still okay with this?"

From his experience, he'd found there were three types of people in the world. Those who owned guns and could use them. Those who fought against the right to own weapons and bemoaned those who did. He suspected Kelly to be the third type—someone who'd accepted the use of firearms as protection but had never been properly taught how to handle one.

She looked up at him with her doe eyes. "Yes, of course." He heard the catch in her voice. "I need to do this."

Nathan understood her frustration. She'd been under the shadow of alarm since he'd been hired to protect her. Now, it was his responsibility to help her regain her independence. He couldn't be by her side every hour of the day, and eventually, he'd need to step down from his position as her bodyguard. Maybe sooner than later, after what he'd admitted today.

"Okay, here you go." Nathan handed her a set of goggles and ear protectors.

Confusion blanketed her expression.

"Trust me, you'll need them."

"People don't wear these when they're in real-life situations."

"No, they don't." He slid on his hearing protection and motioned for her to do the same. "But I don't want you to lose your hearing on this little outing. Besides, it's required."

"Oh, okay." She stuck the bulky grey covers over her ears then slipped on the plastic range glasses. She looked out of place, but to him, she looked adorable.

He smoothed a section of her hair sticking out like a floppy dog ear.

She reached up and pawed at the rest of her head. "I doubt a bit of hair out of place is going to make me look any more ridiculous, Mr. James."

He smiled, but he kept his thoughts of how she really looked to himself.

120

18

As they walked into the shooting range, Kelly jumped at the first shot. Even with her ears protected, the barrage of activity shocked her senses.

Nathan turned. "Everything okay?"

She gave him a thumbs-up and threw him a smile. She was more than okay. The thought of trying something new added a spark of energy to her step. It was ironic how her fictional characters used weapons, but she'd never fired a gun herself. Today that would change.

When they reached their lane, Nathan placed the first paper target on the clips and pushed the button. The target moved several feet away.

Another shot went off beside them, and she flinched.

Nathan moved his hand to the small of her back. "All good?"

She straightened and nodded. After he lifted his hand, the imprint of his touch lingered.

"You'll get used to it." He retrieved a small gun from the case and handed it to her. "This is something you'd carry in your purse, briefcase, or in a holster."

She couldn't imagine ever wearing a holster, but she was glad to have the visual. After she handed it back, he placed it on the shelf.

Nathan lifted his gun out of its holster and passed it to her. "This is the one I carry. It's a little larger but shoots the same size bullet."

After inspecting the gun, she gave it back to him.

"I'll shoot first, then you can have a try. Okay?"

She stepped back, just enough to be out of the way but close enough to get a good view around his broad shoulders.

Nathan let off several quick shots then gestured for her to step beside him. He brought the target in so he could show her where they landed. All the holes were in the center. He flashed her a roguish grin. "This is where you want to shoot. It's very effective in destabilizing your enemy."

"It looks like you've done this before."

"Lucky for you, I have." He winked at her then clipped a new paper target up and sent it back to the wall. After a quick lesson on how to reload, he handed her the gun. "Your turn." He moved behind her and wrapped his arms around hers, guiding her stance. "I'll steady you for the first round."

When Nathan's breath tickled her neck, Kelly stilled.

"Relax. I'm right here with you."

Relax. Sure. She focused on her breathing and tried to ignore his muscular form anchoring her body. "I think I'm ready."

"Okay, go ahead and pull the trigger."

She followed his command. The force of the kickback vibrated in her hands and traveled like an electric pulse through her arms. As the shot took off, she released the breath she didn't realize she'd been holding.

Nathan took the gun out of her hands, checked the chamber, and laid it on the shelf beside them. "What did that feel like?"

"Wow."

He laughed. "Do you want to do it yourself this time?"

"Yes."

"Relaxed stance, two hands, and be ready for the kickback. You have several bullets left, so you can let them all off if you'd like."

He handed her the gun and gave her a quick nod as he stepped out of her peripheral vision.

Taking a deep breath, she aimed and let all the shots go. After she placed the gun on the shelf, she turned to see Nathan's approving look.

"You're a quick study, aren't you?"

"That was amazing."

He chuckled then moved the target in. For a moment, Nathan stared at the marks. "Kelly. Wow." He turned and threw her a surprised look. "Look at where your shots hit."

She moved in and studied the black figure. Most of the combined shots were near the center.

"That's remarkable for your first time."

Pride welled up inside her. "You're a great teacher."

"I really didn't do anything but tell you how to stand. The aiming was all up to you." He looked at the target again then back at her. "Would you like to do a couple more rounds?"

"Definitely."

He pushed the button, and the target floated to the back of the lane. For the rest of the hour, they took turns shooting, finishing the box of ammo he'd bought from the man at the front counter.

"I enjoyed this so much. Thanks for bringing me."

"Any time." Nathan packed up and brought in the paper target. He folded it and handed it to her. "Here, keep this as a memento of your first time."

When she took the target, their fingers touched, igniting the spark already pulsing between them. "I'll always remember today. Thank you."

"Me too." As his tender gaze rooted her in place, the commotion around them fell away.

A gunshot popped in the adjacent lane. This time she didn't flinch.

Nathan grinned. "I told you you'd get used to it."

"Get used to what?" *Staring into the fathomless ocean of your eyes? Or enjoying your handsome smile?* Another shot rang out, and her heart quickened its pace. "Oh. Yeah. The noise." She pointed to her ear protectors. "They work."

Nathan's eyebrows arched with his grin. "They do."

———

Nathan's step lightened as they exited the range and slipped into the SUV. Kelly had amazed him at how well she'd caught on. If push came to shove, at least she'd be able to defend herself.

"You did great today. Thank you for trusting me enough to show you how to use a firearm."

"I couldn't imagine having anyone else show me."

"What about Declan?" As he blurted the question, Nathan cringed. Did he really want her to answer that?

"I don't know if this is really his thing."

"You might be surprised." He stuck the key in the ignition.

"I'm not sure he would've been as patient with me."

He turned and held her gaze, trying to ascertain how she really felt about her agent. Unsure of what he saw, Nathan started the engine and flashed her an impish grin. "If you keep shooting like that, you may just put me out of a job."

He checked the rearview mirror then backed out of the parking spot. As he drove through the warehouse district, Nathan caught a contemplative look on her face. "Care to tell me what's dancing around in that clever head of yours, Miss Landon?"

"Hmm ..."

"Yes?" They pulled up to a stoplight, and he turned to face her.

"If it risks you losing your job, I may never pick up a firearm again."

Heat curled through his chest. If he wasn't careful, he might lose his heart well before he lost his job. He searched his mind for a clever comeback, but his tongue had turned to cotton.

The light turned green, and a soft honk from the car behind them broke through his thoughts. Nathan faced the windshield and pressed the pedal down.

Kelly giggled.

Impressive. I almost missed a green light. As he shook off the brief embarrassment, questions bounced around his brain like stray rubber balls. *Is she flirting with me? If so, what about her and Declan? Am I flirting with her? If so—Have you lost your mind?*

He tugged at his collar then turned down the heat in the car. *You're in way over your head.* His job should've been simple—find out who was stalking the novelist and get out.

Nathan cleared his throat and slipped a sideways glance at Kelly. When her lips curved into a smile, his heart melted. The getting out may be more challenging than expected.

I need to focus. He redirected his attention back to the road. While the threatening notes had stopped, his intuition told him her stalker was just regrouping. If he didn't concentrate on his job, he'd risk putting her in danger.

Don't forget about her agent. The thought made him cringe. She liked Declan, and from what he could tell, Declan liked her. A lot. A quick memory of the art gala flashed through Nathan's brain. Did Declan really care for her? Or did he just enjoy the publicity?

Nathan stole another glance at Kelly as he drove through her neighborhood. There was no denying the chemistry brewing between them. But romance? *Nope, don't go there.* He'd always considered an instantaneous connection between two people to be the thing of myths and fairy tales. Not real life.

Robotically, he punched in the numbers on her gate keypad. He had to get his head together and stop flirting with the possibility they may have a future together. If she knew his history, where his line of work had taken him, Nathan was sure she wouldn't have looked at him like she did today—with such trust in her eyes.

"Is something on your mind?"

Her question yanked him out of his thoughts.

"Uh … no. Why?"

"You just got quiet all of a sudden."

He pulled the car to the front of the house, threw it in park, and turned off the engine. "I was just … thinking."

"About?"

He gripped the back of his neck, contemplating how he should answer. *About you. About us.* "Nothing important. I just remembered I have an appointment on Monday."

"Oh."

Nathan jumped out of the car. *An appointment? You're an idiot.* When he got to her door, he opened it and offered his hand. As she wrapped her fingers around his, a flux of electricity shot through his forearm. He froze.

"Declan's going out of town in a few weeks." Her soft voice floated around them. "I have a signing in Richmond while he's gone. I don't think I have anything to worry about, but I was wondering if—"

"I'll take you." His pulse thrummed in his ears while he continued to hold her hand. "I mean … if you want me to, I can take you."

"I would like that."

I'd like that too. His fingers opened as if he'd gripped a hot coal.

Turning, Kelly scurried up the steps to her door as if running from his awkwardness.

The air grew heavy, and Nathan suddenly wished there was a manual to tell him how to proceed. *You're her bodyguard. Hired to protect her.* He blew out a long breath, then took the steps two at a time and joined her by the door.

"Thank you. Again. For today." Kelly unlocked the door then pivoted to face him.

"Any time." He shoved his hands in his pockets, feigning a relaxed posture. "Would you like me to give the place a check?"

While her gaze lingered on his, a hunger crawled through him with a ravenous prowl.

A hunger for something he'd suppressed years ago.

For companionship? Connection? No—for love. Nathan swallowed hard.

"Please. I'd appreciate that."

He walked over the threshold and waited for her to step inside. Darting from room to room, he did a quick check. "Everything looks in order."

He strode toward the door as his chest squeezed tight. *Kiss her.* A chuckle threatened to escape. Where had that thought come from? Not a good idea. He'd likely be fired, but ... Would that be so bad?

"Nathan?"

The tremble in her voice made him pause. Was she feeling as confused as he was? Or was something else bothering her?

Smoothing his expression, he turned to face her.

"Would you like to stay for lunch? I'm heating up vegetable soup, and I made caramel cheesecake brownies yesterday. I'd be willing to share if you're in the mood for something sweet."

Another vision of him pulling her into his arms traced across his brain. He cleared his throat. "No. I better not." *I better not what? Kiss her? Eat lunch?* His stomach rumbled betraying him.

"Oh. Okay."

"I mean, I can't. Not right now." She moistened her lips, and his gaze fell to her mouth. *Because if I stay ...* He jerked his chin up and forced a smile. "Rain check?"

Disappointment crept over her features. "Rain check. But I can't guarantee there'll be brownies."

"Understood." Mumbling a quick goodbye, he opened the door and rushed to the safety of his car.

Why was he feeling so off-kilter? *You're falling for her.* He shook off the thought. That would prove to be very inconvenient.

He started the engine, loathing how he'd sprinted out of her house as though it was on fire. *Why didn't I stay?*

Being with Kelly tugged at the layers he'd bound around his heart. It was frightening and wonderful all at the same time. Like a rollercoaster where you couldn't see the curves in the track. He enjoyed their talks. The conversations that came so easily. What would it be like if he'd really let down his protective shield? Would she accept him?

Glancing at her front door, he contemplated going back. "Nope. Not a good idea."

He needed to keep his guard up and stay focused.

After he found out who wanted the information Kelly had, then maybe he could entertain letting her into his world.

Maybe.

19

Kelly shuffled through the fallen leaves as she walked up to the Zucker mansion with Nathan following close behind. It had been over a month since they'd gone to the shooting range, and she was still trying to piece together his mixed signals. And her own.

Had she flirted with her bodyguard? Did he take it that way? She pushed aside the thought and slipped a glance at Nathan as they stepped up to the door. They were becoming friends. That was it. And friends asked friends to lunch. She blew out a sigh and pressed the doorbell. Why did navigating relationships have to be so challenging?

After a moment, a tall woman Kelly had never seen before swung open the door. "Good evening, Miss Landon and Mr. …"

"James."

"Mr. James." The woman motioned for them to come in. "I'm Dr. Swanson, Mr. Zucker's doctor." She smiled at them, but her eyes mirrored a grave expression. "I know Abram asked for you today, but I wanted to let you know he's feeling tired this evening. He may not be up for a long visit."

"Okay, we understand." Kelly's heart sank. Abram had been taken by ambulance to the hospital earlier in the week, so she was grateful to receive a call asking her to visit.

"We've moved him downstairs. I'll take you to his new room."

A sense of dread fell over her as she moved through the long halls of the first floor. Before Dr. Swanson opened the door, the middle-aged woman turned to them, and the creases in her forehead pinched together. "There's a button next to his bed. Just ring me if you need anything."

Kelly's chest tightened. She understood Abram was ailing, but the thought of him declining so quickly made her heart want to break in two.

After she stepped through the doorway, Kelly rushed to his side. "Hello, friend."

"Kelly, dear. How are you?"

"I'm good." She leaned in and kissed him on the cheek. His skin had grown paper-thin and cool to the touch.

"Did you bring your bodyguard today?"

"I did." Her nameless tormentor had returned. After an incident that left her SUV vandalized in a parking garage, she felt an urgency to keep Nathan close. She lifted her gaze to Nathan, who stood watch in the doorway. He nodded, his expression somber.

She studied him for a second, recalling his admission that he enjoyed spending time with her. A warm tingle spread through her like a wildfire. Spending more time with him had not been a hardship for her either. Although she wished it had been under different circumstances, their prolonged hours together had only ignited the need to get to know him better. More intimately. As a friend.

"Is that him?"

She turned back to Abram, and heat flooded her cheeks.

"I guess that's a yes." Abram chuckled then slid his glasses up on the bridge of his nose as he glanced around her toward Nathan.

Kelly followed Abram's gaze. Nathan's broad shoulders and six-foot-two frame took up an ample amount of space next to the doorway. Today he'd worn his dark gray suit, with a pinstriped, indigo tie, sparking to life the rich color of his eyes.

Nathan stepped into the room a few feet. "Good evening, sir."

She'd told Nathan Abram's eyesight was getting worse, so she appreciated the gesture.

"Good evening." Abram sent him an approving nod then turned his attention to her. "Very regal, that one."

When he slid back to his place on the wall, Nathan flashed her an enchanting look.

"Yes. He is."

"I have someone I want you to meet today." Abram patted the bedside and gestured for her to sit down. He pushed the button next his bed, and after a few seconds, Dr. Swanson poked her head in the door. "Doctor Swanson, would you be a dear and get my great-granddaughter?"

"Yes, sir, of course."

He turned his attention back to Kelly. "I want you to meet Emersyn. She's home on break."

"I'd love to."

Emersyn Renée Zucker was a bit of a mystery to her. With her boarding at an elite preparatory school a few hours away, Emersyn and Kelly had never crossed paths.

After only a few minutes, a bright-eyed young woman marched into the room. She was tall and slender, and her long, amber-colored hair hung in large, wavy curls, reminding Kelly of a medieval princess.

"Papa, you're awake." Emersyn's airy voice drew back the curtain of sadness and filled the room with life. "How are you feeling this evening?" She glanced at Kelly then back at Nathan. "I didn't know you had visitors."

Abram's face brightened. "Yes. Come here and sit down." He beckoned to her, and Emersyn scooted in next to him. Abram patted Kelly's hand. "I'd like for you to meet a dear friend of mine, Miss Kelly Landon."

"It's nice to meet you." Emersyn's eyes shimmered like blown glass. "You're the author, aren't you?"

Kelly chuckled. "Yes, I am."

"I've heard a lot about you." Emersyn turned to Abram. "She's as pretty as you described."

Abram winked at Kelly. "Of course, she is."

"Who's that man standing by the doorway?"

"He's my bodyguard," Kelly said.

Nathan flashed the two of them an award-winning smile.

Kelly laughed. "Don't let that smile fool you. He can be very stern when he wants to be."

Emersyn studied Nathan for a few more seconds, her cheeks ablaze with pink. "Why do you need a bodyguard, Miss Landon?"

Abram cleared his throat. "Maybe that's a story for another day."

"Yes, of course." Emersyn took another quick peek at Nathan then turned back to Abram. "I just received a list of my classes for the winter semester." As she scrunched up her nose, Emersyn drew her lips into a pout. "It looks like I'll be in Mrs. Barnes's class again for creative writing."

"Not a fan of creative writing? That's hard to imagine when Abram has such a vivid imagination."

Abram's laughter filled the room.

"I prefer investigative writing. And research." Emersyn's expression brightened. "Mr. Ratcliff offered me a spot on the school newspaper. He still believes in using old-fashioned ink and paper."

Abram gave her a bemused look. "Since when is ink and paper old-fashioned?"

"Since everyone started blogging." Emersyn settled back on the pillow next to Abram and rolled her eyes. "Online."

"I still get the old-fashioned ink and paper delivered." Abram shot Kelly a sly look. "I have some really old-fashioned newspapers up in the attic. Would you like to look at them some time?"

"I'd love to."

"I'd like to see them too." Emersyn spoke up, pulling the attention back to her. "Mrs. Barnes wants us to make up stuff. I want to write about real events. She complains I don't have enough description, but I told her flowery words aren't important in a *real* story."

Kelly turned her attention to Emersyn. "A real story, huh? Well, if you need help making stuff up, give me a call."

"You mean it?"

"Sure. I could give you some pointers."

Abram squeezed her hand. "Miss Landon loves research and flowery words. She'd be a wonderful resource."

She shrugged. "What can I say? I'm wordy."

Emersyn laughed.

After a pause, Abram took a shaky breath, and his expression darkened. "Emersyn. Kelly. There's something I need to discuss … with the both of you."

Emersyn shifted to face Abram, and her jubilant expression disappeared into a cloud of worry. "What is it? Is this about your last time in the hospital?"

Abram gave a slight nod. "I've not been feeling well as of late. Well, honestly, I've been feeling worse." He paused and looked from Kelly back to Emersyn. "No matter what happens to me, I want you to know I trust Miss Landon—with everything. I want you to trust her as well. Will you promise me that?"

Emersyn nodded as tears gathered in her lashes.

Abram turned back to her. "Kelly, I'd like you to look after Emersyn when I'm gone."

A weight lodged in her chest. The girl was just a teenager. She didn't know anything about raising children, let alone an adolescent young woman. "I … I don't know what to say."

Emersyn reached out a hand and placed it on her arm. "It's okay, Miss Landon. If my papa trusts you, so do I."

Kelly's eyes welled with tears. She blinked a few times, attempting to push them away.

"Emersyn, you'll be an adult soon, and all of this will be yours." Abram looked past them and out the window. "You'll want for nothing, and you'll be well taken care of. I made sure of that." When he turned back to Emersyn, his countenance dimmed. "I want you to be careful about who you trust. Listen to Miss Landon's advice. Do you understand?"

"Yes, Papa." Emersyn's soft answer pricked Kelly's soul.

"There are people who may want to manipulate you because you're young. Don't listen to them. When the time comes, I trust Miss Landon will give you good direction."

Kelly's throat dried as she tried to quell the trepidation churning in the pit of her stomach. How could she give the young woman advice about her future when she barely had all the kinks of her own life worked out?

Abram patted Kelly's hand as if reading her thoughts. "All will be okay. Just follow your instincts, and everything will unfold as it's supposed to."

She opened her mouth to respond, but Abram cut her off. "Emersyn, I'd like you to take Miss Landon to the library on the third floor." His face lit up as he threw her a wink. "Miss Landon is a bit of a rare book enthusiast, and she'll enjoy the tour."

Kelly forced a smile, still reeling from her new duty as guardian.

Sending her a reassuring look, Abram added, "Miss Landon would never turn down an offer to wander through a room of old books. Would you?"

Shaking her head, Kelly breathed out a sigh. How could Abram throw the mantle of guardianship at her, then whisk her off to another wing of the house?

"Come on, Miss Landon, you're going to love this room. Well, it's more like a hidden chamber than a room." Emersyn giggled as she stood and placed a quick kiss on Abram's cheek. "My papa has been collecting books for years."

With a myriad of questions swirling in her mind, she took Emersyn's outstretched hand. "Abram's right. I can't pass up a chance to wander through stacks of old books." She furrowed her brow, then shot Abram a 'this-conversation-isn't-over' look.

He waved them off. "Go, go. Have fun."

⁂

Both women flashed Nathan a shy look as they breezed through the doorway and rushed down the hall.

Nathan glanced over at Abram, unsure of what he should do now that Kelly had left the room. Should he follow them? Or would he get in the way?

Abram attempted to sit up as a nurse swooped in to rearrange the layers of pillows behind him. "Young man. Why don't you come over here?"

Amusement ignited inside of him. No one had referred to him as a *young man* in quite a long time.

Abram crooked a finger toward the wingback chair next to him, and Nathan took a seat.

"Tell me about yourself." Abram's tone conveyed more of a command than a suggestion.

"Nothing much to tell, sir. What would you like to know?"

Kelly had described many things about Abram, and his assertive nature was one of them. But, meeting him face to face was even more enjoyable than the secondhand knowledge.

"Very wise." Abram clicked his tongue. "I can tell you're a man of few words. Not willing to expound your life all over the rug." The old man's eyes flickered with amusement. "Now, that Mr. McNeary could tell you about himself all day long if you asked him to."

Nathan relaxed in the chair. This conversation was going to be very entertaining.

"Did some time in the military?" Abram stared at him over the rim of his glasses.

"Yes, sir."

"Very good." Abram paused then asked, "Have you been overseas much?"

"Yes."

"Any time in the UK?"

Nathan hesitated only a moment before he answered, "I was stationed there for a bit. A couple of years, give or take."

"Very good, very good." Abram rubbed his chin before he continued. "So, now you're Kelly's bodyguard?"

"Yes."

"Why would Kelly need a bodyguard? Nathaniel, is it?"

"Well, Mr. Zucker—"

"Please call me Abram."

"Of course, Abram." Nathan straightened. "I think I'll let her answer that question if she hasn't already."

Abram stayed silent for a moment. Pondering his next move like a master playing a game of chess. "She told me some things about you."

"Is that so?"

"Yes." Abram held his gaze. "She told me you knew your way around a dance floor."

"She did? I hadn't realized I made an impression with Miss Landon in that area." *She told him about our dance. Tchaikovsky, was it?*

"You know, between you and me, I think Mr. McNeary has a thing for our Kelly."

The way he said *our Kelly* made Nathan smile. "Is that so?"

Abram nodded. "Between you and me." He paused and urged Nathan to move closer. "I don't think he's the right guy for her. I think there might be someone better suited."

Nathan leaned back and grinned, but he kept his thoughts to himself.

"What do you do in your free time, Nathaniel?"

Nathan relaxed as he and the older man conversed. He could see why Kelly gravitated to the man's friendship. As Abram asked him about his family, Kelly ambled through the doorway with Emersyn on her heels. She stopped short when she saw him sitting near Abram's bed.

"Did you have a good time?" Nathan sprung out of his seat, nearly coming to attention.

"Yes." She turned her gaze to Abram. "Thank you for letting me check out your amazing collection."

"Of course. Besides,"—a sly smile spread across Abram's face—"I needed to send you somewhere so I could have a chat with your bodyguard."

Kelly's jaw dropped, then she quickly recovered and pressed her lips into a thin line.

Nathan shifted on his feet and tried not to chuckle at her reaction.

"He's a nice young man." Abram looked up at Nathan. "I think we had a very pleasant talk. Don't you, Nathaniel?"

"Yes, sir, we did."

Kelly glanced at him then looked back at Abram. "What did you two talk about?"

"We talked about dancing," Abram said.

Her face blanched, and Nathan coughed.

"Don't worry, we talked about other things too." Abram did little to hide the amusement in his voice as he tittered like a schoolboy. "Did you know Nathan served in the military?"

Kelly's pale expression transformed into a strawberry pink. "I ... well, I suspected maybe he had."

Nathan grinned. The tidbit that Abram had given him about his dance moves sweeping her off her feet was invaluable. He'd have to remember to thank the old man later.

A wheezy cough rose from Abram's chest, and Emersyn moved next to his side. "Can I get you some water?" She lifted the cup from the side table, and he took a few long sips from the straw.

"Thank you."

"It looks like you may have had enough excitement for today,

Mr. Zucker." Everyone turned toward the door as Dr. Swanson breezed into the room.

"I think you're right." Kelly turned to Abram. "We're going to head out and let you get some rest. We'll talk again soon."

The hitch in Kelly's voice made Nathan's heart tear in two. *This can't be easy for her.*

"Yes. Soon." Abram coughed again, and Emersyn lifted the straw in the water cup to his lips. He took a quick drink. "Nathaniel, make sure you come back with Kelly when she comes to visit."

"I will."

Emersyn placed the cup on the table and rushed over to Kelly. "It was nice meeting you."

"You too. Let me know when your creative writing class starts."

Emersyn's brow's shot up. "I will."

After both women hugged and said their goodbyes, Nathan followed Kelly down the hall and out the front door.

20

Nathan turned onto the interstate as the sun slipped past the horizon. Abram's probing into his life had been an interrogation he'd not prepared for. *She remembered our dance.* He cut a glance at Kelly sitting in the passenger seat. He'd grown accustomed to her being up front. He even preferred it now. Tonight, however, her proximity filled him with nervous energy. What other memories had she tucked away in her heart?

"Nathan?"

"Yes." His heart jumped at the sound of her voice.

"I don't feel like going to my house just yet. I keep thinking about what happened in the parking garage, and—"

"Where would you like to go?" Nathan didn't need to let her finish. He knew the latest visit from her stalker had shaken her. If he was honest, the event rattled him too. The attacks were getting more personal—angrier. There'd been enough damage done to her SUV to leave her car in the shop for weeks.

"You mentioned your apartment was in Newport News."

"It is." *What about my professional boundaries?* His jaw clenched. Tonight, she needed a friend more than she needed a bodyguard. "I'm anticipating a delivery this evening," he said. "Would it be okay if we stopped at my place for a minute?"

"That would be great."

Hearing the relief in her voice made him forget any boundaries between his personal life and hers.

In fact, if he was honest, he was growing weary of holding the line.

***

Kelly studied her surroundings as they continued to drive. Had she really just invited herself over to her bodyguard's place? Maybe she should have just gone home. *I didn't feel like being alone.*

She pressed back in the seat, suddenly feeling self-conscious. Abram looked so frail tonight. Time sped forward in her thoughts, and the familiar pang of loss shadowed her like an unwanted companion.

"It's not too much farther." Nathan's words yanked her out of her melancholy thoughts.

"This is a nice area."

He nodded. "It seems to be."

In less than twenty minutes, he pulled into a gated community filled with modern, multi-level condominiums. The newly built homes with ebony doors and white pillared porches stood shoulder to shoulder along the landscaped road.

"These are cute. Are they new?"

"Fairly new." Nathan pulled his car into one of the narrow driveways. "This is me. Number one-zero-eight. I needed something temporary and found an owner who could provide a flexible lease."

Sadness fell over her. Nathan wasn't a local. He'd only moved to this area because his job in DC. ended. She wanted to probe him about the intricacies of his profession. Did he take jobs all over the world? Or did he try to stay close to the East Coast?

Nathan came to the passenger side and opened her door. As

her hand slid into his, their first meeting flashed across her mind. *Those intense, sapphire eyes.* That day, having a bodyguard had been an inconvenience—an intrusion into her once idyllically quiet life. Heat spread from her palm to her heart. Nathan was no longer an inconvenience.

He released her hand, and they walked to the front door.

"Have you ever thought of staying?" She twisted her purse strap as the question flew off her lips.

"In Virginia?" He unlocked the door and stepped aside so she could walk in. "I guess it depends on where my work takes me."

She shrugged out of her coat, and Nathan swept in to help.

"What about you?" he asked. "Is Virginia your final stop?"

"I'm not sure." She pivoted to face him. When she'd daydreamed about the future, she'd never really considered location.

Nathan hung her coat on the hook by the door then turned to face her. "They say home is where your heart is. For now, I guess it's Virginia."

Her heart grew wings. *Yes, it is.*

"Please make yourself comfortable." He walked toward the kitchen and flipped on a light. "Can I get you a water? Or a soda?"

"Sure, I'll take a glass of water. Thank you."

She walked around the living space, taking in every detail. It was an open concept floor plan, with masculine grays and bold, inky colors. In the center of the room sat a dark leather couch and a bulky walnut coffee table. Nothing appeared untidy. With one exception. The sizeable antique desk in the corner. She chuckled. It looked like something Bob Cratchit from *A Christmas Carol* might have sat behind while he warmed himself next to the flame of one dimly lit candle.

"This is a beautiful piece of furniture." She moved toward the desk and ran her hands over the weathered wood. "It looks well loved."

"I picked it up a few weeks ago at an estate sale. The

warehouse was amazing. There were rows of antique doors and stained glass from old churches." Nathan described a couple more bygone pieces, then apologized for the mess as he muttered something about antiques and research.

Kelly's gaze swept across the room to where Nathan stood filling two glasses with water from the fridge. A trio of bare lightbulbs dangled over a rustic concrete bar, giving the space a rich, industrial feel. After he set the glasses on the bar, Nathan slipped off his suit jacket and slung it across one of the leather stools flanking the counter.

The modern look usually came off as cold and sterile, but with Nathan in the picture, it projected class and tranquility.

He looked up and caught her studying him.

"I love your place." She turned away and pretended to be interested in a painting of what appeared to be a medieval church. "It looks exactly like what I'd imagined it to be." Pulling in her bottom lip, she bit down. *What I imagined it to be? Really?*

Glasses clinked together as Nathan sidled up to her. "It took me a few weeks, but I think I finally got it set up the way I wanted."

"I've never been a fan of dark, industrial décor." She swallowed back her awkwardness then turned to face him. "But your place feels comfy and ... secure." *Like you.*

His eyes flickered with something she couldn't decipher. "I'm glad you think so."

After handing her a glass, Nathan took his gun out of the holster and placed it on the coffee table. "Please. Take a seat."

He sank into the couch as she nestled into an oversized gray, wingback chair across from him. For a few seconds, it was quiet. Not uncomfortable—but peaceful.

She took a drink then set her glass down on a coaster and leaned back against the velvety fabric. The chair's cushions tugged at her strength as Kelly struggled to keep her eyes open.

If home was where his heart was, then Nathan's heart had just wrapped her in a warm embrace.

As he watched her relax, a tingle swept across the back of his neck. Having Kelly here, in his home, made the place feel tranquil—homier. He'd been solitary for so long he'd forgotten what it felt like to have the presence of another human invade his personal space. *Don't get too comfortable.*

Nathan ignored the warning and continued to study her. She shifted in the chair and sighed. A smile tugged at his lips then at his heart. He could spend every evening winding down like this.

After a few minutes, her eyes fluttered open. "I'm sorry. I didn't mean to doze off."

"It's okay." Fire rushed around his neckline when he realized he'd been caught staring. "You've got a lot on your mind."

"I guess I do."

"Abram's a nice man," he said. "I'm glad I got to meet him."

"He is."

"It seems you two have grown close after collaborating for the memoir."

"We have. He's like a grandfather to me." Her expression fell. "I just wish meeting him wouldn't have thrown me into … well, into whatever I've been thrown into."

Nathan's fingers flexed around his glass. He wished the same thing. "What happened to your SUV …" Struggling to find the right words, he set his drink down and frowned.

The chaos in Kelly's life had been relatively silent; then, like a cobra, out of nowhere, the tormentor decided to strike again.

"I don't know what to do anymore." Frustration coated her words. "Everything seems so upside down."

Nathan's heart sank. Tonight, it was evident Abram was dying, and there was no denying Kelly's heart was breaking from the thought of losing her friend. That, compounded with the return of her stalker, had to be overwhelming.

"I shouldn't have let you get so far ahead of me in the parking garage." His throat constricted. "It won't happen again."

That night, he'd been a few steps behind when her scream pierced the air and propelled him to her side, with his gun drawn.

The car window on the passenger side was shattered, and all her seats had been sliced apart with a box cutter or a knife. When he looked inside, the glove compartment was open, and the contents were strewn all over the floorboards. Somebody was looking for something.

Or leaving a message.

Kelly pulled one of her legs up under her. "I guess I didn't imagine this profession would be dangerous. I'm just a writer. It's not like I'm some undercover agent in a mob den."

"You're a crime fiction writer. Maybe one day, when this is behind you, you can put all your trials in a book." He smiled, hoping to lighten the mood.

"Right, but this all came about because I wrote a memoir about love." Her gaze tugged at his soul. "Who knew love could be so precarious?"

Nathan swallowed hard. *I'm starting to wonder the same thing.*

Shaking his head, he scolded himself again about that evening. He'd been at the restaurant to shadow her while she met another writer for coffee. Before that, he'd made a promise to himself to keep his guard up and give her some space. It was getting too personal.

Nathan glanced back at Kelly, sitting across from him with her feet tucked casually under her. *Like it is now. Too personal. Too comfortable with her here.*

He shook off the thought and mentally retraced their steps in the restaurant.

After her friend had left, he waited for her cue to leave. Instead, she waved him over to her table and asked him if he'd join her for dinner. Without much prodding, Nathan agreed and took his place in the seat across from her.

While they ate, she expressed her need for some freedom.

Maybe even a change of location. She explained how her creativity felt suppressed, and she wanted to find a place where she could go and write again without having to look over her shoulder all the time.

Nathan let himself believe the evening was just a meal between two friends. Not an assignment.

I got sloppy.

She leaned her head back again and closed her eyes. The peaceful look on her face kindled a soft flame of guilt inside him. The perpetrator could have been waiting for her in the car that night.

Fury surged through him like molten lava. It was time to pour all his resources into tracking down the person making her life a living nightmare.

After that?

After that he'd find out her agent's intentions and then maybe …

As if eavesdropping on his internal struggle, she cleared her throat and opened her eyes. "I don't mean to keep drifting off."

"It's okay. I'm glad you feel secure enough around me to unwind."

Nathan nodded toward the weathered world map on the wall. "You mentioned the other night about wanting a change of location. Where would you like to go?"

Maybe if he got her out of the country he could focus.

Her face brightened, and he was relieved to see this topic brought her some pleasure.

"There are so many places. Where do I choose first?"

"Let's start with where you've already been."

"I've traveled around Europe—Germany, France, and the UK. My dad worked for Homeland Security and was stationed overseas."

"Really? How interesting."

"It wasn't, really. My father worked in the IT department."

"You're right. IT sounds anything but adventurous. How was your relationship with your father?"

"He was obsessed with antiques, so if we had any father-daughter bonding moments, it was over old, dusty relics."

Nathan waited for her to elaborate.

"He had numerous metal detectors in the closet, and the smell of silver polish permeated our home."

"Ah, he was a treasure hunter." He'd heard about the Nighthawkers in the UK, but it was hard to believe Kelly's father dabbled in any of the illegal stuff.

She shrugged. "I guess."

"What about your mom? Did she share your dad's regard for treasure hunting?"

"No. She despised it."

"I'm sorry. That couldn't have been easy."

"It's okay. My mother got tired of Dad's misuse of his family's money. Her words, not mine. Later I realized she suspected my dad of having an affair."

Nathan arched a brow. "Because he collected antiques?"

"For a time, my father was overly interested in buying antique jewelry. My mom thought it was for another woman."

"Was it?"

"I don't think so. After my mother left, my dad stayed single. One day, when I was a bit older, he laid a black velvet bag in front of me and said, 'it's all there, all of it.'"

"What was in the bag?"

"Jewels."

"Wow."

"Yeah, just a sack of random gemstones. My father had taken every jewel out of its setting." She rubbed her temples. "I was a teenager. I had no idea what treasure was in front of me."

Nathan took a drink while he tried to unravel everything she was saying.

"My father was terrible at communication. He handed me a ledger explaining the jewels totaled around half a million dollars and would more than pay for my college. Whatever was left, he told me to save for a rainy day."

"You're kidding. Did you keep them?"

"I went to college, if that's what you're asking."

"Did your dad ever mention what he was looking for?"

"No."

It was quiet for a moment, then Kelly got up and walked over to the bookshelves lining the wall. While she read the titles, her fingers glided over the books' spines.

"This is an interesting book. May I?" She pointed to a tattered children's book on the shelf.

"Of course. It's rumored there were only twelve of those ever in print."

"Really?

He nodded.

She pulled the book from the others and opened it like a reverent prayer. "I've never seen anything so unique."

"It's a retelling of Jewish history for children. Those books were on the list of banned books during World War II. It's believed some of them were burned, and the rest were smuggled out by people willing to preserve them."

"That's an intriguing history."

"The story is the books were distributed at random, but I have another theory."

"You do?" Kelly closed the book.

Nathan set his glass down and joined her next to the bookshelf.

"What's your theory?" She asked as the gold in her eyes sparkled. "I love a good hook."

"Hmm …" Rubbing his chin, he pretended to string her along. "I don't know. It's some pretty clandestine stuff. Secret treasures. Family legacies."

"Nathan." She replaced the book and pushed her bottom lip out into a pout.

His eyes swept over her mouth, and a trail of fire wrapped

around his collar. *Don't tempt me, Miss Landon.* When he lifted his gaze, her eyes smoldered with longing.

She wasn't playing fair.

He leaned in, and his lips nearly brushed against her earlobe. "I believe they were given to people for a purpose. A calling. Those who hold the books have a commission from the past to keep them safe until they're reunited with the rightful owners."

"That *is* an interesting theory, Mr. James."

A grin tugged at his lips as he took a step back. "I think we're past using Mr. James. Don't you?"

"I think you may be right—Nathan."

Nathan's heartbeat pounded in his ears. Or was it her heartbeat?

"Kelly." He traced the contours of her jawline with his finger then gently lifted her chin, so her gaze met his.

"Yes."

Was that a question? Or an answer?

"You make me want to let down my guard." Nathan rested his hand on the shelf beside her, hemming her in on one side. "I haven't decided how I feel about that."

"Your secrets are safe with me, Nathaniel James."

"Are you sure? I hold some weighty secrets." His pulse rumbled through his veins like a freight train. "If I can trust you, then … ask me anything."

"Anything?"

Ask me to kiss you.

"What do you think your calling is?" she asked.

"My calling?" Nathan drew in a steadying breath. "My calling is to protect you."

The doorbell's chime sliced through the quiet, and he backed away.

"I better get that."

That was too close. My calling needs a boundary. And maybe a moat.

Releasing a lungful of air, Nathan stalked away and answered the door.

With a shaky hand, Kelly brushed a finger across her lips. They were trembling. *Was he going to—No. That's crazy.*

After he accepted the package, he placed the box in the front closet and rejoined her in the living room. Trying to focus on something other than his proximity, she turned and continued reading the titles on a row of books.

"Have you read all of these?" She ran her finger along the spine of *The Count of Monte Cristo.*

"Yes, I have."

"This one, with the floral scrollwork on the spine, written in French." She twisted to look up at him. "*Parlez-vous français?*"

"*Oui,* a little."

"You're quite the character, Nathaniel James." She zeroed in on a row of English authors. "I see Tolkien, Dickens, and Austen, to name a few."

Nathan shrugged then returned to the kitchen and turned on the electric kettle. "I guess you could say I'm a fan of all things British."

She smiled. They'd already spent hours chatting about the island across the pond, both having lived there at some point during their childhood.

"Can I get you some tea?" he asked.

Kelly turned as Nathan held up two clear glass mugs. "Do you have any coffee?"

"It's almost ten in the evening. Won't that keep you up all night?"

"Not really."

"Sorry, I don't have any coffee." Nathan shook his head. "You're quite a character yourself, Kelly Landon."

"Yes, I guess I am." She continued to survey his collection as the kettle bubbled to life. If books reflected the owner, then Nathan was an eclectic mix of classical romance, historical non-fiction, and Gothic thriller.

"I'll get some coffee for next time."

He'd walked up behind her, and his words tickled the back of her neck. *Was he inviting her back?*

She turned to face him. "I like cream and sugar too."

"So do I." He chuckled then took a long drink of his tea. "In my tea." Nathan put his mug down on a coaster then reached up to the shelf above her and pulled down a book. "There's something I want to show you." His mouth curved into a boyish grin as he showed her his treasure. It was a first edition Charles Dickens.

Taking the book, she gingerly opened the cover. "It's beautiful."

"I remembered you liked Dickens."

"I do."

"Kelly."

She glanced up and tried to decipher his expression. "Yes?"

"I need to tell you something."

The Westminster chime broke through his words.

"It's getting late." He glanced at the clock then looked back at her.

"It's only ten. What did you want to tell me?"

"It was nothing. Another time."

She handed him the book, but as she took a step to turn, Nathan reached out and gently pulled her back toward him.

"I want you to have this." He laid the book in her hands, letting his fingers glide gingerly across hers.

"I … No, you don't have to …" The scents of Earl Grey and sandalwood circled around her, making her mind a tangled mess. "This is your copy."

"I want you to have it. Think of it as a memento of our time together." He picked up his mug and took another drink.

Her throat constricted. *Was he leaving?* Maybe not today, but someday he would. "I'll cherish it. Thank you."

While she cradled the copy of Dickens close to her chest, Nathan holstered his weapon and picked up their glasses.

What was he going to tell me?

After he unplugged the tea kettle, he shrugged on his jacket and glanced in her direction. "Let's say we get you home, Miss Landon."

The spell had shattered. Nathan was back to the professional who'd been hired to guard her. Halfheartedly, she followed him out the door.

As they drove to her house in silence, she was unable to quell the prattle in her mind.

What was Nathan going to tell me? Did he want to kiss me? I wanted him to kiss me. What am I doing? I can't fall for my bodyguard. That's a trope that never plays out well.

He threw the SUV in park but kept the engine running. "Would you like me to give the place a look around?"

Her vision blurred. "Not tonight." She'd rather not attempt to decipher his secret thoughts while she tried to organize hers.

He gripped the back of his neck then blew out a quick breath. "Kelly, I feel like tonight—"

She gripped the handle and opened her door.

"Wait. Kelly." Nathan jumped out of the car. By the time he reached the passenger side, she'd already stepped out and shut the door. "What's wrong?"

"Nothing." She smoothed her expression. "Like you said, it's getting late."

He studied her for a second then pivoted and paced the length of the car twice before coming to a stop in front of her. "Look, I—"

"Nathan. I'm tired. You're tired." She pulled the novel in closer to her chest. "Let's finish this conversation when the sun's up."

"Okay."

She turned and walked up the steps to her door.

He didn't follow.

And she didn't want him to.

Instead, he waited at the bottom of the steps until she stepped across the threshold and shut the door.

21

Nathan stepped into the elevator with Kelly's visit to his apartment still fresh on his mind.

He was getting too close to her. To the whole situation.

He'd spent the past week researching the Zucker family memoir, trying to piece together any valuable information she might have included to make her a target. Anything to bring this chaos to an end. He'd found nothing. Maybe the old man really did only want to print a story about his family.

Shoving away the thought, Nathan stepped out onto the fourth floor. *There's got to be something I'm missing.* He blew out his breath and rounded the corner as another thought popped into his mind. *Maybe she's doing her own research.* He pursed his lips. Does she even know what she's looking for?

Standing in front of Declan's office, Nathan knocked twice before he heard a muffled "Come in."

He squared his shoulders and strode into the room.

"Nathaniel." Declan pointed to the phone next to his ear. "Go ahead and sit down. I'll be with you in a minute."

He slid into the leather chair in front of Declan's desk and continued to siphon through his internal debate. *If nothing important is in the book, then it's got to be in the journals. But why doesn't she trust me with the information?*

"Yes, of course. I'll get right back to you." Declan placed the phone on the desk, then leaned back in his seat. "Thanks for coming in today."

"Of course." Despite Declan's friendly greeting, Nathan's body failed to relax. He suspected he'd been asked here to talk about the vandalized SUV. Or worse, dinner. He wouldn't be surprised if Declan believed he was no longer able to protect Treasure House's favorite author.

Then where would he be? Back to square one.

Tension coiled in his shoulders like an angry snake. Wouldn't that be perfect?

"I've got some news." Declan grinned like the cat that ate the canary. "We've finally got info on the house break-in."

"Really?" Nathan tried to smooth the surprise in his voice. "That was ages ago."

"Yes. It looks like we'll no longer be needing your services after the new year."

As if punched in the gut, Nathan's stomach muscles contracted. *Of course. I screwed up. He's letting me off easy.* He pressed his lips together and waited for Declan to explain.

"The police picked up someone last week." Declan said. "He confessed to everything and mentioned he'd been in Kelly's neighborhood the exact night of the break-in."

That doesn't explain the SUV. Or the notes. "Receiving threatening notes can be very unsettling. Don't you think someone's still out there plotting to do Kelly harm?" Nathan threw out the question, and Declan didn't bat an eye. "She received another one right after her car was ransacked." He recalled the words scribbled in red.

Maybe we need to take you on a little trip down memory lane and find those journals together.

He couldn't help but think it was a direct threat to kidnapping—or worse.

Declan laid his elbows on the desk and steepled his fingers. "Most likely it's just a crazy fan. Writers with her notoriety deal with it all the time. I don't think we should give them much weight." He relaxed his hands and tapped his fingers on the smooth, dark wood. "Kelly writes crime novels. Sometimes people want to jump in and feel like they're part of the experience."

"Experience? That's absurd." Heat flooded Nathan's veins. "Shouldn't *you* be concerned about a crazy fan? The threats have escalated. The latest note mentioned a set of journals."

"She showed you *all the* notes?"

He held Declan's stare. "All of them."

Declan didn't flinch, and neither did he.

"Do *you* know where the journals are, Mr. McNeary? Have you read them?"

A flash of irritation leaped across Declan's expression. "No."

He sensed Declan was lying, but for what reason, he wasn't sure.

"Have *you* seen the journals, Nathaniel?"

"No."

Declan leaned back in his seat and waved a dismissive hand in the air. "The journals were mentioned in the book. Anyone could've known about them."

"However, in the book, the journals came off as love letters written between a married couple. Hardly worth anyone's villainous interest."

"You read the book?"

Again, Nathan didn't like Declan's tone. Maybe he was on edge because he'd just been fired.

"It doesn't seem like your style." The right side of Declan's mouth quirked up. "The book."

"It's not. I was curious." He held Declan's gaze. "I was curious as to why it was causing havoc in Miss Landon's life. I thought it might help me do my job better if I knew where the animosity was coming from."

"Did you find anything that piqued your interest?"

"Nothing worth tormenting a writer over."

Declan relaxed his shoulders and folded his hands in his lap.

"What's your theory on the car break-in?" Nathan asked. "Whoever broke into Miss Landon's vehicle was looking for something specific." He measured Declan's reactions. Declan didn't balk, so he threw out another question. "If the journals were *just* love letters, can you think of another reason why anyone would want to get their hands on them?"

"No," Declan said, "but I can see you're thinking of something. What's *your* theory?"

Nathan had several theories, none of which he was willing to share with the man across from him. "I think there may be something deeper going on with Kelly and Abram. How much do you know about Abram Zucker?"

"Not much." Declan threw out his answer like a ninety-mile-an-hour fastball.

Is that some animosity I'm sensing?

"He's a rich old man who sought Kelly out to write his memoir. You aren't insinuating a romantic relationship, are you?"

"No. I'm not." Abram was like a grandfather to Kelly. That was the farthest thought from Nathan's mind. He studied Declan. There was a possessiveness in his eyes he'd not seen before. The look made him pause. Was Declan jealous of him as well? If so, he might not be thinking clearly about the notes or the SUV. Or letting Nathan go.

"The thing is,"—the timbre in Declan's voice dipped into a euphoric tone—"I think some things are going to change for Kelly and me next year."

He reached into a drawer, and Nathan's hand twitched for his sidearm. When Declan placed a small, light-blue ring box on the desk, his stomach clenched. *A ring?* This was worse than being fired. Part of him still contemplated drawing his gun.

"I guess congratulations are in order."

"I hope so."

A protective ache raked through Nathan's chest like hot coals. *I need to get out of here before I do something I'll regret.*

"I haven't asked her yet, but we have a connection. I think we'll be a good fit."

A good fit? Are you kidding me? Nathan swallowed back his aggravation. *Is he even in love with her?*

A smile spread across Declan's face. "I plan to ask her on New Year's Eve. I think a January elopement will be just what she needs to get her life back on track."

Nathan gripped the armrests, considering his next move. With Kelly married, she'd have Declan's full attention—and protection—at her disposal.

Nathan shot to his feet and extended his hand across the desk. "I'd like to thank you for the opportunity to work with one of your authors." When he withdrew his hand, he tried to ignore the storm churning in his gut. "With the holidays around the corner, I think I'll resign. It will give me a chance to make plans to fly out to see my family."

"Now, Nathan. There's no need to leave in haste." The smug look on Declan's face said the opposite. "The date has not been set, and there are still a few occasions when we may need your services—as a couple."

Nathan's shoulders stiffened. *I don't think so.* He'd seen how Kelly looked at Declan when they were together. Her eyes lit up like he'd hung the North Star.

Clenching his jaw, Nathan recalled how she looked at him. *With trust.*

"I think, since there's been a break in the case and you don't seem concerned about the notes, it would be best to give her back her privacy." Nathan held Declan's stare. "I'm sure *you* will do everything in your power to keep her safe."

"Aye, I will." Declan rose and walked him to the door. "Should I give Miss Landon a message from you?"

"No, no need." Every muscle in Nathan's back coiled into an

unbendable knot. "Miss Landon wanted me to be released as soon as her safety was assured. I'm sure she'll be relieved."

"I'm sure she will."

Nathan reached for the door handle as Declan cleared his throat.

"Oh, Nathaniel, one more question."

Glancing over his shoulder, he tried to neutralize his expression.

"I read the police report," Declan said. "Miss Landon's statement leads me to believe she approached the SUV before you did. Why is that?"

Fiery heat wrapped around Nathan's neck and spread down his back. "It's true. I followed her to the car that night."

"Ah, I see." Declan's jawline pulled taut. "You both left the restaurant pretty late. The timeline's a little fuzzy. Maybe you can clear it up for me?"

He pivoted to face Declan. *You just showed your hand, McNeary. Jealousy doesn't look good on you.*

"Miss Landon met someone at approximately five o'clock. They conversed for just over an hour. After that, I asked Miss Landon if she'd like to return home. She explained she'd not had dinner yet, so she ordered a meal, and we left when she was done."

Declan's eyes darkened. "I see. Thank you for shedding light on how the night unfolded."

Nathan clenched his jaw.

"I appreciate all you've done for Miss Landon during this tumultuous time." Declan's tone cooed with sarcasm. "I really just want Kelly to get back to doing what she loves—writing." His lips quirked into a cool smirk. "I'm sure over time, things will quiet down over that blasted best seller."

"I'm sure you're right." Nathan turned the knob, threw Declan another courteous nod, and stepped into the hall. After he heard the click of the door closing behind him, he made a beeline for the elevator. *What is in those journals?* As the floors clicked off their descending numbers, the question moved through his mind like a slow train.

Scowling, he walked to his car. He pressed the button on his key fob and jerked open the door. *He's going to ask her to marry him.* He slid into his seat and slammed the door shut.

"A good fit. What a jerk."

He started the car as his mind siphoned through a thousand questions. His instincts told him Kelly was hiding something. But not out of deceit. Out of loyalty. Which led him to believe there was more to Abram's story than what was written in that book.

"Why won't she trust me?" Frustration pooled in his gut. If his hunch was correct, Abram had pulled her into his confidence and handed over all his family secrets just like he'd handed over guardianship of his great-granddaughter.

Nathan hit the palm of his hand on the steering wheel and glanced back at Declan's office window. For now, his hands were tied. After Declan's news today, nothing was keeping him in Virginia. Nothing.

You're a coward.

He huffed out a groan. "If she won't open up to me, I can't do any more to help her."

Pulling out his phone, Nathan punched in a few details then purchased an airline ticket.

He needed to leave today.

Before anything—or anyone—tried to change his mind.

22

Dread washed over Kelly as she walked into Abram's room.

It was too quiet. Too still. Too much like a deserted church in the dead of night.

"Abram."

His eyes fluttered open. "Kelly, dear, it's so nice to see you."

Her heart skipped at his greeting. It was as if God whispered a greeting as well. *Your friend's still here. You have time to say goodbye.*

She grasped Abram's hand and smoothed an errant wisp of gray hair from his forehead. "How are you?"

"Better with you here." He lifted her hand and inspected the ornate cluster of rubies propped up on a gold band. "A ring? Is this the bodyguard or your agent?"

Her chest constricted. "My agent."

"Hmm …" Letting his eyes drift closed, he murmured, "The bodyguard must have failed to do his research."

As her hand fell from his grip, she slipped into a chair and glanced out the window. The rosebushes, which in the summer peppered the garden with bright hues, were now barren and pallid. Her heart sank. So many seasons had passed since they first walked through the rose garden and shared stories of make-believe. Now the bleak winter season seemed to seep into every corner of her life.

"Kelly?"

"Yes." She glanced back at Abram and wanted to weep.

"I may not be on this earth much longer." His eyelids hung between closed and open as labored breaths crawled from his lungs.

Please God, give me more time.

"Before I go, I have something else I want to give you."

He'd already given her so much with his kindness and friendship, she couldn't imagine what else would have any meaning.

"Not just yet. But soon."

When his eyes fluttered closed again, she studied his profile. Despite the nearness of death, his cheeks still held a hint of a rosy glow. A hint of the beauty to come.

"I want you to watch over Emersyn." His eyes opened, and worry wrenched his features. "She's still so young. It breaks my heart to think how lonely she'll be."

"Of course, I will." Her heart tore from the ache of his burden. She didn't know the first thing about guiding a young woman through life, but because it was Abram who asked, she'd try her best.

"I've kept her sheltered." He released a ragged sigh. "I don't know if I made the right decisions. For her. For her future. People can be cruel. Manipulating. Please … please keep her safe."

It saddened her to think about Emersyn losing Abram—the only family she had left. Kelly understood aloneness, and that wound burrowed deeper than a canyon.

"I promise, Abram. I promise to keep her safe."

"Kelly, dear?"

"Yes." She leaned in as Abram's feathery breaths circled around them.

"Emersyn's mom …" He stopped as if weighing what he was about to say. "I found Emersyn's mom."

Wasn't Emersyn's mom dead? "What do you mean?"

"Her heart." Abram took another strained breath. "I needed to find out about her heart."

Emersyn's heart? Was there something wrong with Emersyn's heart?

"Expect a package in the mail soon." Abram's words interrupted her thoughts. "It will tell you what you need to know. You must guard its contents."

"I'll guard it with my life." She'd grown familiar with his riddles, but today, they made her weary.

"There are people out there that want the information I have. The information *you* now have."

She picked up his cup and offered him a drink. "I know."

"You do?" After sipping from the straw, he frowned.

"Yes." She set the cup on the table and slipped back into the chair. "Someone's searching for the journals. Why are they so important?"

"Is this why you needed a bodyguard?"

She nodded. The mention of her absent bodyguard pricked her heart.

"I've gone about this all wrong." Abram shook his head as if fighting against a tormenting thought. "I should've never sought you out."

"You've been such a dear friend to me. I just want to do what you've asked and keep the journals safe."

"Are they safe?"

"Yes."

"Does Mr. McNeary know where they are?"

"Nobody does."

"Not even the bodyguard?"

Her heart twisted. "No. Not even him."

After a few beats of silence, Abram pointed to the bookshelves beside the door. "I need you to get something."

Kelly stood and walked over to the wall of books.

"Go to the second shelf. The one near the door. There's a children's book, the only one like it. Bring it to me."

She did as she was told and scanned the row until she found the book. Her breath caught. *It can't be.* She wrapped her fingers around the tattered spine and pulled it out. *It's the same book.*

"What is it?"

"This book." She walked back toward Abram's bed. "I've seen this book before."

"You have?" Abram tried to sit up, and she rushed to his side to move the cushions. "Where?"

Her throat tightened as she glanced down at the cover. "In Nathan's apartment."

"The bodyguard?"

She nodded and sank back into the tufted chair beside the bed. "He said it was rare." Her voice quivered as she tried to wrestle with the confusion bubbling inside of her. "What are the odds you two would have the same rare book?"

"Dear girl, I'm afraid that is a mystery you'll have to solve on your own."

"I don't understand." She slapped the book closed and placed it on the side table. "Why does everything need to be a puzzle I have to solve?" She got to her feet and walked over to the window. The exposed rosebushes bent and swayed in the frosty wind. "I never wanted any of this. I never wanted to be in the middle of this mystery."

"But it's your destiny."

"My destiny?" Her shoulders slumped as she turned back to face him. "I'm just a girl. With no family. I want to write and live a quiet life."

"You're so much more than you know, Kelly."

His words startled her. She longed to be more. To feel like she was a part of something. Something that mattered. To be loved and cherished.

Slumping back into the chair, she released a frustrated sigh.

"My life's been turned upside down because someone out there thinks I harbor a deep, mysterious secret. What's the secret? And why did you give it to me?"

"Sweet Kelly." Tenderness filled Abram's expression. "The secret is the love story. God's love story."

Her vision blurred as she fought to restrain her sorrow. "I don't want to lose you, Abram. I can't—"

"My dearest. You won't lose me. I'll always be with you."

But he wouldn't. Would he? Not in this life at least.

She pulled the children's book into her lap. As she turned the pages, she couldn't help but admire the beautiful artwork and the ornate script. What was it about this story that intertwined with her own?

"I've scanned those journals a thousand times, and there isn't anything life-altering in them. What am I supposed to be looking for?"

"I needed to know if you were the one."

"The one?" She shut the book and groaned. His riddles were looping in circles.

"The one that I could pass my family's legacy to and keep the treasure safe."

"Do you mean the story of your parents?"

"Yes, that and … other things." Abram blew out a breath, visibly exhausted. "Did you write their story?"

"I did." Kelly cradled her head in her hands as sorrow wrapped around her heart like a thorny vine. "It made the best-seller list, and I brought you a copy."

"That's great. I'm so happy you did. I knew you were the one."

She lifted her chin and caught his weary look.

"Read the journals again. This time, focus on the wedding. Focus on the church."

What's the point? She tried to mask her frustration. "Okay. I'll see what I can find."

"I want you to have the children's book as a memento of our time together."

An empty pit grew in her stomach. Nathan had said the same thing when he gave her the Dickens book, and now he was gone.

She reached across the bed and gathered Abram's frail hand in hers. "Nathan had a theory about this book. He believed people were given these books for a particular reason—a calling."

"I believe his theory is correct." Abram's pale lips lifted into a thin smile. "He was a good man, the bodyguard. He was a true treasure."

"He was." Tears tumbled down her cheeks as the memories of her time with Nathan tumbled through her mind. *I miss him so much.*

"Don't cry, dear. Please don't cry." Abram tried with slow, jerky movements to wipe away her tears. "Why didn't you say yes to the bodyguard?"

"He didn't ask."

"What was that?"

"Nothing, Abram. It was nothing."

"Do you have the book, Kelly?"

She placed her hand on Abram's cheek. It was colder than usual, and his droopy eyes proved he needed to sleep. "Yes. Thank you. I'll cherish it."

"I know you will. Keep it safe. Along with the journals. And Emersyn."

So many responsibilities. Her shoulders sagged under the weight of them.

"I think it's time I rest now."

"Of course." She stood and pressed a final kiss on his forehead.

"Kelly?"

"Yes."

"Don't forget, love is a mystery. And often it's the missing piece."

"I won't forget." A weight filled her limbs as she picked up the children's book and turned to leave. "Goodbye, Abram."

With a broken heart, she walked down the shadow-filled hallway to the front door. Would today be their last conversation? Would she ever solve the mystery he'd left her to unravel?

As she slipped into her SUV, a sob caught in her throat. She was tired of losing people she loved. Tired of walking through life alone. But more than anything, she was tired of fighting the dull ache of loneliness that clung to her soul like a barnacle. *God, help … I need You.*

She swiped the back of her hand across her tear-stained cheeks and placed the children's book in the passenger seat. As she stared out the windshield at the gray winter sky, her tears fell.

Was it a coincidence that Abram and Nathan had the same book? Or was there a connection between the two she'd failed to see? Maybe she was reading into things. Imagining a bond that wasn't there.

Maybe I should reach out to Nathan. A weight tugged at her soul. *No. He left without even a goodbye. Remember?*

She started the car, and as the pale moon peeked between the clouds, she looked back at the Zucker mansion. "Goodbye, sweet friend. I'll miss you."

While she drove away, her mind filled with more questions than answers. She wasn't sure whom to trust with the riddle she'd been commissioned to solve.

But she had to be careful.

Somebody wanted those journals.

Which meant there was still a target on her back.

K elly stood outside the entrance of The Bookend and waited for Rhett to open the door. The sign read closed, but Rhett Sullivan, proprietor of the quaint bookstore in Newport News, had extended an open invitation for her to use his overflow room for research.

The door creaked open. "Good evening, Rhett."

"Good evening." He held the door for her and beckoned her inside. "I was sorry to hear about Abram. If you want to talk, I'm here. It's not easy to lose a close friend."

A pang wedged itself in her gut. "Thank you."

Rhett locked the door behind them, then strode ahead and slipped behind the counter. "I'll be here a few minutes counting the till. You know how to lock up, so please take as much time as you need."

"I appreciate it."

As she wove her way through the aisles of books toward the back room, she recalled the day she'd met Rhett. It was a balmy, spring afternoon when an unexpected downpour sent her bursting through his doors to seek shelter.

After she'd wandered the aisles, Rhett introduced himself and asked if he could help her find anything. She explained she'd been out perusing the antique shops and needed something to distract her while her editor took red ink to the story she'd just submitted. For the next hour, they conversed about dead authors over a package of Linzer cookies and steaming cups of creamy coffee.

Before she left, he'd offered to let her use the book storage room any time she needed it.

Kelly pushed through the door and flipped on the light. Oak floor-to-ceiling bookcases wrapped around the room while old books with tattered covers lined the shelves. The wood beneath her feet creaked, and she paused to inhale the rich scent of leather and worn pages. It was the first real breath she'd taken in weeks.

After shutting the door behind her, Kelly walked to the far corner of the room, where a group of well-worn red velvet chairs huddled around an antique worktable. Slumping down into one of the chairs, she sighed. This room held so many happy memories for her—*but after today*—she shook her head to push away the thought. *No. Abram wouldn't want me to continue in my grief.*

She pulled the bulky mailer out of her bag and laid it on the table. Opening the envelope would mean reading Abram's final correspondence. His final words to help her unravel the puzzle she'd fought to protect and preserve. She exhaled a lungful of breath, then drew out the stack of papers and spread them in front of her.

"Okay Abram, let's finish this puzzle."

Clamped to the top of the pile was an envelope. She broke the wax seal and unfolded the pages, reading each word as if it were a sacred script.

Abram began the letter with a riddled greeting then flowed into his wish for her to learn to trust in God's love and the importance of her role in Emersyn's life. He talked of their early friendship and their walks around the rose garden.

I've set a few items aside for our time capsule. I'm sorry I won't be around to watch you hide it under our majestic rose.

Snatching a tissue from her bag, she swiped at the flow of tears. "Dear, sweet friend, I miss you."

Through a blur, she continued to read.

Abram mentioned the journals and explained how each child his parents helped escape was listed in the documents. He'd hidden the complete list of names until now to ensure the safety of a hidden treasure. A treasure that, in time, she'd understand was the reason he sought her out to write his book.

Find out what you can about Emersyn's mom.

Her eyes skimmed over an address from an adoption agency in New York.

I need you to do more research. Ease Emersyn's concerns.

She flipped to the last page of the letter. Abram instructed her to read through the documents and only trust in the 'mystery of love' when it came to whom to share the information with.

God is love.

Your friend, in life and in death—Abram Zucker

Gripping the note, she pinched her eyes shut and tried to wade through the torrent of memories flooding her mind.

It had been a Thursday, the weather cold and rainy with slivers of sunshine pushing their way through the gray, wintery clouds. She recalled how the frigid rain mingled with her tears while the minister attempted to soften the blow of grief. Her heart ripped in two as the ebony casket was lowered into the ground and disappeared from view.

Taking a deep breath, she opened her eyes and pushed the gut-wrenching memory aside. Abram had told her to expect a delivery, but now, staring at its contents, she was unsure of where to begin.

Each stapled stack contained family names, handwritten as black-and-white genograms. The data included genetic history, religious and political affiliations, occupations, and psychological attributes. She turned to the final genogram. *Kelly Rea Holt Landon. English, German, Irish, and Swedish. Eidetic memory.* As she read her name and the notations that followed, her blood iced.

"Why did you have my family's history?"

As she traced the lines with her finger, she recited the following names aloud. "Father, Jacob Henry Landon the second. Grandfather, Jacob Henry Landon. Grandmother, Elsa Renée Lyman."

Her pulse thumped like a bass drum, as her eyes continued to scan the spidery veins of her family tree.

"Mother, Elizabeth Rea Holt. Grandfather, Edmond Dolph Holt. Grandmother, Claire Ann Kelly."

She flipped to the final page in the stack. A single column of names was typed in bold italics.

Dennis Michael Mueller
Kelly Rea Holt Landon — X
Miriam Dawn Sharp
Betsy Ann Sanders
James Edmond Taylor III
Beryl Abram Jakob Zucker
Jacob Henry Landon II
Garret Dean Sullivan Jr.

Staring at the X next to her name, she struggled to understand why hers had been singled out. Only recognizing Abram and her father other than herself, she skimmed over the list again and attempted to pinpoint a connection between the names.

"Think, Kelly. Think. Have you ever seen these names before?" A cat yowled outside, and she stilled. "It's only a cat." She shook off a shiver and scanned the empty room. "There's no one out there."

Or in here. She grabbed her phone and looked at the time. Almost midnight. Where had the time gone? After she shoved her phone in her pocket, Kelly gathered the papers and slid them back into the mailer.

The quiet in the room grew heavy. She rushed to the antique

safe in the closet and spun the knob forward and back until the door swung open.

Her pocket vibrated. firing her pulse into overdrive.

She laid the mailer next to the journals and shut the door. After a quick spin of the knob, she grabbed her cell and opened her messages.

Do you really know your fiancé?

Her gaze jerked to the number. It wasn't local.

She grabbed the notes she'd taken and shoved them into her messenger bag. *I should've asked Rhett to stay with me.*

No one had bothered her since Nathan left. Why would they sneak out of the shadows now? An uneasiness settled around the room as her heart pumped louder in her ears. *Because Abram left you the final set of clues.*

She inhaled and exhaled, hoping to slow her pulse. "It's only a text. From an out-of-state number." Did her tormentor know she was at The Bookend tonight? Alone?

A creak echoed in the hall. *God, please help me.* She eyed the closed door and prayed the doorknob didn't turn.

Tick. Tick. Tick. The clock on the wall counted off the seconds while disturbing memories left behind by her stalker floated across her mind. Had someone followed her here? Declan was out of town, and Rhett had gone home. Maybe she should dial 911?

She listened a few more seconds. Nothing.

Nathan, I wish you were here. The startling thought made her heart sink. *Why didn't he at least call? Or drop in to say goodbye?*

Weeks after he'd left, she'd received an impersonal note explaining how Treasure House Publishing no longer needed his services. In closing, he'd added a simple sentence about how much he enjoyed getting to know her. The scribbled note did little to quell the longing in her heart that made her wish Nathan was still around. If not as her bodyguard, then as her friend.

You still have Declan. Kelly glanced down at the sparkling ring on her left hand. A New Year's Eve surprise. Twinkling lights. A candlelight dinner. It was the thing fairy tales were made of.

A car engine revved in the alley, and she held her breath. After a few seconds of pounding bass music, the car sped away.

"I need to get out of here." Kelly slung her bag over her shoulder and twirled her engagement ring with her thumb. She didn't want a bodyguard. She wanted a husband. And a family. She wanted the fairy tale. Her gut twisted. *Then what are you waiting for?*

She shook off the question and glanced back at the text. *Who would want to warn me about Declan?*

Delete. It didn't matter. She wouldn't allow anyone to fracture her idyllic plans for her future—a future where she would become Mrs. Declan McNeary.

Releasing an exasperated breath, she pressed an ear against the door leading to the hall. Nothing.

As she flipped off the lights and turned the door handle, another shrill beep broke through the silence.

She sucked in a breath and glanced at her phone. Declan.

> I know it's late, but I wanted to say good
> night.
> I'll be home next week. Stay safe.

Good. When the time was right, she'd tell Declan everything. Everything about Abram. Everything about the best seller. Everything about the journals. With his resources and contacts, he'd be able to make sense of the conundrum her life had become.

> I can't wait to see you.

After she sent the reply, she opened the door and scurried down the dark hall to the back door. *Just get to the car.*

The streetlamps hummed with energy, and shadows danced and bobbed along the fences. She pushed the button on her key fob, and her headlights blinked a greeting. Kelly imagined

Nathan waiting by the car wearing his dark suit and serious expression that held just a hint of a grin. She frowned. "Girl, it's time to move on. That's a path you can never travel down again."

A branch creaked in the wind, and she stepped up her pace. *Get your head out of the clouds. Nathan's gone.*

She jumped in her car then locked and relocked the doors. "I'm going to tell Declan everything when he gets back."

While she drove through the quiet streets, the genograms Abram had sent her raced across her mind with pinpoint accuracy. What did they mean? And why did Abram have a dossier on her family?

It's your destiny.

Abram's words screamed at her from the grave.

He'd mentioned it was her destiny to know his family's history and preserve it.

Now she just had to understand why.

N athan sat in the tinted SUV contemplating his next move. *I need to call Henry.* He pulled out his phone and tapped in a handful of numbers. In three rings, his brother Henry picked up.

"Did you make it to the States?" Henry asked.

Nathan hesitated. "Yes. I've been here for a week." After spending the holidays with his family, Nathan had tried to make sense of his stay in Virginia. He'd hoped the time and distance would tamp down his thoughts of Kelly. He was wrong. Instead, the bleak, rainy days only amplified the ache in his heart.

"A week? And you just now called me?" Henry blew out an exasperated breath.

"I've been … thinking." Regret washed over Nathan. When he learned of Abram's passing, he'd wanted to kick himself for not being there for her. *Don't worry, she had Declan's shoulder to cry on.* He scowled.

"Thinking about what?"

"I'm trying to decide the best way to approach Kelly and talk with her privately."

"Any luck?"

"No."

"You could always do something stupid like you—"

"Henry, stop." Nathan clenched his jaw. He and his brother usually got along, but lately, they'd been butting heads about his recent assignment.

"Okay, okay. Truce?"

"Truce. I'll admit it. You were right." The words soured on his tongue.

"And?"

"And what?"

"And next time, you'll listen to me."

"Don't push it, Henny."

"That's enough of that."

It had been years since they were schoolboys, but the nickname he'd given his younger brother still got a rise out of him.

"So, back to why I called." Nathan checked his side mirrors and made a mental note of the cars parked along the street. "Can you get me info on where Declan is and how long he'll be gone?"

"Give me a minute." Henry's fingers tapping on the keyboard carried over the line. His brother was being a good sport, even if he thought Nathan's plan was idiotic.

As he waited for Henry to do his thing, Nathan glanced out the rearview mirror where the morning sun filled his back window. It was still cold outside, but at least today would be sunny. *Unlike my mood if I don't get to talk to Kelly.*

"Declan's in California." Henry's voice cut through the line. "His ticket shows a return date for next week."

"Okay, I'm outside Kelly's house now." Nathan ran his hand over his budding five-o'clock shadow. He wasn't looking his best, but it would have to do. "I'm going to see if I can get inside."

"Be careful. Did you take your gear?"

"I'm not breaking in." He shook his head as he blew out a sigh. "I'm going to knock on the door and see if she'll invite me in."

"Really? That's a bold move, brother, even for you. What makes you think she will?"

Nathan pursed his lips.

"Is there something you aren't telling me about your relationship with Kelly?" Henry paused. "This isn't just about the assignment. Is it?"

"I haven't decided."

"How does she feel about that? Hasn't *she* already decided?"

Henry's words cut deep. He'd been privy to how Nathan and Kelly first met, and Henry was adamantly against this new course of action—one that included full disclosure.

"What makes you think your charm is going to work this time?"

Nathan cringed. "I think Declan's a snake."

"You flew back to tell Miss Landon her boyfriend's a jerk? Scratch that, her fiancé. Aren't we still looking for proof he's directly involved somehow?"

Nathan detected the reprimand in his brother's voice. It was true. He hadn't found anything substantial on Declan, other than a gut instinct. The literary agent's background drew no red flags, but that didn't mean he didn't have wicked intentions.

Henry's voice sliced through his thoughts. "If he's involved, he's done a great job covering his tracks. Everything I've found has traced him back to two deceased parents in Ireland. Nothing about McNeary is exceptional."

"I believe we're missing something. This whole time, we've been focusing on Abram and Kelly. I can't help but think maybe Declan is involved in the chaos that's plagued her."

"Are you sure it isn't because you've developed feelings for her?"

Nathan ignored Henry's probing. He wasn't ready to comment about his feelings. He wasn't sure how to interpret them. Was he here out of duty? Protection? Loyalty to his calling? A surge of adrenaline shot through him. Love?

"Is there anyone else in her life we should be looking at?"

"No. She has no family, no siblings, and she intimately knows two people in this town."

He thought back over the brief time he worked for her. She frequented a bookstore called The Bookend, but he'd already checked into Rhett. The bookstore's owner had no contact with Kelly prior to her moving to Virginia. Her connection to him was purely coincidental.

"Think hard, brother. You don't want to miss anything and go storming into her house, spouting off—with no proof—that Declan is of a bad lot." Henry snorted. "Most women I know wouldn't respond well to that."

"I'm not going to storm in there." He rolled his neck back and forth and tried to release the tension. "First, I need to apologize for leaving without saying a proper goodbye."

His gut wrenched. He should have stayed. He should have been there for her when Abram passed.

"Just be careful. She may not want anything to do with you this time."

Nathan massaged the back of his neck while he let Henry's words sink in. "Just let me know if anything changes with Declan's itinerary. Got it?"

Without waiting for a reply, he ended the call and tossed the cellphone into the passenger's seat.

He had one more chance with her.

This time, he hoped he wouldn't blow it.

Kelly relaxed in her living room, enjoying her first cup of coffee while she flipped through a bridal magazine. After she'd dodged Declan's idea to elope, he'd tried to convince her that hiring a wedding planner and hosting an event for a few friends from Treasure House would be more fun. Now, she just needed to come up with a theme.

She thought back to the photo in Abram's study of his wife,

Rachel, in her wedding dress. The gown was the epitome of classical elegance. However, more breathtaking than the dress was the joy in Rachel's expression. Who needed a theme when you were in love?

After she fanned through a few more pages of the magazine, she landed on a story about choosing the right flowers for centerpieces. *What do your centerpieces say about your relationship?* Kelly snorted a laugh. Did flower arrangements really communicate the love story of two people?

Her gaze flicked to the bouquet of deep red roses Declan had sent her while he was away on business. They reminded her of her friendship with Abram.

"I should go with roses for centerpieces. Something simple and elegant." She slapped the magazine closed and flung it onto the couch next to her. "Maybe we should've eloped."

The buzzer from her front gate called from the security screen on the wall. *Who could that be at this hour?*

She rose and checked the screen. *Nathan?* Her pulse leaped at the sight of him waiting at her gate. *What's he doing here?*

Without responding to him, she pushed the button to open the gate, then rushed to the mirror in the hall. She wore no make-up, and her hair was pulled back into a low ponytail. Glancing down at what she was wearing, she cringed. A V-neck T-shirt and leggings. *Why does it matter? Who am I trying to impress?* After she tightened her ponytail, she pinched her cheeks. *I'm being ridiculous.*

Nathan knocked. Kelly counted to three, then opened the door and did her best to act unbothered. "Nathan. What are you doing here?"

"I … uh." He gripped the back of his neck. "Can I come in?"

"Sure." She waited for him to enter, then she shut the door. "Is there something wrong?"

"No, nothing's wrong."

After a moment of uncomfortable silence, she gestured for

him to follow her into the living room. "Can I get you anything? Some tea or water."

"No. I'm good. Thank you." He took a seat and scrubbed a hand down his face. "Kelly, I'm sorry."

"Sorry? For what?" She sat on the couch across from him and slid the magazine under one of the throw pillows.

"For …" He hesitated. "For leaving the way I did. Without saying goodbye."

She fiddled with the edge of the throw pillow. What did he want her to say? That it didn't matter. That would've been a lie.

"Declan mentioned you went to see your family for the holidays. How was that?"

"It was good. Cold." His gaze traveled over her left hand, then he looked away. "How have you been?"

"I've been good. Busy." She smoothed her thumb down her ring finger. It was bare. Good. She wasn't in the mood to answer questions about her engagement. "I've been writing, but the story's coming slow. I've had a lot on my mind."

When he turned back to face her, his expression fell. "I should've been here. For you." His voice hitched as he continued. "I should've been here when Abram passed."

Her throat dried. He should've been here. She needed him. But he'd left without even saying goodbye. *That's history. Declan was my shoulder to cry on.*

The clock on the mantle chimed, breaking through her thoughts. Their awkward conversation twisted a knife in her heart. Had time really erased their connection? Or had it all been a figment of her imagination?

"I hate to cut our meeting short." She rose and smoothed a hand down the front of her rumpled shirt. "I have an event to attend tonight, and I have a few errands I need to run before I go." She waved toward the garment bag hanging by the door. "Declan garnered us some tickets to a dinner with a local production company. They want me to pitch them Abram's story."

Nathan stood. "Kelly, I …"

She turned and walked toward the door, hoping he would follow. Having him here, this close, curled her emotions into a tangled mess. "Declan's convinced Abram's story would make a great made-for-TV movie. I just wish he wouldn't have left town on business. He's much better at shmoozing than I am."

"Kelly."

Nathan walked behind her toward the entryway. She exhaled, trying to ignore his presence. *Just get him out the door.*

"Declan mentioned something about wildfires in California. Have you heard anything about them? He wanted to make sure the west coast office had come out unscathed." She reached for the door handle, and Nathan laid a hand on her arm.

"Kelly. Look at me."

Her bottom lip quivered. *Don't turn around. Do. Not. Turn. Around.*

"You don't need to go alone tonight." His voice turned husky as he pulled back his hand. "I can be your plus-one."

After a second of hesitation, she turned to face him. "I don't know if that's a good idea."

"I need a quick shave." He rubbed a hand across the stubble on his chin. "But I've got a suit. Or is it black tie?"

"No." She shook her head. "I mean, no, it's not about you needing to shave." *Keep the stubble. It looks great.* She shifted on her feet. *Ugh. Stop staring at him.*

"Okay?"

"It's just … I don't need a bodyguard." *I need a friend.*

"I know." He reached for her hand. "Think of it as an act of penance for leaving how I did."

This is not a good idea. "Okay. You can be my plus-one." She pulled her hand from his and folded her arms. "But no bodyguard stuff. It's just dinner. Deal?"

"Deal."

I'm so glad he's back. Her skin heated.

"What time should I pick you up?"

"Be back here at five." She reached for the door handle and opened the door. "Oh, and Nathan, it's black tie. Wear a tux."

He pulled his keys out of his pocket and shot her a wry grin. "Will do."

As she followed his retreat, a shudder twirled in her middle. Nathan was back. But for how long this time?

25

Kelly straightened in her seat as the vehicle accelerated along the shadow-filled highway. "Why are you speeding up?"

"I think we're being followed." Nathan scowled. "They've been on our tail for a few miles."

"What?" She turned and looked out the back window. "I don't see anyone."

"I've moved ahead of them." His gaze landed on the rearview mirror. "I'll keep an eye out in case they return."

This can't be happening. She wrung her hands in her lap.

"The car's staying back." Nathan flashed her a pensive look. "Maybe I read it wrong."

"That's good."

When he turned his gaze back to the road, she noticed how the rays of the moonlight highlighted the scar under his jawline —a scar only noticeable when he shaved. A tingle whispered across her neck. *That's not how he'd shown up this morning.* This morning, thick, ebony stubble covered his chin and cheeks, making him look rugged and unkempt. A look she'd only seen him wear on the weekends—but she liked it.

"If I haven't said it already, thank you for taking me tonight."

"Of course." He cut another look her way. "As a friend this time, not your bodyguard."

Warmth trickled through her. He'd kept his word this evening. After escaping for a few hours, he'd returned freshly shaved and dressed to kill. The sight of him in a tuxedo again made her insides warm like molten lava.

Nathan's grip tightened on the steering wheel. "They're back."

The angry sound of a roaring engine lassoed a panicked chokehold around her throat. "What do we do?" She cut her eyes to her side mirror. A vehicle flipped on its high beams and sped toward them.

"Make sure your seatbelt is on tight, in case I can't shake them." He pressed his foot down on the accelerator, and their vehicle sped up.

Nathan watched Kelly check her seatbelt, then he turned his eyes back to the road. He'd shown up at her door that morning to persuade her something didn't seem right about Declan. He hadn't expected to slip into the position of her guardian again.

The driver behind them lay on his horn, and the rumble of the engine raced closer. He grasped for her hand and gave it a reassuring squeeze. "I'll get us out of this. I promise." His pulse soared as a thousand scenarios of how this night could end tumbled through his thoughts.

Tears pooled in her eyes. Sensing her panic, his training kicked into high gear.

I'm glad I rented a sporty SUV. Nathan pushed the pedal to the floor. He needed every bit of the vehicle's horsepower to break the car off their tail. *Please, God, get us out of this.*

"Brace yourself." He pressed his body into the leather seat as they took the low, banked corner at a high rate of speed.

"Why would someone want to follow us?"

He glanced back at the mirror. "I'm not sure."

"I thought I put all of this behind me when you left."

"This could be a random idiot out for a joy ride." Another honk sounded from behind them.

"You don't really believe that, do you?"

He ignored her question, but he didn't believe it. "If I can't lose them, we're going to take a detour." He'd studied the roads around the area and vaguely remembered there were two options for him to choose from up ahead.

Now to choose the right one.

Kelly clutched the door handle with a death grip.

He brought his eyes back to the road and threw another silent plea to Heaven for their protection.

"What really made you come back to Virginia?" Her breath hitched as they accelerated.

Nathan shifted in his seat while the headlights in the rearview mirror moved back and disappeared around the bend. He'd hoped for a more peaceful setting to explain his mistrust in Declan, but he didn't want to ignore her prodding any longer. "I found out some information."

Information that lit a fire in him and had been kindling since he left. Declan was quickly rising to the top of his list of people he did not like or trust.

Documents showed large sums of money going in and out of an account in Europe connected to Declan's literary agency. The account's transactions added merit to his belief that Declan may be involved in the underground transfer of black-market antiquities. That and a brief perusal around Declan's home and office proved he was a collector of relics. Gathering antiquities was not an illegal hobby, but someone blinded by an obsession with sacred artifacts might be tempted to go down a crooked path.

"Information? About what?" The quaver in Kelly's voice pulled him out of his thoughts.

"I have something to tell you about Declan."

He understood she was not a collector, but her father had been. And from what he'd deduced, Declan may suspect Kelly had clues to treasures she knew nothing about.

"What?"

Nathan glanced back at the rearview mirror. Nothing. Good.

"What about Declan?"

"Kelly, I ..." A disturbing thought flashed across his mind. If someone was following them tonight—*No.* He scowled and gripped the steering wheel with white knuckles. *Why didn't I see this before?* Every time Declan leaves town, something happens.

"You what? What do you know about Declan?"

Two headlights reappeared in the mirror. An idea danced around his thoughts as he sped along the unlit road. *If Declan planned this pursuit tonight, Kelly would've been driving alone.* Nathan slammed the steering wheel with his hand and brought his gaze back to the mirror. A set of high beams rounded the corner, closing the distance between them.

"They're back. I'm going to try to get us off this highway." He slowed, looking for his turn. Without warning, a delivery truck shot out from a concealed dirt road and smashed into the rear passenger side. Kelly screamed and flung out her hand to clutch his arm.

Pressing on the brakes, Nathan jerked to the right. The SUV was no match for the one-ton truck, and it continued to skid across the shoulder.

"Nathan! Watch out!" Her cry pierced through the chaos as the moonlight shimmered against the backdrop of a body of water.

No! He gazed back at the rearview mirror and scowled. The vehicle that had been following them skidded around the corner and rammed into the back of their SUV. The impact propelled them down the pebbled embankment and tipped the SUV's nose into the water.

"We're sinking!" Kelly shrieked.

Nathan groaned as the dashboard lights blinked several

times before going dark. In a knee-jerk reaction, he clicked free his seatbelt then released Kelly's.

Grabbing his tactical pen out of his jacket, he banged it against the bottom corner of the window. It shattered, and with his sleeve, he pushed as much of the glass out of the car as he could.

"Water's coming in. We need to get out." Kelly's voice quaked as water seeped over the floor mat. She kicked off her heels and pulled her feet up to the seat.

The lights blinked on. Nathan held his finger to his lips and pointed behind them. He didn't want to risk crawling out of the SUV only to be met with a bullet to the head.

She pursed her lips and nodded. After a flicker, the lights cut off again, leaving them to adjust their vision to the pale moonlight. The water now reached the level of the front seats.

Please God, get us out of here. Alive. Nathan slipped his phone into his shirt pocket before he tugged off his jacket and laid it across the shards of glass in his window frame. Grabbing Kelly's hand, he pointed to the window then held his finger up to his lips again.

After he helped her slide out of the vehicle, he pulled himself out and signaled for her to wade to a secluded bank behind a copse of trees. If someone meant for them to die tonight, he didn't want to be treading water as he tried to fend them off.

They reached the shore and staggered up the bank.

"We need to call for help." Kelly's teeth chattered as she sucked in a quick breath.

Her hand trembled in his as he helped her sit down behind a cluster of rocks and tall grasses. The form-fitting dress did little to aid her movements. Tugging on the fabric, she ripped the slit farther then pulled her knees in and folded her arms in a tight hug around her body.

A rustle on the hill made the hairs on Nathan's neck stand up. He scanned the embankment. After several seconds of silence, his gaze shifted to the roof of the SUV as it bobbed in the water. He guessed if anyone wanted to finish them off, that was where they'd check first.

His attention went to the dark road. It was empty. For the first time since he saw the headlights careening down on them, he breathed a sigh of relief. *Thank you, God.*

He turned and sat down next to Kelly. With one arm, he drew her close, and with the other, he pulled out his phone. When he tapped on the screen, it blinked to life. Only one bar. Great. *Please, God, let this call go through.* Forcing his fingers to still, he struggled to dial 911.

After three rings, his frustration buoyed to the surface. "Pick up the blasted phone."

"Nine-one-one. What's your emergency?"

"There's been an accident." His voice shook from the cold. "A lorry slammed into us and pushed our SUV into a waterway."

Kelly's head jerked up, and her face blanched.

Oh, no. When the fear and confusion in her eyes registered in his brain, his gut clenched. Reflexively, he tightened his grip on her shoulders and moved the phone away from his lips. "I'm sorry, luv."

She looked away from him.

Moving the phone back to his lips, he rattled off the highway number and their approximate location to the dispatcher. "We need an ambulance and officers immediately." The call dropped, and he looked at his screen. "Spotty service. Perfect."

She trembled, and he rubbed her frigid skin with his hand. *God, help us. Please.* He forced his trembling fingers to push down another group of numbers on his cell. After two rings his friend, Frank Collins, picked up.

"Frank, I'm in a bit of a mess, mate." The phone alerted him to a low battery and disconnected. "Brilliant."

He redialed the number, relieved when Frank picked up after only one ring. "The service is a bit dodgy mate, and I'm about out of battery. Can you still hear me?"

Kelly glanced back up at him. Terror and rage kindled in her expression.

"There's been a collision." Nathan kept his eyes level with hers as he quickly tried to explain the situation to Frank. "A lorry hit us and slammed our car into the waterway just off the road. It wasn't an accident." He rattled off a quick description of the lorries that had bowled into them.

Frank mumbled a curse. "I'll get the word out."

"Thanks, mate, I—" Before he could complete his sentence, the call dropped.

26

Kelly shuddered as Nathan's icy fingers pressed into her skin. *It's him.*

The first time she'd heard it, she thought she was hallucinating. But the second time, the thick, velvety English accent rolled off his tongue, she knew exactly who he was.

As he shoved his phone into his shirt pocket, guilt blanketed his expression. "I can explain."

God help me. I need to get away from him. She inhaled a deep breath, and the pungent, woodsy scents of Nathan's cologne mingled with lake water and circled up her nose.

She pinched her eyes shut then forced them open. How had she ended up here? With him. Her stalker. Twisting out of his grip, she turned and slammed a solid kick square into his leg. She rolled onto her knees and scrambled to stand, but her legs buckled.

Nathan's arm shot out, and he pulled her back toward him. "Kell. I can explain."

"Let. Me. Go." She struggled in his grip like a trapped rabbit, and the pebbles under her legs tore against her frozen skin. "I know who you are. You're him!"

He squeezed tighter, stealing her breath. "Kell. Stop." The

low, guttural tone of his British inflection ignited her fear into a blaze of panic. "There's nowhere for you to go."

Bile crawled up her throat. He was right.

Nathan relaxed his grip. "You've got to be quiet. We don't know if they're coming back to finish the job."

His warm breath brushed against her cheek, and she started to sob. The shadow-man from her nightmares now had his arms coiled around her body like a snake. *What if he set this whole thing up? The accident, the …* She gulped for breath as her throat tightened. He'd been her bodyguard. Someone she trusted. Someone she … *No. Don't think about that.*

"Kelly, please, listen to me. I'm not going to hurt you." Headlights approached, and Nathan leveled his gaze toward the road. "No sirens. Just a car. Keep your head down." While he kept his hands on her, he continued to scan the embankment.

She sniffled a shaky breath. *Like he said, there's nowhere for me to go.*

The car slowed but didn't stop. He expelled a breath. "They're leaving."

Her pulse raced as the taillights danced along the water then faded into the night. No one would see them from this angle or suspect there was a black SUV floating in the lake. *No one will ever find me.* A cold shiver traveled over her body, and she started to shake. Had he really called for help? Or had it just been a ruse?

While Nathan continued to scan the road, he rubbed his hands up and down her arms, trying to warm her.

She tried to shake off his touch, but she was too weak. "Why are they taking so long?"

He looked at her, then gently brushed dirt off her forehead. "You've got a cut. You'll need stitches." As his gaze held hers, his voice hitched. "I'm so … so very sorry about tonight."

She pinched her eyes shut. "Who are you?"

"Look, I know you're scared, but—"

She opened her eyes and scowled. "Don't patronize me,

Nathaniel James. I know you're the man who held me in my hotel room in Philadelphia. I'd recognize *that* accent anywhere."

"I can explain. Everything." His lilting words fell over his lips like warm honey. "I didn't mean to scare you that night."

Her gaze moved to his mouth. The same lips she'd dreamt of kissing now looked like they belonged to a stranger.

"I'll admit, it wasn't my most brilliant moment."

She jerked her chin up. "If you wanted me out of the picture, why didn't you just leave me in the SUV to drown?"

"I don't want you—" Nathan groaned as he released his hold on her and raked his fingers through his wet hair. "I'm trying to protect you."

Sirens yowled in the distance as she tried to muddle through her foggy thoughts. "Protect me? From what? You're the one I was afraid of." Her lips quivered with each word. "And now, I'm here … with you … and I'm cold—and tired." Lowering her chin, she closed her eyes and wrapped her arms tighter around her body. "I just feel so tired."

Nathan curled his fingers around her jaw and lifted her chin. "Kelly Rea Holt Landon, open your eyes."

Her eyelids were heavy, but she forced them open. "We … need … someone to find us," she said.

He wrapped his arms around her and tucked her head under his chin. "They're coming. In the meantime, you need to stay awake."

"Why? I feel like a popsicle. I just found out my bodyguard is my stalker, and my hundred-dollar shoes are at the bottom of a lake."

His chuckle rumbled in her ear. "Just keep talking and don't close your eyes. The ambulance is almost here."

"Is Nathan even your real name?" Another round of icy shivers wracked her body. Craving warmth more than security, she pulled herself into a tighter ball and snuggled closer to him.

"No, it's James." His grip tensed. "James Edmond Taylor, the third."

While her teeth clacked together, his name rolled around in her brain like change in a vending machine. *Where have I heard that name before?* After several seconds, her lagging synapses broke through, and an image flashed across her mind. *The list.*

"I've seen that name before. It was on a piece of paper." She attempted to connect her words, but a soupy fog impeded her thinking.

As the sirens grew louder, Nathan shifted and brought her closer. She didn't fight him.

"That name, your name ..." Another tremor racked her body. "I'm cold."

"I know, luv. Help's coming."

"You said you wanted to kill Declan." A haze rolled over her mind as she struggled to remember why she wanted to flee.

"I thought you were an ace with details, Miss Landon."

She lifted her head to look at him and the moonlight swept across his eyes, reminding her of an ocean at dawn.

"What I said was, if you told anyone about me questioning you, your boyfriend *might* end up dead." He paused and nodded in the direction of the submerged SUV. "I was afraid since Declan was close to you something like this might happen. To you both."

"You weren't going to kill him?"

His brows shot up. "No. I wasn't going to kill him."

A cacophony of activity stirred around them as the paramedics and police officers rushed in.

James leaned forward, and his eyes darkened. "On second thought, Miss Landon, I may have to change my mind about that."

She blinked, but she was too exhausted to respond.

The next voice she heard was an EMT shouting commands into the headset attached to his ear.

27

James sat in a vinyl chair next to Kelly's hospital bed and took a couple of minutes to make three calls. One to the airport, one to the car rental company, and one to his brother, Henry.

"What happened? You did what?" Henry didn't sound pleased as James explained how the night had unfolded.

"I need to go, mate. Frank's at her house, picking up some things for her."

"Fine, but don't get into any more trouble. Get yourself on the next flight out of there."

James assured Henry he would, then took an incoming call. "Hey, Frank. Bring several outfits for cool weather and a raincoat." He looked down at her feet. "Yeah. Bring a pair of trainers and a pair of wellies." He rattled off a few more items to pick up then passed on the security code to get Frank into Kelly's home.

She flashed him a glare. "You've got someone breaking into my home?" A nurse walked in, and she clamped her mouth shut.

He moved the phone from his lips. "Not breaking in, luv. I gave him the code."

Kelly scribbled her name on the paperwork as she scowled at him.

James shrugged then directed his comments into the phone. "That will be good. Pick that up too."

After the nurse left, Kelly folded her arms like a spoiled child.

He slid the phone away from his lips again. "The clothes you were wearing are out with the rubbish." He waved a hand over his black jeans and charcoal pullover. "Frank already grabbed what I needed. However, your beaded gown, while I'll admit looked gorgeous on you, was covered in dirt, and ripped to the thigh. I could go retrieve the gown or," James pulled his lips into a grin. "Or you could walk out in what you're wearing now."

She yanked the blanket up to her chin and stared down at the mint green fabric barely covering the front half of her body.

He laughed then moved the phone back to his lips. "Yes, I'm fine. Bruises, no broken bones, a few stitches, and some whiplash. Nothing I haven't been through before."

A second nurse came in and handed him a clipboard. He scratched out his signature and glanced at the papers while he continued his conversation with Frank.

"Kelly's fine too, a nasty gash on the head from a piece of glass, but all the tests came back normal. They've given her fluids. She was a bit dehydrated." He smiled at the nurse as he signed a few more documents. "We'll be released shortly. We've already made our statements to the authorities." He listened to Frank rattle off a few more things over the line, then he ended the call.

In less than an hour, Frank arrived with a duffel bag full of clothes. James handed Kelly the bag and ducked out into the hallway while she changed.

When she opened the door, he held a hand out to her. "Rental's in the car park. We've got to go."

She glowered at him and jerked her arm to her side.

"Kelly." James drew back his hand. "Look, I'm truly sorry about before. If I could go back and—"

"Before?" She stepped into the hall and cut him off. "Do you mean before in the hotel in Pennsylvania? Or before when you lied to me about your name? Or before when you left without even saying goodbye?"

He gripped the back of his neck then hissed out a sigh. "I've gone about this all wrong, and for that, I'm truly sorry."

"This? What *this* are you referring to?"

"I'm sorry I lied to you."

Soft floral scents floated from her freshly washed hair. Even dressed in a sweatshirt and leggings, she looked amazing. He reached out and moved a stray strand of hair away from her cheek.

"I'm not sorry I was hired to protect you. Or for the dance we shared." His chest squeezed. "I'm not sorry for any of the time I spent with you."

Her eyes glistened as she stepped out of his reach. "I'd like to get out of this hospital."

"Understood." Convincing her to trust him again would not be easy. Convincing her he cared for her wouldn't be either.

After they took the elevator to the lower level, he led her to the rental car. She climbed into the passenger seat and pulled the door shut before he could get to it.

"This is going to be a long trip." He rounded the front of the car, ducked into his seat, and started the engine.

Pulling out of the car park, James tried to untangle his thoughts. *I need to keep her safe. There's only one place I trust to do that.* "If you know anything about where the journals are or any other information Abram gave you, you need to let me know. Before this escalates any further."

Her lips formed a tight line.

"Kelly, you're an intelligent woman. If you haven't figured it out yet, someone is trying desperately to get all the information you have in that head of yours."

"I don't know what a big deal these journals are. Why should I trust you with what I know?" She shot him an angry glare.

"Why did you come back, Nathan? Or James. Or whatever your name is."

"I came back to ..." He had no idea how to articulate what he was feeling. *I came back to protect you. I came back because Declan's a snake. I came back because I couldn't live with myself if something happened to you.*

"To?"

"To warn you."

"Warn me? About what?"

"Don't you see how much danger you're in? We could have been killed tonight." Frustration kindled in him as he pulled out of the car park and drove through the city streets.

"I wasn't in any danger until you showed up."

"That's not true." He kept his voice even. "You're in a lot more trouble than even *you* could imagine."

"How am I supposed to believe I'm not in danger with you? You blindfolded me. In my own hotel room."

He thumped his fingers on the steering wheel. "I'm not the bad guy, Kelly."

"Is that so? Then who is?"

He didn't want to say it aloud. Now that he'd blown his cover and her trust, he didn't want to risk showing his hand, but he was running out of options.

"Well?"

When he pulled up to a red light, he turned to face her. "Declan."

"What?"

"Listen to me. I have some information leading me to believe he does not have your best interest in mind." When the light turned green, he turned and veered down another street.

"He's always had my best interest in mind. It's you I'm not so sure about."

He glanced at her, and she threw him a fiery glare.

"Where are you getting this information? Declan's been nothing but honorable with me."

James stared out the windshield. Of course, she wouldn't see another side of Declan. She was in love with him.

"Did you send me the text warning me about Declan?"

He jerked his head to look at her. "What text?"

"Nothing. Never mind."

Gripping the steering wheel, he volleyed back and forth about how he could convince her he wanted to help. *Why can't she see she's in trouble?* "When did you get this text?"

"I told you, never mind."

He measured his words as he drove through the side streets. "I just don't think Declan is who you think he is."

"Nobody is, it would seem."

James shook his head then inadvertently glanced down at the cluster of rubies on her left hand.

Kelly followed his gaze. She'd slipped the ring on in the hospital after taking it off a chain she'd hidden beneath her dress.

"How long have you been engaged?" The words tasted acidic on his tongue. He thought he'd come to terms with Declan proposing. He was wrong.

Kelly folded her hands and tucked them into her lap.

"I saw the ring. How long?" Jealousy sprouted in his gut like a venomous vine. *I'm too late.*

"Not long."

"Have you set a date?"

"No." She hesitated. "Declan wanted to elope, but I needed more time to …"

Nathan's heart did a little jig. *Time to what?* Clearing his throat, he shoved aside the possibility her waiting had anything to do with him. "I think Declan may be connected with the break-in and the car vandalism."

He watched her in his peripheral vision as she shook her head.

"I don't want to scare you," he said, "but I think you deserve to know everything before you make a lifelong commitment to that bloke."

Kelly played with the antique ring on her finger as a knot grew larger in the pit of her stomach. The night had been too long, with too many unsettled emotions converging in a span of one day. When her ex-bodyguard showed up on her doorstep, she couldn't suppress the thought that her engagement to Declan felt all wrong. Now she'd found out the man who'd been her friend and protector was the same one who'd haunted her dreams and filled her with fear for months. It made her question everything she'd ever believed to be genuine.

While they were at dinner, she'd wanted him to give her a reason to change her mind about Declan. But not like this. Not by accusing Declan of some nefarious plan to ruin her life.

"I just don't believe he would hurt me."

James remained silent while he focused on the road.

"Where are we going?"

"We're going to Baltimore." A muscle in his jaw twitched. Then increasing their speed, he flipped on his turn signal at the light and pulled onto Interstate 64.

"What?"

"After we get to Baltimore, we're getting on a plane to London."

"Are you out of your mind?"

He threw her a wicked grin. "Not this time."

"I don't have anything with me. I don't have my passport, my ID, or any money."

He motioned to the back seat.

She looked over her shoulder, and her heart sank. Two small pieces of luggage sat on the floor of the back seat.

"Frank was able to retrieve your license and your passport from your house." His mouth tugged at one corner. "Thankfully, the only thing you carried in that tiny purse of yours was your phone. I'm afraid that's at the bottom of a lake."

"You can't force me to get on a plane with you."

"True." He hesitated. "I need you to trust me. Give me one more chance to show you what I'm involved with, then you can draw your own conclusion." James looked over at her. "To show you that when I approached you in Pennsylvania, I intended to help you, not harm you."

The look in his eyes made her heart melt. For a brief second, she'd probably agree to follow him anywhere despite his previous deception. *Can I really trust him?* She folded her arms. "I need to make a phone call."

"To whom?"

"A friend."

"You must think I'm a fool. I'm not going to let you call Declan. Not until you hear me out."

"I'm not calling Declan, and I don't think you're a fool. A deceiver, but not a fool."

28

James tapped on the steering wheel, debating if he should trust her. Tonight had been a nightmare. It was time to come clean with everything—everything about his past, his profession, and his calling.

From the corner of his eye, he studied Kelly. *I missed her.* He shook off the thought. *You need to focus.*

"Are you kidnapping me, James?" She drew out his name as if she wasn't sure she should say it. "Because if you are, I won't go quietly."

Getting her to comply would be tricky, but he had just under four hours to convince her. "If I were kidnapping you, do you think I would have told you where we're going? I'm asking you to trust me. One more time."

"I'm asking you to trust me also, mate." Her tone mocked his accent. "One phone call. I need to make a stop before we leave Virginia."

James reached into his jacket pocket and pulled out the prepaid phone Frank had procured for them. He hoped the gamble would pay off. At this point, if she ditched him, he was afraid the next accident would end her life. "Put it on speaker."

Kelly cut him an angry look. "What exactly do you do for a

living, James? Are bodyguard and interrogator your only qualifications?"

"No."

"Care to share?" She tapped in some numbers then pressed the speaker button with a dramatic flair of her hand.

"Occasionally, I fill in as a teacher. I teach boys physical education in a London primary school."

She pushed the volume up to the max level, and obnoxious rings screamed from the phone. "Is that so? Makes sense, with you being so …" She waved her hand down the length of him. "Well, so fit, I guess."

He chuckled and focused on the traffic.

"How does the primary school feel about your kidnapping habits, Sir James?" Again, she mimicked his accent with a woeful imitation.

He flashed her a steely glare then glanced back at the road.

"Any other jobs you're qualified for?"

"Hello." An older man's voice interrupted her questioning.

"Rhett, it's me, Kelly."

Rhett from the bookstore. Makes sense.

"Oh, hey. Is everything okay?"

"Yeah. Why do you ask?"

James cut his gaze toward her, waiting for Rhett to answer.

"Declan called not long ago and asked if I'd heard from you."

"Yep. Everything's great."

She's a terrible liar.

"Kelly," Rhett sounded worried. "Are you sure you're okay?"

"I'm okay, but I need your help."

"I'm listening."

"I need to stop by your store. I know it's late. Can you let me in?"

"Any time. You know that."

"And Rhett, if Declan calls again, don't let him know I called."

"Understood."

"Rhett?"

"Yeah?"

"I really appreciate all you've done for me."

"Your father was a good friend to me years ago." Rhett's tone softened. "I made him a promise that if I ever heard his little girl needed help, I'd be there."

James whipped his head back at Kelly and stared at her in disbelief. Had her father been working with Rhett? His mind spun in circles as he tried to piece together Rhett's involvement in her life.

"I know. It means so much to me to have someone in my life I can trust." Kelly motioned for him to keep his eyes on the road. "I'll be there in a few minutes."

"Sounds good. Oh, and Kelly ... Is your bodyguard with you?"

James sneaked a look to catch her reaction.

Lifting a brow, she said, "Uh ... yes."

"He's a good guy. You can trust him too."

For a second, the air stilled.

Rhett's voice broke through the silence. "I'll have everything ready when you get here. See you within the hour."

After she disconnected, James asked, "How long have you known Rhett?"

"A few years."

"Did you know he knew your dad when you met him?"

"Not at first. Rhett's always been kind to me. He let me use the back room of his bookstore to write and do research. It was nice to get away from the noise sometimes." She pulled down the visor and ran a finger-comb through her hair. "We shared some family info, and I found out he and my dad worked together on some antiquity projects when they were in college."

"You've mentioned your dad and his search for rare artifacts, and yet I didn't see many antiques in your home."

She flipped up the visor and turned to face him. "Were you trying to steal something?"

"Really? Is that your opinion of me?"

Kelly ignored his question. "I have a few small items of my father's, things he insisted were special to our family. I already told you about the jewels. I sold only what was needed to pay for my education. There was a beautiful set of emeralds I had inserted into some jewelry. The rest of them are in storage." She shrugged. "Saved for a rainy day and all that entails. After tonight, I might buy a cabin in the woods and not give anyone the address."

James shook his head. After tonight, he might need an escape too. "Emeralds? How many?"

"There were twelve of them."

"And the rest of the antiques?"

"He sold it all and left me the money."

"What?"

"Yeah. He knew I had no interest in all the junk he collected, partly because I believed it was why my mom left."

James tried to organize what she was telling him into ordered compartments in his brain. It wasn't working.

"When he died, I was shocked at how much he left me." She relaxed in her seat and laid her head on the headrest. "I knew if I invested the money wisely, I would never be in need. I left Europe the day after I received my inheritance, flew to California, and never looked back."

"Why California?" he asked.

"I somehow thought I'd be closer to my mom's memory. She was born in Sacramento. I guess I took the time to try to understand who I was—what my purpose was." She paused, then added, "That's when I started writing."

"Then Declan made you an offer you couldn't refuse?" As he threw out the question, the muscles in his jaw pulled like a taut rubber band.

She huffed out a breath. "I'd just lost my agent. Declan reached out to me, and he had a great reputation."

"I'll bet."

Brushing past his comment, she continued. "We met a few times, and just connected. He loved Virginia and—"

"You moved out here to be with him."

"It wasn't like that. I have no family. It's easy for me to relocate."

James winced when he heard the sadness in her voice. She was lonely, and Declan had been the one to fill that void.

"And then you found Rhett?" He pushed out the question, trying to redirect. The green-eyed monster stirring inside him wanted to ask more questions about her and Declan, but it was none of his business.

"Well, I found Rhett's bookstore. I might not collect antiques, but rare books are another story."

"Interesting."

"I have a storage shed in Pennsylvania with a few collections my dad left me. Some paintings as well. They've been boxed up for years. They're probably more valuable to me than anyone else."

"You'd be surprised."

The rest of the drive ticked away in silence, and finally, they pulled into the alley behind The Bookend. He glanced up at the historic stone and siding building nestled between a coffee shop and an understated antique store. He turned off the ignition. "Biblical history."

"What?" She stalled before grasping the door handle.

"You asked what I do, other than specialized security duty. I research biblical history. On occasion, I speak at conferences and go on archeological digs. It's a hobby." He shrugged. "Or a passion. I majored in history and minored in biblical studies."

"Really?"

"Not as dark as you hoped for?"

A shadow covered her face as her lips bowed into a frown.

"Stay in the car while I take a look around."

She started to protest as he laid his hand on her arm. "It comes with the territory. You could've been killed in that car accident, and for better or for worse, Declan, at one time, did hire me to keep you safe."

"I thought he let you go?"

James held her gaze for a moment. "I left because I was getting too emotionally involved with the client. In my line of work, that's a liability." He looked down at the shimmering ring on her finger. "I knew *that* was coming." Silence pressed around them as he drew his gaze back to hers. "I didn't think I was ready to see an engagement ring on your finger."

The streetlight highlighted the pink ombré filling her cheeks.

"Turns out, I was right." He pushed open his door. "Give me a few minutes, and keep the doors locked."

James stepped out of the car and clicked the door closed. After he inspected the alley, he opened her door and held out his hand. "It's safe. Let's go."

Kelly refused his hand, hopped out quickly, and scurried to the back entrance of the bookstore.

He sighed then turned to follow her. "Are you sure you can trust Rhett not to tell Declan we've been here?"

"Yes." Kelly knocked on the back door with a red *Employees Only* sign nailed to it. "I feel like he's the only one I can trust right now."

Her words punctured like a dagger. But he didn't want to try to defend himself standing out there in the predawn light, so he clamped his mouth shut.

The door opened with a low creak, and Rhett looked them over with a grim face. "Kelly. You look terrible. What happened?"

"I'm fine." She shrugged as Rhett waved them in. "So, Declan called you?"

They followed Rhett down a dimly lit hall and into a small room.

"He did. He heard secondhand that you were in a car accident." Rhett turned on a glass lamp in the middle of a table, illuminating a wall full of books. "Is he out of town again?"

She nodded then waved a hand at James. "Do you remember Nathan?"

Rhett stared at him with a confused look.

"Right, he never came in, did he?" She walked toward the closet. "Anyway, he's my old bodyguard, but now his name is James."

Neither man spoke.

She went on, "Yes, well, supposedly, James is taking me to London tonight."

James tensed. How much would he have to explain now that she had told of his plans to take her out of the country?

Rhett raised an eyebrow then pulled his gaze back to Kelly. "Decided you needed a last-minute vacation?"

"Something like that."

Rhett glanced back at him and stuck out his hand. "Rhett Sullivan."

"James Taylor." He shook Rhett's hand and gave the older man a once-over.

"I know."

James lifted his brows, hoping the man would explain. But, instead, Rhett turned from him and unlocked the closet, revealing a sizeable antique safe.

Kelly gave the knob a few turns, then opened it. She grabbed a small notebook that looked as though it had seen better days. "I took down some notes. They might be helpful to us." She moved a few items, then pulled out two children's books.

"Where did you get those?"

"Abram gave me one." She hesitated. "After he passed, he left me a letter explaining I should check for the same book in my dad's belongings."

James moved closer and tried to look over Kelly's shoulder. Inside the safe was a stack of leather-bound journals.

"These are the infamous journals? I feel a bit like that bloke looking for the lost Ark of the Covenant.."

She turned and rolled her eyes.

He grinned, hoping she'd laugh.

Instead, she pursed her lips and grabbed the journals and a mailer out of the safe. "Rhett, did you know this British man is the very same one who accosted me in the hotel in Pennsylvania?"

James shook his head as he stepped away from the safe.

Rhett straightened, and his face contorted into a glower. "Is that so?"

She smirked. "Yep."

"I wouldn't say accosted." James held up both hands. He had no desire to fight this man in the back of a book shop tonight.

Kelly glared at him.

"I was merely trying to find out some information."

"He threatened to kill Declan."

"I did no such—"

Rhett held up a hand. "Maybe we should hear where he's coming from."

James smiled. He liked Rhett. "First of all, I did not threaten to *kill* Declan." He looked back at Kelly. "I told you. *You* misunderstood me."

"Of course." She grabbed a duffel bag out of the closet.

"And second, I was trying to keep you out of this debacle you're in now." He shoved his hands in his pockets and leaned against the wall. "You have no idea what all of this is really about, which I plan to remedy when we arrive in London."

Rhett's expression turned serious. "What *did* happen tonight?"

"James was driving me home, and someone followed us." Kelly exhaled a long breath then recounted the evening. "A truck came out of nowhere, hit us from the side, and submerged the SUV in a small lake near the road."

Rhett's eyes widened.

"I know, I know." She loaded the journals and her notebook into the duffel.

Rhett turned his attention back to James. "I didn't know what she was keeping here, but I was afraid it wasn't just some random collection of letters."

James looked at his watch while he ignored the obscure question. "We need to go if we're going to catch our flight."

When he looked up, she shot him a heated look then glanced at Rhett. "Thanks, for everything."

"Of course, any time. What should I tell Declan if he calls again?"

Kelly frowned. "It's probably best if you don't tell him you've seen me at all."

"Sure thing."

James turned and gave Rhett another hearty handshake. "Thanks, mate. For helping Kelly."

"I think it's me that should be thanking you."

"What do you mean?"

Rhett didn't elaborate but turned to Kelly. "I need to talk to James for a minute."

She sent him a confused look.

James shrugged then followed Rhett to the front of the store. "What's up, mate?"

Rhett moved around the counter and spun the dial on a smaller safe. "I have something for you." He pulled out an envelope and handed it to him. "Don't open it until you get on the plane."

James tilted his head at the cryptic instructions.

Rhett closed the safe and grinned. "They weren't my rules. I'm just the messenger."

Understanding flooded James's thoughts. He nodded, then joined Kelly by the door.

"Take care of yourself." Rhett gave Kelly a quick hug then opened the door and waited for them to leave.

James moved ahead of Kelly and opened her door. "Thank you for giving me one more chance."

She paused and looked up at him. "Please don't make me regret it."

His jaw hardened while he waited for her to slip into her seat before he shut the door.

He hoped after he told her everything she wouldn't regret anything. Especially not meeting him.

29

Kelly's eyes fluttered open as a sliver of light played peekaboo from behind a set of heavy velvet curtains. *I'm in London.* She glanced at the clock and squinted. It was nearly two in the afternoon local time. *How long have I been sleeping?*

After a lengthy, exhausting day of travel, James had driven her to his townhome in the city. While he explained he'd stay at his brother's home across the street, he showed her to his guest wing on the third floor. All she could recall after that was changing, brushing her teeth, then collapsing onto the bed in a heap.

Rubbing the sleep from her eyes, she propped herself up on her elbows and glanced around the room. The space was cozy and warm, decorated in a mixture of rustic charm and Victorian architecture. A single arched, floor-to-ceiling window encased with thick cream-colored molding anchored the room to her right. Behind her, a curved metal headboard stood against an exposed brick wall. She scooted to a sitting position, tugged on the ivory duvet, and nestled back into a mound of pillows. Closing her eyes, she released a contented sigh. "I could stay in this bed forever."

A childlike giggle escaped her lips as Kelly opened her eyes and surveyed the rest of the homey space. In one corner sat an ornate desk with a cushioned, high-back chair, turned out, as if beckoning her to come and sit. *I could write a million stories here.*

Every piece looked as if it had been plucked from history and placed with care in the room.

Reluctantly, she pulled her legs out of the warm blankets and walked over to the window. When she drew back the curtain, light flooded the room. Blinking, Kelly gave her eyes a few seconds to adjust.

The room faced a quiet street where a winding sidewalk led to a front courtyard with an iron gate and a row of hemispherical bushes.

"This place is magical."

She stepped back from the window, and a chill brushed across her skin. Kelly eyed the plush, rose-colored robe hanging on a hook behind the door. Perfect. She slipped on the robe, and the smell of fresh laundry and flowers wafted up to her nose. Every detail in the room reminded her of an upscale B and B.

After she ran a quick finger comb through her pillow-tangled hair, Kelly escaped to the hall and followed the rich notes of Tchaikovsky down the stairs.

The sounds led her to a closed door. Was James in there?

She knocked then pushed the door open. Sunlight dappled the walls from a partially open curtain, filling the space with a warm, beckoning glow. When she caught the outline of James's form lounging in a bulky leather chair, she cleared her throat. "Good morning. I mean … good afternoon."

James lowered the newspaper he was reading and peered over at her. "How did you sleep?"

Will I ever get used to that voice? "I haven't slept that well in weeks."

"Good to hear. I'm glad you feel comfortable here."

She trembled and pulled the robe snug around her. With Tchaikovsky playing in the background and James surrounded by plush leather, the strong, masculine aesthetic drew her in like a moth to a flame. Comfortable wasn't the word she would use.

More like … secure. Protected. Miles away from the reach of her worries.

With a flick of his wrist, he folded the newspaper and laid it on the table beside him. "If you need anything while you're here, don't hesitate to ask."

"Thank you." She pulled her gaze away from his and scanned the room.

Three windows, arched and crowned in molding, faced the same street she'd looked over from the third level. Behind James was another exposed brick wall. Chocolate-brown leather furniture faced a towering ebony fireplace, where a fire crackled and danced.

Glancing up, she caught her breath. A massive ornate, medieval chandelier hung from the center of the ceiling with flickering amber lights that mimicked the look of candles.

"This room …" She looked back at him. "I've just stepped into a Gothic fairy tale."

His lips stretched into an inviting smile. "Just a couple of well-placed antiques."

"Right." She walked back to the door and peered down the hall.

"There's a loo and a library down the corridor. Feel free to investigate."

"Are you sure you don't mind?" Like Lucy, she'd just stepped through a wardrobe portal, and she couldn't wait to explore.

James waved her on. "Be my guest."

The first room she'd entered was a teal-painted washroom with a black-and-white mosaic floor and an ivory pedestal sink. A petite brick fireplace sat nestled in the corner adjacent to the porcelain clawfoot tub. Next to the tub hung one window, small and round with thick, heavy molding.

From there, she wandered to the library. The room smelled of antique book bindings and sandalwood soap. Along the walls stood floor-to-ceiling dark walnut shelves that held a plethora of colored spines. She ran her fingers down the shelves, then paused when she caught James leaning against the arched doorway, his arms folded nonchalantly across his chest.

"Your home is beautiful." Her gaze darted around the room one more time. "If it's not too forward of me, how do you afford this on a teacher's salary?"

His mouth quirked at the corners. "Well, like yours, my father left me a generous inheritance and some properties in Europe as well."

She waved a hand at his library. "Your collection is amazing."

"I thought you might like this room."

The calming scent of leather and sophisticated, spicy aftershave floated to her nose as James moved beside her. "Please make yourself at home." He indicated to one of the Queen Anne chairs in the middle of the room. "You can read any of the books you'd like."

She turned to look up at him, and his eyes darkened like the ocean after a storm. "I'm not sure where to begin."

"If it was me, I'd start with *The Count of Monte Cristo*." He took a second to hold her gaze, then he reached out to place an errant curl behind her ear. Clearing his throat, he took a step back. "But I imagine after a day of travel, you must be starving."

Her stomach rumbled in response. "Yes. I guess I am."

"I've stocked the fridge. I'll show you where the kitchen is."

"Sounds perfect. How many levels is this house?"

"Four." James signaled for her to follow him into the hallway. "The garden level is below where we are now. It's where the kitchen and dining areas are."

She trailed behind him as he explained a little of the house's history.

"The second level has a bedroom, a sitting room, the master bedroom, and of course, another washroom."

"The architecture is remarkable."

"Thank you. It's what drew me to this place." He pivoted to face her. There were only centimeters between them as they stood in the narrow hallway. "The top level is for guests. It's not been used in a while, so I asked my neighbor to come in and spruce it up a bit."

She looked down at the oversized robe she wore, and a sting prickled her cheeks. It was mid-afternoon in London, and she was still walking around in her lounge pants and a robe. When she looked up, Kelly tugged the robe closer, relishing the luxurious feel of the fabric against her skin. "The robe was a great touch."

"I can see that." James's heated gaze lingered over her as they stood in the hallway suspended in time.

Her stomach rumbled, breaking the spell.

He chuckled. "Let's go see what we can find in the kitchen."

James's heart skipped faster as he reluctantly pulled his eyes away from Kelly and continued down the hallway to the stairs. *She's here, in London, with me.* Being with her as she walked the halls of his home in an oversized robe filled him with more pleasure than he'd expected. He turned once more to face her before they reached the kitchen doorway.

"I wanted to be here when you woke up today." He caught the subtle scent of lavender, and his blood heated in his veins. "But you'll have the whole place to yourself. I'm staying with my brother Henry while you're in town. I'll leave my number. Feel free to ring me anytime you need something."

A concerned look covered her face.

He reached out and held her cheek in the palm of his hand. "If it makes you more comfortable, I could get a suite for you at one of the hotels. There are some lovely ones a few streets over."

"I'll be okay here. It's just such a large home, and I ..." Her skin warmed in his palm. "I mean, I'll be all the way up on the top floor. By myself."

He leaned in but did not give in to the temptation to place a gentle kiss on her forehead. Instead, he let the back of his fingers brush against her cheek. "You're safe here. I promise. I'll be over first thing every morning and leave you before you go to sleep."

"That sounds perfect."

He turned and pushed the kitchen door open. "The refrigerator is stocked, but if there's anything else you need from the store, don't hesitate to ring me." He pulled a phone from his pocket and handed it to her. "This is a pay-as-you-go, but it will work until your replacement gets here."

She took the phone. "Thank you."

James shoved his hands in his pockets as he fought the urge to gather her in his arms and reassure her she'd be safe. *Don't go there. She's engaged. Remember?* A muscle in his jaw twitched. He'd not forgotten, but he wanted to.

"Take some time to rest a bit more, and don't forget to eat something. The jet lag can take a toll on you."

"Are you leaving?"

He didn't want to. He wanted to tell her to take the ring off and throw it into the fireplace.

"I need to meet with Henry. He's anxious to hear about what happened in Virginia." James looked at his watch. "I'll be back over around seven, and we can go into town for dinner."

"Okay."

Without another second of hesitation, he turned and left.

As he walked to Henry's, he contemplated all the ways he might convince her to stay.

Kelly watched James step out the door and noticed he wasn't wearing his holster. A wave of relief washed over her. If he didn't feel threatened for their safety hundreds of miles over the Atlantic, then she wouldn't either.

Her skin still radiated from the warmth of his gentle touch.

James's chivalrous concern for her was endearing, but she still wasn't sure she should trust him.

She shuffled into the kitchen and tried to piece together everything she'd been through since the Zucker memoir had been published. Her thoughts flashed to the recent car accident. James was right about one thing; someone had tried deliberately to force them off the road. She shuddered to think what would've happened had he not been there.

Kelly opened the fridge and grabbed a yogurt, an apple, and a bottle of water and sat down on one of the stools at the counter. What had James's motive been, when he arrived on her doorstep out of the blue that morning? *He couldn't have known about my plans that night. Could he?* He'd never said why he'd come back, only that he didn't trust Declan.

She sighed and took a bite of her apple. Everything about James Taylor confused her. Especially the emotions he stirred up when he looked at her the way he did just now. He'd been nothing but protective; however, she couldn't help but wonder why he'd acted so duplicitously while he was employed as her bodyguard.

She dipped a spoon into her yogurt as the contradictory questions about James and Declan swirled in her mind. *What about Declan?* She studied her left ring finger. Declan had not even crossed her mind until now. Instead, her thoughts were preoccupied with James. The comforting smell of English leather and the penetrating looks of his subterranean eyes were enough to make her heart skip around like a spring pony.

She shook her head. *You're engaged. Why are you thinking about James that way?*

After she rinsed out her yogurt cup, she dropped it in the recycle bin. Then she threw the apple core in the compost receptacle before giving the countertop a quick wipe down.

Fingering the phone in her pocket, she again thought of Declan. *I need to call him.*

She drew out the phone but hesitated. *What if James's concerns are right?* Blowing out a frustrated breath, she decided to email Declan instead.

"I should at least let him know I'm alive."

She flipped through the screen, inserted her email details, then jotted a quick note to Declan. Her finger hovered over the send button. *Should I wait until I hear what James has to say?*

Kelly deleted the email. Tonight, she'd make James tell her everything, starting with the day he'd blindfolded her in her hotel room. She needed to have all the pieces of the puzzle before she could finally find the answers to the dangerous conundrum her life had somehow become.

She took a few more minutes to explore James's home before she picked out a book from his impressive library and headed upstairs to take a long, hot bath.

She hoped after dinner she'd understand why he'd brought her to London.

But more importantly, why did he suspect Declan was the villain in their story?

30

Kelly yawned as she sauntered down the stairs and into the kitchen. She'd only slept a few hours the previous night, but she hoped getting up with the dawn would reset her internal clock.

"Morning." James grabbed two mugs from a cabinet and motioned to a seat at the island. "You're up early."

"I am. Too early." She slouched into the seat and glanced out the window. The rain tapping on the glass pane, and calming aromas of brewed coffee and tea floated through the air, tickling her senses.

She rubbed her eyes as she turned to watch James glide around the kitchen dressed in black slacks and a snug gray sweater. The way he moved reminded her of how he'd led her around the dance floor. Blinking, Kelly looked away. The curve of James's biceps were imprinted on her thoughts. *Goodness. Does he always look so … put together?*

Glancing down, she took stock at what she'd thrown on after her shower. Dark jeans and a white button-down. Straightening her back, she casually tucked the front of her shirt into her jeans and fluffed her semi-dry hair. *At least I'm not wearing a robe.* "Don't you remember writers prefer to sleep in?"

"Oh, I remember." He shot her a saucy look as he placed a mug of coffee in front of her. "We have a lot to discuss today. I was anxious to get an early start." When he slid over a plate of scones, clotted cream, and raspberry jam, her stomach rumbled. "Hungry?"

"I am." After pouring a healthy serving of milk into her coffee, she yawned again. "This all looks and smells delicious."

"My neighbor sent the scones over for you."

The way he said *scone* rhymed with *brawn*. She still couldn't get over the smooth English accent flowing over his lips. Her eyes lingered on his mouth. How long would it take for her to become accustomed to his face with that voice? *Stop staring.* She jerked her chin up. "Well, when you kidnap a writer, meals are important."

"You wound me, Miss Landon." He held his hand to his heart. "I thought you came willingly."

She shook her head while she plopped a dollop of cream on the warm scone. As she bit into the pastry, her mouth melted with pleasure. "Oh. My. Goodness. Tell your neighbor I said thank you."

"I will." He placed his mug on the island and poured steaming water over a tea strainer.

After she finished off the pastry, Kelly moved her gaze to the adjacent counter where several brown banker boxes were stacked in neat rows. "What are those?"

"Well, now that you're rested—and have eaten—I thought I should explain precisely what I do and how you and I came to meet."

"By meet, you mean scared the life out of me by blindfolding me in my hotel room?"

He tipped his head back and laughed. "That was not one of my finer moments."

"No, it wasn't." She took another sip of her coffee as he unpacked some of the files and laid them in stacks in front of her.

"I guess I should start from the beginning." He pulled the tea strainer from his mug and placed it on a small plate.

"Yes, that sounds good." Kelly wrapped her fingers around her mug, and warmth spread across her palms. She'd pressed him last night at dinner to fill her in on why he'd brought her to London, but he'd insisted they enjoy their meal and start from scratch in the morning.

"I belong to a group called H & G." James pulled out a stool and sat next to her.

When the masculine scents of his aftershave wafted to her nose, she resisted the urge to scoot closer.

"H & G is a private society with members spanning across the globe."

She looked at the documents and noted an imprinted H & G in gold calligraphy script on the front of all the files. "What does H & G stand for?"

"Hunters and Gatherers. The society can be traced back to medieval times." He rested his elbow on the island. "My father, James Edmond Taylor, the second, was a Hunter. Which in turn, makes me one too. Well, I chose that path. Had I been better at research, like my brother, I'd have joined the Gatherers."

"So, what exactly does a *Hunter* do?"

"We hunt for stolen religious heirlooms and return them to their rightful owners." He opened a file and showed her a few pictures of fine art and jewelry. "We aren't thieves, nor do we get paid for our job." He tugged at the collar peeking out from his sweater and pointed to a dime-sized pin in the shape of a shield. "It's more of a calling."

She leaned in and studied the pin. She'd not noticed it before. Maybe he'd always been discreet about its placement.

James folded his collar back under the ribbed neck of his sweater. "For centuries, religious heirlooms have been stolen, sold, or hidden, and we try to find them."

"Sounds like a plot from an action-adventure movie."

"That's fiction. This is all very real." He slid another stack of pictures over to her. "During times of religious persecution, sacred items are taken from families or churches. The items we're concerned with often have more emotional value than financial. There are times, though, when the item we're looking for is worth millions. It all depends on the mission."

She nodded and continued to listen.

"Imagine a family forced from a town or village because they are Christians. They have one family Bible. In that Bible, they keep a list of their family lineage and notes in their own language. Their last and final link to their spiritual heritage as related to their culture." James opened a file and sorted through a few documents. When he found the one he was looking for, he placed it in front of her.

She read the missive and noted the list of countries hostile to religious freedom. "There are so many countries listed."

"In some parts of the world, believers struggle to find Bibles in their own language." He flipped through a few sheets and pointed to a document with a photo paper clipped to the corner. "Here's a family Bible from a convert in Afghanistan. We found it in an auction on the dark web as a war trophy after the family was evicted from their home."

"That's horrible. What happened to the Bible?"

"I posed as a buyer and retrieved it." The muscles twitched along his jawline. "If the seller ever knew an *infidel* had that Bible—"

"You have the Bible here?"

He nodded, but his expression remained somber. "I'll show it to you this afternoon. Henry traced down some of the owner's distant relatives here in London. I plan on returning it to them as soon as I have an open door to do so."

He stood and pulled out another folder from one of the banker boxes. "There's always at least one story that hits harder than the others. One that keeps you up at night." He slid into his seat and glanced down at the file he'd retrieved. After a few moments, James opened the folder and pulled out a document with the reverence of a curator. "For me, this is that story." On the document were two photos of an ornate oval pendant.

She inspected the elaborate Arabic inscription drawn on the back of the pendant. "What does it say?"

"It's John 3:16."

"The detail is stunning."

"It's the basic gospel on a piece of jewelry. It belonged to a young pastor." James hesitated. "He was thrown into prison, and the necklace was confiscated."

"Did you ever find it?"

A grave shadow crossed his expression. "Yes, but the pastor was executed before I could help him."

She remained silent and waited for James to continue.

"We—a couple buddies from my RAF days and I—decided to take things into our own hands." The battle sparking in his eyes supercharged the air around them. "The government was taking its time. He was just another pastor in the wrong place—a lawbreaker. But he was …"

Her chest squeezed as she laid her hand on his arm.

"He was my friend." James glanced out the window while the rain splashed spatters of mist on the glass. "We played at the pitch together. We swapped stories about the best curry in town. I …" He hung his head and whispered, "I dated his sister."

As a weight landed in her gut, Kelly slid her hand down James's arm and curled her fingers around his. "I'm so sorry, James."

"Thank you." His voice caught. "It was a fool's errand. But I had to try. I had to do something."

The weight of his story pressed in on her. How close had he come to rescuing his friend? How close had he come to being captured himself? "Where is it now? The pendant?"

James slipped his hand from hers. "I returned it." He stood, then proceeded to gather the documents.

She curled her fingers around her mug and tried to reclaim the warmth of his skin.

"I returned the pendent to his sister." He placed the files back in the banker box then resumed his seat. "After that, well, after that she asked me not to contact her ever again."

Her eyes stung. She was beginning to understand his duplicity was born out of a commitment to finding these precious stolen objects, and not for nefarious purposes.

"What made you decide to be a part of this? Surely, you had a choice as to whether you wanted to be involved?"

"In the beginning, it was out of duty to my family's legacy. Later, after I became a believer, I saw it as my duty to my faith. My purpose. A calling."

She quieted at the mention of James's calling. Seeing the energy in his eyes as he talked about his faith sparked a longing in her that she'd pushed into the hidden caverns of her soul. But now, listening to James explain his calling, the yearning surfaced again. Was it possible that God could save her from a life of loneliness and isolation and give her a purpose? Did He really care? More importantly, could she trust Him?

"You look like you have something on your mind," he said. "Do you want to talk about it?"

She blinked then looked away. She didn't want to open up to James with her questions. Not just yet. Not until she knew she could trust him.

"No. I'm fine." Kelly waved her hand over the stacks of files, hoping to redirect. "Your calling, it sounds dangerous."

"I guess it is, but not any more dangerous than anything else in life." Shrugging, he added, "I served in the RAF for a few years. Secret stuff. I enlisted just past my seventeenth birthday. I got my degree, then when I got out, I decided I wanted to invest in my community. I applied for a job at a London primary, and they hired me to teach physical education." His expression lightened. "You want to talk about danger? Those tykes at school are a handful."

She laughed, grateful the heavy mood had lifted.

"I work for H & G in my spare time." He sat back and relaxed with his hands behind his head. "If I have a free moment in my week, I like to get in a game of football down at the local pitch with a few of my mates from the RAF."

"The military background explains—" she stopped herself, embarrassed her thoughts had become words.

James quirked an eyebrow. "Do tell. Explains what?"

"Well, you know, you seem, so … so ready to meet danger head-on. You're giving off MI6 vibes while you sit across from me speaking the Queen's English and sorting through documents about stolen artifacts. I'm still trying to make sense of your double life, James."

He flashed her an impish look. "I understand."

"Do you work with the government?"

"No, but they know we exist. For the most part, they leave us be. We have a lot of contacts all over the world who have pledged to aid in our searches."

"I still don't understand. What does this have to do with me?"

Gripping the back of his neck, he said, "Well, that's what I wanted to explain to you." He got up and walked over to the boxes. Moving a few aside, James lifted a lid and pulled out a leather document holder. After he handed it to her, he folded his arms and propped his hip against the counter. "Take a look at what's in there. It should answer a lot of your questions."

Kelly fished out the contents and studied the first picture. It was a black-and-white photo of a young man standing next to some old church ruins.

"That's your father." He pointed to the man in the photo. "He was a Gatherer."

"My father?" Kelly's heart raced as she shuffled through the stacks of pictures. "What does that mean? What does a Gatherer do?"

"A Gatherer investigates. They keep records. They track down the last known location of the missing item. It's a lot of research and compiling of facts. Connecting the dots and piecing together puzzles."

She drew her hand over the last photo. It was in color and more recent.

"Gatherers need to make contacts. They often make trades for any information they garner. It can be hazardous also. If word gets out they're snooping around, it can end in disaster."

She looked up, and her eyes misted. "He never told me any of this."

"He died before your twenty-first birthday. Most of us were told around that age." James reached out and placed a hand on her shoulder. "I was seventeen when I enlisted in the RAF, and my father never told me anything until after I turned twenty-one. I had clearances in the military and had no idea H & G ever existed."

"I still don't understand. Why did you seek me out? I didn't know about any of this." She looked over the documents her father had written. There were dozens of pages of scribbles in his own handwriting.

"That dreaded night when I made the most foolish decision of my life."

A weight filled her chest, and she nodded. "You had to have known I was in the dark. That I didn't know what my father was doing."

"We'd been following information about Edna and Otto for a long time. They were involved in hiding what we at H & G refer to as *The Twelve Story Stones*."

"Like the children's book?"

"Yes." He pushed himself away from the island and paced the room. "We don't always know the Gatherers intimately. It's better if the Gatherers working on a specific mission stay concealed for their safety. I heard of your father and his involvement in looking for the precious stones. The information he gathered was priceless. After his death, a note arrived at H & G, revealing another former Gatherer held information."

"You thought it was me?"

He stopped and faced her. "No. It was Abram." He slipped back into his seat and took a long drink of his tea. The face he made told her it had cooled to lukewarm. "Abram was not only a Gatherer, but the Zucker family was directly connected to the preservation of *The Twelve Story Stones*. When we heard about the published memoir, H & G sounded the warning." His look turned pensive. "Then, we started to look into you."

"Why?"

"I knew the basic things about you. Your father died unexpectedly, and you moved to California to attend university." He raked a hand through his hair. "What I didn't know was how much you knew about H & G. I thought you'd turned on H & G, which would explain why you were writing the book and put the info out there to catch the eye of someone who wanted to buy the stones."

"You thought I was a turncoat?"

James shrugged. "It's happened before."

He didn't expound on his answer, but she could tell by the icy tone of his voice, he'd seen the betrayal firsthand.

"The other option, you had no idea what H & G was, and your father passed before he was able to bring you in." He tapped his fingers on the counter. "Which meant Abram handed you a puzzle you had no idea how to solve."

Her throat dried. The information about her father was overwhelming. She'd always believed there were areas in his life he kept from her, especially after her mother's death. Now she understood that the secrets from both him and Abram could take her a lifetime to unravel.

"If the information was so precious, why did Abram want me to write about it?"

"Abram knew your father was a Gatherer, and he knew you were a writer. Maybe he wanted to get you interested, so you could take up where your father left off." James's expression grew serious. "The one thing about working with H & G, it's a choice."

Kelly pondered his words, and a thousand questions converged in her mind.

"If you look at the memoir in detail, it merely whets the appetite of someone who knew anything about the stones. For the basic reader though, they wouldn't have a clue what it was trying to reveal." He reached out and took her hand. "Ultimately, I think Abram wanted to honor their story, and he trusted you to write it."

Heat traveled from his fingers and trailed up her arm. Whether it was from his touch or his kind words, she wasn't sure.

"In the story and the journals," he went on, "Abram most likely left you a road map of clues. Clues to complete the hidden story of the precious jewels."

He gave her hand a quick squeeze before releasing it and retrieving a manila envelope from across the counter. After he opened it, James handed her another black-and-white photo.

"Where did this come from?" She studied the photograph as her palms slicked with sweat. Rhett Sullivan, her father, Abram Zucker, and another man she didn't recognize, sat in chairs in front of a giant English oak. The same oak she recognized from her childhood.

"When we went to the bookstore, Rhett handed me an envelope with instructions to open it on the plane. He said it would help us connect the dots." He pointed to the men in the photo. "You probably already know, but that's Rhett, your father, and Abram. The other man in the photo is my father."

"What?" She stared at the picture.

"I had my brother do some digging. Abram was indeed a Gatherer, but after his wife died, he stepped back from the society. I don't know why. Maybe he just wanted to retire." He pointed at Rhett. "Rhett's not connected to the society through familial ties. He served as an outside contact for my father and Abram many years ago."

"If Abram was a Gatherer, where does that leave Emersyn? She doesn't know. Does she?"

"Most likely, no. She was too young to know before he passed away. Also, with Abram stepping back, he may have wanted to disconnect from H & G permanently."

"How did Rhett know who I was?"

"You two meeting was purely coincidental."

She wasn't convinced.

"Your pen name is your birth name." James smoothed his expression. "Most likely after you spent time together, he realized who you were."

"Do you think that's why he was my friend?" She hated the way her voice quivered, but she was beginning to question who her friends were. Even her father had hidden this from her.

"I checked more into it. The Bookend has been there for years. Also, Rhett only did research on the side. He's not part of H & G. It was pure chance you showed up in Virginia and stumbled upon his bookstore."

Relief washed over her. *It's true, nobody but God could've orchestrated a downpour that day. Maybe He's been working behind the scenes this whole time.*

"Not to say that after Rhett found out who you were, he didn't feel a kinship with you. Or maybe a protectiveness. He seems to play the role of guardian in your life quite well."

She sat in silence for a few seconds. It was so much to take in. Finally, she lifted her gaze to his. "Thank you, James."

"For what?"

"For trusting me with all of this. Most of my childhood, I wanted to understand why my father was so unsettled. This helps put a lot in perspective."

"I'm glad."

As she stared at the photo of her father and Abram, her mind ran in circles. Had working for the society made her father into the paranoid person he was before he died?

If so, what had he found that made him that way?

31

James released a pent-up breath and leaned back in the stool. He was glad to finally let Kelly into his family's secrets. He hoped it would explain why he acted so irrationally the first time they met. Nevertheless, it still pained him to think about that night, and he wished he could go back and do things differently.

"What do you think was Abram's real motive behind me writing the book?" Kelly's brow furrowed.

"My theory? He wanted to get to know you. He knew the best way to do that was to come at you from the angle of Edna and Otto's story. It would be the perfect reason to get involved in your life."

"But why give me the information? I have no idea what the clues mean or where they're supposed to lead." Her shoulders slumped. "I'm not a Gatherer."

"No, but you were born into a family of Gatherers."

"But why me? Why not you? You obviously know what you're doing." Anxious frustration dripped from her voice. "Abram told me to look for things, and most of the time, he spoke in riddled phrases I didn't understand."

"Maybe he wanted to give you a chance. To see if you wanted

to take up where your father left off. Unlike you, I don't have a talent for details or untangling puzzles."

"What do you mean?"

He leaned forward, placed his elbows on the counter, and steepled his fingers. He'd known that after he'd disclosed the information about the society, she'd have a mountain of questions.

"I'm a Hunter. Gatherers tell me where the items are, and I retrieve them. I've dropped into some dangerous places, but I've never been great at memorization or gathering facts." James pointed to one of her father's documents. "I study history, but Gatherers are special. They see things differently and have an innate way of making connections with people from all over the world. Gatherers are an integral part of our mission."

She glanced down at the paperwork strewn in front of them. "That's a lot of expectation."

"*You* notice details, and your eidetic memory—while it isn't perfect—it's an asset. You feel awkward in crowds, but you never let it show. You lack confidence in your abilities, but with the right teacher, you're not afraid to try new things."

When her gaze met his, she smiled. Was she remembering their day at the range? A day he'd tucked away as one of his favorites.

"Your love for languages and different cultures makes you an asset to our group." He let his statement sink in for a moment before throwing out a random question. "Can you tell me what our flight attendant's name was? The one who brought us our meal."

"What?"

"Take your time. You've gathered the facts. Now tell me what you remember." He'd recorded all this information on the flight over just for this moment.

"Okay." She closed her eyes and tapped her chin with one finger. "Let me see …"

While she thought about her answer, James took the time to study her. *Beautiful, creative, intelligent —*

"Jackie."

When her eyes popped open, he cleared his throat. "Correct. Now tell me what the person seated next to you on the plane wore?"

"James, I don't … I wasn't even paying attention to him."

"Sure, you were. How do you know it was a him?"

She shot him a look. Closing her eyes again, she released a long breath. "He was wearing a *Versace* suit. Pinstripes. And an ecru button-down shirt." Nibbling her lower lip, she opened her eyes.

"Very good. What else do you remember?"

"I remember thinking how odd it was that his suit was so expensive, but his cologne was a cheaply made, drugstore brand."

James grinned. *She's a natural.*

"He was older, in his mid-sixties, and he wrote with his left hand. He was listening to an audiobook in German. From what I picked up, it was about World War I. He only drank water. No ice. And he had a slight tremor in his right hand while he dozed off."

"You got all of that on a rushed flight to London, with little sleep, after a traumatic event. To think, you weren't even supposed to be observing that poor man."

She laughed.

"I'd hate to hear everything you've observed about me," James said.

"Well, for one thing—"

He held up his hand. "No, really, I don't want to know. I'd rather not hear about how bad my Yankee accent was the first time we met."

"It did throw me off a bit." She shrugged. "I figured it was your straitlaced demeanor that made your jaw sit so rigid while you spoke to me."

For some reason, you made me nervous. James tugged at his collar. "I was glad to have made it past your scrutiny the first day." Shifting in his seat, he sat back and folded his arms. "I did my homework, Miss Landon. I knew what I was up against."

Her brows shot up, and she grinned. "So, you're saying I'm the brains, and you're the brawn?"

"I guess you could say that."

"There is one thing I'm curious about."

"Yes?"

"I might be good at details, but I didn't guess your deception."

He grinned. "That's true. But you did question some things. Didn't you?"

"I guess I did."

"I'm good at my job too."

Her brows lifted. "Oh, really? What job is that?"

"Hiding in plain sight."

She narrowed her gaze at him. "Let's remember, after the car accident, I knew immediately who you were. It was the cadence of your voice mixed with the smell of your cologne. It wasn't the same scent you wore as my bodyguard."

James sighed. He'd been careless the night of the accident when he slipped into his native accent. And the night in the hotel. He'd not even considered what scent lingered on his clothes the first night he was with her. He only remembered the feelings she stirred in him. Feelings he'd not visited in years.

"There is one thing I question." She tilted her head as if pulling a thought from the recesses of her mind.

"What's that?"

"If Declan is somehow involved in all the chaos in my life, how did I not see that?"

He clenched his jaw. She still didn't want to believe Declan was a criminal, and he still had no solid proof. "Sometimes, we allow our judgment to get clouded. We only see what we want to see."

His words stung. Had he just accused her of not keeping her eyes open when it came to Declan?

Kelly glanced out the window for a moment and pondered what he'd said.

"You said you were becoming too involved, that's why you left." She drew her gaze back to him. "What did *you* see when you were with me?"

"What do you mean?"

"In me? In Declan? What did you see? You were around us a lot. Did you observe anything to make you suspect Declan was involved in any of this?" *Did I really miss something that was right in front of me?* "You don't seem to have any proof."

James didn't answer right away. Instead, he looked at the ring on her finger. Kelly followed his gaze, but she wasn't ready to end the questioning.

"What did you see, James? Did you see a lonely writer who fell for her agent? A woman so shadowed by a fear of being alone for the rest of her life that she let the first guy who'd taken notice of her claim her heart?"

He jerked his gaze up to meet hers. "No. Of course not."

"I fell in love with Declan, and I believe he loves me too."

His eyes darkened to the color of pure sapphire. "Did he tell you that?"

"What?"

"Did he tell you he loves you?"

Her eyes pooled with tears, and she looked away.

"Did he?" James's voice lowered as he continued to prod.

She pushed back from the counter and scrambled to her feet. *Has Declan ever said he loves me?* Wrapping her arms around her middle, she turned and walked toward the door. Pursuing this line of questioning had been a bad idea.

Her mind retraced every conversation she'd ever had with Declan. Finally, realizing the truth James had pulled to the surface, her heart splintered like broken glass. No. He'd never said he loved her. He'd promised to protect her and advance her career—but he'd never said he loved her.

"I think I need to go rest. This is a lot to take in." Kelly struggled not to cry as she shot out a hand to steady herself against the door jamb. *He never said he loved me.*

"Kell, wait." James sprang from his chair and reached for her. "I'm sorry. I didn't mean to question Declan's feelings for you. It's just ..." He tugged at her arm, so she'd turn toward him. "It's just, I don't want you to get hurt."

She stared at the floor, praying it would open and devour her. "You've made your point. Please, just let me go."

"Miss Landon." He lifted her chin with the crook of his finger. "You asked me what I saw while I was your bodyguard."

Her lip quivered as the dam threatened to break.

"I saw you."

"What do you mean?" she whispered.

"I saw you, Kelly Landon."

As she stared up at him, untethered energy hummed between them.

"I know you drink coffee with way too much cream, and you love licking peanut butter right off the spoon." His lips curved into an enchanting smile. "I know if you walk into a bookstore, I won't see you for hours. And I know you like Dickens and Bronte and Austen, but for the life of me, I don't understand why you won't drink tea."

Wrapping his arms around her, James pulled her close and rested his chin on her head. "I know you're afraid to be alone, but you need your space. And I know you need security, but you don't want to live in a fortress."

Kelly snuggled into his chest, breathing in the comforting scents of Indian spiced tea and laundry soap. *I want to stay in your arms forever.* She pinched her eyes closed, trying to iron out her wrinkled emotions. *What about my feelings for Declan? How could I have been so wrong about him?*

After several heartbeats, she stepped back and turned away from James. "I ... I can't ..." She didn't trust what her heart was telling her to do. *Stay.*

"Kell, don't go."

Ignoring his plea, she bolted for the stairs and ran to her room.

By the time she'd burst through the bedroom door and collapsed on the bed, tears were streaming down her face.

32

The door opened, and Kelly pulled her attention from the window and the sweeping view of the St Martin-in-the-Fields church.

Henry Allen Taylor, James's brother and a senior director at H & G London, marched in and dropped a stack of folders onto the conference table. "He's been there the whole time, and we didn't see it."

When she noticed Declan's picture paperclipped to the front of one of the files, her stomach dropped. "Why do you have a file on Declan?"

She slipped into the seat next to James, still feeling on edge after their conversation about Declan's feelings for her. She doubted he'd meant to be hurtful, but his prodding had thrown her insecurities into a tailspin. However, he'd been a gentleman and not probed any further.

"I don't understand. Is Declan a CG?" James flipped through the first pages of the file while Henry paced in front of the gallery of antique maps on the back wall.

"A what?" Kelly looked at Henry then back at James. The past two days she'd spent with the Taylor brothers had felt like an immersion into an alternate realm of unfamiliar acronyms and clandestine tales of hidden treasures. She loved it, but at times, she felt like an outlier.

"A counter-gatherer, or CG, as we call them." James dropped the file and sat back in his seat. "Their group is the antithesis to what we do. They hoard stolen religious heirlooms as trophies or sell them to the highest bidder on the global black market."

Henry stopped pacing and turned to face them. "To the CGs, it's a game, and some of them even set up competitions to liquidate their pilfered goods. They don't care about the human story behind the items they've seized."

"I checked and rechecked Declan in all of our databases." James's brow furrowed. "We try to keep info on the CGs, but sometimes, they slip under the radar."

"Or new ones matriculate." Henry straightened one of the iridescent glass paperweights on the table.

"Is this what you think Declan is involved in?" Her stomach churned.

"No. I don't." Henry opened another file. "I think it's worse." He waved a hand over a document, then walked to the window and peered out over the misty city.

She surveyed the detailed genogram. The drawing resembled those she'd seen in the mailer Abram had sent to her.

Henry turned and scowled. "The jewels we are looking for are linked to World War II, and because of your incessant prodding, James, I started to think we missed something with Declan."

The churning in Kelly's gut intensified. James was looking for his proof.

"What's that?" she asked.

"We've only investigated the McNeary family." Henry walked back over to the table and traced his finger along Declan's ancestry line. "His father was an Irish farmer. The McNearys come from generations of farmers, and most of them have never left Ireland." Henry paused for a second and showed them another document. "Patrick, Declan's father, left the island once."

"Where did he go?" James asked.

"Virginia. He wasn't there long," Henry said, "but that's not the disturbing bit of information I found."

Kelly looked at Henry, afraid of what he would say next.

"We didn't check into Helen McNeary. She was a McNeary by marriage, and she listed her maiden name as a Belinski, from Poland." Henry unbuttoned his jacket then slid into a chair at the head of the table. "I decided to run her picture through some facial recognition websites, and what I came up with was unbelievable." Henry pulled out a folder from the stack. "Her maiden name was actually Mueller."

Staring up at them was a tattered black-and-white photo of a young woman, barely out of high school. James pulled out the documents. Across the top was the name: *Helen Annora McNeary, formerly Helena Annora Wolfgang Mueller of Berlin.*

Kelly read over James's shoulder while Henry paused and allowed the words they read to sink in.

"She joined the German Red Cross when she was sixteen." Henry blew out his breath as he rubbed a hand across his clean-shaven jawline. "We have documented proof she worked as a nurse with some of the most disgraceful doctors from that dreadful war."

As Henry read off the list of doctors, Kelly recognized the names from the stories she'd read detailing the post-war crime tribunals.

"After the war, Helena fled the country and moved to Ireland. The marriage record states she was born in Poland. She lied about her homeland and married an obscure Irish farmer to cover up any involvement in the war." Henry paused and shot Kelly a warning look. "Helena Mueller is Declan's grandmother."

Her throat constricted as she tried to swallow back the uneasiness stirring inside her.

James turned the page and pointed to a photocopy of what appeared to be family names scribbled in German. "What's this?"

The names were the same on the documents Abram had given Kelly. She pursed her lips together and waited for Henry to explain.

"We traced Helena back to the beginning of the theft and destruction of *The Twelve Story Stones* children's books and the precious stones that go with them." Henry leaned back in his seat, and a flash of anger traced across his face. "The very stones we're trying to find and give back to the rightful owners."

James shook his head. As he pointed to a document, he relayed what he was reading. "Helena stripped people of their dignity and their history before shipping them off on German death trains." He slid the documents over to Kelly. "How did Helena get involved in the missing stones?"

"According to one Gatherer, the children's books, *The Twelve Story Stones,* were to be confiscated and burned." Henry pulled out a picture of the book. It resembled the ones they already had in their possession. "The books talk about the unique and precious stones representing the twelve tribes of Israel." He pointed to a colored drawing. "They also represent the same stones that are in the priest's ephod mentioned in the Old Testament. The book explains the history of the Jewish people in a way a child would understand."

She pulled to her memory the intricate drawings she'd seen inside the book. James had explained that H & G were looking for any surviving books and the stones that accompanied them.

Henry broke through her thoughts. "If a family had one of these books, they also had a corresponding precious stone. According to what we've uncovered, families would pass the gemstone down from generation to generation along with the story."

"Shortly after the regime took over, the *Deutsches Rotes Kreuz,* or the German Red Cross, was brought under the umbrella of

Hitler's deadly political agenda." A muscle twitched in James's jaw as he tapped on Helena's photo. "Helena must have found out about the books and used her credentials to invade Jewish homes to search for them."

Kelly rubbed her temples then continued to scan the documents before her. "Here's a note written by an unnamed Jewish journalist." She pointed to the photocopied note and read it aloud. "A German nurse tore through a neighbor's home after she confiscated a children's book. Everyone stood in terror as she directed the soldiers to bring her all the jewelry in the home. The family was beaten and left for dead in the street for their silence and lack of cooperation." Kelly pressed through a tremble in her throat as she read the last line. "We called her *Helena the Wolf*, and we knew she would be back."

For a moment, the room was silent.

"Any books she confiscated were likely burned while the German Student Union built their angry fires and torched banned literature." Henry straightened his tie along with his posture. "We can assume Helena took the jewels and kept them for herself as some sort of war trophy."

Kelly winced as she thought about the three banned books in their possession. What had the owners gone through to preserve them?

"Is that why my father brought home jewelry all the time?" She spoke aloud, but it was more for herself than anyone else in the room.

"There were people who passed around the idea that your father found two of the books, along with the jewels they go with." Henry shot James a look. "And our father knew about them as well." Leaning forward, he folded his hands together and rested them on the table. "*The Twelve Story Stones* are embedded in political history and intrigue. I'll warn you both, it's a perilous mission for anyone to be actively looking for them."

"I don't understand. When I unpacked my dad's book

collection, I only found one." Kelly glanced at James. "We have three copies with us. One from my dad's collection, one from yours, and one Abram gave me."

"It's possible your dad hid one someplace else, so they wouldn't be together."

She nodded. "True."

"That still doesn't help us with the precious stones." Kelly blew out her breath. "Trying to find them would be like the proverbial needle in the haystack."

"Yes. It will prove difficult." The line in Henry's brow deepened as he settled back in his chair, smoothed his hands down his shirt, then crossed his arms.

James pointed to the final paragraph of the page. "It says here there'd been a report of stolen property at the home of the McNearys."

"Yes," Henry said. "According to the local law enforcement, Helena, then called Helen, did not want local authorities notified of the missing jewels. Her husband, Josef McNeary, was probably completely in the dark about his wife's evil past and worried about the theft. He called in a family friend who had ties to the local police."

Henry slid a photocopy of a vague scribbled report from years ago across the table, and James accepted it.

"Here's the information that Josef gave. There isn't much to go on, since they lived in a small, out-of-the-way farming community. Josef issued a brief statement about his wife's missing jewelry and the date. Josef died two years later, without knowing who his wife was or what she'd been a part of in Germany."

"How much of this do you think Declan knows?" Kelly looked at James, then back to Henry.

Henry shrugged. "I'm not sure. If he does know anything, he might feel like it's his familial duty to find these gemstones and make sure they never get back in the hands of God's chosen people."

James stared at Helena's picture. "Helena might have left him a missive and explained to him everything before she died. We see it all the time in our line of work. Death doesn't always mean the death of a vendetta."

Her pulse pounded in her temples. Even if Declan didn't know any of this, how could she marry a man whose veins pulsed with the blood of Helena the Wolf? Acid crawled its way from her belly into her throat. *I think I'm going to be sick.* While she twirled the engagement ring around her finger in mindless circles, her thoughts raced ahead with a million what-ifs before settling on one. *What if Declan knows everything?*

If he did, then she'd pledged herself to a monster.

33

ater that night, James sat next to Kelly in his formal dining room overlooking the back garden. Files and papers lined every inch of the table, and several banker boxes sat stacked in rows next to them on the floor.

"I'm making a pot of tea. Would you like something?" He pushed back his chair and walked into the kitchen.

"I'd love some coffee."

He laughed. It was almost nine in the evening. The way she could crawl in bed after a cup of the dark brew never ceased to amaze him.

As he plugged in the kettle, his thoughts went to their conversation about Declan's feelings for her and how the chat ended so abruptly. He'd avoided bringing it up again, and so did she. Until they connected all the dots in this investigation, he didn't feel it was the right time to try to explain how he felt. *I wouldn't even know where to begin.*

James flipped on the single-shot coffeemaker and dug through the drawer for a flavor Kelly might like. He enjoyed sharing everyday life with her more and more with each passing day. But how long would she stay? He prayed he'd have an opportunity to tell her how he truly felt before she slipped through his fingers and flew back to the United States.

Mugs in hand, he strolled around the corner and noticed Kelly's fingers tapping on the children's books in front of her. "What's on your mind?"

"This list of names." She pointed to the document she'd brought with her from Virginia.

"What's your take on it?"

"Well, there's your name, Abram's, mine, my father's, and there are four others."

"Do you see any connections there?" He slipped into the chair next to her and placed their mugs on the table.

"I think everyone on that list has a book. That means four books are unaccounted for." Kelly pinched the bridge of her nose. "They were either burned, or they're missing."

"True." He took a drink of his tea, and the smells of hazelnut coffee and English Breakfast tea circled around him. "You have an X by your name. That means you should have a book. Right?"

"I should. If that's what the X means." Kelly blew out her breath. "I feel like I'm working in circles."

"It is a bit of a puzzle. Isn't it?"

"It is." She leaned back and groaned. "Let's pause on the names and think about the jewels."

"Okay."

"I had a crazy idea." She picked up her coffee and took a long sip. "Do you trust me?"

He grinned. "I guess that depends."

Kelly got up, walked into the kitchen, and came back with a knife.

James threw up both hands in surrender. "Whoa. I thought we put all that animosity behind us."

She rolled her eyes and sat down. After she opened her father's copy of the children's book, she slid the knife under the aged book paper.

An urge to stop her fired off inside him, but he held his tongue. Instead, he watched as she guided the knife along the inside cover so as not to rip any of the wilted bindings. Working her way through the tape with the care of a surgeon, she stopped at the spine. With the tip of the knife, Kelly pricked at the edge of the binding. As soon as it tore, a tiny blue stone fell out onto the table.

"What?" His pulse skyrocketed as he reached for the gem. "Is that … no, it can't be."

She tilted the book, and more stones trickled out.

James pulled his chair closer and studied the jewel in his hand. It was one of the purest sapphires he'd ever seen. "You found the Story Stones, luv."

Tears pooled in her eyes.

"What's wrong, Kell? This is amazing—you're amazing." Pivoting in his seat, he opened his arms to her. Without hesitation, she fell into them and started to weep. "It's okay, luv." He tightened his hold and placed a row of kisses on the top of her head. "You found them. You unlocked the mystery."

After a few seconds, she pulled back, leaving behind a trail of moisture on his shirt. "James … it's just … I know where these gems came from and why they were hidden." She sniffled while she swiped her eyes with the back of her hand. "The horrendous stories we've heard about—what Helena did. People died, James. Millions of them. My heart aches to think about what the guardians of these books went through to keep them safe."

He tugged her back into his arms and wrapped her up tight. "I know, Kell. I know. We can't go back and change what happened, but we can find the families these belong to and return them."

She pulled back and looked up at him. "These families deserve to know their heritage was preserved. Even amid all that carnage, somebody out there kept a remnant of these books safe. Promise me you'll find the rest of the books, James. Promise me."

Lifting his hand, he brushed her tears away with his thumb. "I promise, Henry and I will do whatever it takes to find these books and return them."

James returned his attention to the table. *One, two, three, four, five* ... His pulse heated as his mind registered what lay before him. "Kell, look."

She turned and followed his gaze.

"There are twelve stones. But they're all the same."

"What? You're right."

"Do you know what this means?"

She straightened and reached for one of the gems. "Yes. Wait. Really?"

He nodded. "I think there are twelve of each kind of precious stone. What made you think to look in the spine of the book?"

"I was just thinking about something Abram said."

He waited for her to explain.

"During one of our talks, he told me if I wanted to step into my calling, I needed to be willing to trust that God will protect me and preserve me." She laid the stone back on the table. "Like a book whose story would fall apart without one, you need a backbone." She picked up the children's book and studied the cover. "If someone is said to have backbone, they have the courage to stand up for something. Those who protected the legacy of *The Twelve Story Stones* had backbone."

"That's true. They did."

"Abram always spoke in riddles. Did you know another name for the spine of the book is a backbone?" Her expression brightened as she ran her fingers along the hard edge of the book. "The backbone of these books protected and preserved these stones for the next generation." Looking back his way, she added, "After I saw what H & G does, and what it meant to my father, I wondered if maybe Abram *was* trying to tell me something. I need to step back and revisit everything he said."

James picked up another of the children's books and studied each page. Each vivid drawing described a different colored stone, and each stone shared the history of another tribe of Israel. "The book talks about twelve different specific stones." James handed the book to Kelly. "Will you do the honors?"

She nodded, then sliced the inside cover and nudged her way

up to the spine. After she found the folded tab, she disconnected it from the backbone of the book. When the flap dislodged, violet-colored stones trickled onto the table.

He picked up a jewel and held it up to the light. "It's an amethyst. Look at them. They're stunning."

Kelly reached for Abram's book and lifted the tape. After she dislodged the hidden tab, twelve smooth, green stones fell onto the table. "Beryl." She picked up a gem then looked at James. "Do you know what this means?"

"I do."

"Each person on that list has a copy of this book and unknowingly is hiding an amazing treasure." Kelly grabbed the list of names. She started at the top of the list and scanned them.

Dennis Michael Mueller

Kelly Rea Holt Landon

Beside her name was already scribbled a large red X. But she made a note that the book was still missing along with the stones.

She continued to study the list of names.

Miriam Dawn Sharp

Betsy Ann Sanders

James Edmond Taylor III

Next to James's name, she wrote amethyst.

Beryl Abram Jakob Zucker. Next to his name, she wrote beryl.

She paused, and her finger lingered on Abram's name. She thought it was fitting that his name would represent the exact stone he'd fought so hard to protect. She blinked back a bit of moisture at the memory of her dear friend and continued to move down the list.

Jacob Henry Landon II

Next to her father's name, she wrote sapphire.

Garrett Dean Sullivan Jr.

"What do you think the X next to your name means?"

"I don't know."

James pointed to the last name on the list. "Look at this name."

"What about it?"

"Rhett's last name is Sullivan."

Kelly rubbed her chin. "And Rhett could be short for Garrett."

"It could be," James said, "or it's just a coincidence. It wouldn't hurt to look into it."

She ran her finger over the name *Garrett Dean Sullivan Jr.* one more time, then looked at James. "If it's him, I wonder why he didn't say anything?"

"Maybe he wanted to give you time to put the puzzle together. Or maybe he doesn't even know the jewels are hidden in the book."

"True." Her mind reeled. They'd learned so much in just a few days—about each other, Declan, and *The Twelve Story Stones* —it was hard to process it all. As she continued to study the gems on the table, Kelly raised her hand to her throat and gasped.

James jerked his head to look at her. "What's wrong?"

"I know where another group of twelve are. My father gave me twelve emeralds. Remember?" She stood and grabbed her purse. After rummaging through her wallet, she held up what she'd been looking for—a crumpled four-by-six photo of her and Declan having dinner. The one with a red circle drawn around his head.

James stood and moved next to her.

As she studied the photo, the memories from the fear of being held in her hotel room rushed back. For months, she'd lived in the shadow of that night, and now she didn't know what to think. Was James the villain? Or was Declan? Or were they all thrown together by chance?

"Kell."

She looked up, and regret blanketed his expression.

"I can't say this enough. I'm so sorry for what I did. I should have never deceived you. If I could do it all over again ..." His words caught in his throat.

"After you explained everything about H & G, I think I understand why you did it."

"There's nothing to understand. It was a rash, idiotic decision."

James pivoted and strode to the fireplace. He nodded toward a tattered photo of a man in military fatigues. "That's my dad. He was an asset to H & G. He'd be so disappointed in me. Dazzled by the hunt, I didn't think about the people who were involved. I didn't think about what it would do to you."

"James—"

He turned to face her. "There's something you need to know about that picture you're holding."

"What?"

"I didn't take it. The photo was anonymously delivered to H & G. Whoever took it, pointed us to you—and Declan."

"Who do you think sent the photo?"

"I'm not sure. It could've been one of our contacts. Sometimes they're willing to help, but they want to stay under the radar. Or it could be someone on the outside." A moment passed before he added, "Maybe it was someone working for Abram. Or your dad."

A shiver whispered across her skin. Someone had been watching her the night she had dinner with Declan. But who?

James took a step toward her. "There *are* others looking for the stones. Others who only care about how much they're worth, not about the story behind them. When your father passed away, we lost a lot of ground trying to find them."

"So, you tried to get close to me? You wanted to see what I knew about my father's research."

The soft curve of his Adam's apple bobbed as he swallowed.

"Yes, but ..." He reached out and took her hand. "Something happened that night in Pennsylvania. I can't explain it. I'm drawn to you. Like something missing in my life was finally discovered." A longing stirred in his gaze as he added, "After that night, all I wanted to do was keep you safe."

Kelly blinked. She'd felt the same way the first time they were introduced. She felt that way now.

"That's why I took the job as your bodyguard." James released her hand and took up pacing in front of the mantel. "I wanted to make sure whoever took that photo, if they wanted to get to you, they'd have to go through me first." When he turned back to face her, his forlorn look melted her heart. "Can you ever forgive me?"

She pulled in a shaky breath and nodded. "I forgive you, James. I understand now what all this means to your family and to the families whose memory you're trying to preserve."

"Thank you. Your forgiveness means the world to me."

She held up the picture and pointed to the earrings and the necklace. "There they are. My dad gave me twelve emeralds, and I had a jeweler set them for me. I have a feeling they belong to the book."

He took the picture and studied it. "The jewelry is exquisite."

"Thank you. Declan thought so too."

His eyes darkened as he handed the photo back to her. "Where's the jewelry now?"

"In storage. After my house was ransacked, I thought I should move the jewelry."

"That was smart." He surveyed the gemstones scattered on the table. "I need to call Henry and tell him what we found."

"That's a good idea."

James grabbed his phone and opened the screen. After a few rings, Henry picked up. "You're not going to believe this."

Kelly listened as he shared everything with Henry.

He tilted the phone away from his lips. "Henry's on his way over."

She nodded as thoughts raced through her mind about Declan. *I still can't believe he's the bad guy. Wouldn't I have seen a darker side of him?*

She looked down at her engagement ring, and a twinge of sadness pressed a bony finger into her chest. At one time, she'd been head-over-heels in love with Declan. What about now? *I can't deny the feelings I have for James.* Pinching her eyes shut, she tried to make sense of her jumbled emotions.

"Kell?"

She snapped her eyes open. "What?"

"Did you hear what I said?"

"No, I'm sorry."

"Henry may have found another person on the list."

"Really? That's wonderful news."

James escaped into the kitchen with their mugs, leaving her to glance once more at the photo in her hand. With a heavy heart, she studied the handsome face of her agent. He'd never acted like someone with a vendetta. Had he?

Frustration rolled through her like a storm. Every kiss, every caring gesture, every touch from Declan circled through her mind in a loop. Never had he acted duplicitously. Never had he given her any cause to fear him.

Folding the photo, she placed it back in her wallet. *Maybe the person who took the photo is after us both?* The idea pushed a shudder through her veins.

She needed to find out the truth about Declan. And the photo.

Eventually, if she wanted answers, she'd need to return to Virginia and confront her fiancé.

34

Time ticked away as one week stretched into two. After spending her days investigating *The Twelve Story Stones* with James, Kelly had started to feel connected to the inner workings of H & G. More than that, she'd begun to understand James's calling—and her father's.

"What do you say we take a break and catch a movie?" James leaned back against the leather couch and threw her a boyish grin.

"That sounds—" A shrill ring from her phone sliced through her answer. Her heart stalled. "It's Declan."

"How did he get your new number?"

"What am I going to tell him?" She ignored his question. She had bigger problems to deal with. She'd avoided Declan's calls for almost two weeks. Instead, they emailed while she attempted to explain she needed time to sort things out after the accident.

Another ring carved through the room.

If she answered, she'd be obliged to give him an explanation for leaving the country. If she didn't answer—*he'll only call again.*

After the third ring, James spoke up. "Take it. See what he has to say. Just let him do most of the talking."

As she answered the call, her stomach clenched. "Hey,

Declan. How are you?" She pushed the speaker button and set the phone down on the table in front of them.

"I'd be doing better if you were here."

Kelly brought her finger up to her lips and sent James a warning look. He grabbed his phone and silenced it.

"I'm a little confused by something." Declan's lilting voice hung in the air and blew a shiver across her skin. "Why London, Writer Girl? What's there?"

She took a deep breath and released it. "I was scared, and you were out of town. I just needed to get away. Take a break. I'm familiar with London. Remember? My family lived here for a while."

"So, you decided to take Nathaniel with you?"

The name made her pause. *That's right, James went by Nathaniel.* Kelly fought to steady her voice. "I asked him to get me out of the city for a while. I could've been killed that night. It was a last-minute decision." Catching herself mid-ramble, Kelly took a deliberate pause. "I told you where I was going. It's just for a few weeks of R & R."

"Where are you staying?"

Her gaze darted to James. "Downtown." Not entirely a lie.

"Okay? Which hotel?"

James scribbled something down on a piece of paper and held it up.

"It's a flatshare." She drew in a quick breath. "You know, where you can rent a few rooms from a private owner."

Silence carried over the line, then finally Declan spoke up. "I was thinking …"

She pinched her eyes shut and waited for him to continue.

"Maybe I should head across the pond, and we can do some sightseeing together. I could use a few weeks of R & R as well."

Her eyes darted open. "No. I told you, I need some time to myself. And …"

"And?"

"And, well, I don't think we should be traveling all over Europe together until we're married."

Declan blew out an exasperated breath. "I think you're acting irrational, Kelly."

"What does that mean?"

"It means we're engaged. Do I need to remind you that you're the one who flew to Europe with another man?"

She cringed. As she glanced over at James, something dawned on her. By flying to London with her bodyguard turned treasure hunter, she'd inserted herself as a player in this game of duplicity—a game she was in no way qualified to play.

James's gaze locked onto hers. The irritation in his expression conveyed he did not appreciate Declan's accusation.

Thinking quickly, she decided to throw a claim back at Declan, learning the game as she went. "I thought you trusted him. It made sense at the time, and I believed he'd keep me safe."

"Is Nathaniel with you now?"

"No. He's out. Getting dinner." Her face burned with the lie.

James nodded as if to tell her she was playing her part well.

"Do you know why he left?"

"I assumed you fired him." Her body tensed as she remembered the conversation with James when he saw her engagement ring. *Oh, no.*

"I didn't fire him. But I do think he has feelings for you."

"What?"

James shook his head and looked away.

"I could tell by his expression—his body language. When I told him I was going to ask you to marry me, he looked upset."

Her mouth dried. *I can't believe this is happening.* She swallowed hard. "That's absurd."

"It's true."

A weighty silence permeated every crevice of the room.

Declan cleared his throat. "I want you to be honest with me. Do you have feelings for him?"

Kelly pinched her eyes closed. *Yes.*

"I need to know if the woman I'm going to marry has a divided heart. Or are we in this together?"

When her eyes opened, James's smoldering look penetrated her soul.

"Can I assume by your lack of response you *do* have feelings for him?" Declan's voice shifted from hurt to hostile. "After all I've done for you. This is how you treat me?"

"Declan, it's not like that." As she found her voice, a cold tremor raked through her body.

"Tell me. What's going on with you and him?" Declan's icy tone sliced through the phone. "Why was he even with you the night of the accident? Why was he back in town the week I was gone?"

James jumped to his feet and paced the room like a caged tiger.

"I don't know."

"Did you ask him to come back to you? Do you enjoy humiliating me by running off with your bodyguard?"

A ribbon of anxiety twirled inside her as more charges were hurled over the phone.

"Do you know what a laughingstock I'll be if word gets out you left me for the man I hired to protect you?"

James pivoted to face her, and the blue in his eyes ignited into an angry flame.

"You pursued me, Kelly. You gave me all the signs." Declan's voice deepened to a dark growl. "If it's over between us, don't you think I have the right to know?"

She opened her mouth to respond, but the words clung to the roof of her mouth.

"You were always so pious, Writer Girl. Now you're flouncing around Europe with your bodyguard." A soft chuckle escaped over the line. "If we're over, I'd like the ring back."

Clammy sweat clawed around her neck. This was a mistake. Coming here.

"That's quite enough." James's expression darkened as he snatched the phone off the table.

"Ah, Nathaniel, so you are there. You sound a bit more British than I remember, mate."

"And you sound a bit more like a jerk than *I* remember."

She listened to the control in James's voice while her emotions toppled like dominoes to the floor.

"I can't believe you'd treat your fiancée like this. She was nearly killed. Now, she's here trying to pick up the pieces of her life." James glanced at the ring on her finger. "And the ring you demanded she give back is staring at me from her left hand. She's done nothing but defend you since we've been here."

Her stomach flipped over.

"Let me talk to her again. Am I still on speaker?"

"No. You aren't." It was a lie, but James continued. "I can pass on whatever message you'd like me to—later. Unfortunately, she's too upset to take the phone right now."

"Tell Kelly I'm sorry. I'd like for her to come home so we can talk about this face to face."

"I'll let her know."

"Oh, and Nathan? Thanks for taking care of her, but as I said before, we aren't going to need your services any longer."

The muscles along James's jawline twitched like arcing power lines.

"Do we understand each other?"

"Perfectly." James ended the call and plunked the phone back onto the table. "Kell?" He sat down next to her, taking her hand. "Are you okay?"

She shook her head while she stared at the file on the table. Helena Mueller's photo stared up at her from the top of the stack. "I'm going back."

"What? Are you mad?"

"I need to go back." She jerked her hand from his grip and bolted from the couch.

"You can't go back to Virginia. Not right now." James stood and moved next to her. "Declan's a—"

"He's right."

"What? Right about what?"

"I pursued him."

"That doesn't matter."

"It does to me." She took two steps toward the hall then turned. "My life is in Virginia, James. After Declan proposed, I signed another contract for two more books. So, for better or worse, I'm tethered to that man one way or another."

James reached out and tugged her back toward him. "None of that means you have to marry him."

"I know. But I need to figure this out. I need to unravel what I've done." Kelly blinked back the tears threatening to fall.

"You don't have to do this alone. I'll go back with you." The golden specks in his eyes blazed with energy. "How long can it take to write two books?"

"James, you don't understand."

"Explain it to me."

"I thought I loved him. Then I find out he's related to this horrible person." Kelly inhaled, and the arborous scents of James's cologne circled through the air. "We don't know for sure what Declan's motive is, but I know I can't judge him by the sins of his grandmother."

"I don't believe he's a good person."

"I know. You don't believe Declan really cared for me either." She took a step back, needing to put space between them. "I'm going back to figure things out. It's humiliating to think I was such a poor judge of character."

"I can't let you do this. It's illogical."

"You can't stop me."

James gripped the back of his neck. "I'm not trying to stop you. I'm trying—"

"Stop. You can't protect me from everything. You're not my bodyguard anymore, James. And besides, we don't know if

Declan's behind the notes or anything else relating to the jewels."

"But ..."

She shook her head. "You don't have any proof."

"Did you hear him just now?" Worry blanketed James's expression. "He was angry, Kell. You don't know how he'll react when you go back."

"Wouldn't you be angry if your fiancée flew to another country with someone else?"

"That's not the point."

"Why? He asked, and I said yes. From the outside, I've reneged on that promise." She wrapped her arms around her middle, trying to ward off the chill filling the room. "Declan doesn't know I know anything about his family. I can't hide here in London forever. What about Emersyn? Now that Abram's gone, I'm her guardian. She needs me."

"What about the jewels? What about the mission?"

"I can't stay with you until you find all the jewels. That could take years."

"What are you saying exactly?"

"I'm saying that I'm going back to sort out my life. I'm a writer, James. My career is just taking off, and I need to fulfill my obligations." She waved a hand toward the files. "This is your calling, not mine. You and your brother have more than enough information to continue the hunt."

A storm churned in his expression.

"I need to do this. I need to sort this out between Declan and me, if ..."

"If what?"

"If I'm ever to move on."

Before he had a chance to reply, she fled up the stairs and prayed she wasn't making a mistake.

35

As Kelly tapped on the keyboard, the chime of the doorbell interrupted her scattered thoughts. She hadn't made any headway on her story, and now—she closed her eyes and took a deep cleansing breath—now she'd need to jump through the awkward hurdle of this visit.

She opened her eyes and pulled herself to her feet. She'd been back in Virginia only a few days, and she hoped that after she smoothed things over with Declan, she'd finally get some words on the page.

Kelly walked to the entryway and nibbled on her fingernail. For reasons unknown, first date jitters sparked in her veins. *It's only been a couple of weeks. You can do this.*

Tugging open the door, she forced a cheerful smile. "Declan. Thank you for coming over."

He leaned in and placed a chaste kiss on her cheek. "Thanks for inviting me."

"Please, come in."

He looked good. He always did. But today, his shoulders sagged, and there was a hint of uncertainty in his posture. She followed him into the living room and took a seat beside him on the sofa.

"Can I get you some coffee?"

"No. Thank you." He glanced down at her left hand. "I see you're still wearing my ring."

Warmth wrapped around her neck as she unconsciously twirled the ring around her finger.

"I'll admit, I'm a little surprised."

"Oh?"

"I was afraid after you ran off with Nathaniel to London, I'd be getting a ring back in the mail."

"That's not fair." She shifted to face him. "You know the car accident scared me. I didn't know what else to do. It was a rash decision, but ..." Forcing a hitch from her voice, she added, "England is familiar to me. It reminds me of my dad."

He glanced away.

"You trusted Nathan to protect me at one time. Remember?"

"I did." He turned back to face her, his expression a mixture of disappointment and suspicion.

"You were out of town. With everything that's happened, I was frightened." She laid her hand on his arm, hoping the tender act would allow her back into his heart.

"You didn't have to fly out of the country—with him."

"I know you don't understand." Kelly withdrew her hand and glanced out the window. "I told you, I needed time away to think. I needed to get my head together."

"He's British."

"What?" She swiveled her head back to face him.

"You heard his voice."

"What does him being British have to do with anything?" She sank back into the couch and crossed her arms. "Are you referring to some Irish-British schoolboy, rivalry thing? That's ridiculous."

"No, of course not." Declan flew out of his seat and paced in front of her. "He pretended to be someone different the whole time. Doesn't that bother you?"

"Of course, it does."

"Really?" He did an about-face and drilled her with a cold

stare. "But not so much that you wouldn't think twice to fly across the pond with him?"

Don't respond. Just let him vent.

"He has feelings for you, Kelly."

"No. I'm sure he doesn't." She stood and walked toward the kitchen. She wasn't ready to have this conversation with him and couldn't possibly look him in the eye when she did.

"You mean to tell me Nathaniel never gave any indication he has feelings for you?" Declan stepped in front of her, cutting her escape. His bottle-green eyes darted back and forth as if trying to read her reaction.

Every time he looked at me. "No. Never."

He trailed a finger down her arm. "I need to know if you want to go through with this engagement. Are you still willing to be my wife? If not, then I guess I'll bow out gracefully."

Kelly's throat constricted. She hated what this was doing to him. To her. To James.

"I'll take your lack of response as an answer." Declan flashed her a heated look.

"I just need some time."

"Time? You've had months, Kelly. I …"

Was he finally going to say what her heart had longed to hear?

"I want us to join forces. Together, we can battle anything that comes against us."

A blade carved at her heart. "I don't want to battle anymore. Ever since the memoir was released, my life's been nothing but chaos. I just want a reprieve."

"I said I would protect you, Writer Girl."

"Yes, I know." She willed her hand to stop trembling, but when she looked at Declan's face, all she could see was Helena's square jaw and straight nose. "Give me another month. Marriage is a big step for me."

"A month?" He reached for her hand. "I can wait a month."

She exhaled the breath she didn't know she was holding.

He tugged her closer. "You know, I was thinking. Maybe what we both need is some time. Away from all the chaos." When he brought her knuckles up to his lips, her stomach coiled into a knot. "Time to reconnect. Time to rekindle the flame." Turning her hand over, he placed a trail of kisses from her palm to the inside of her elbow.

Kelly shuddered. "I …"

"My touch still leaves you breathless." His eyes shone like a pair of emeralds. "That means something. Doesn't it?"

Recalling the photo of her necklace, she pulled her hand back and brushed her fingers across her collar bone.

"I care for you, Kelly. Let me prove to you how much."

Did he tell you he loved you? James's question crashed into her thoughts. *I know he cares for me.* Swallowing back a pang of sadness, she asked, "What did you have in mind?"

"A road trip." Declan's expression brightened.

"What kind of road trip?"

"Let's get out of the city. It might be just what we need to patch things up."

"Do you think that's wise? Have they found the people who tried to run me off the road yet? Wouldn't our time be better spent trying to piece that debacle together?" She nibbled on her bottom lip. "Then we can put all of this behind us before we walk down the aisle."

Declan wrapped his arms snugly around her. "That's not our job, Writer Girl." He placed a quick kiss on the top of her head. "Let's leave that to the professionals."

Wrapped in his embrace, she breathed in the crisp maritime fragrances of his soap and aftershave. *Like the shores of Ireland.*

"I've hired a private investigator to look into everything."

She stepped back and looked up at him. "You did?"

"I want to put this behind us as soon as possible."

As she studied his face, her anxious thoughts warred inside of her. He was still just as handsome as she remembered, but was there anything in his expression to make her believe she'd been wrong? Wrong to trust him. Wrong to fall in love with him.

"I have a cabin not far from here." Declan's mouth unfurled into a wide grin while his eyes tracked hers like an animal stalking its prey. "It may just be the peace and quiet we need to rekindle what we had before."

Her stomach flipped over. She'd been adamant in their relationship about boundaries. Why was he pushing the issue now?

"Darling, you look like a frightened rabbit. I know you have your rules." He traced his thumb along her bottom lip. "I'll respect them. I always have."

Am I that easy to read?

"There are divisions in the cabin. It's two separate vacation rentals."

She listened as he continued to rattle off the details of their impromptu trip.

"We'll have separate entrances and separate keys." He flashed her a roguish grin. "You don't even have to let me past the threshold if you choose not to."

"It seems as if you thought of everything."

"I always do."

Declan released her and moved toward the door. Before he clasped the knob, he glanced over his shoulder. "It's good to have you back, Writer Girl. I missed you."

A lump crawled up her throat and settled.

"Go ahead and pack. We'll leave in a few days." He threw her a wink before he let himself out the door.

In stunned silence, Kelly stood rooted to the floor. A cold disquiet wrapped its arms around her soul and compressed.

"God, help me." *What did I just agree to?*

36

"James?"

"Kelly?" It had been weeks since James had heard Kelly's voice. He'd kept his promise and remained in London while she went back to Virginia. But, with so many things left unsaid between them, he had difficulty focusing on his work.

Within hours of their awkward phone call with Declan, Kelly was back on a plane to Virginia. She'd stepped out of his home and his life just as quickly as she'd stepped in.

"Yes, it's me."

He looked at the screen. He didn't recognize the number. "Why are you whispering?"

"I'm at Declan's cabin."

"What?" He tried not to sound as punctured as he felt.

"It's not what you think."

"I'm not sure what to think."

"I don't have time to explain right now. I found something in an old wooden chest in Declan's room."

"Why are you in Declan's room?"

"James, are you listening to me? I finally found the note his grandmother left for him."

It took a moment to register what she'd just said. "Are you out of your mind?"

"The letter clearly explains the history of *The Twelve Story Stones* and how it's now his duty to find them."

The sound of papers shuffling floated over the phone.

"It's a lengthy letter. Declan's been charged with preserving his grandmother's memory. She wants him to destroy the books and retrieve all the missing stones. Not just the ones she confiscated during the war."

"You shouldn't be doing this alone. We don't know what that man is capable of."

"I know, I know."

For a second the phone went silent, and James's entire body twisted with tension. "Kelly?"

"I'm here. I thought I heard something. We're only here for a few more days. This trip was his plan for us to rekindle our relationship."

James gritted his teeth. "How's that going?"

Another string of silence.

"Kelly?"

"I think I may have lost our connection for a second. What did you ask?"

"Nothing. Don't worry about it."

"There's another document. It looks like it was part of a will." Her voice trembled. "It mentions the families the children's books were taken from. There's a hand-scribbled list of surnames."

"Declan's been involved in this the whole time." He pinched the bridge of his nose. *This is not good.* "It seems as if the grandson has inherited his grandmother's lust for stolen artifacts."

"From the numbers listed on one of these forms, the precious stones are worth millions." Kelly murmured a few numbers and notations, then added, "Here's something odd. There's another letter. It mentions other stolen antiquities. There were crates of heirlooms carried out of Germany."

"Does it say where they took them?" He listened for an answer, but none came. "Kelly?"

"James ..." Her voice dipped into a strained whisper. "There's a picture of my dad, and I'm in the photo. There's a note attached."

"What does it say?"

"The father knows, and so will the child."

Adrenaline soared through his veins like a bolt of lightning. "Where is Declan right now?"

"He drove into town to get some groceries."

"You've got to get out of there. He's known who your father was this whole time."

"Someone's coming. I've got to go."

"Kell!" As he shouted her name, a loud thud echoed over the line. "Kelly! Kelly!"

"Now that you know all my secrets, Kelly, it's time you tell me yours." The controlled, whispered tone of Declan's words shot a pang of alarm through James.

God, please protect her.

After a long moment of silence, a loud, hollow thump echoed in the background. *The antique chest.* He listened to Declan struggle for a few seconds, and James's heart sank. Where is he taking her? *He'll keep her alive—for now.* That thought brought him little comfort since he was an ocean away and had no idea where Declan's cabin was located.

The connection remained open. He assumed Kelly must have dropped the phone to allow him to listen. He strained to hear something—anything that could give him a hint of where Declan had taken her. The only sounds he could decipher were the clangs of an old water pipe and the distant sound of a screeching hawk. Then, after a few seconds, the phone disconnected. With a shaky hand, he lowered his cell from his ear.

Shoving aside the terrifying thoughts of what Kelly might be going through, he punched in Henry's number and sprinted up the stairs to his master suite. After he grabbed a duffel from his closet, he made a mental inventory of everything he'd need to take with him.

"Hello, mate. What's up?"

"He has Kelly." James harnessed his panic as he shoved a few items into his bag.

"Who?"

"Declan."

"I thought she went back to be with him."

James winced. "It wasn't like that."

"Okay? Then explain it to me."

"Kelly found evidence proving Declan was commissioned by his grandmother to find the stolen jewels."

"You're kidding?"

"While we were on the phone, there was an altercation." He darted to the master bath, grabbed his toiletries, and continued to pack. "She dropped the phone, Declan said something to her, then …" He plunked the bag onto his bed and scrubbed a hand across his five-o'clock shadow. "Then it went silent."

"That's not good."

"To add to that, she found a picture of her and her dad." Yanking the zipper closed on the bag, he snatched his passport out of a drawer. "Declan's known who she was this whole time."

"What are you going to do?" Henry asked.

"I'm getting on a plane, and I'm going to find her."

"What can I do?"

"Find out where Declan owns a cabin. See if you can trace her last call." He shrugged on his field jacket and texted for a ride while he put Henry on speaker. "Start in Virginia. I don't think he took her far."

"Got it."

"Put a call in to Liam. I could use some backup." Liam Campbell, his mate from the RAF and fellow Hunter, worked in specialized security around the globe. If anyone could connect the dots to Declan's next move, he could.

"I've already messaged him. He's in DC."

"Brilliant. He's not far." James shut off his lights and peered out the front window for the cab.

"Besides," Henry said, "Liam owes us a favor after our two-week detour in the Czech Republic."

James stifled a laugh. "That he does." He shot off another text, this one to Frank. "I've got a message in to Frank. He'll contact Rhett Sullivan. From the bookstore. They're the closest to the situation right now." He spotted the black cab and bolted out the door. "I can't believe I let her go back without me."

"Come on, mate. It was her choice to go back."

"I didn't think she'd jump in like this." He hopped into the back seat of the cab. "Heathrow Airport."

The cabbie nodded and accelerated into the city.

"She must have decided to pick up where her father left off." James shook his head, frustrated at himself and furious with Kelly. He'd only told her about H & G so she'd understand where he was coming from, not to convince her to jump into the investigation. "She has no idea who she is dealing with. He could ..." James let the sentence trail off, aware of listening ears in the front seat. "I'll call you when I land."

"I'll expect it. And, James ..." Henry paused. "Be careful."

James ended the call and looked down at his screen. There were new messages from Frank, Rhett, and Liam. All had agreed to start piecing together where Declan's cabin was located. He sent a quick text back to Liam. He'd need to get a team from H & G ready to extract Kelly as soon as he landed.

After what felt like an eternity, the taxi pulled up to the airport's departures. He snatched his duffel off the seat and handed over his payment.

What was Declan's plan to extract information from Kelly? And what would he do to her once he got what he wanted?

Dread sank into James's gut as he raced through the doors to the ticket counter.

With Helena the Wolf's vendetta haunting them from the grave, there was no predicting what Kelly was up against.

He just prayed he got to her before it was too late.

37

"We've got to stop meeting like this."

Kelly turned her head in the direction of James's voice and strained to make out his face through the black cloth impairing her vision. *He found me.*

"Is this your way of telling me you're joining H & G?" He sliced through the zip ties digging into her wrists and ankles. "Next time, just send me an email."

I need to warn him about Declan. Shaking her head back and forth, she fought to speak past the gag wedged between her lips.

"Just a minute, Kell." He released the cloth around her eyes then untied the gag.

"Declan has cameras. Everywhere." Licking her parched lips, she pointed above the door.

"I expected as much." James held out the shoes he'd retrieved from outside the door. "Put your trainers on. We're getting out of here."

She took her shoes from him, and with trembling hands, slipped them on.

Instead of his usual suit and tie, James crouched in front of her, decked head-to-toe in black tactical gear. Her gaze roamed from his black fingerless gloves, past the knife sheath on his belt, to the intimidating weapon strapped to his thigh. *Who is this man?*

He caught her staring, and his lips unfurled into a wide grin. "No suit today, luv."

"I hope you don't dress like that to teach kids."

"No. But they might listen better if I did." He opened his arms to her, and with a nod, he coaxed her toward him. "We need to talk. Lean in and pretend like you're glad to see me."

This wouldn't be an act. She slid her arms inside his jacket, skimmed past another holster and wrapped him in a death grip. "How did you know where to find me? Declan threatened to kill me if …"

James pulled her closer, and the warmth of his breath tickled her ear. "Relax, luv. Take a couple of long, deep breaths. I'm going to get you out of here."

"How? He can see everything."

"I know. Right now, I need all eyes on us. We need to distract him while the rest of my team moves in." He kissed her temple then placed a trail of kisses down her cheek.

Kelly's body warmed as she continued to cling to him. If he wasn't distracting Declan, he was definitely distracting her. She breathed in, then exhaled. He smelled like the forest and masculine body soap. "I didn't come back to patch things up with Declan."

"I know."

"I thought if I could find out what he knew, then I—I'm so sorry I came back without you."

"It's okay. I'm here now." James curled his fingers through her hair as he continued to console her in deep, soothing tones. "I brought a few specialized security guys with me, and my mate Frank isn't far behind with the local police."

She pressed closer to him, relishing the security of his arms. *I could stay here forever.*

"There's a holster on the inside of my left ankle. If anyone comes through that door, you grab the pistol and start shooting. Center of the paper. Do you understand?"

"I understand." She shivered as she snapped back to the present. "There are more men here. Not just Declan."

"How many?"

"I counted six different voices, and they're armed."

"Tell me everything you know."

"Declan's fluent in both German and Russian. The men with him call him *Wolfe*."

His muscles coiled taut beneath her grip. "Fitting."

"They're searching for more than just a couple of missing jewels. There's a group of stolen heirlooms, and they think I ..." Kelly pushed through the lump expanding in her throat. "They think I know where they are."

"It's going to be okay. I promise."

James leaned back and fished a phone out of his jacket pocket. After a quick glance at the screen, he clicked the microphone on his lapel. "I've got the author." Throwing her a wink, he stood and held out his hand. "Everyone's in place. It's time to go, Miss Landon."

When James pulled her to her feet, Kelly's legs buckled.

"Are you okay?" He circled an arm around her waist and drew her to his side. "Did that bloke give you any food or water while you were down here?"

"A little. Yesterday." Kelly squared her shoulders and smoothed a hand down her rumpled shirt. "I'm fine. I just need to catch my bearings."

"When I get my hands on him ..." While he muttered a threat, James dug out a thin, black nylon pullover from his thigh pocket. "Put this on. If we make a break for the woods, it will be easier to blend in if you're wearing dark colors."

She looked down at her white T-shirt then pulled on the windbreaker. "Looks like you thought of everything."

"It's in my job description."

"Did you happen to bring a latte in one of those pockets?"

James shot her an amused look. "No. But we'll stop at a café on our way out of here."

"Promise?"

Taking a step toward her, James zipped her windbreaker the rest of the way to her chin. "I promise. Now let's get out of here before your ex-fiancé tries to kill me."

38

J ames looked Kelly over one more time. If they were lucky, his team would be able to subdue most of Declan's cohorts before they made their way down the hall.

"Shots fired! Shots fired!" Liam's warning blasted through his earpiece as a barrage of gunfire erupted in the house.

"James! What's happening?"

He reached out and curled his fingers around hers. "Don't let go of my hand, and do exactly what I tell you to do."

She moved in next to him as he pushed open the door. The hallway was empty, but footsteps and voices echoed on the floor above them.

"We're going to exit through the back door."

Two more shots reverberated through the house, and Kelly stopped, rooted to the floor.

"It's okay. We're almost there." He tugged her closer and prayed the melee had moved to the front, giving him more time to get them out. They scurried down the hallway and up a small flight of stairs leading to the kitchen.

"James, wait." Kelly pulled him in the direction of a closed door. "It's Declan's room. I need to get a file."

"No. We need to get out of here."

She yanked her hand loose, pushed through the door, and

bolted toward the chest. As two more shots rang out, thundering footsteps rushed toward the front door.

"Kell, hurry."

She grabbed the file, slipped it into the waistband of her jeans, and they took off toward the kitchen.

"Hold it." A male voice shouted over the commotion. "It seems you're trying to leave with something of mine."

The thick, agitated accent told James precisely who it was. He turned in the Irishman's direction and shoved Kelly behind him. "I doubt that, McNeary."

A red laser danced across James's chest as Kelly whimpered. He lifted his gaze. "Did someone call for a bodyguard?"

Declan sneered. "Hardly. Leave the author with me, and I'll let you live, Taylor."

James forced a calm expression.

"Yes, I've discovered your secret, James." Declan glanced around him to Kelly. "But does she know?"

Frank called out several orders that fed into James's headset. They had three men in custody, and police were in position along the road leading to the cabin. *God, please provide a way for Kelly to escape.*

Shouting reverberated from the second story above them. James strained to pick up any of the dialogue but was left in the dark. He narrowed his eyes at Declan. "Friends of yours?"

"I wouldn't call them friends." Declan said. "More like business partners."

Kelly leaned in and hissed out a shaky whisper. "They have explosives. We …we need to get out of here."

"Okay, McNeary. I guess you win."

Declan cocked an eyebrow and waggled the red beam in a circle. "I always do."

Don't let him win, God. Please don't let him win. "Mind if I say goodbye to Kelly?" James asked. "I did fly across the pond to see her."

"Of course." Declan nodded toward the holster fastened to

his thigh. "Take your weapon out and lay it on the floor. Slowly. And don't do anything stupid or …" He smirked. "I'm sure I don't need to spell it out for you."

While he kept his eyes level with Declan's, James unsheathed his weapon, then crouched and laid it on the ground.

"Very good. Now, put your hands up where I can see them, and turn around."

When he turned to face Kelly, the terror in her eyes made his heart splinter in two. "I'm sorry, Kell. I didn't think it would end this way."

"No. What are you doing? We—"

"Kell. Look at me."

She lifted her gaze, and her eyes glistened with tears.

"Do you remember the day of the accident? When you finally realized who I was and how I had deceived you?" He prayed she would understand where he was leading her with these questions. "Do you remember how you responded?"

Her expression morphed from confusion to a look of recollection.

He nodded, hoping to prod her along.

"You're a jerk, James Taylor, and I hate you." She pulled back her foot and kicked him in the shin. James let out a painful gasp as he dropped to one knee.

Declan tipped his head back and howled with laughter. "Not the farewell you "

Grabbing the pistol strapped to his ankle, James pulled Kelly to the floor and fired off a shot at Declan. Kelly screamed as the bullet sliced through Declan's chest, and he let off a shot toward James.

Gritting his teeth, James shoved his pistol back in the ankle holster and swiped his Glock off the floor. "Are you okay?"

Wide-eyed, she nodded. "But …" She pointed to his shoulder. "Your …"

He followed her gaze. "I'm fine."

"You're not fine. There's blood seeping out of your jacket."

A herd of footsteps stomped above them, followed by yelling.

"We need to go." James pressed the mic on his lapel. "Frank, get your guys out of the cabin. They've got explosives."

"Copy that."

Kelly turned and stared at Declan. "Is he …"

Footsteps hit stairs, and James tugged on Kelly's arm. "Let's go." Pushing the screen door open a few inches, he surveyed the wrap-around porch. It was quiet. He motioned for Kelly to follow him down the steps.

They took off across the gravel drive and into the shadowy copse of trees. Holding his injured arm close to his body, he prayed they could put several yards between them and the cabin before Declan's goons decided to follow.

"One down. One just fled out the back door. He's heading east. I repeat, he's heading east." Liam's voice crackled in James's ear.

James motioned Kelly toward a natural cave carved out of a stack of bulky rocks. "Get in. Keep low."

She hesitated only a moment then crawled into the cave.

James crouched next to her, and searing pain crawled across his shoulder. He inhaled a quick breath. It wasn't a deep wound, but he was losing blood. And it would grow more difficult to handle his weapon.

A twig snapped, tearing his focus from his injury to the shadowy figure gliding across the moonlit forest floor. His muscles pulled like a taut rubber band. *Focus. Listen. Breathe.*

He pulled the pistol from his ankle holster and slid it into Kelly's hand. At least if he passed out, she'd be able to fend off their attacker. *Please, God, keep her safe.*

The footsteps drew closer.

I need to get him away from us. With his left hand, James scraped through the dirt next to his foot. *Got it.* He wrapped his fingers around a rock. With his injury, he'd need to throw with his left hand. It'd be awkward, but he had to try something. He shot to his feet and hurled the rock down the moonlit path.

The footsteps stopped.

James gripped his gun and propelled himself out of the cave. "Put your hands up, and don't move." He winced as the pain in his shoulder clawed down his arm. *Give me a few more minutes of strength, God. Just a few more minutes.*

"Oh, come on now, James. You wouldn't shoot a man in the back. Would you?"

The hairs on his neck prickled to life. "I told you to put your hands in the air."

The man turned to face him. "Surprise!"

"Declan?"

"In the flesh."

Kelly gasped.

"Is that you, Kelly? Where are you hiding?"

James gripped his gun tighter as he studied the doppelgänger standing in front of him. *It can't be.* He must be losing blood faster than he thought.

"I always wondered which one of us you fell in love with, Miss Landon. I think I'm the better-looking one." Although he couldn't see her, Declan winked in the direction of the cave. "And I know I'm the better kisser."

James's finger hovered over the trigger. *Just one shot. That's all it would take.*

"What's wrong? Cat got your tongue, James?"

"Shut up and put your hands in the air." He growled out the order through clenched teeth.

"It looks like your shoulder is a bit of a mess, mate." Declan shifted his stance. "At least my imbecile of a brother got off one shot before he hit the floor." He glanced in Kelly's direction. "I'm definitely the smarter one."

He was a twin. James couldn't believe Declan had played them both with such a detailed double-cross.

The ground beneath him sagged as pinpricks blinked across his vision. *I'm running out of time.* "I don't want to shoot you, Declan, but I will."

"Oh, I know you will. You proved that just a few minutes ago when you shot my brother." Declan sighed with a dramatic flair. "You're going to have to pay for that, by the way."

A glint flashed in Declan's hand, and James stilled.

"I'll be taking payment for that in three, two, one ..."

A fiery explosion rocked the ground. Kelly shrieked as a second blast shook the earth, and flames flew up from the direction of the cabin.

Declan sprang at him like a trained fighter. James wrestled him back, but because of his injury, Declan knocked the gun out of his hand.

James landed a punch. Declan stumbled.

Shaking off the hit, Declan lunged a second time and took a crack at his jaw. The taste of copper seeped into James's mouth.

He blinked and shook off the punch. As his vision swayed, Declan rushed in like a linebacker and pinned him to the ground.

"James!" Kelly darted out of the cave.

Panic surged through him like a trail of ignited gasoline. "Kell, stay back."

Declan got in a second punch, and strobes of light flashed across his vision.

"I'd listen if I were you, Writer Girl." Yanking the knife off James's belt, Declan flicked it open and shoved the tip into James's inflamed wound.

James released a guttural yell.

"No!" Kelly's scream speared his soul as he struggled to push Declan off.

Declan cackled, then bent and whispered in his ear. "When you've taken your final breath, she's mine."

As Declan pushed the knife deeper, James gnashed his teeth. With his uninjured hand, he clawed at the ground, searching for anything to fight back with.

"I'd stop moving, mate. The more I push this blade in, the worse it's going to get."

James's combat reflexes fired inside him as Declan pushed the blade deeper. *I've got to save Kelly.* He fisted a handful of dirt and shoved it in Declan's face.

Declan cursed and spat on the ground. "You're not playing fair, James." Declan shot a seething look at Kelly. "You should've just walked down the aisle quietly, my dear."

"Run." James's vision clouded as he growled out the order. "Kell, run."

The expression on Declan's face shifted from grotesque satisfaction to confusion.

James twisted his neck, straining to follow Declan's gaze.

With tears streaming down her face, Kelly raised the pistol and pointed it at Declan. "Get. Off. Him."

"You can't seriously think I believe you know how to shoot one of those." Declan's words gushed with ridicule.

"Well, here's the thing. A few months ago, you hired a bodyguard to protect me." Her voice hitched, but she kept the gun steady. "And for some reason, he thought I needed to learn how to use one of these."

"Is that so?" Declan glared at James. "He's losing a lot of blood, sweetheart. I'm not sure how much longer he'll be with us."

"I wouldn't make her angry, *mate.*" James's breath came out in quick bursts. "She's a brilliant shot."

Declan ignored him and pushed the knife down theatrically with the tip of his finger.

James sucked in a ragged breath.

Declan's sardonic laugh floated in the breeze as he lifted his hand off the knife and waved his blood-streaked fingers in the air.

Kelly sucked in a breath. "I'm giving you one more chance, Declan. Get off him."

Declan held her stare.

"James? Can you hear me? James?"

Please God, protect her.

Kelly's pulse pounded in her ears. *I need to save James.* She looked at Declan's hand dripping with James's blood, and her stomach curled into a knot.

"He's not answering, Writer Girl." Declan's sing-song pitch floated in the air. "That's not a good sign."

Without a second thought, she fired off a shot.

Declan grunted a curse then rolled off James.

"The next shot, you won't survive Mr. McNeary." Kelly kept the gun leveled on Declan. "Roll on your belly and put your face in the dirt."

Declan did as he was told but continued to hurl a slew of threats in her direction.

As she glanced back at James, a tremor of dread circled through her. Even when she fired the gun, he hadn't flinched.

"Declan, if he dies ..." Her voice shook as much as her hands. *God, please don't let him die.*

James moaned, and she jerked her gaze back to him. With his uninjured arm, he grasped his lapel mic and pushed the button. "Frank ... got him. Head ... east." After completing the transmission, James's arm went limp, and his eyelids fell shut.

Kelly fell to her knees and snatched the microphone off his lapel. "Frank. James is hurt. We need an ambulance." A quick sob escaped her lips. "Hurry."

She dropped the mic and swiped at her tears. "James. Stay with me."

As she reached for the knife sticking out of his shoulder, James's eyes shot open.

"No, Kell. Too much blood."

"What am I supposed to do? I don't know how to help you." Tears tumbled down her cheeks as his eyes drooped shut. "God. Please. Help us."

As the plea escaped her lips, Frank and two other men ran up the hill.

One of the men yanked Declan off the ground, making him yowl.

"My hand. She shot my hand."

"You're lucky, mate. I wouldn't have aimed for your fingers."

Kelly turned in the direction of the familiar voice.

"I wasn't about to let my brother come here alone." Henry winked at her then glanced at James. Concern streaked across his expression.

"Don't worry. I got him." The other man pushed past Henry then fell to his knees next to James. Throwing his backpack on the ground, he ripped open the zipper and dug through what looked like a four-star first aid kit. "This might hurt." He mumbled something under his breath as he tore open James's shirt and surveyed the wound.

"He's in good hands, Miss Landon." Henry flashed her a reassuring look as he turned and dragged Declan, still issuing his threats, down the hill.

She stumbled back onto a log and closed her eyes. *I think I'm going to be sick.*

"Miss Landon?"

Kelly's eyes shot open.

Frank crouched in front of her, frowning. "Are you injured anywhere?"

"No, no." She glanced down at the blood and dirt smeared across her hands. "This blood ... it's James's blood. I didn't know what to do. I didn't know how to help him."

"I need you to hand me the gun."

With shaky hands, she offered the weapon to Frank. "I didn't know what to do. He was hurting James, and ..."

Frank tucked the gun in his waistband, then he grabbed her wrist and checked her pulse. "I need you to start taking deep breaths. Do you understand me?"

She did as he said and looked back at James. "Is he going to be okay?"

"He'll be fine."

"Who is he?" She nodded toward the man moving over James like a skilled surgeon.

"That's Liam Campbell."

She glanced back at Frank, waiting for him to explain.

"They served together a few years back in the RAF. They were in an intel unit together."

"James told me he was a PE teacher."

As she studied James, she realized how little she still knew about him. He'd told her he worked as a teacher, but he'd shown up today dressed to kill and ready for a fight. The unshakeable poise he'd kept with a laser pointed at his chest made her believe he'd done all this before.

"James teaches on occasion. Fills in, that sort of thing. He also works private security. But he has a history in the RAF too." Frank sat down next to her on the log. "I guess he worked with some top secret things. Of course, I didn't ask the details."

"How do you know him?"

"His dad and I go way back. I served in the Air Force years ago, and his dad was in the RAF."

She tried to sort through all her questions as Frank continued to explain. "I was stationed across the pond. His dad was in at the same time. We just hit it off. We were friends for years after I left the military, until he passed away." Frank looked from her to James. "There isn't anything either one of us wouldn't have done for each other's family. So, when James contacted me and asked for my help, I didn't hesitate."

James moaned.

She pushed off the log and fell to her knees beside him. "James, James. Can you hear me?" She glanced up at Liam. "Is he going to be all right?"

"He's looked worse." Liam grinned and tipped a nod her way. "I'm Liam Campbell. One of James's mates." A velvety, smooth Australian inflection rolled off his lips. "You must be Kelly."

She nodded. "Are you sure he'll be okay?"

Liam glanced back at James. "No worries. He'll survive." James groaned, and Liam leaned in. "Take it easy, mate. I gave you some of the good stuff. There's no telling what you might start confessing."

"I'll give you twenty quid if you give me some more." James pinched his eyes shut and grimaced.

Liam picked up his gear. "My job's done. The ambo's here."

Henry rushed up the hill with two medics in tow. "Someone's taking care of Declan. Looks like he won't be typing any time soon." Henry turned to face her. "You're quite a shot, Miss Landon."

Kelly swallowed past the acid coating her throat. *I shot Declan.*

As a cool clamminess crawled over her skin, her vision rippled like a mirage.

"Kell?"

Her name on James's lips was the last thing she heard before her world went black.

# 39

Kelly took a long sip of her double-shot latte as she slipped into the hospital room. It had been another long, sleepless night, so she'd rushed over early to check on James.

"Morning, handsome." She leaned in and placed a soft kiss on his cheek.

The glow from the morning sun filtered through the curtains and cast a warm orange haze over the bed. Her heart squeezed. The bruises he'd acquired from his tussle with Declan now had a deep, purple hue, and the laceration on his bottom lip appeared red and painful, all proof he'd borne a lot to rescue her.

"Morning, luv." James's mouth tipped into a groggy smile as he opened his eyes. "Did you bring any tea? The stuff they have here tastes like watered down ash."

"I did." She dug through her purse and pulled out the contraband. "Look, it even has the British flag stamped on the package."

"Perfect." His goofy grin proved he was still sleepy from last evening's pain meds. "Now I just need a kettle."

"I knew I forgot something."

A soft chuckle escaped his lips.

"How's your shoulder?" She laid the box on the bedside table.

It had been a few days since he'd undergone surgery to repair the damage done by the knife and the bullet. Now his arm was wrapped from collarbone to elbow and hanging in a sling.

"Better. Numb." His eyelids drooped closed. "The doc assures me I'll be as good as new. Or maybe he said almost new."

"That's good."

She lowered herself into the chair next to his bed and tried to stretch the kinks in her shoulders. Since her rescue, she'd been surviving on caffeine and broken sleep. The images parading through her mind of Declan's twisted face while he inflicted pain on James, did little to allow her to rest.

"Knock, knock."

She glanced up as the door opened. "Hey, Frank."

Frank walked in balancing a crate and a few packages. "How's the patient holding up?"

The motor on James's bed hummed to life as he lifted the angle of his head. "Ready to get out of this bed."

Frank and Kelly both laughed.

"I stopped by your house, Kelly, and picked up your mail. There was a large box delivered to your home." Frank set a rectangular box down on the table. "It's from Abram."

"Abram?" As she rose from her seat, her heart squeezed at the memory of her friend.

"I have a few things Rhett wanted me to bring by as well." Frank placed a wooden crate next to the box, along with a file and a few manila envelopes.

She stood and examined the stack on the table. "What's in the crate?"

"I'm not sure."

She opened the lid and pulled out a bulky, worn leather Bible. Tears gathered in her eyes as she recognized the handwriting inside the cover. "It's my grandmother's Bible." A flood of memories washed over her while she opened the pages and ran her fingers along the notes scribbled in the margins. For weeks, she'd been reading scripture and asking God to help her understand His love for her. Now she'd be able to read the spiritual notes left behind by the grandmother she'd adored as a little girl.

"What a special treasure." James spoke up and flashed her a knowing look.

"It is." She pulled the leatherbound book close to her chest, and it felt like a warm hug from the past. *Thank you, God.*

"How did Rhett find it?" James directed his question to Frank.

Frank shrugged. "I'm not sure, but there are some other books in there you might be interested in."

Kelly laid the Bible down and pulled out two children's books from the crate. *The Twelve Story Stones.* One was discolored and faded. The other had burnt edges. Kelly examined the spines. Both books had slices along the bindings. *No jewels.*

"Rhett said he'd received this stuff in the mail years ago with instructions to give it to you when he thought the time was right."

She held up the discolored book and handed it to James. "This one must have been the book that was mine."

"You're right."

"Look at the charred edges of this one." She ran her hand along the burnt cover of the second book. "Do you think it was pulled from a fire?"

When she opened the cover, an aged piece of paper slipped out and floated to the floor. She bent over, picked it up, and looked at the script. "It's in German." She scanned the words and did her best to translate them.

"Dear Rachel,

I rescued your book, and I'll keep it safe.

Your friend,

Abram"

"Who's Rachel?" Frank looked from her to James.

"Abrams's wife." As she examined the book in her hands, a

trace of warmth ribboned through her. "Not only did he rescue her book, but his family rescued *her* as well."

Kelly took her book from James and laid it next to the Bible on the table.

"What's in the box?" Frank tapped the top of the cardboard lid.

"I'm not sure." Lifting the tape, she tugged on the lid and peered inside. "Oh, my." She raised a cotton garment bag out of the box and hung it on the hook next to the door.

"What is it?" James sat up straighter, trying to get a better look.

"It looks like a dress." She unzipped the zipper and pulled back the flaps. A collective hush fell over the room. "It's gorgeous." Encased in the bag was a long-sleeved, ivory, vintage-style wedding dress.

"Why would Abram send you a wedding dress?" Frank peered inside the garment bag then brought his gaze back to her.

"I don't know." Kelly peeked in the box and found a note. After she read it silently to herself, she glanced at James. "He said this was a gift for my wedding day."

Frank cut in. "To Declan?"

"No."

The room grew silent.

James smiled. "To whom then?"

"I ... I'm not ..." She looked back at the note.

Love is a mystery.

When she lifted her gaze, the longing in James's expression heated the blood coursing through her veins.

Frank cleared his throat. "That's an extravagant wedding gift."

Kelly pulled her attention from James and drew her fingers over the silky fabric. "I noticed Rachel's wedding dress in a photo at Abram's home. It was a classic. Gorgeous lines. Something you'd hand down to your daughter. I hoped I might find one in a vintage shop—someday." She turned and looked back at James. "I never thought he'd have one made for me."

"It will look amazing on you." James's voice hitched, and he looked away.

She scanned the note again, searching for any other clues to her unexpected gift. "Abram recommends having it altered. He suggests I should let the hem out myself." She glanced up. "Why would he say that? I don't even know how to sew."

"It's no telling with Abram." James sent her a bemused look. "He was an unusual old man."

Reaching into the garment bag, she slid her hands over the sleeve's intricate lace details. Everything she remembered about Rachel's dress had been replicated.

Love is a mystery. Focus on the wedding. Alter the dress. Find the church.

What did these riddles mean? And what did it have to do with this dress?

As she fingered the elegant fabric on the bodice, she imagined what it might be like to become Mrs. James Edmond Taylor. Goosebumps crept across her skin. *It would be the most wonderful day of my life.* "Abram, what are you trying to tell me?"

A knot twisted in her stomach. The last time she spoke to Abram she'd worn Declan's ring. What if she'd eloped? She'd be Mrs. Declan McNeary. The wife of a criminal. The wife of a villain.

"Kell?"

She jerked her head toward James as a shiver crept down her spine.

"Does the note give you any more clues?"

"No. He mentions a church. Maybe he's talking about the church where he and Rachel got married." Her shoulders slumped. "Abram often talked in riddles, but sometimes he didn't answer them."

What shall we talk about today? The mystery of love.

A pang of sorrow wrapped around her heart and compressed. *I miss you, dear friend.*

She ran her hand over the worn children's book with the singed edges. The spine had been cut, and the jewels were no longer there. *Where are Rachel's jewels?* As she studied the book, thoughts clicked in her mind like gears snapping together in a clock.

"Wait!" She turned to the wedding dress and moved her hands along the skirt until she reached the hem. Letting her fingers slide across the silky fabric, she pinched her fingers along the fold. When a pebble-like object glided under the pad of her finger, her pulse ratcheted. With a gentle push, Kelly pressed the tiny bauble through a narrow opening in the thread.

"Is that what I think it is?" James leaned forward, straining to see.

She couldn't help but laugh. "Yes." Moving her hand along the inner edge of the dress, she slid out more of the gems until she had twelve shimmering diamonds in her hand.

"I can't believe it. Another group of twelve." James's excitement carried around the room.

Frank ran his fingers over the diamonds in her palm. "Amazing."

"They're the jewels from the burned book." Kelly placed the diamonds on top of the children's book. "Rachel's diamonds."

"So, if the book was Rachel's,"—Frank rubbed his five-o'clock stubble—"then her family was targeted during the war?"

"Yes. The Zuckers helped Rachel's family flee." Kelly thought back to everything Abram had told her. "Rachel was sent to London, where she grew up and attended college. When the war ended, she flew back to Germany to make peace with the past. By then, the Zuckers had closed their bakery, and Abram was living in the United States."

"How did Abram and Rachel find each other again?" Frank folded his arms and leaned against the wall. "It wasn't like they had the means back then to just look someone up on the Internet."

"Abram told me it was written in the stars." She paused, pulling at the memories Abram had entrusted to her. "He flew to Germany to settle his parents' estate. Of course, he visited the town he grew up in, the home of his last memories of Rachel."

Her throat tightened as she recalled how Abram had found Rachel. "While he strolled down the street near his family's old bakery, he stopped and stared in the window. It was evening, and the stars reflected in the glass, along with the outline of a woman. As he studied her lingering shadow outside the old dressmaker's shop, his heart knew without a doubt it was Rachel."

The room quieted. She grabbed a tissue from the box on the table and dabbed her tears.

"That's a wonderful story, Kell. God was working behind the scenes the whole time. Even amid that abominable war."

It was true, God was working behind the scenes. For Abram and Rachel. And for her. Even though her mother had left and her father's obsession had thrown a wedge between them, God had never abandoned her.

"Kelly," Frank blew out a breath then frowned. "I know you've been through the ringer, but there's something I need to tell you."

"What?"

"I've uncovered some information that may be connected with what happened out at the cabin."

"Let's hear it, mate. What did you dig up?" James adjusted his posture as he shot Frank a concerned look.

"After I found the address to Declan's cabin, I couldn't get it out of my head that I'd seen that address before."

Her pulse thrummed in her veins while she slipped into a seat by the table.

"I did some digging." Frank slid a large envelope across the table and tapped on it with his forefinger. "You need to take a look at these."

With shaky hands, she opened the envelope. "It's photos of my mom. I don't understand." Kelly shot out of her seat and handed the photos to James. "Where did you get photos of my mom?"

"What's all this about, Frank?" James scanned the pictures then handed them back to Kelly.

"There's a private investigator's case I checked into." Frank nodded toward another envelope. "The paperwork's in there."

She pulled out the documents and scanned the notes. "She was kidnapped?"

"That's her story." Frank reclaimed his place against the wall and shoved his hands in his pockets. "In her statement, Elizabeth Landon asserts that whoever took her asked about missing jewels and about her husband's research."

"How long did they keep her? Was she hurt?" Kelly's heart dropped. "Why didn't she go to the police?"

"That's a good question." Frank's expression remained stoic. "According to what I dug up, Elizabeth escaped from her captors and stumbled across some campers, who helped her to safety."

Kelly glanced back at the documents. "The date shows she was taken a few months before she left my father."

"Do you know why your mom was in Virginia?"

She nodded as she looked up. "She was sick. Dad found a specialist back in the States. She had an appointment to get some tests done."

"Well, while she was here, she hired a PI. She wanted to know what they could dig up on the cabin."

"Did they find anything?"

"The PI that checked it out claimed it was vacant. Not one hint anyone had been there." Frank shook his head. "I mean, it was scrubbed. Wiped. A professional job. Not one scrap of evidence was left in that cabin."

"Is that why she left my dad? Because someone had kidnapped her?" Kelly's mouth dried as she slumped onto the hospital bed next to James. "Or was she lying about that too?"

James reached out his hand and curled his fingers around hers. "Maybe she realized your dad was keeping something from her. You mentioned he'd never told her about his work with H & G."

"Why didn't she take me with her?" The question floated off her lips in a whisper. "Why didn't my dad try to bring her back? Why didn't he try to explain?"

James's expression filled with compassion. "I don't know, luv."

She squeezed James's hand as tears welled in her eyes. "I was her child. Her only child. How could she just leave me?"

"Often when people are scared, they make rash decisions." Frank shot her a sympathetic look. "If she was sick, maybe she had no other choice but to leave you with your father."

"I guess I'll never know for sure."

Frank exhaled.

"Something else on your mind, mate?" James shot Frank a probing look.

"You might be able to get your questions answered." Frank pulled out his phone and handed it to her. "I think your mother may still be alive."

"What?" She stared at the picture displayed on the phone. *Mom? It can't be.* As she stared at the photo, her pulse raced. Her mom's hair was lighter than she remembered, but the distinct contour of her cheekbones—the cheekbones they shared—confirmed her identity. Kelly glanced up at Frank. "Where did you get this?"

"I went on a hunch and decided to put an old picture of her through facial recognition. This popped up."

She studied the photo a few more seconds then handed the phone to James.

"That photo was taken at a pharmacy." Frank said.

"Checkouts, airports, traffic cameras—they're all places where your image is taken and stored. They're easy to find."

James handed the phone back to Frank then looked at her. "Is it possible your father told you that your mother died because she was scared?"

Frank interjected before she could answer. "It seems like whatever Declan wanted with the two of you was deep-rooted in history and dangerous. Your father might have been protecting your mother from all of this."

Her heartbeat skipped. *But why would she leave me? Why didn't he send me away to be with her?* "Do you know where she is?"

"I don't have an exact location. I could find out." Frank held her gaze. "I wanted you to make that call before I dove into an investigation."

"I think I'd like some time to think about it."

"Of course."

Her stomach roiled. Did she want to know where her mother was?

As she shuffled through the pictures again, she studied her mom's face. Did she want to be reunited with someone who could just walk out of her life without a glance back?

And if they were reunited, could she forgive her for leaving?

40

The doorbell rang, and Kelly's heart jumped. *Who would be at the door at this hour?* She blinked, acclimating herself to her surroundings. Guest room. James's townhome.

A few weeks after the doctors had released James from the hospital, they'd flown back to London. Naturally, he wanted to have all the resources of H & G at their disposal to track down the rest of the jewels. That, and he wanted to put some distance between them and the scene of her kidnapping. He wanted to make sure Declan wasn't working with anyone else.

"Maybe I was dreaming."

She settled back onto her pillow. If James was surprising her with breakfast, he would've just let himself in.

The doorbell chimed again, and she froze.

Slinking out of the bed, Kelly peeked through partially open curtains and eyed the street below. There were no cars, except the ones parked along the street. Without a clear view of the door, there was no way to identify her early-morning visitor.

Her gaze flicked to Henry's townhome across the street. No lights were on, save the porch light illuminating the three steps leading to the front door. Her pulse ratcheted up a notch. *I'm sure it's nothing.*

She pulled on her robe and slipped her cell into the side

pocket. As she fingered the buttons, she considered calling James before she walked downstairs.

"Don't let your overactive imagination take over." A tremble crawled under her skin as she took the stairs to the main level. Warily, she peered out the window and surveyed the front steps. Nothing. Kelly released her breath. "See. Nobody."

When she pulled open the front door, a whoosh of empty air greeted her, and a shoe-sized box fell with a thud against the threshold. Her throat constricted. She looked up and down the street, attempting to catch a glimpse of her caller. The fog-covered sidewalk was abandoned.

Kelly took a step back and curled her fingers around her phone. She'd received enough unwanted packages in the mail to be leery of anything unaccompanied on a doorstep.

Don't be silly. She swallowed and inched out across the threshold. *You're not in Virginia, and Declan's behind bars.* After one more glance at the street, she picked up the box and cautiously lifted the lid. "Oh, my. How beautiful."

Inside, wrapped with burlap and creamy-white satin ribbon, sat a small bundle of baby red roses and an envelope stamped with a looping H & G.

After Kelly shrugged off her initial trepidation, she tucked the box under her arm and carried it into the townhouse. "Flowers before breakfast. What a fun surprise."

She nestled into an oversized club chair, pulled out the note, and read it aloud. "To the Gatherer. I know you love a good mystery, so I've hidden some clues for you to find today. Follow the instructions and enjoy your journey. Remember ... love is a mystery. From the Hunter."

Warmth rushed over her. They'd only been back in town for a few weeks. How had he had time to plan this out?

Lifting the flowers, she noticed a book lying at the bottom of the box. *The Old Curiosity Shop* by Charles Dickens. She ran her fingers over the cover then opened the book. A small notecard with the same elegant writing stared up at her.

Treasures await you at The Old Curiosity Shop
Your taxi will arrive at 10:00 a.m.
Enjoy your adventure, luv

Kelly checked her watch. She had several hours to get ready.

After a quick shower, she stared indecisively at the armoire filled with her clothes. At least on this trip to London, she had more than just the basics to choose from.

Finally, after several outfit changes, she decided on a creamy cashmere sweater, a dressy pair of black slacks, and ankle boots. She wanted to look nice, but Londoners walked everywhere, so she needed to be prepared with comfortable shoes. Her heart did a quick little jig. Would James be waiting for her in the taxi?

She put the finishing touches on her hair, then threw on a pair of diamond stud earrings and a dainty rose gold bracelet. When the clock struck ten, she peeked out the window. As promised, a black London cab waited at the curb.

Grabbing her purse, a jacket, and an umbrella, Kelly glided down the stairs and bolted out the door.

"Morning, Miss Landon." A sharp-dressed cabbie stood on the sidewalk and tipped his flat cap at her.

"Good morning."

He opened the back door and waited for her to slip inside. "It will be just a few minutes until we reach our destination."

She bit back a giggle as she slid into the cab and glanced at the third floor of Henry's building. James wasn't joining her this morning. Was he watching as she drove away?

After snaking through a few city streets, they pulled up to the *Charles Dickens Museum.*

"This is it, miss." The taxi driver sprang out of the cab and opened her door.

She stepped onto the sidewalk and glanced up at the terraced house on Doughty Street. The quintessential London building beckoned her to go back in time and revisit the life of one of her favorite authors. She looked back at the cabbie. "Should I wait for James?"

"Just go in and tell them your name. You'll get the rest from there." The driver winked at her, jumped back in the cab, and took off down the narrow street.

Butterflies took flight in her belly as she walked the black-and-white tiled entrance to the museum's door.

When she stepped inside, a woman greeted her and waved her over. "Hello, ma'am. Are you here to visit the museum?"

"My name is Kelly Landon. I was told you'd be expecting me?"

"Yes, of course." The woman's eyes sparkled. "A very smart-looking man left you some instructions with a ticket to the museum."

Warmth wrapped around her like a blanket. *He is a very smart-looking man.*

"The instructions were for you to ..." the woman looked down at the small notecard in her hand. "To take your time and enjoy all the treasures of the museum." She lifted her gaze and handed her a sealed envelope. "This is for you. Following your time in the museum, you're requested to go to the gift shop, where you'll need to open the envelope."

"Thank you." *This is so much fun.*

As she made her way through the museum, Kelly took in everything—the rows of photos, the display of books Dickens had read from, his desk, and the drawing room. Every inch of the home gave her a glimpse into the life of Charles Dickens.

After she finished soaking in every detail, she found the gift shop and scanned the shelves. There were so many Dickensian gifts, she could scarcely contain herself. She reached in her purse, pulled out the sealed notecard, and opened it.

Dear Gatherer,
There is a gift bag for you at the gift shop desk.
Give them your name and enjoy your treasures.

Yours always,
The Hunter

She walked up to the cashier. Bolder this time, she approached the young woman behind the counter. "Hello, my name is Kelly Landon. I think you may have a package for me."

The teen girl with rosy cheeks flashed her a knowing look. "Yes, I do." She pulled a gift bag down from a shelf and handed it to her.

Kelly opened the bag and sifted through the goodies inside— a copy of *A Christmas Carol*, a souvenir guidebook, a post card of the museum, and an *Oliver Twist* bowl that had, '*Please, sir, I want some more,*' written in script around the edge. At the bottom of the bag, she found a note. She pulled out the note then looked back at the cashier.

The girl waggled her eyebrows. "What does it say?"

Kelly laughed. "Let's see." She opened the card and read it aloud to her new friend. "Miss Landon, would you please join me for a drink in the café?" Her pulse quickened as she glanced around. *He's here.* "Could you tell me how to get to the café?"

"Yes, ma'am." The girl's expression brightened. "Just pass through the gift shop. It's in the adjoining room."

When she entered the room, her heart sank. The café was empty.

"Can I help you, miss?" An older gentleman, who looked as if he'd stepped out of a Dickens novel himself, approached her.

"I'm looking for someone."

"There are more tables out in the garden, miss." The man winked at her. "You can leave your gift bag behind the counter if you'd like."

"Oh, thank you." She handed the man her bag then rushed toward the entrance to the back garden. When she pushed open the door, her heart almost pirouetted out of her chest.

"Good morning, Miss Landon." James stood in the middle of

the garden wearing a slate gray, slim-fitting suit, and the same sapphire tie he'd worn the day they'd met.

Kelly's breath caught. "Good morning."

"Did you enjoy your adventure?"

"I did." Her words came out breathlessly. "I'm sorry I took my time."

His lips pulled into a tender smile as he handed her a sealed envelope.

"What's this?"

"Open it."

Reluctantly, she tore her gaze from his, opened the letter and read it aloud. "Kell, I have a confession to make. When you sit next to me in the car, it's a distraction." Looking up, she smiled, recalling his first weeks as her bodyguard. It had been a distraction for her too.

James nodded for her to continue.

She returned her attention to the letter. "But dancing with you is a whole other story. That night with you in my arms, gliding across the dance floor, will remain in my memory forever. I need to confess this too. That night, I wanted to take you in my arms and kiss you. Above anything, I longed to take away all your fear and uncertainty. To make you feel safe and secure."

Warmth dotted her cheeks as she stole a glance at James.

He grinned.

Kelly continued reading. "I always want to be your plus one. I want us to unravel puzzles and find treasures together." Her voice hitched. "I promise to guard and protect you, but also to give you space to breathe. I'll serve you creamy coffee in bed and peanut butter on a spoon, if you promise to let me have my tea."

Her pulsed jumped as she read the last line. "Let's start a new story—together." Through misty eyes, she looked up at him. "Oh, James …"

"It looks like we have an audience." He nodded toward the building behind her.

Peeking over her shoulder, she caught the museum staff peering through the window. "I think we do." When she turned back, he'd lowered himself to one knee.

"Kell, I love you." He blew out his breath and laid a hand on his chest. "My heart's about to beat out of my chest, luv."

A tear trickled down her cheek as she placed her hand over her own heart. "So is mine."

He smiled then held out a ring box and opened the lid. "Will you do me the honor of becoming my wife?"

She gasped. Nestled in satin sat a ring with a teardrop diamond encircled with twelve stones—a replica of the twelve precious stones they were searching for. "Yes, James. A hundred yeses."

He stood, slipped the ring onto her finger, then circled his arms around her waist, and drew her close. "A hundred yeses. That works." He slipped a hand behind her neck, and his mouth found hers.

Kelly's eyes closed as her lips melted into his. She'd waited a lifetime for this. His kiss was warm and deep and spoke of security, unconditional love, and adventure. Lifting her hands, she let her fingers brush against the edge of his lapels. She could kiss him like this forever.

After several heartbeats, they parted.

Her eyes fluttered open, and she murmured a sigh.

"Forever, luv." James brushed his thumb across her bottom lip, and his irises altered between a thousand shades of blue. "I'm going to kiss you again, Miss Landon."

She tugged on his lapels. "Please do, Mr. Taylor."

James didn't rush. Instead, every slow, deliberate movement spoke of his commitment and his love for her.

Several oohs and aahs rippled from the small crowd that had now gathered behind them in the garden.

When he lifted his lips from hers, she was breathless.

"I can't wait to start a new adventure with you, Kelly Landon." He stepped back and waved toward a bistro table draped in a white tablecloth. "I thought you'd like to have brunch this morning at the home of one of your literary heroes."

He pulled out a chair, and she slipped into the seat.

"What a perfect idea."

The staff went back inside while a young woman brought out a tea set and scones.

Kelly reached for a scone and placed it on her plate. "Those look delicious."

"I'm beginning to think scones are your favorite treat."

She laughed. "I think you may be right."

As she bit into a scone, the older gentleman from the café brought her a large, creamy cup of coffee. "For the bride-to-be."

"Thank you." Kelly looked at her drink and caught a foam heart swirling in the center.

James shook the man's hand. "Thank you, Robert, for all your help today."

"It's my pleasure." The gentleman nodded then shuffled back into the café.

"How long did it take you to do all of this?"

"Let's just say I've been plotting this for a while." James waved a hand around the garden. "How I'd propose. What I wanted to say. I had several ideas."

"Is that so?"

"It was on the tip of my tongue to ask you to marry me while Liam patched up my shoulder." He flashed her an impish grin. "But I was afraid you might think I was delusional."

She took a sip of her coffee. "We nearly died, and you were thinking about proposing?"

"Yes." He rubbed a hand across his chin. "Now that I think about it, as soon as I took the blindfold off you, I thought about asking you to marry me."

"Well at least it wasn't when you put the blindfold *on* me."

He shot her an amused look over his cup of tea. "Will you ever let me off the hook for that?"

"Probably not." Looking down at the ring on her left hand, she sighed. "This ring … it's gorgeous."

"I'm glad you like it." He reached for her left hand and brought the back of her fingers up to his lips. A shiver tiptoed down her arm and ribboned through her entire body.

James's gaze smoldered with desire. "The *Story Stones* brought us together. I can't wait to spend the rest of my life going on adventures with you, Kelly." His lips curved into an inviting smile. "You already have the dress. What do you say we elope?"

"Elope?" Molten lava filled her veins as the thought of spending a lifetime with James tumbled through her thoughts. *Adventure. Love. Family.* "That sounds perfect. Where would you like to go?"

"I've heard you can procure documents in Denmark in less than two weeks."

"Really?" She took a sip of her coffee, trying to chase off the nervous jitters dancing in her belly. *Was he serious?*

"Really."

"What about Henry?" *I'd be Mrs. Taylor in less than two weeks?* She set her mug back on the table. "Will he be upset if we don't include him?"

"Henry. He's so … organized." A flash of mischief streaked across his expression. "If he had his way, he'd have me petitioning His Majesty before I made *any* decisions."

She laughed. Henry had become as dear to her as a brother, quirks and all. "Well, there's one thing I've learned since I've been with you, Mr. Taylor."

"What's that?"

"You sure know how to keep me guessing."

James's brow quirked. "Wait until you see what I have planned for our honeymoon."

41

Kelly followed James into the shadow-filled visitors' building of the Virginia correctional facility. It had been just over six months since the trial, and as she walked through the sterile hall, she'd begun to think twice about their visit today.

After checking in, they deposited their things into a locker then stepped through a metal detector.

"Follow me." A female guard stepped out of the shadows and signaled for them to go down a narrow hall.

Kelly's legs turned to rubber. How would Declan react to seeing her again?

James rested his hand on the small of her back as they moved through the maze of corridors policed by security cameras. "Are you doing okay, Kell?"

"I'll be fine." She swallowed past the dry lump forming in her throat. Would she be fine? She wasn't sure. This had been her idea, but maybe it had been a bad one. *I need to do this.*

They pushed through a final set of doors, and a guard behind a metal desk tossed them an indifferent look then lowered his gaze back to the security screens. When they entered a room lined with plexiglass partitions, she shuddered.

It was the smell that hit her first.

The harsh scent of cleaning products intermingled with the musky odor of the aging building. How many others had entered this room over the years? The walls crept closer as anguished whispers from shattered lives called out to her from the peeling paint. How many others had come face-to-face with their tormentors?

She gripped her hands together and exhaled a long breath. She needed answers. Answers only Declan could give. Then, she could put this behind her.

"Go ahead and take a seat at window four." The guard pointed toward the enclosure with a couple of chairs. "Mr. McNeary will be in shortly." After she gave the room a passing glance, the guard set up camp by the door.

James pulled out a chair and waited for Kelly to sit. "Ask what you need, then we'll leave. Okay, luv?"

She nodded.

He took a seat beside her, crossed an ankle over his knee, and eyed the clock on the wall. Despite his history with Declan, every body movement remained at ease and under control.

How does he do that? Tapping her foot on the floor, she nibbled on one of her fingernails. They had thirty minutes. She hoped it wouldn't take that long.

The door on the other side of the glass opened, and she paused mid-chew. *Ask your questions and get out.* James dropped his foot to the floor, slid his hand over, and gave her knee a reassuring squeeze. She glanced at him, then, needing an anchor, she threaded her fingers in his.

Turning back toward the window, she blew out a long breath. With James at her side, she had nothing to fear.

A gray-haired guard directed Declan to the orange chair and unlocked his cuffs. "You've got thirty, McNeary. Keep your hands where I can see them."

Declan lifted his eyes and caught her stare.

Kelly blinked.

Irritation. Disappointment. Hurt. A litany of emotions flitted across Declan's expression.

God, help me to forgive him.

Gripping James's hand tighter, she straightened and kept her gaze level with Declan's. She'd forgive. That was what God commanded her to do. A shudder tip-toed across her shoulders. But would she be able to forget?

Declan's mossy eyes darkened as he leaned toward the mouthpiece and pressed his scarred hand onto the glass. "Did you come to say you're sorry, Writer Girl?"

Guilt raked through her as she stared at his marred fingers. She'd never intended to harm him. Only to save James. "I *am* sorry, Declan. But you gave me no choice."

"I'm sure."

A weight jerked at her heart as she recalled the times Declan brought with him the breezy scents of the ocean along with his winsome personality. Those days had vanished. Now his presence carried the burden of restraints and bad decisions.

Declan drew his gaze from her and glared at James. "You two seem quite cozy."

James released her hand and laid an envelope on the metal shelf in front of them. "So do you, mate."

Declan's brows pinched together as he eyed the envelope. "I hope you aren't trying to buy my forgiveness."

"This isn't money, McNeary. It's some information you might be interested in." James pulled a piece of paper out of the envelope, then added, "Maybe this info, along with your scars, will help you learn a little humility while you're in here."

Declan rolled his eyes.

"Wait." Kelly yanked the document out of James's hand. "Before we show him anything, I have a few questions."

Declan's brows shot up. "Whoa. Look who's grown assertive after all this time." His attention shifted back to James. "It looks good on her, doesn't it?"

"Just answer her questions, McNeary."

"Why should I tell you anything?" Declan cut a dead-eyed look back at her and sneered. "After all, *you* betrayed me."

"Maybe the jilted fiancée has a right to know why her betrothed was masquerading as one person when there were actually two." She laid the folded document on the shelf and settled back in her seat.

"So, now you're the jilted fiancée?" Declan choked back a laugh. "Well, when you put it that way, I may just have to let you in on a few of my family secrets." He tossed her an award-winning smile and asked, "Would it change your mind about me and give us another chance?"

"Hardly." James hissed under his breath.

She sent James a sideways glance, then looked back at Declan. "Tell me about your brother. That was quite a ruse you pulled off."

"It was, wasn't it?" Declan paused a moment then began his story in a sing-song voice. "Once upon a time … there was a woman that had two little boys." With his marred hand, he scratched at his scruffy beard. "Twins as it were. Identical."

Her gaze fell from Declan's stubble and narrowed on his damaged hand. It still wasn't easy to accept his injury and her part in it. *God, forgive me.*

Declan cleared his throat, and she jerked her chin up. "You were saying. Twins?"

"They were identical in every way. Except one. Ivan had a raised, red birthmark, stretched across his shoulder blades." Declan's lips twisted. "My mother most likely believed he was touched by the fairies or some other folklore nonsense. If anyone ever found out about the mark, people would've talked."

"What if your grandmother found out?"

"Ah, my beloved grandmother. God rest her soul."

James shook his head and muttered something under his breath.

"My grandmother wouldn't have appreciated the deformity." Declan glowered at James. "She liked things … a certain way."

"What happened to Ivan?" Kelly rubbed her clammy palms on her jeans.

"My mother didn't tell anyone about the twins. Except her sister. From what I've deduced, she handed Ivan over to an adoption agency." Declan eased back into his chair and sighed. "We weren't well off. I assume she had good intentions. After some digging, I found Ivan eking out a living on a farm in Russia. Worlds away from Ireland. Worlds away from the judging eyes of our family."

"If your mother kept it secret, how did you find out about Ivan?"

"I overheard my mother talking about missing a part of herself. Lamenting to my father that she wished she'd had more children." Declan shrugged. "As twins do, I always felt like there was a part of me missing. Back then, there wasn't much paperwork for that sort of thing, so I called in some favors."

"Did your mother have any other children?"

"What? No." Declan straightened in his seat. "I was the only one left. That's why I decided to search for Ivan. I wanted to bring him into the fold. My grandmother had given me a mission, and I needed him. He needed me too." The lyrical tone of Declan's voice grew serious. "As you know, family means everything to me."

Kelly tugged at a wrinkle on her jeans. She almost felt sorry for him. The man across from her acted nothing like the fun-loving, poised professional she'd fallen in love with. Instead, he was a dark and lonely soul, tethered to an even darker family vendetta.

"I know what you're thinking, Writer Girl." Declan's expression morphed into a fake look of concern. "You're thinking, how did I fall in love with this monster?"

Her throat dried. *Yes. How?*

"I drew you in." He leaned toward the glass and whispered, "It was easy. I had all the qualities you were looking for."

How was I so blind? She inhaled a steadying breath.

"You were drawn to what I let you believe." Declan's cat-like eyes glinted under the amber lights as he rested his elbows on the metal shelf. "You were attracted to the illusion of what we could be—together."

Kelly studied the contours of Declan's face. Even with a tawny beard shadowing his jawline and dark circles cradling his eyes, there was a handsome quality to him. *I was attracted to the illusion.* Living in the clouds had always been her Achilles' heel, but falling head-over-heels for the wicked Irishman had nearly cost her everything. Swallowing back her humiliation, every moment she'd spent romanticizing Declan raced through her mind. When had she interacted with Declan? When had it been Ivan? *How did I not see the difference?*

"I wouldn't think about it too hard. It may drive you insane."

"That's enough, McNeary." James curled his fingers into fists and rested them on his knees. "Explain your side, or don't. It makes no difference to me. But your audience with us is dwindling."

Declan's lips pulled into an angry line. "Very well. When I found Ivan, I was stunned. Our features were identical. Not one iota of difference."

"How did he respond when he saw you?" Kelly folded her hands in her lap and forced herself to relax.

"Shocked, of course." Declan eased back in his seat and crossed his arms across his chest. "But he was glad I came for him. It didn't take long for me to see his value. However, there were a few problems."

"Like what?"

"First, he wasn't educated like I was, and he was brought up considerably poor. He spoke only Russian and a smidge of English."

She shook her head in disbelief. "So, you taught him a few languages, cleaned him up, and brought him to the United States to play your second."

"Exactly."

"How did Ivan fit into your plan with you and me?"

"That's easy. He was there to do my dirty work. It wasn't a hard sell. I took excellent care of his family—even moved them into a nicer farmhouse. He wanted to be close to me, so he did what I asked." Declan gave her a sweeping glance. "You were an enticing part of the package."

James reached for her hand under the shelf. The tension in his grip proved his irritation was growing.

"He took care of the house toss and the car break-in." Amusement blanketed Declan's face. "I had a key to your place and knew all the security codes, but Ivan enjoyed getting to know you."

Her breakfast curdled in her stomach.

"Ivan wanted to get closer, but I didn't think he was ready. He proved that the night of the gala."

The black-tie event rushed through her thoughts like a whirlwind. *That was Ivan?* With a trembling hand, she brushed a finger over her lips. *No. Please, no.* Her gaze dropped to Declan's hands. His knuckles were bruised that night. James noticed right away. But were they bruised the day after? She pinched her eyes shut, trying to recall. *No. No. No.* The internal chant did little to chase away the nightmare that had once been a fairytale. She opened her eyes and peered at the man on the other side of the glass. What else had she failed to notice?

Declan's mouth hitched at the corner. "Ivan was a lover. A poet. Loved studying archaic languages. He was a little overzealous at times, and I didn't want to scare you away."

A rumble of disgust escaped James's lips.

"Ivan was interchangeable with me when I needed him to be." Declan paused and glanced at the ceiling as if pulling a thought from the past. "He even visited your good friend Abram on occasion."

She recalled the night Declan had shown up at Abram's house unannounced. His personality seemed off, but she'd excused his behavior because she only wanted to see the fantasy. The illusion.

When he glanced back at her, Declan's brows lifted. "The subterfuge was brilliant if you think about it."

"What about the accident?"

"Ivan wasn't happy about that plan. He was okay when I just wanted to ruffle your feathers a bit. But—"

"He wasn't keen on almost killing me."

"Pretty much."

"That's a comfort." Sarcasm coated her words.

Declan snorted. "We had to join forces that night." He tipped his head to acknowledge James. "In case you're wondering, I was driving the lorry, *mate*."

James's face flooded with rage as he released his grip on her hand. "What was the point of the accident? If Kelly had died, you wouldn't have gleaned any information from her."

"True. I didn't want Kelly to die. Just scare her a bit." Declan slumped back in his chair, and his shoulders sagged. "Oh, come on. You can't see it? It was the perfect setup. I was going to sweep in and rescue her. It was going to be brilliant. I'd explain how flew home early and I just happened to be driving to her house when I came across the accident."

"You're sick, McNeary." James pulled his shoulders taut and glared at Declan.

He'd planned the entire accident. If James hadn't shown up

…

"Ivan brought up the idea of you becoming my wife." Declan's attention turned back to her. "He'd grown fond of you."

Fond of me? Her gut twisted. She'd been such a fool.

"Don't get me wrong, I believed we had a connection as well, but Ivan adored you. In the end, his devotion probably cost him his life."

"Don't put that on her." James's voice dripped with disgust. "Did you forget your brother had a laser pointed at my chest?"

"How *is* that shoulder of yours doing?" Declan shot James a bemused look. "I've seen you readjust your posture several times. Got an ache that just won't heal?" He waggled his injured hand in the air. "I can relate."

"I can still handle a weapon, if that's what you're wondering." James turned to Kelly. "Did you get what you needed?"

"I think I did." She picked up the document they'd brought with them and held it up to the glass. "There's some information we both need to share with you."

Declan squinted at the H & G drawn across the top. "Nice touch. You two have your own stationery."

She ignored the snide remark. "After you read this, you'll understand there's nothing more for you to pursue."

Declan scanned the document and scowled. "You found them?"

"Yes." Kelly folded the paper and slipped it back in the envelope.

"We," James pointed between him and her. "Found everything."

"Where did you find them?"

She looked from James then back to Declan. "Most of the jewels were hidden inside the spines of the banned children's books."

"Most of them?"

James pulled a photo from the envelope and held it up to the window. "Some of them were hiding right under your nose."

Declan studied the photo of her emerald jewelry, then frowned.

"It took loads of research to track down the children's books Helena tried to destroy." James's lips curved into a boyish grin as he pulled the photo back. "But we did it. There were twelve books in print and twelve of each stone. And they've all been returned to their *rightful* owners."

"So, you see, Declan." She leaned toward the glass, hoping to punctuate her statement. "There's nothing for you to pursue anymore. Nothing."

Declan blew out a resigned sigh. "I see." After a few moments, he said, "I do have one thing I'm still interested in."

She tried to read his thoughts but failed. "What?"

"I want my ring back."

"Ah, yes, the ring."

"It was my grandmother's."

James muffled a cough.

Kelly gave James a sideways glance, then looked back at Declan. "I wanted to melt it down, pour it into a hole and bury it forever."

Declan's brow's shot up. "That's a bit dramatic, even for you."

James suppressed a laugh. "She's a writer, mate. What do you expect?"

"The ring wasn't your grandmother's." Kelly shoved the photo back in the envelope.

"What?" Declan's face blanched.

"She pilfered it before she fled Germany."

"How do you know that?"

"I did some digging. The history of that ring is quite fascinating. But as a good friend of mine would say, that's a story for another day." She turned to James, and they shared a knowing look. Then, glancing back at Declan, she said, "Don't worry, it's in a safe place."

Declan pulled his gaze from her and looked at James. "Care to share?"

"Don't look at me." James held up his hands, palms out. "I have no idea where she hid the ring."

Declan blew out his breath as he massaged his damaged skin. "You truly do have the blood of the Gatherers running through your veins. Don't you, Writer Girl?"

"It seems that I do." She searched Declan's expression for any sign of remorse. She didn't see one. "You don't have to finish your life tethered to Helena's legacy. You *can* change."

Declan pursed his lips as he held her gaze.

"Think about it. Living your life devoted to a vendetta didn't work out. Maybe you should try a new path. Something for good this time."

"What's the point?" Declan surveyed the visitor's station. "I'm not getting out of here for a while. When I do get out, I could never be one of you."

"No, of course not. It's in our DNA." James thrummed his fingers on his knee. "But you *can* change."

Declan snorted. "Does a tiger really change his stripes?"

"That's up to you, McNeary." James stood and pushed in his chair. "You'll pay for your crimes, but God can forgive anything. You can have a new identity, even behind bars."

Kelly gave Declan one more cursory glance, then rose to her feet.

She doubted Declan would change, but she prayed they'd given him something to think about.

42

Kelly went through the barred door when James held it open for her. "That was kind, what you said to Declan."

James wrapped an arm around her waist, pulling her close as they followed the sidewalk to the parking lot. "What good is our calling, if I don't share the hope of forgiveness?"

As they continued to the car, she thought about what he said. It was hard to imagine Declan would ever change, but it was not up to her to decide his fate. "You're right."

As she thought back to the handwritten notes left behind in her grandmother's Bible, tenderness enveloped her in a hug. She was grateful someone in her life had left a road map for her own path to God's love. Maybe in time, someone would help Declan see God's restoring love was meant for him too.

"What about the ring?" James threw her a concerned look as they approached the car. "Are you sure you wanted to provoke him like that?"

"Like he said, he's not getting out of there for a long time. It doesn't even belong to his family. I doubt he'll give it a second thought."

"Are you going to tell *me* where you hid it?"

"I'm not sure Hunters need to be privy to all the Gatherers' information." She lifted her brows. "At least, that's what I'm told."

"Is that so?" James pulled his wedding band out of his pocket and slipped it on his finger. "Do you think he knows?"

She shrugged and slipped on her bands. "It doesn't matter now. I found out what I needed to."

Keeping their marriage a secret had been a joint decision. Declan might not have been so open about his past if he felt he'd lost in love as well as failed to recover the jewels.

She relaxed her hip against the side of the SUV and looked up at James. "I think maybe as Mrs. James Edmond Taylor I might be willing to disclose some of the information about where I hid the ring to my husband."

He leaned in and kissed her slowly. When he stepped back, a bemused look filtered across his expression. "I appreciate that, Mrs. Taylor."

Kelly glanced past him at the plain façade of the jail. She hoped their visit had quenched the flames of Helena's vendetta for good.

James opened her door, and she slipped into her seat. While the quiet of the vehicle wrapped around her, the night she shot Declan and pulled the ring off her blood-stained fingers raced through her thoughts.

She'd had no idea what to do with the ring. Sell it to a pawn shop, melt it down, throw it in the ocean—all of them seemed like viable options.

Instead, she did what came naturally, researched its history. When she found out the ring's circular rows of ruby stones were used as a signet for spy work by the Allies during World War II, she couldn't destroy it. There was too much history there.

James slid into his seat and turned to face her. "Are you doing okay after seeing Declan? He can't hurt anyone now. Not while he's behind bars."

An undercurrent of worry sloshed in her gut. It wasn't the

location of the ring she dreaded telling James about. There was something more pressing weighing on her mind.

"It was difficult to see him." She inhaled, then released her breath. "But that's not what's bothering me."

"What is?"

"After Abram sent me a packet of genealogy documents, I found out Declan had an older sister."

"What? How? How did Abram know?" James gripped the back of his neck and released a groan. "When was she born? Why wasn't there a record of that? Wait. When did you find out about—"

She held up a hand. "One question at a time."

"Sorry, luv. That's a development I wasn't expecting."

"I know. Neither was I."

"Do you know who she is?"

She fiddled with the seam on the seat. "You're not going to like this. She's Emersyn's mom."

"What?"

"Before Abram died, he said he'd found Emersyn's mom." Kelly stretched out her legs, uncurling and curling her toes to release the tension. "Emersyn's mom died of a heart condition. His statement didn't make sense. Later, when Abram mailed me all the genealogy records, there was an unfinished study of Emersyn's genealogy." She paused, recalling the conversations she'd had with Abram. "Abram wanted to know if her heart condition was hereditary, so I took up where he left off."

"And you stumbled upon something more sinister. A connection to Declan."

Shifting her gaze back to him, she said, "I thought I was doing Abram a favor. He was worried about Emersyn, and I wanted to give her the gift of knowing who her family was."

"What about Emersyn? Does she know? About any of this? About you and me?" James's jawline twitched with his questions. "The idea that she's connected to H & G and related to Declan doesn't sit well with me."

"Emersyn doesn't know anything." A knot coiled in her stomach and twisted. "Abram wanted me to tell her about H & G after she finished college."

"And the information about her mother?"

"Emersyn knows her mom was adopted, but she doesn't know any of the details."

"What are the details?"

"The short version?" Kelly settled back in her seat. "Years before Declan was born, and I suspect maybe before she was married, his mother made a trip to New York with her older sister."

"The sister seems to play the part of protector in all this."

"That, or manipulator." She glanced back at the sand-colored walls of the prison. "The records from the New York adoption agency are pretty spotty. There was some scandalous stuff going on with adoptions back then."

"It sounds like it."

"It's likely Declan's mom went back to Ireland, got married, and pretended nothing happened. It happens a lot." She pulled her seatbelt over her shoulder and clicked it in place. "No wonder she was heartbroken to give up one of her twins. She'd already gone through the tragedy of handing a child over to a stranger."

Silence ribboned around the SUV as a cool shiver feathered across her skin. What would Declan do if he found out Emersyn was his niece? Would he use her to get to H & G?

Family means everything to me.

Finally, after several seconds, James broke through the quiet. "Declan can't find out about any of this."

Her heart twisted. "I agree."

"Did you find out if the heart condition was hereditary?" James buckled, then started the car.

"Thankfully, it's not."

"Good. Maybe you don't need to tell Emersyn anything."

Kelly leaned back against the headrest as her mind

cartwheeled with questions. *What am I going to do? What am I going to tell Emersyn about her mom? What am I going to tell her about H & G?*

Abram had entrusted her with Emersyn's welfare, and now that included keeping her protected from Declan too. *God, give me direction.*

They drove in silence for a few minutes before James spoke up. "So … are you going to tell me where you hid your *old* engagement ring?" He shot her a teasing look. "Or do I need to launch my own investigation?"

"Maybe."

"Maybe?" He glanced back at the road, and his lips curved into a grin. "As you might recall, I'm not above using a variety of tactics."

"Oh, I know, Mr. Taylor. I know." Her shoulders relaxed as she settled back into her seat. "I found some interesting history surrounding that ring, but first, let me start by telling you a story."

James pulled onto the interstate and stole a glance in her direction. "Of course. I hear you're rather good at that."

Clearing her throat, she dipped into a dramatic tone. "My story begins in a rose garden. In the center of this garden is a fragrant, purple rose."

As she shut her eyes, a highlight reel of her time with Abram rolled through her mind in vivid, living color. *I miss you, my friend.*

"The rose is called the Ebb Tide rose. Under this majestic rose, I've hidden a treasure."

"Is that so?"

Her eyes fluttered open, and she faced James. "Yes. The ring's in a time capsule."

"A time capsule?" James flashed her a confused look. "Was that Abram's idea?"

"Yes. He gathered a few things for Emersyn to find later. I

added the ring." She cleared her throat and continued. "Back to my story."

James laughed.

"The owner of this rose garden was an eccentric, elderly gentleman with a heart of gold."

Remember, Kelly, love is a mystery. A mystery worth solving.

Her vision blurred as she glanced out at the landscape rushing by the vehicle. "In his golden heart, he held a mystery. A mystery that would unlock doors from the past and plot a new course of one woman's story—forever."

EPILOGUE

Kelly reached out and took her mom's hand. "Looks like we're going to have beautiful weather when we land at Heathrow."

"It does." Elizabeth Landon shifted to face her. "Thank you for asking me along. You don't know what it means to me that you've invited me to stay with you for a while."

"You can stay with us as long as you like." Peering out the curved window, Kelly followed the trail of white puffs floating across the afternoon sky. It was a perfect day for flying. It was a perfect day. Period.

"I only plan on staying in London a few weeks."

She turned her attention back to her mom. "Just don't rush things." After years of experimental treatments, Elizabeth was in remission. Since God had given them a second chance, Kelly wanted to spend as much time with her mom as she could.

"I don't want to invade too much of your life." Elizabeth pulled her hand back and took a sip of her water. "We have some wrinkles in our relationship we still need to smooth out."

"We do."

"I hope you know I thought I'd made the right decision."

"I know that, Mom." Her mother had admitted she'd watched Kelly's writing career from afar while she went through treatment on her own. She'd even hired a private investigator to find out where her daughter had moved to in Virginia, with the hopes of one day reconnecting. But after years of separation, Elizabeth was unsure of how to bridge the divide.

Then God intervened.

"And about the photograph—"

"Mom, it's okay." Kelly reached for her mom's hand again. "Everything worked out. Didn't it?"

Elizabeth nodded. "I guess so. I just wanted to keep you safe."

Call it mother's intuition, or God's hand of providence, Elizabeth had sent the photo of Kelly and Declan to H & G. Given her husband's past with H & G and Kelly's connection to Abram's book, she wanted to make sure Declan was just who'd he'd claimed to be—a literary agent. Even though she mothered behind the scenes, neither time nor distance could cut the ties of Elizabeth's love for her daughter.

"I'm safe now." Kelly said. "And the time we have together is precious. A new start."

"Time *is* precious, sweetheart." Elizabeth's eyes glistened. "I'll stay for the month, and we'll take it from there."

James snapped the newspaper he was reading closed and whispered out of the corner of his mouth. "Have you told her yet?"

Kelly shook her head. She was still trying to wrap her own thoughts around the news.

He grinned as he bent forward and turned his attention to Elizabeth. "You might not want to stay away too long once you hear Kelly's news."

"Oh?"

"James." Kelly released her mom's hand and playfully batted his arm. "I thought we were waiting a few weeks to tell everyone."

"Go on. Tell her." His expression brightened. "I'm telling Henry as soon as we land."

Warmth traveled through her veins, circled around her heart, and squeezed. He was as excited as she was. "We're going to have a baby." Kelly blurted out the announcement, unable to hold back the smile tugging on her lips.

"Are you really?" Elizabeth's eyes sparkled to life. "That's wonderful news. Do you have a name picked out?"

"We have a few in mind."

"The only thing we haven't decided is whether this new little Taylor will be a Hunter or a Gatherer." James threw them a wink then opened his newspaper to the world news section.

A concerned look stole over Elizabeth's features.

"Don't worry, Mom, we have years before we need to think about that." Kelly laid a hand on Elizabeth's arm. "Years."

"You're right. It's just the thought that you—" Elizabeth sucked in a nervous breath as she dug in her purse for a tissue. "With what you've been through, and your father, well …" She waved the tissue then dabbed her eyes. "I'm sorry. It's not my call to tell you how to live your life."

"I'm sorry Dad hid his work with H & G from you." Kelly gave her mom's arm a reassuring squeeze, then withdrew and squared her shoulders. "But James and I are in this together. It's my calling as much as it's his."

"It's dangerous. This group." Elizabeth looked away. "They put their lives on the line and sometimes …"

As her mom's words trailed off, a weight landed in Kelly's chest. Elizabeth refused to talk about the incident at the cabin in Virginia. But Kelly understood why. Her mom had been held captive at the same location she had, and later uncovered the real reason Kelly's father was obsessed with antique jewelry. Elizabeth blamed the society for her husband's disconnect, and now she wanted nothing to do with H & G.

Elizabeth turned back to face Kelly. "Are you sure you know what you're getting into?"

"I'm sure." Kelly folded her hands across her abdomen. "With a baby on the way, we're taking a step back. I'll focus on my writing, and James will ..." She glanced quickly at James then back at her mom. "If I do anything with the society, it will be research. Sitting at a computer. In the safety of my office."

Elizabeth nodded but didn't look convinced.

As the plane sliced through the wispy clouds on its descent into Heathrow, Kelly leaned forward and glanced across the aisle. Wielding her pencil like a magic wand, Emersyn scribbled notes in her leatherbound notebook. Emersyn was an old soul who preferred typewriters to laptops and paper and ink to digital note taking. Kelly chalked that up to Abram's influence.

Joy blossomed in Kelly's chest. She was glad Emersyn agreed to spend a few weeks with them in London before her classes started. Maybe over time, their bond would deepen, and she'd become a trusted confidant and friend to Emersyn.

Sitting back in her seat, a niggling of worry shot through her. What would she tell Emersyn about Declan? And about H & G?

Kelly shoved the thought away. Emersyn needed to finish college, leaving Kelly a couple of years to figure out how much she'd need to disclose. If there was one thing she'd learned, a lot could happen in a couple of years.

She turned just as the breathtaking city of London sprawled below them like a scene from a movie.

"We're almost home, Kell."

The affectionate tone of James's voice wrapped around her like the first sip of creamy coffee on a cold day. She leaned her cheek on his shoulder. "I can't wait to get home."

When he kissed the top of her head, the anticipation of what was to come bubbled inside of her.

She was going home.

Home with a man who loved and cherished her. Home to start a family. Home to make a few more memories with her mother.

More than anything, she was going home to a calling that God had prepared just for her.

And all of this because of one best seller.

ACKNOWLEDGMENTS

First and foremost, I thank Jesus, the author and finisher of my faith, for the gift of imagination. Thank you to the best husband in the world, Steve, for understanding writer's hours aren't always during the daytime. I'd like to give a shout out to Kristy Werner, my friend and fellow writer, for your hours of brainstorming help and beta reads over creamy cups of coffee. Someday I may even be an outliner! Finally, I'd like to say thank you to my daughter, Katelyn, for your input on the details of Best Seller and our endless discussions about World War II.

ABOUT THE AUTHOR

Author Christina Rost is a mother to three amazing children and is married to her high school sweetheart, Steve.

An avid reader, she can still remember the first box set of sweet romance stories her mother bought her as a young teen —*The Canadian West Series* by Janette Oke. Reading about the rugged landscape of the west and handsome Canadian Mounties, Christina daydreamed about writing her own love stories.

After spending twenty-four years as an Air Force wife, her husband retired, and they settled in Oklahoma. Seeing this as an opportunity to pursue writing full time, she jumped in with both feet and in 2020 she attended her first writer's conference— WriterCon in Oklahoma City. That weekend confirmed she'd found her people and writing was a part of her soul.

In 2021, one of her unpublished romantic suspense novels took first place at WriterCon and in 2022, the same story was a finalist for the ACFW Genesis Contest. She's also won several awards in Flash Fiction.

Writing inspirational romance has always been Christina's passion, and she loves to craft relatable characters with redemptive qualities that reflect the importance of her faith.

Her literary hero is Jane Austen, and like Jane, she hopes her own contemporary romances can sweep her readers away for a swoon-worthy, enjoyable experience.

When she isn't spending time with her family or writing, you'll find Christina chatting with friends over creamy cups of coffee or perusing antique shops for tattered books and hidden treasures.

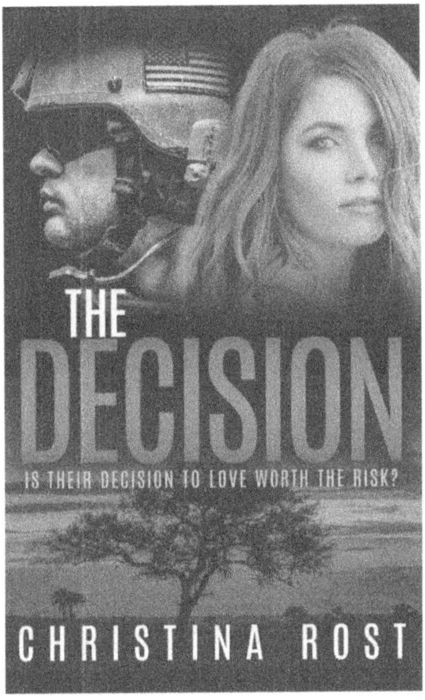

The Decision

Running from her grief, interior designer Ava Stewart makes a hasty decision to join a missionary group heading to Uganda. She's in the country only a few days before tragedy strikes and a mistaken identity leaves her with an uncertain outcome.

Special Operator Blake Martin is assigned to a humanitarian mission when he's captured by a group of armed men. Wounded and miles away from his team, Blake's brought to Ava, and she's ordered to care for him.

Thrown together in chaos, with the threat of danger pressing in from all sides, Ava and Blake are forced to rely on each other—and God—to escape. An undeniable bond is formed during their flight to safety, but opening their hearts to love carries its own risk. A risk they aren't sure they're willing to take.

Now, miles apart and living separate lives, they need to decide if the connection they shared in the untamed, wilds of Uganda is strong enough to confront the future. A future where Ava's fragile heart and Blake's hazardous job collide, and only God knows the outcome.

Get your copy here:

https://scrivenings.link/thedecision

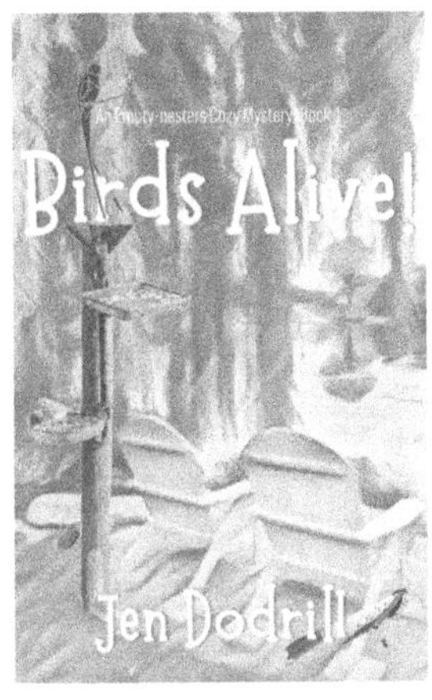

Birds Alive

by Jen Dodrill

An Empty-nesters Mystery—Book One

Peg—widow, mom blogger, and empty nester—is desperate for a new hobby. After a late-night blog post leaves her dedicated Mamma Birds followers fearful that she's closing her blog, she adopts a reader's suggestion and forms the Empty Nesters Birding Group. On their first outing overlooking beautiful Pensacola Bay, a birder dies from an allergic reaction to peanuts in the birdseed. Seed that should be peanut-free.

A hurricane barrels toward the Gulf Coast, and Peg's overbearing, animal-collecting, but well-meaning mother-in-law crashes Peg's empty nest. After the hurricane passes, Peg checks on her new birder friends and finds one wounded and dying. The assailant is still there and knocks Peg down a steep staircase. Stuck in a boot with a broken foot and still reeling from the two murders, Peg recruits a fellow birder and her mother-in-law to help solve the crime. She even teams up with the detective investigating the case, whose dimples draw her in a way she hasn't experienced in years.

Get your copy here:

https://scrivenings.link/birdsalive

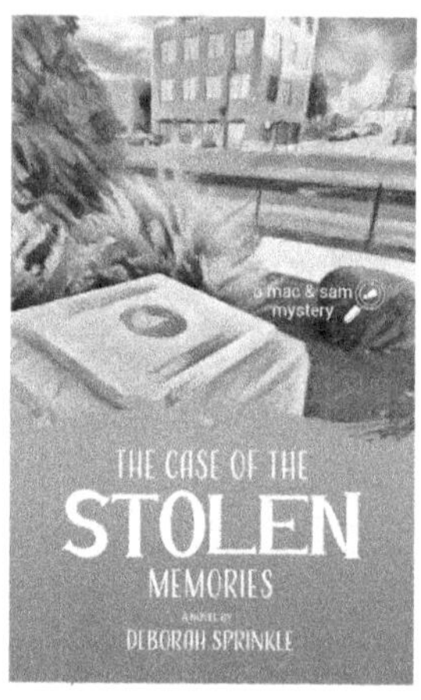

The Case of the Stolen Memories

by Deborah Sprinkle

A Mac & Sam Mystery—Book Three

It's the beginning of a new year and Private Investigator Mackenzie Love resolves to get in better shape. But after only one week of walking before work she interrupts a burglary in progress and ends up in the middle of a murder case.

Detective Jake Sanders, the man Mac's dating, is assigned to the murder, and Mac along with her partners Samantha Majors and Ms. Prudence Freebody are hired to find the memorabilia stolen from the time capsule in Rennick Park. The two cases intertwine and Mac finds herself once more on the wrong end of a gun!

Can Mac and Jake find the killer and the stolen property before the killer finds them?

Get your copy here:

https://scrivenings.link/stolenmemories

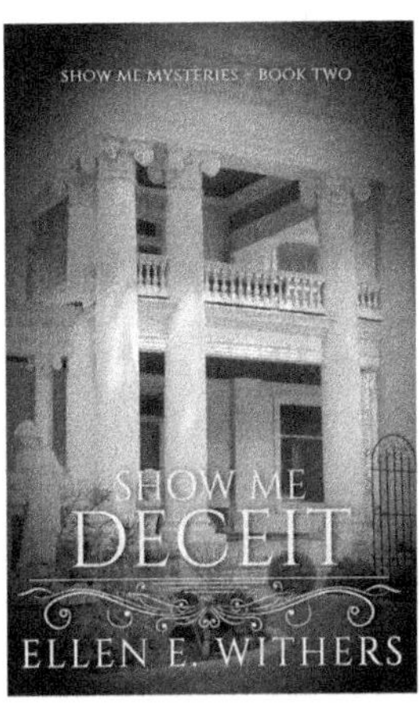

Show Me Deceit by Ellen E. Withers

Show Me Mysteries—Book Two

Present Day: Liesl Schrader is once again involved in death investigations. A body is discovered inside a charitable museum where Liesl serves on the board of directors. She and her best friend Nicole are drawn into a police theft investigation stemming from the death at the museum.

When Liesl and Nicole uncover a set of historic bones, questions arise. Are they related to the Civil War-era encampment in their town? The unit, commanded by General Pope, guarded one of the biggest supply chains of the Union Army—the railroad lines located in Mexico, Missouri, throughout the war. Was this a battlefield death, or was it murder? Surrounded on all sides by Southern sympathizers, did the Rebels kill this Union soldier?

1862: United States Army Lieutenant Cormac O'Malley has a problem. He knows there is a Rebel spy in his camp, and he needs proof of the spy to save the lives of Union soldiers. He has no choice but to work with his sweetheart from town, Enid Connelly, and her local friends to uncover the proof. Are they trustworthy and loyal to the Union in a state divided between North and South? Can he reveal the identity of the spy before the spy can silence him—possibly forever?

Take a walk through time with Show Me Deceit, book two of the Show Me Mystery Series. The mysteries are set in Mexico, Missouri, where death encompasses two eras—Civil War and contemporary times. Liesl, Nicole, and Detective Kurt Hunter, have previously put a killer behind bars. Now they must combine their skills again to stop the plunder of local charities and solve the mystery of a Union soldier's death. Can Liesl and Kurt work together again as friends, putting aside their former romance, to solve these mysteries?

Get your copy here:

https://scrivenings.link/showmedeceit

Stay up-to-date on your favorite books and authors with our free e-newsletters.

ScriveningsPress.com